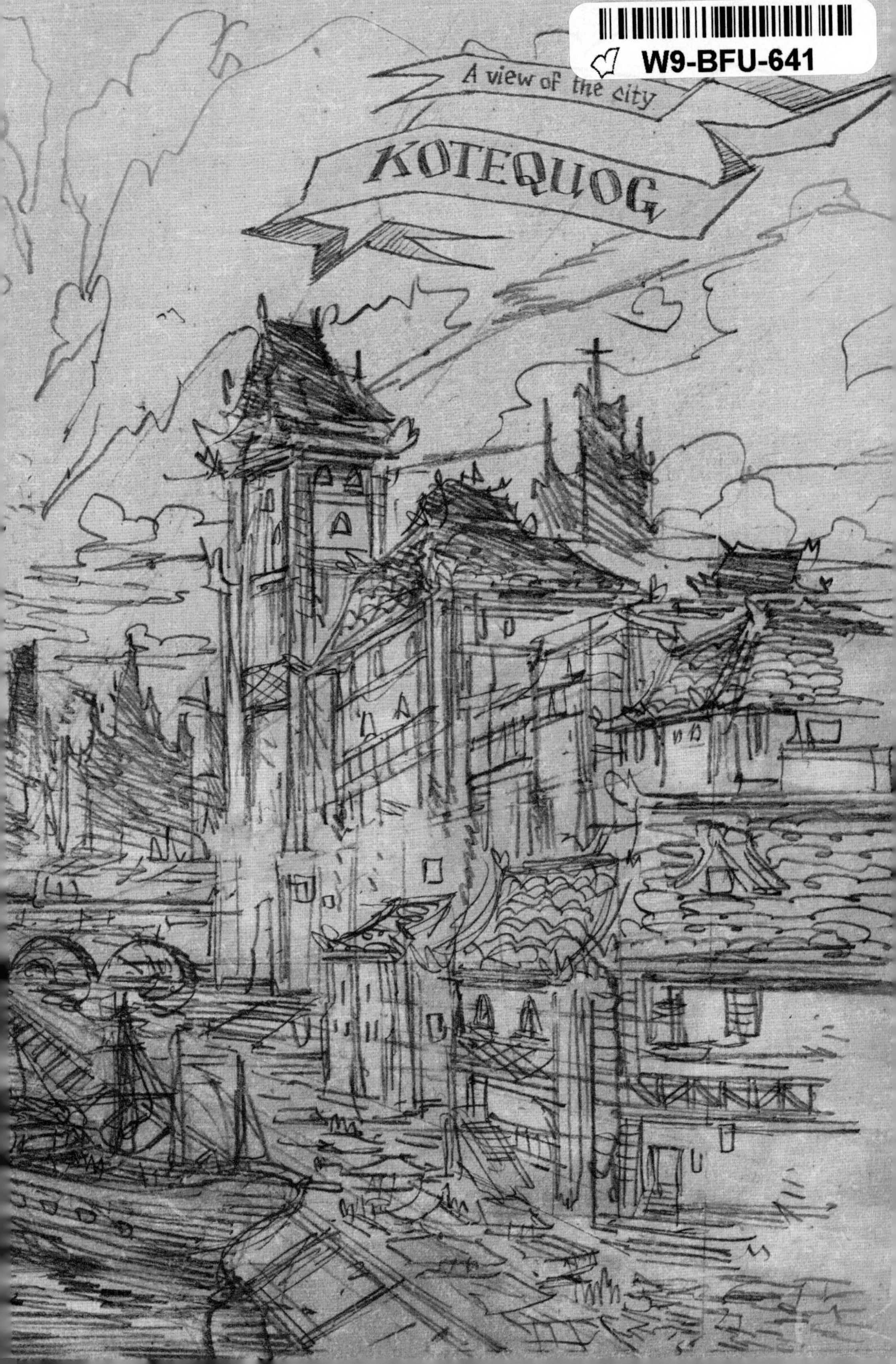
A view of the city
KOTEQUOG

THIS BOOK
and the spirited adventures contained within
BELONGS TO:

....

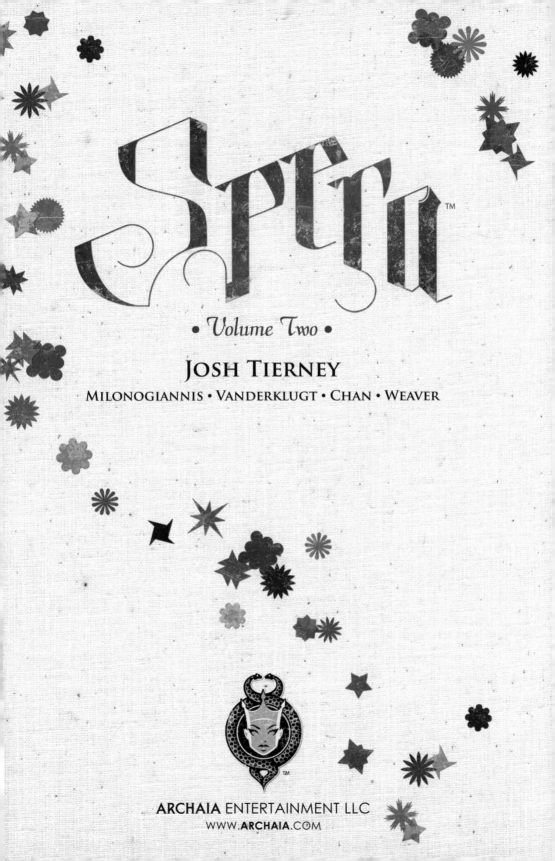

Spera™

• Volume Two •

JOSH TIERNEY

MILONOGIANNIS • VANDERKLUGT • CHAN • WEAVER

ARCHAIA ENTERTAINMENT LLC
WWW.ARCHAIA.COM

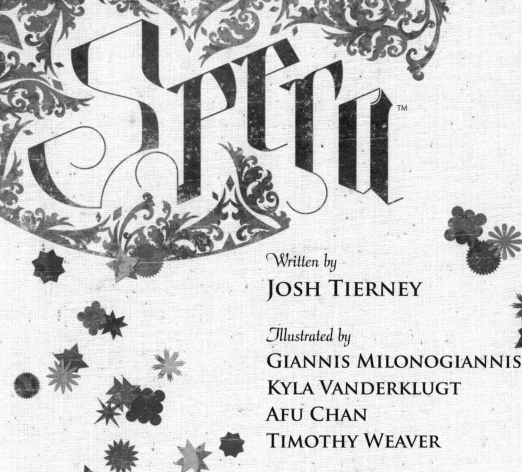

SPERA ™

Written by
JOSH TIERNEY

Illustrated by
GIANNIS MILONOGIANNIS
KYLA VANDERKLUGT
AFU CHAN
TIMOTHY WEAVER

Character Designs and Cover Art by
AFU CHAN

Design by
SCOTT NEWMAN

Rebecca Taylor, *Editor*
Scott Newman, *Production Manager*

Archaia Entertainment LLC
PJ Bickett, *Chairman*
Jack Cummins, *President & COO*
Mark Smylie, *CCO*
Mike Kennedy, *Publisher*
Stephen Christy, *Editor-in-Chief*
Mel Caylo, *Marketing Manager*

Published by **Archaia**

Archaia Entertainment LLC
1680 Vine Street, Suite 1010
Los Angeles, California, 90028
www.archaia.com

SPERA Volume Two. Original Graphic Novel Hardcover. February 2013. FIRST PRINTING.

10 9 8 7 6 5 4 3 2 1

ISBN: 1-936393-76-X
ISBN 13: 978-1-936393-76-3

Printed in **China**.

TABLE OF CONTENTS

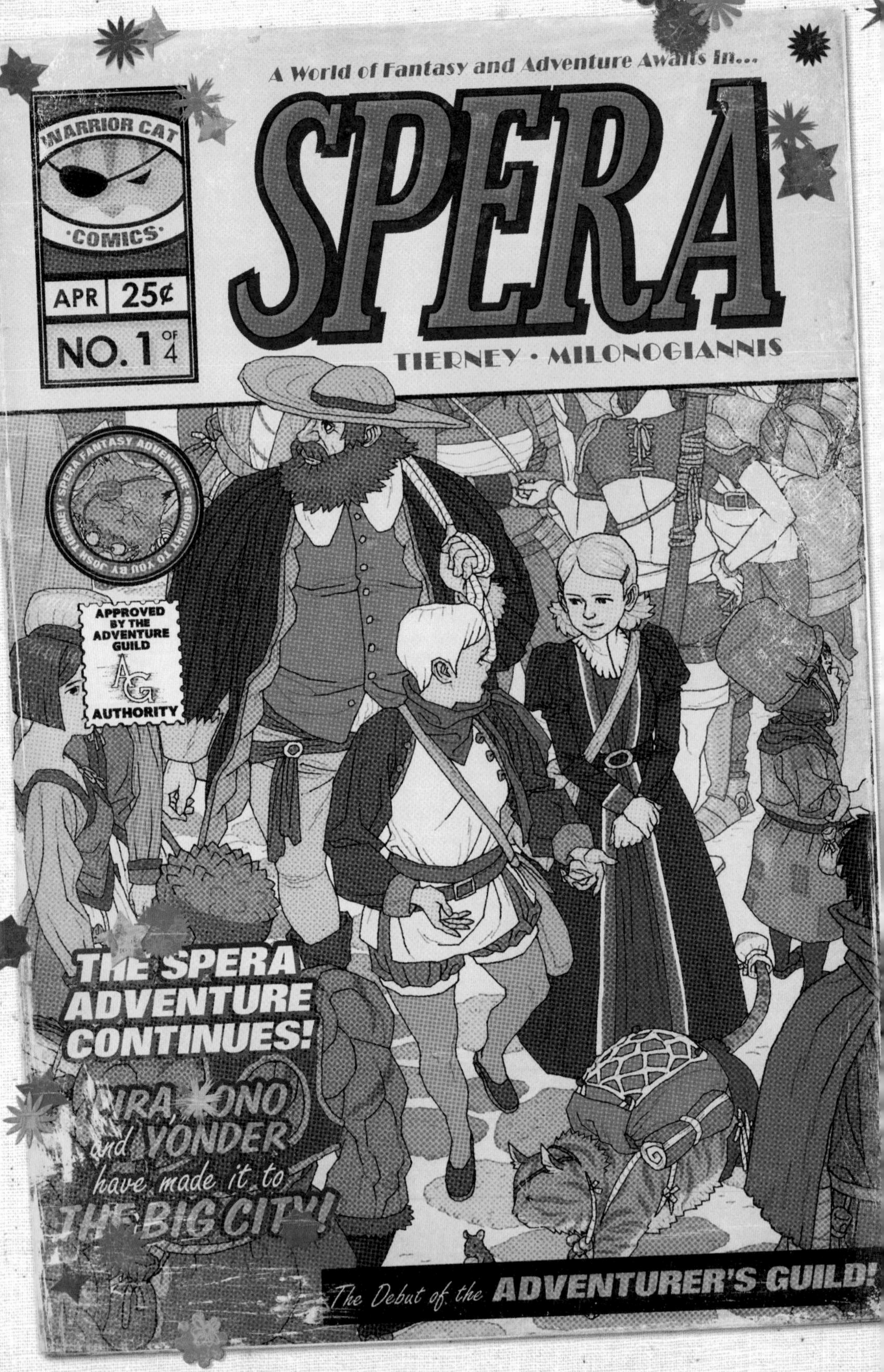
A World of Fantasy and Adventure Awaits In...
SPERA
WARRIOR CAT
·COMICS·
APR
25¢
NO. 1 OF 4
TIERNEY · MILONOGIANNIS
SPERA FANTASY ADVENTURE · BROUGHT TO YOU BY JOSH TIERNEY
APPROVED BY THE ADVENTURE GUILD
AG
AUTHORITY
THE SPERA ADVENTURE CONTINUES!
and YONDER
have made it to
The Debut of the ADVENTURER'S GUILD!

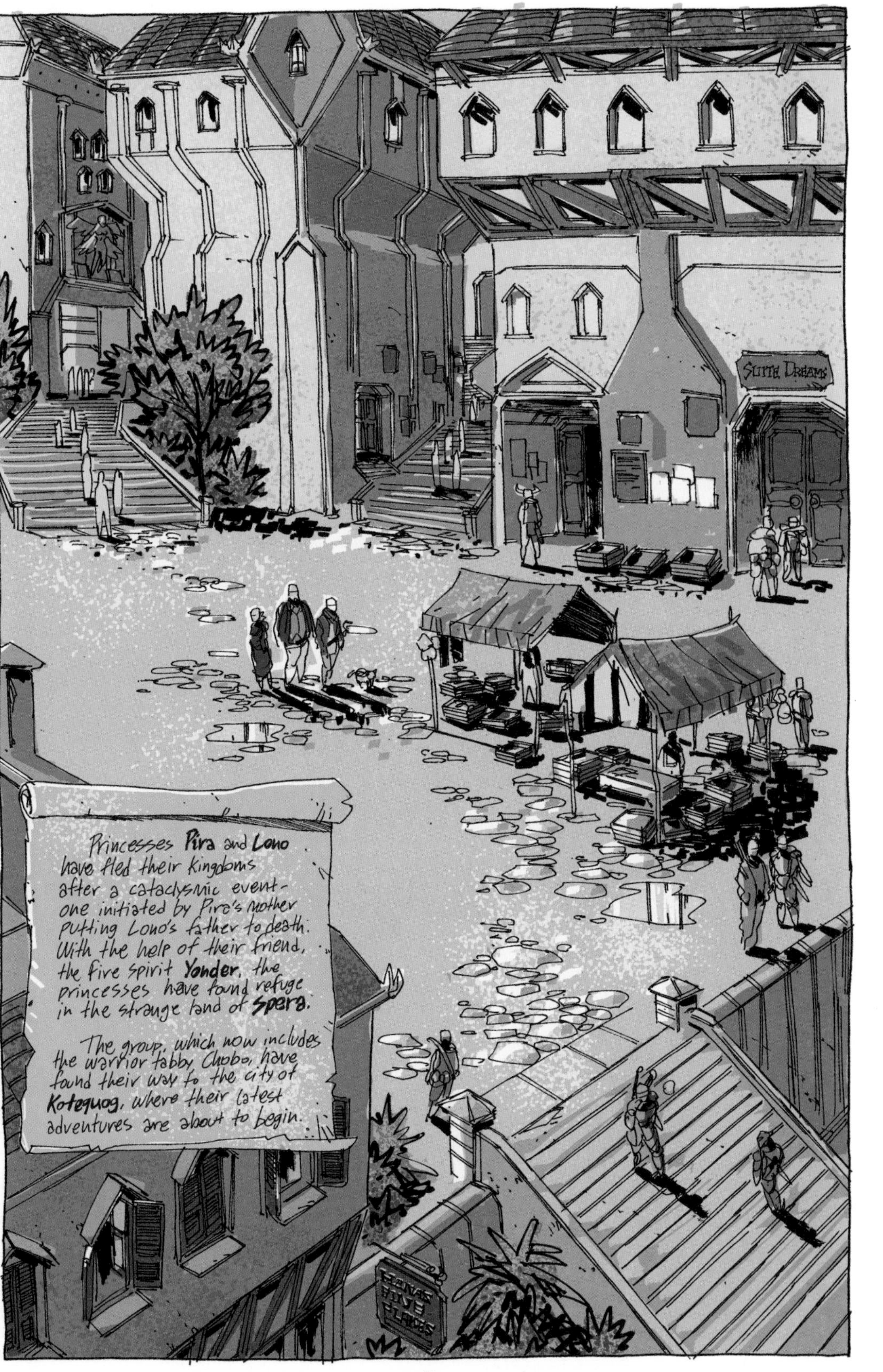

Suite Dreams
Princesses Pira and Lono have fled their kingdoms after a cataclysmic event - one initiated by Pira's mother putting Lono's father to death. With the help of their friend, the fire spirit Yonder, the princesses have found refuge in the strange land of Spera.
The group, which now includes the warrior tabby Chobo, have found their way to the city of Kotequog, where their latest adventures are about to begin.

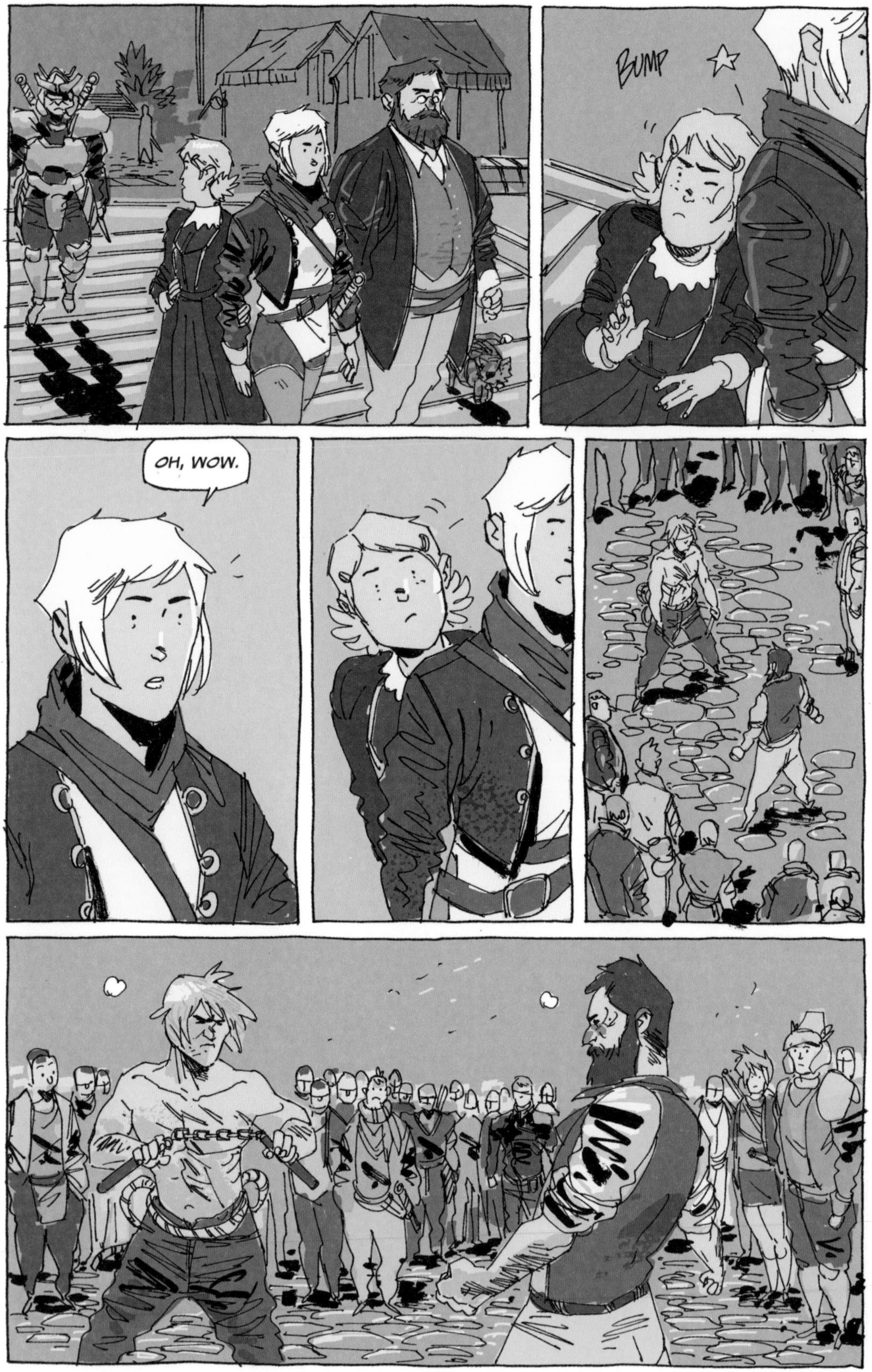
BUMP
OH, WOW.

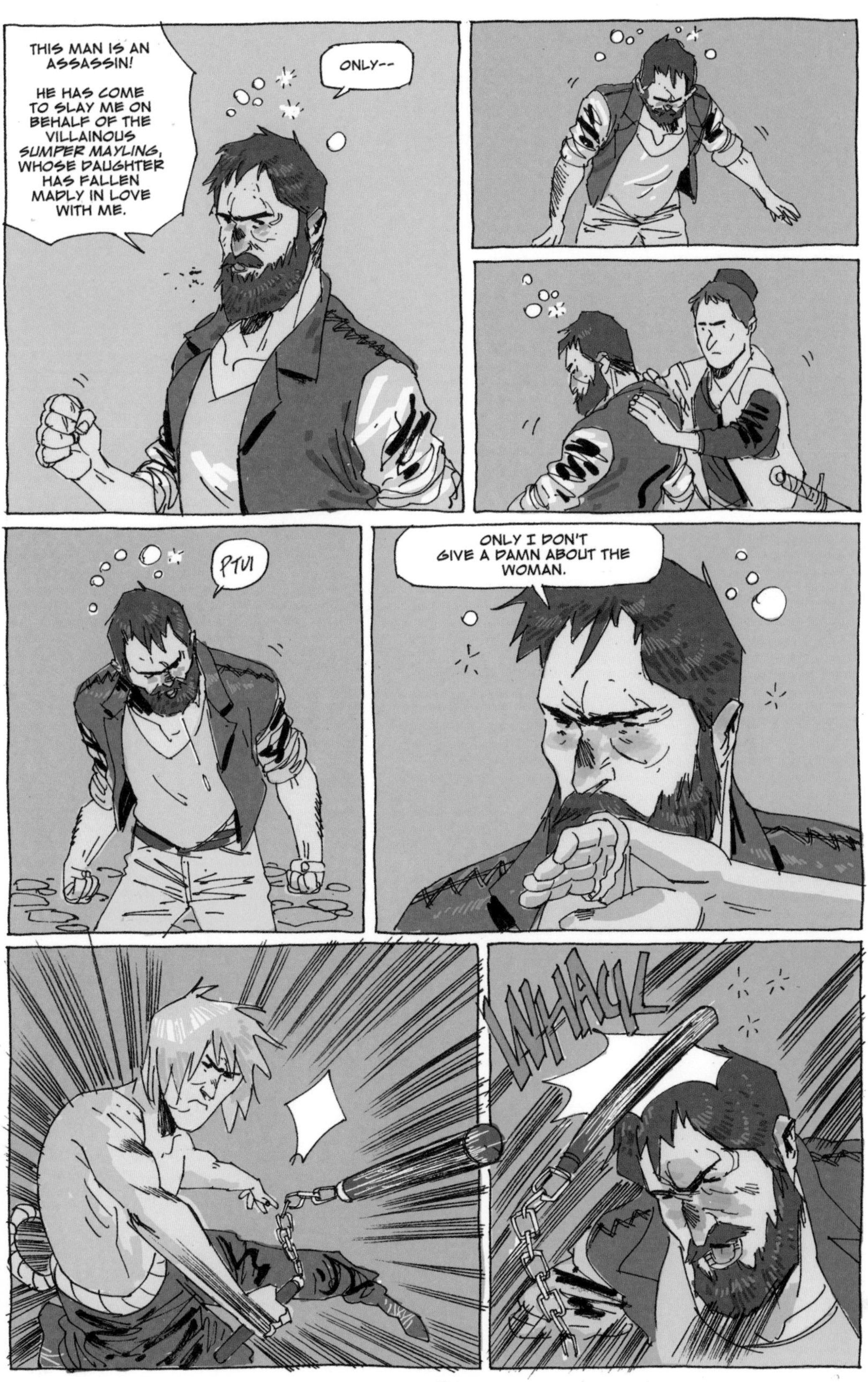
THIS MAN IS AN ASSASSIN!

HE HAS COME TO SLAY ME ON BEHALF OF THE VILLAINOUS *SUMPER MAYLING*, WHOSE DAUGHTER HAS FALLEN MADLY IN LOVE WITH ME.
ONLY--
PTUI
ONLY I DON'T GIVE A DAMN ABOUT THE WOMAN.
WHACK

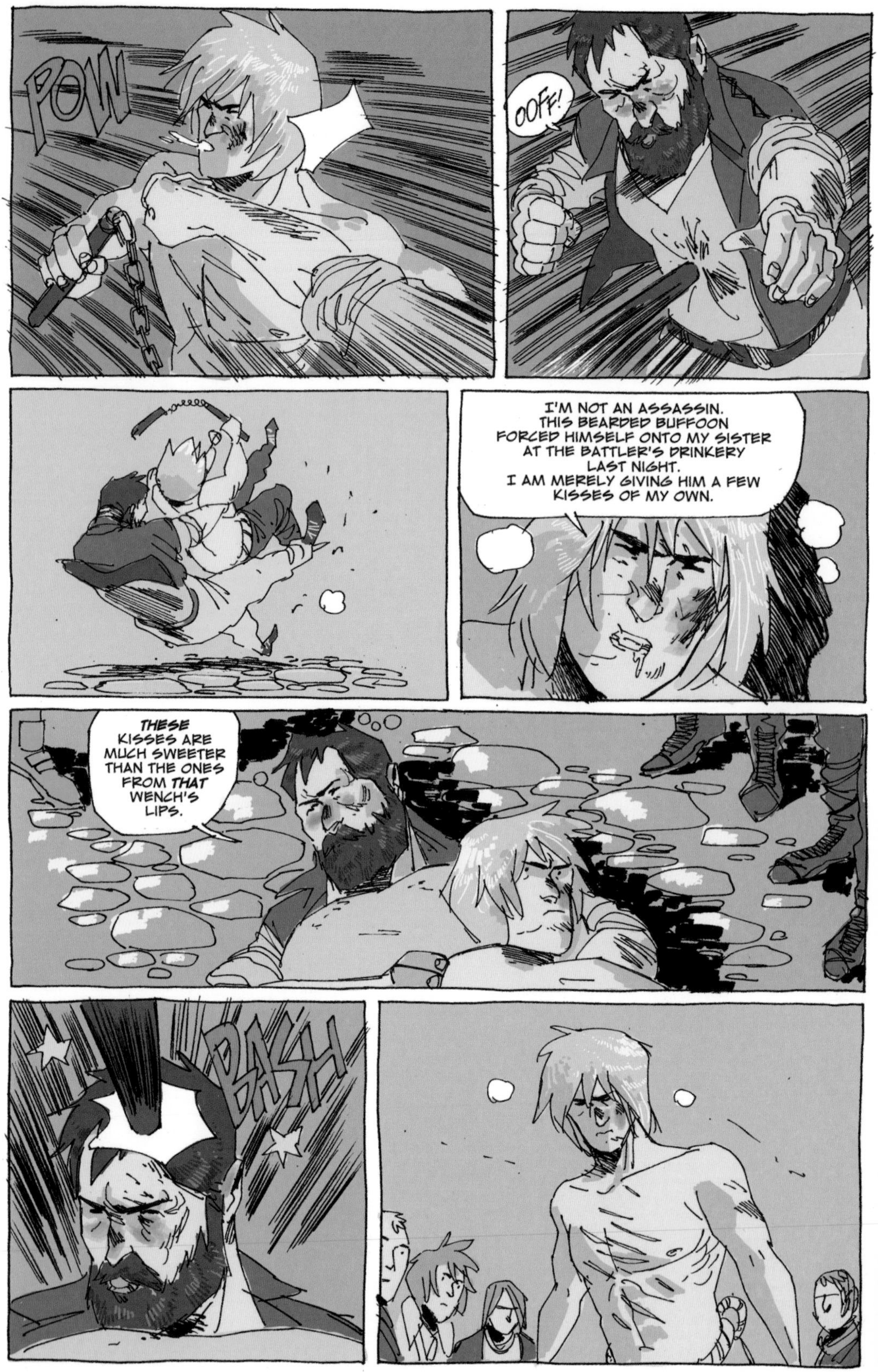
POW
OOFF!
I'M NOT AN ASSASSIN.
THIS BEARDED BUFFOON
FORCED HIMSELF ONTO MY SISTER
AT THE BATTLER'S DRINKERY
LAST NIGHT.
I AM MERELY GIVING HIM A FEW
KISSES OF MY OWN.
THESE KISSES ARE MUCH SWEETER THAN THE ONES FROM THAT WENCH'S LIPS.
BASH

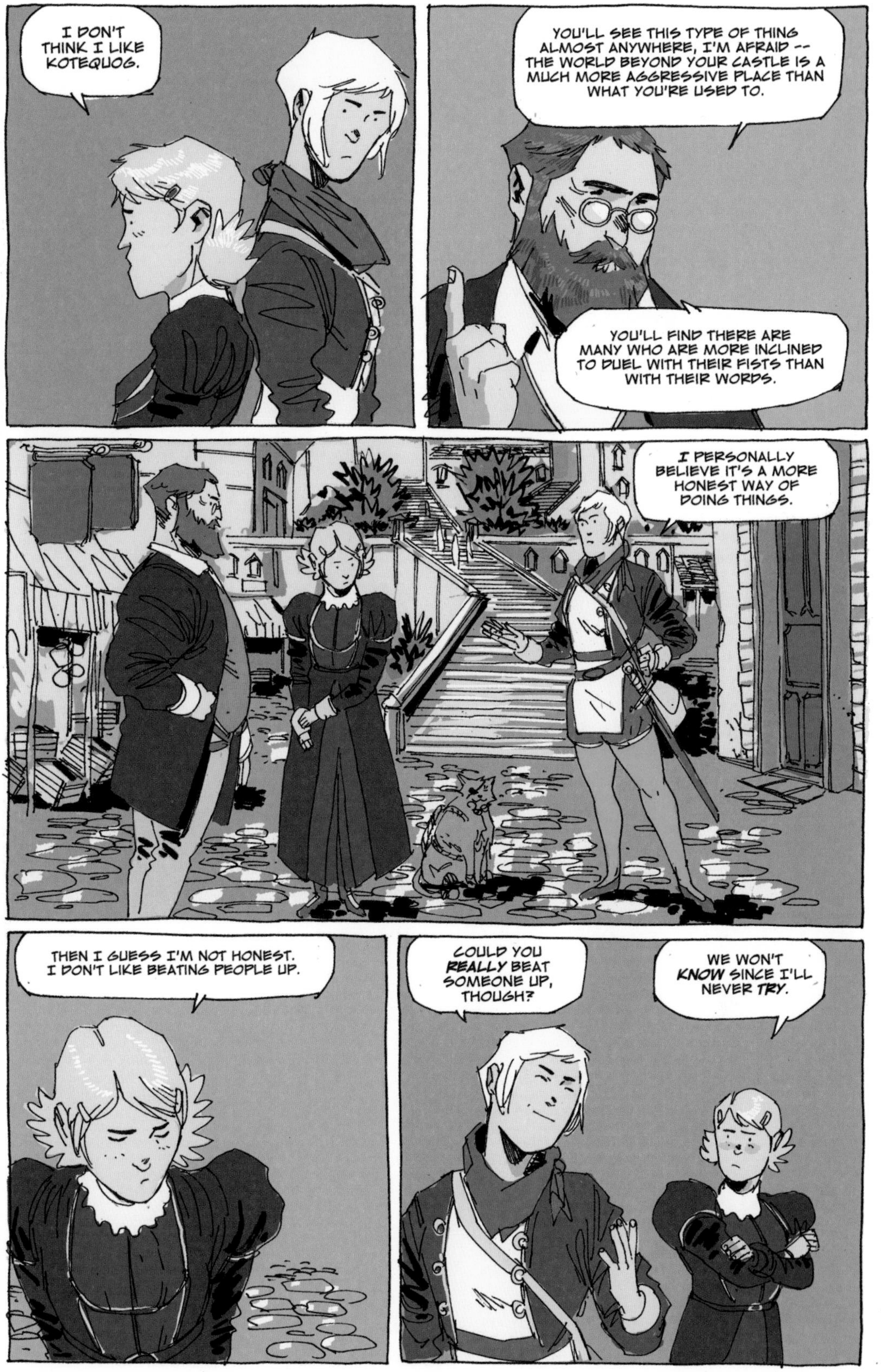
I DON'T THINK I LIKE KOTEQUOG.
YOU'LL SEE THIS TYPE OF THING ALMOST ANYWHERE, I'M AFRAID -- THE WORLD BEYOND YOUR CASTLE IS A MUCH MORE AGGRESSIVE PLACE THAN WHAT YOU'RE USED TO.
YOU'LL FIND THERE ARE MANY WHO ARE MORE INCLINED TO DUEL WITH THEIR FISTS THAN WITH THEIR WORDS.
I PERSONALLY BELIEVE IT'S A MORE HONEST WAY OF DOING THINGS.
THEN I GUESS I'M NOT HONEST. I DON'T LIKE BEATING PEOPLE UP.
COULD YOU ***REALLY*** BEAT SOMEONE UP, THOUGH?
WE WON'T ***KNOW*** SINCE I'LL NEVER ***TRY***.

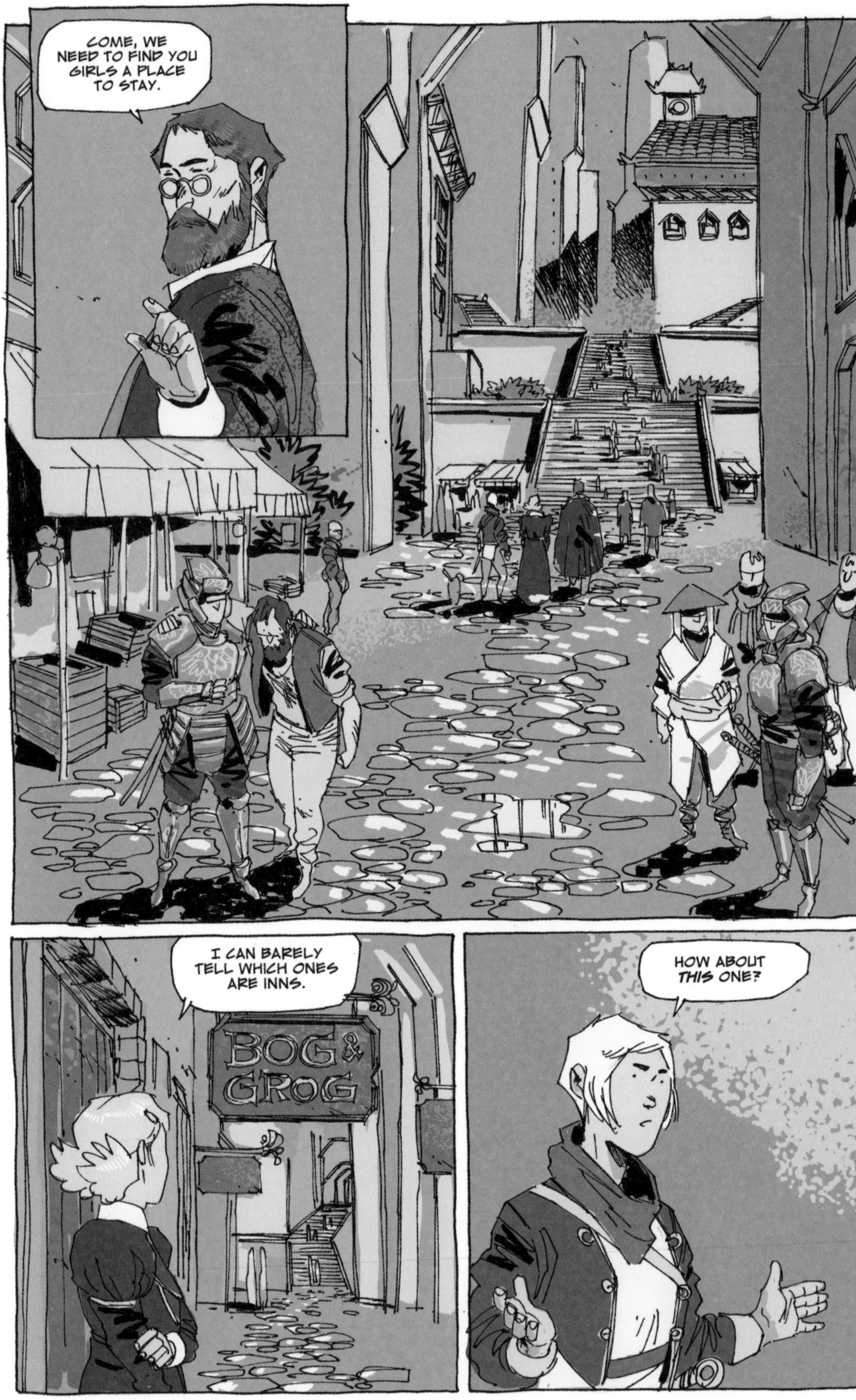
COME, WE NEED TO FIND YOU GIRLS A PLACE TO STAY.
I CAN BARELY TELL WHICH ONES ARE INNS.
BOG & GROG
HOW ABOUT *THIS* ONE?

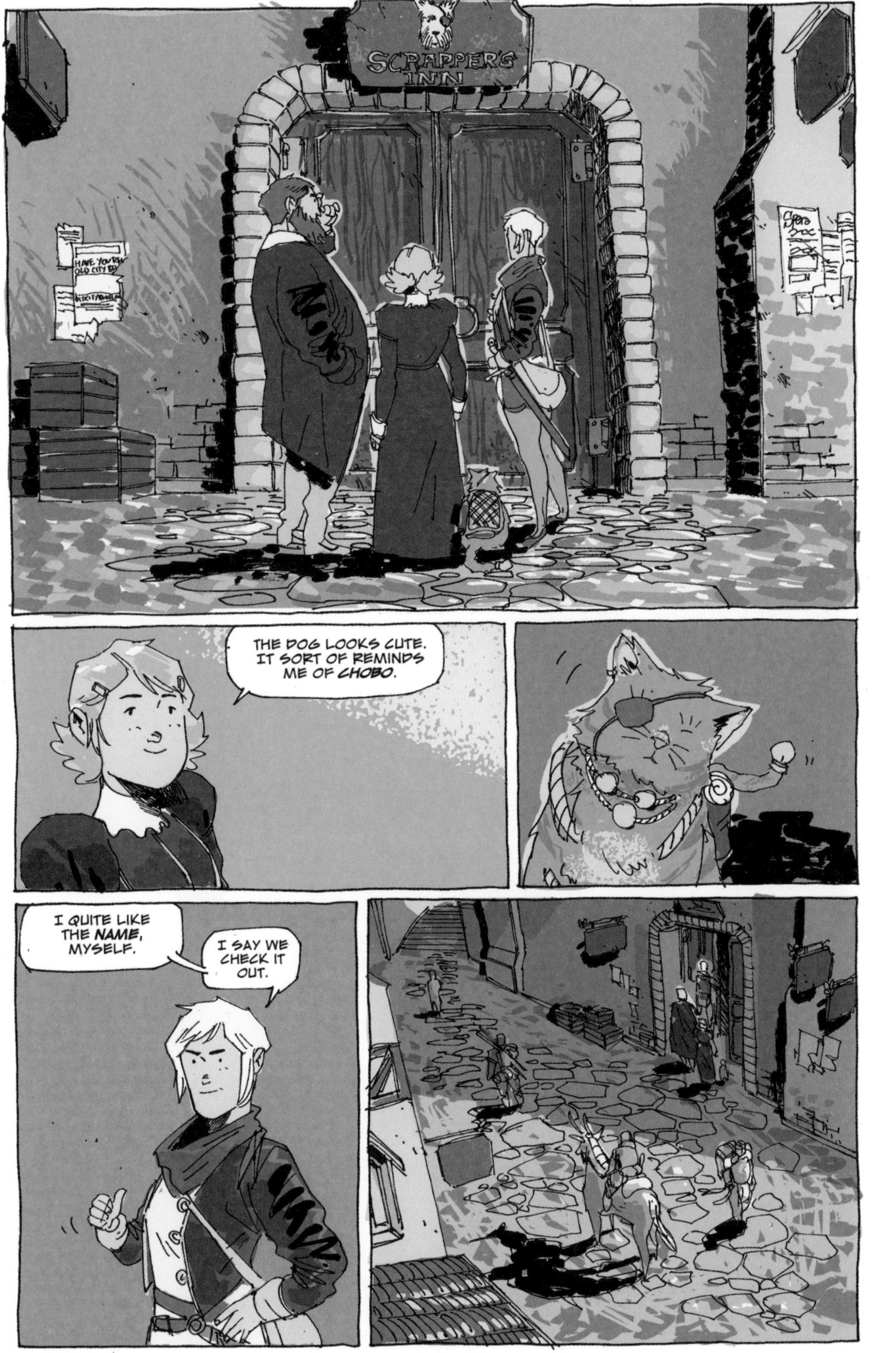
SCRAPPER'S INN
THE DOG LOOKS CUTE. IT SORT OF REMINDS ME OF CHOBO.
I QUITE LIKE THE NAME, MYSELF.
I SAY WE CHECK IT OUT.

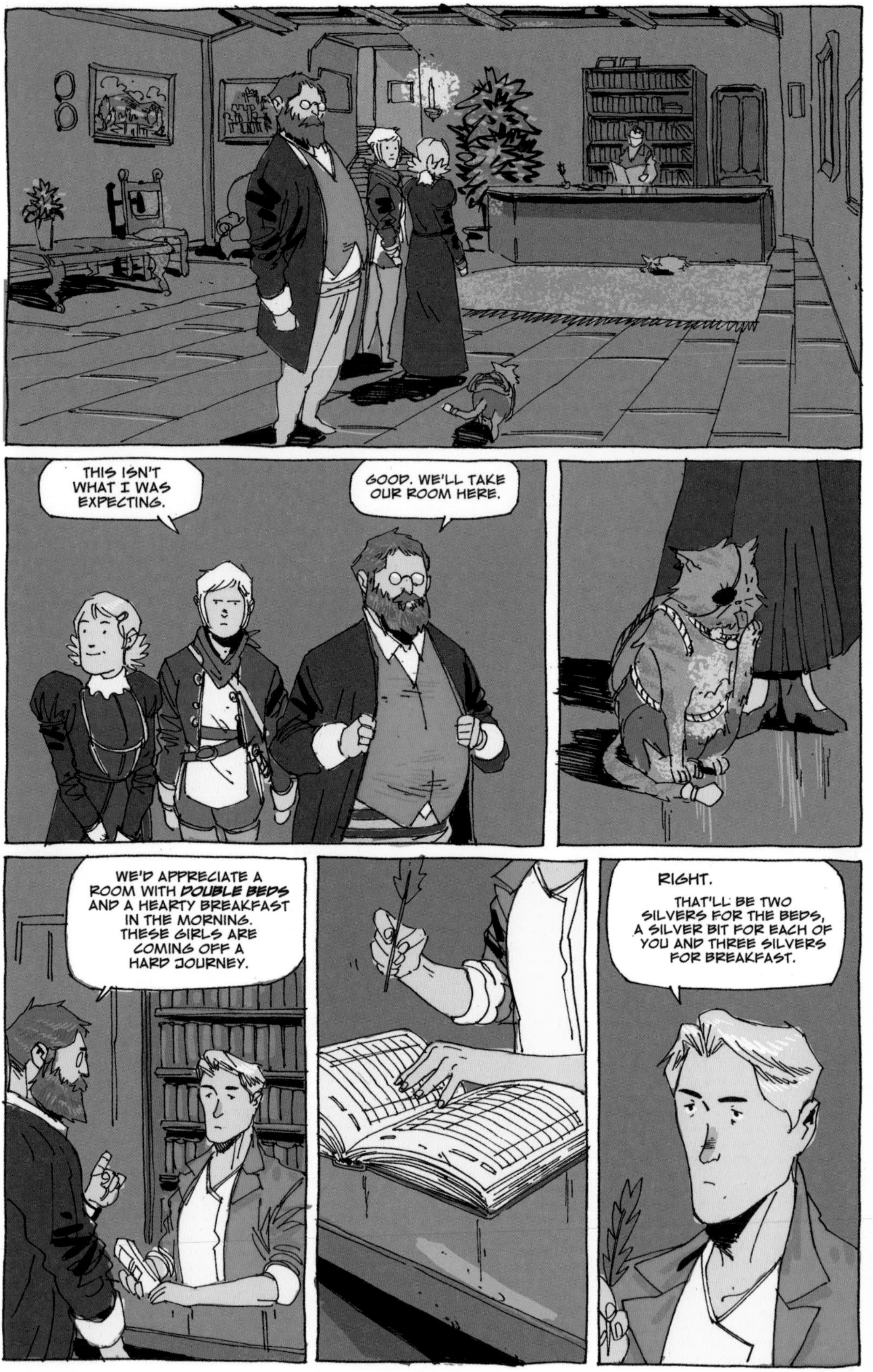
THIS ISN'T WHAT I WAS EXPECTING.
GOOD. WE'LL TAKE OUR ROOM HERE.
WE'D APPRECIATE A ROOM WITH *DOUBLE BEDS* AND A HEARTY BREAKFAST IN THE MORNING. THESE GIRLS ARE COMING OFF A HARD JOURNEY.
RIGHT.
THAT'LL BE TWO SILVERS FOR THE BEDS, A SILVER BIT FOR EACH OF YOU AND THREE SILVERS FOR BREAKFAST.

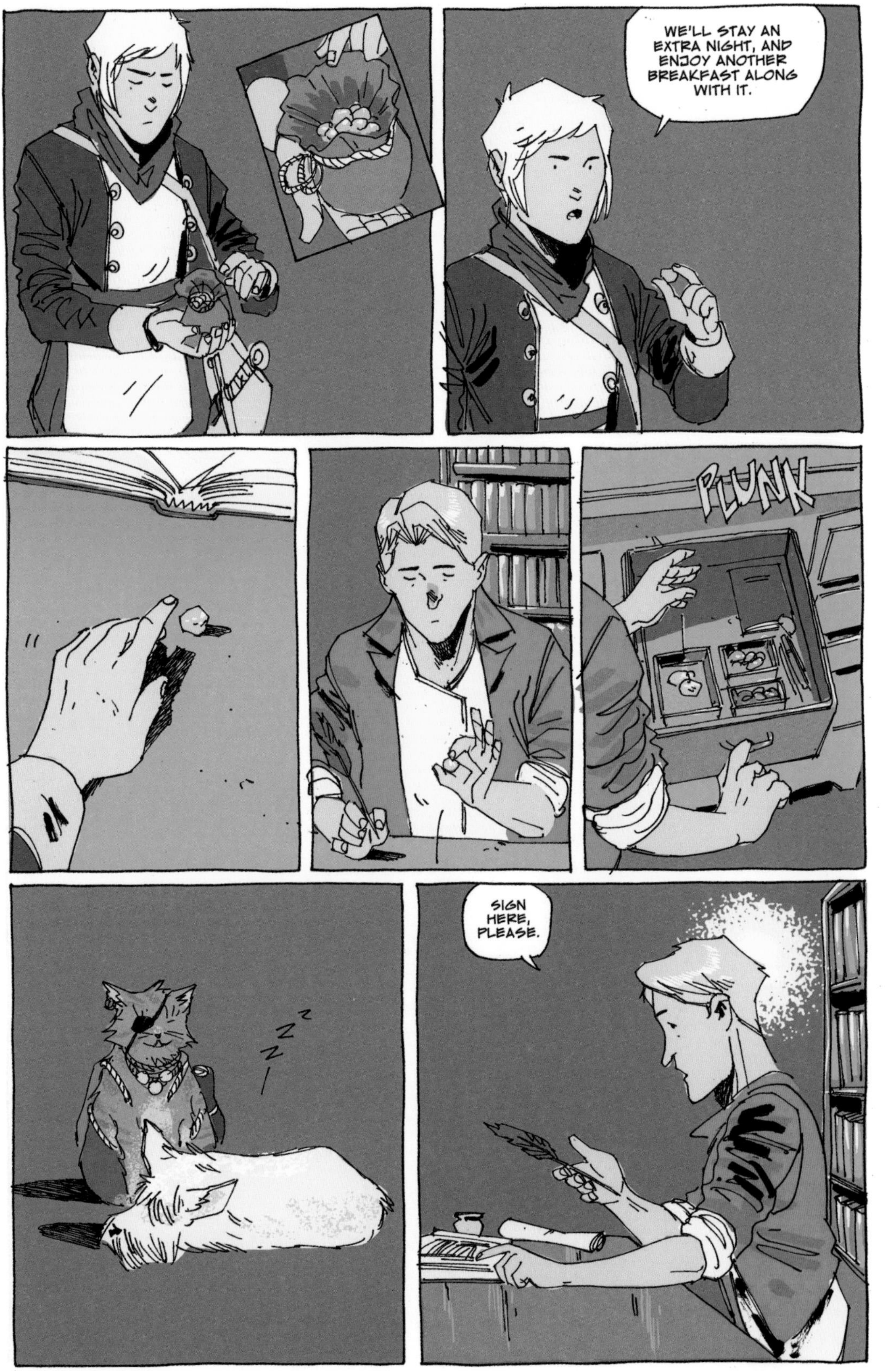
WE'LL STAY AN EXTRA NIGHT, AND ENJOY ANOTHER BREAKFAST ALONG WITH IT.
PLUNK
SIGN HERE, PLEASE.

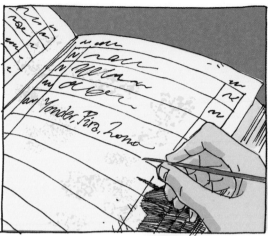

YOUR ROOM'LL BE THE SECOND DOOR UP THE STAIRS. WE ASK THAT YOU DO NOT DISTURB THE OTHER GUESTS DURING YOUR STAY.

SCRAPPER'S INN THANKS YOU FOR YOUR PATRONAGE.

RUSTLE

RUSTLE

YAAWWN

COME ON, CHOBO.

MRRROW

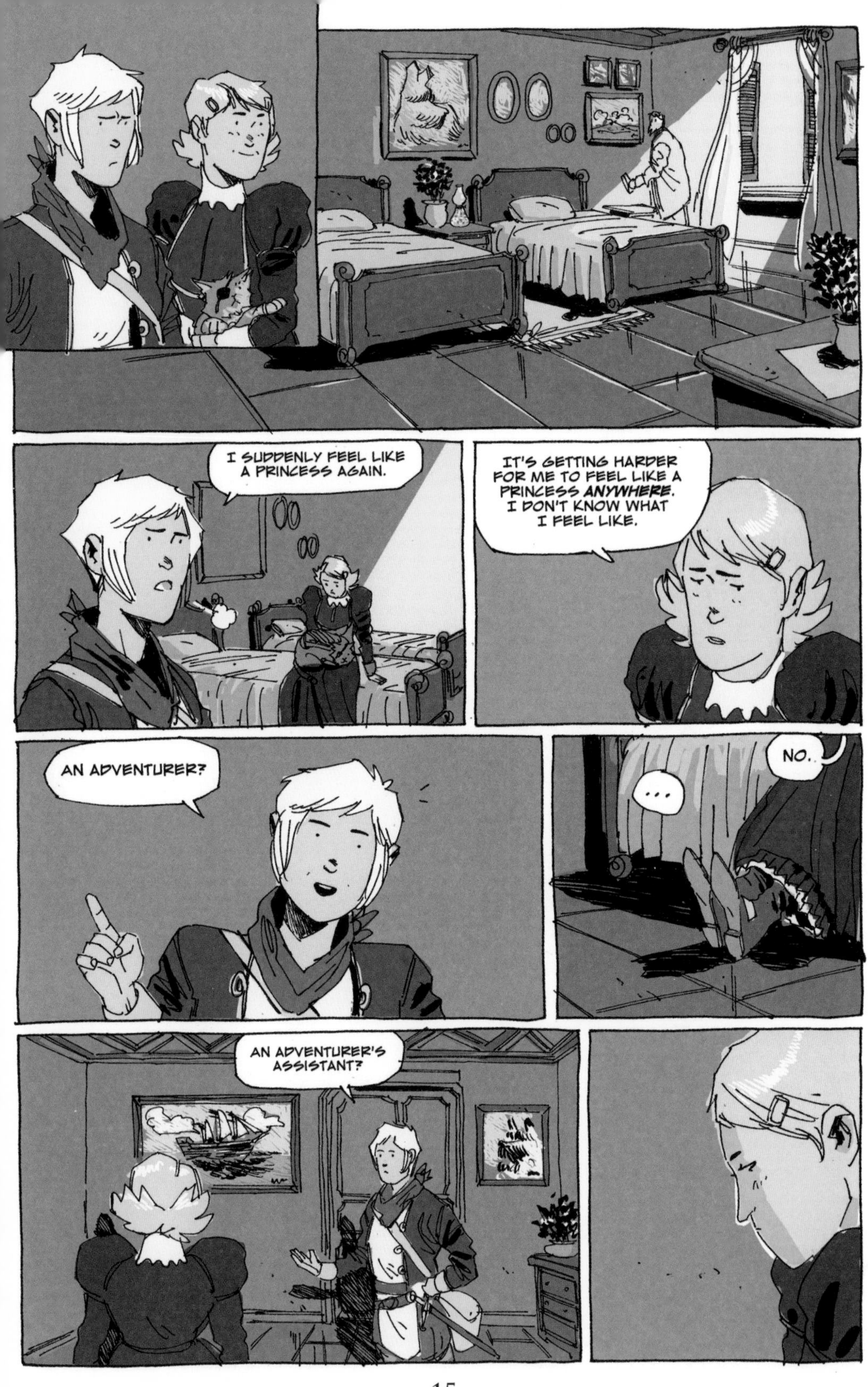
I SUDDENLY FEEL LIKE A PRINCESS AGAIN.
IT'S GETTING HARDER FOR ME TO FEEL LIKE A PRINCESS ANYWHERE. I DON'T KNOW WHAT I FEEL LIKE.
AN ADVENTURER?
...
NO.
AN ADVENTURER'S ASSISTANT?

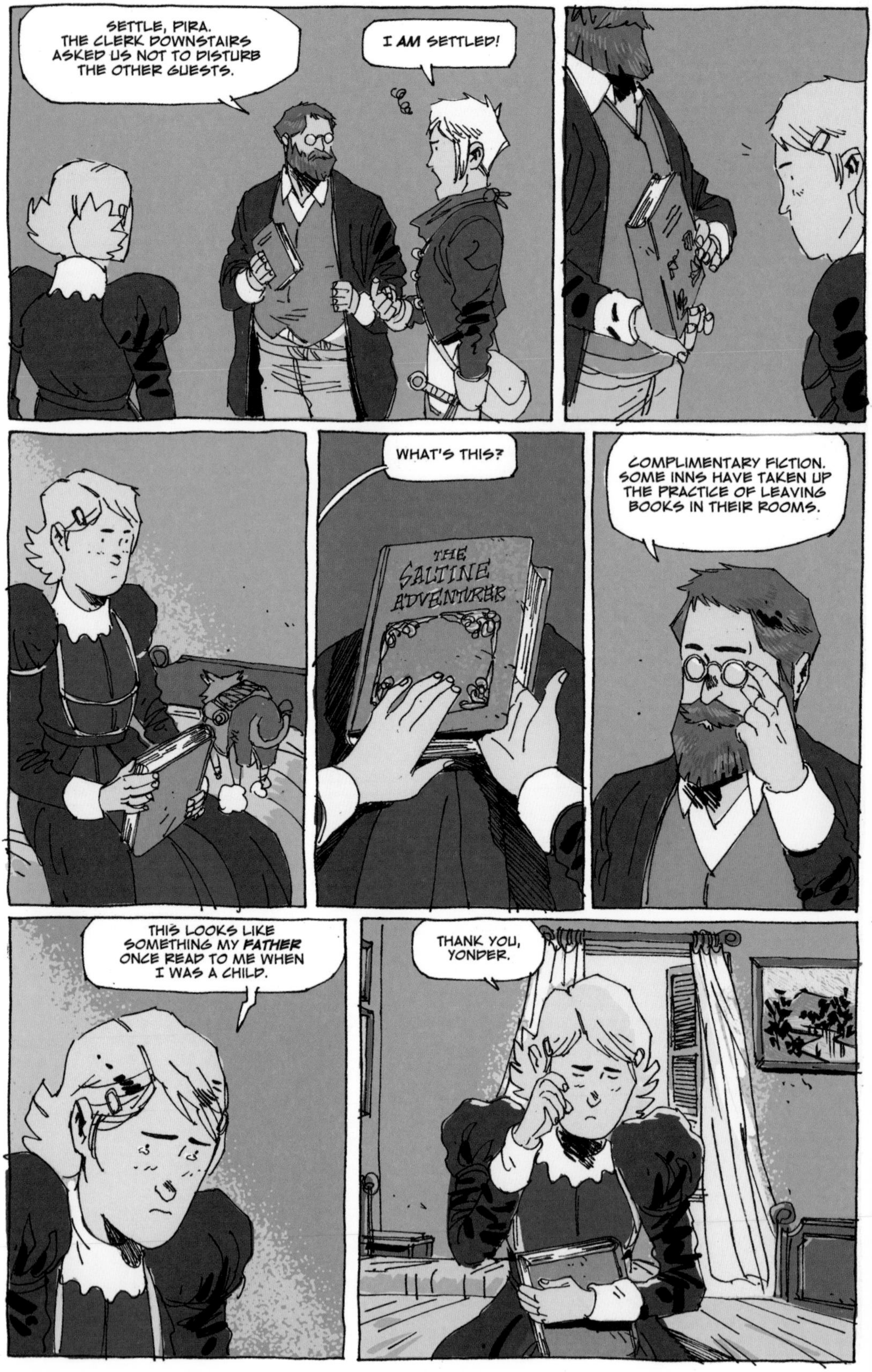
SETTLE, PIRA. THE CLERK DOWNSTAIRS ASKED US NOT TO DISTURB THE OTHER GUESTS.
I AM SETTLED!
WHAT'S THIS?
THE SALTINE ADVENTURER
COMPLIMENTARY FICTION. SOME INNS HAVE TAKEN UP THE PRACTICE OF LEAVING BOOKS IN THEIR ROOMS.
THIS LOOKS LIKE SOMETHING MY FATHER ONCE READ TO ME WHEN I WAS A CHILD.
THANK YOU, YONDER.

THANK *PIRA* FOR PAYING FOR OUR ROOM. UNTIL WE FIND A WAY TO MAKE MONEY, EVERYTHING WE DO WILL BE ON HER COIN.

THANKS, PIRA.

I KNOW YOU'RE *REALLY* THANKING ME BECAUSE YOU NOW HAVE SOME *BOOK* TO READ, BUT YOU'RE WELCOME.

I DON'T UNDERSTAND WHY WE ONLY GOT *TWO* BEDS, THOUGH. WHERE'S *YONDER* GOING TO SLEEP?

I'VE ALWAYS PREFERRED THE *FLOOR*, WHAT WITH BEING A *DOG* AND ALL.

TAP

TAP

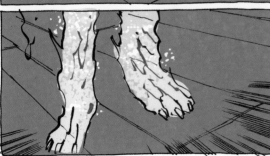

IS IT OKAY?

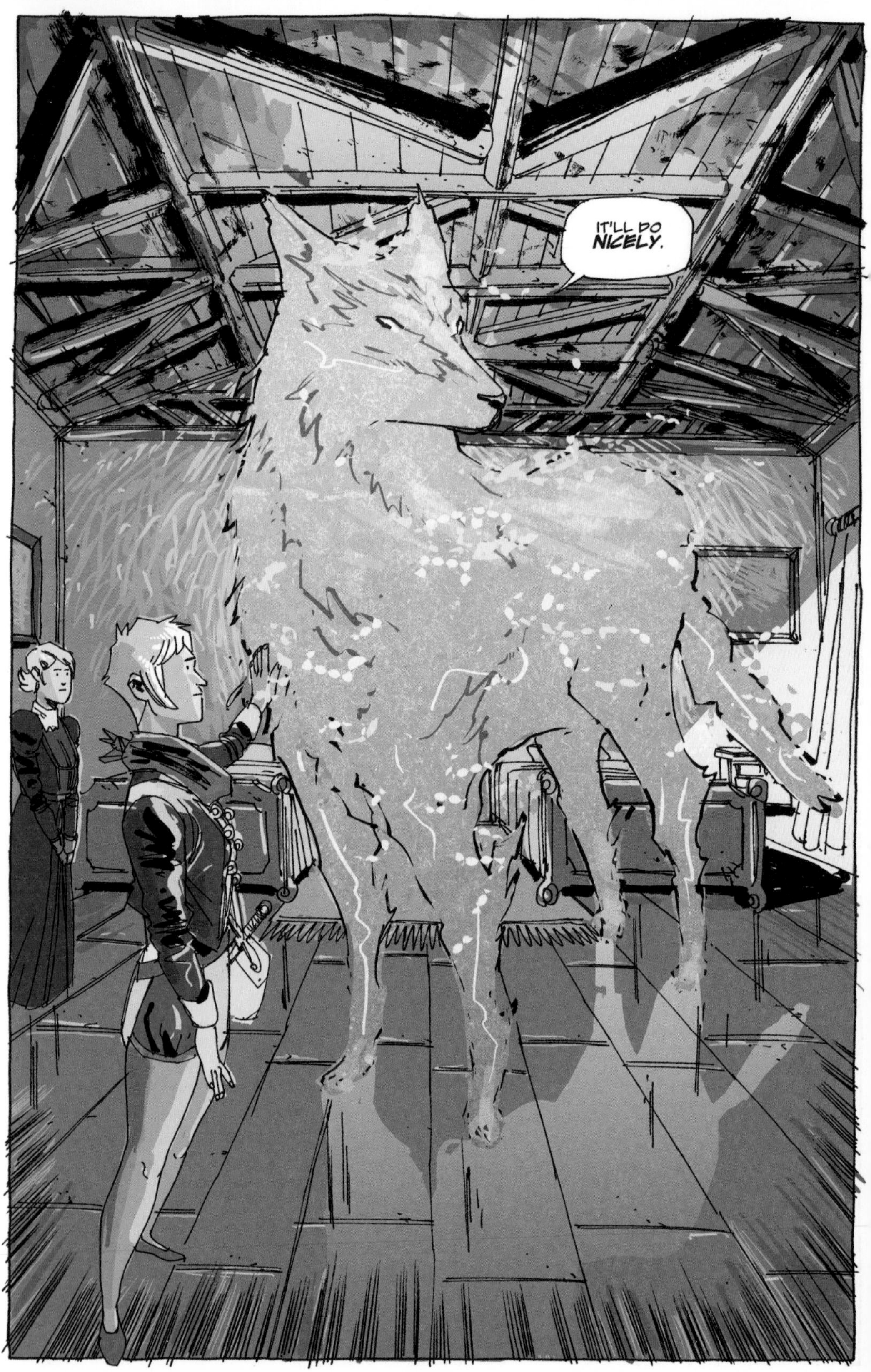
IT'LL DO NICELY.

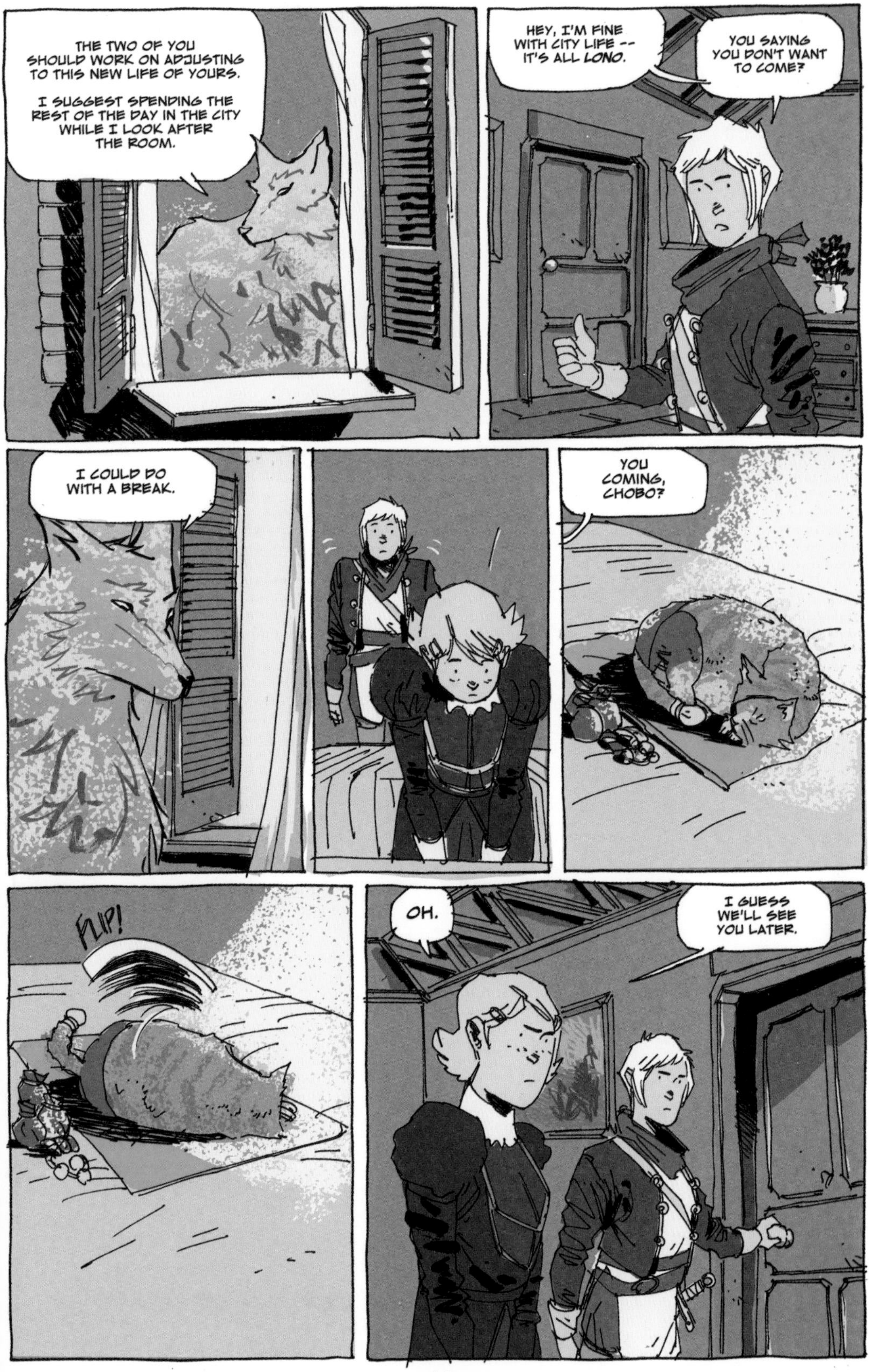
THE TWO OF YOU SHOULD WORK ON ADJUSTING TO THIS NEW LIFE OF YOURS.
I SUGGEST SPENDING THE REST OF THE DAY IN THE CITY WHILE I LOOK AFTER THE ROOM.
HEY, I'M FINE WITH CITY LIFE -- IT'S ALL *LONO*.
YOU SAYING YOU DON'T WANT TO COME?
I COULD DO WITH A BREAK.
YOU COMING, CHOBO?
FLIP!
OH.
I GUESS WE'LL SEE YOU LATER.

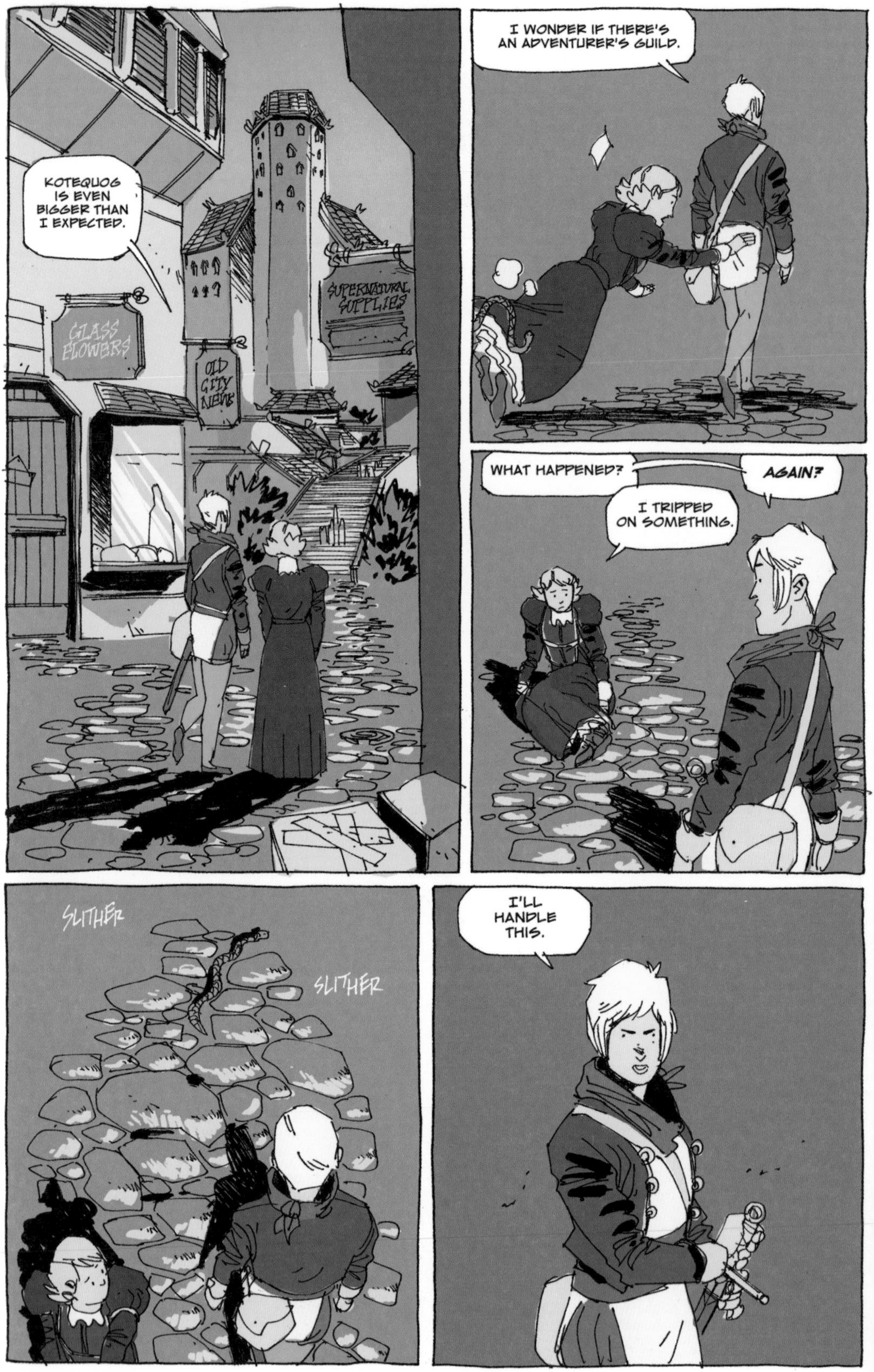
KOTEQUOG IS EVEN BIGGER THAN I EXPECTED.
GLASS FLOWERS
OLD CITY NEWS
SUPERNATURAL SUPPLIES
I WONDER IF THERE'S AN ADVENTURER'S GUILD.
WHAT HAPPENED?
AGAIN?
I TRIPPED ON SOMETHING.
SLITHER
SLITHER
I'LL HANDLE THIS.

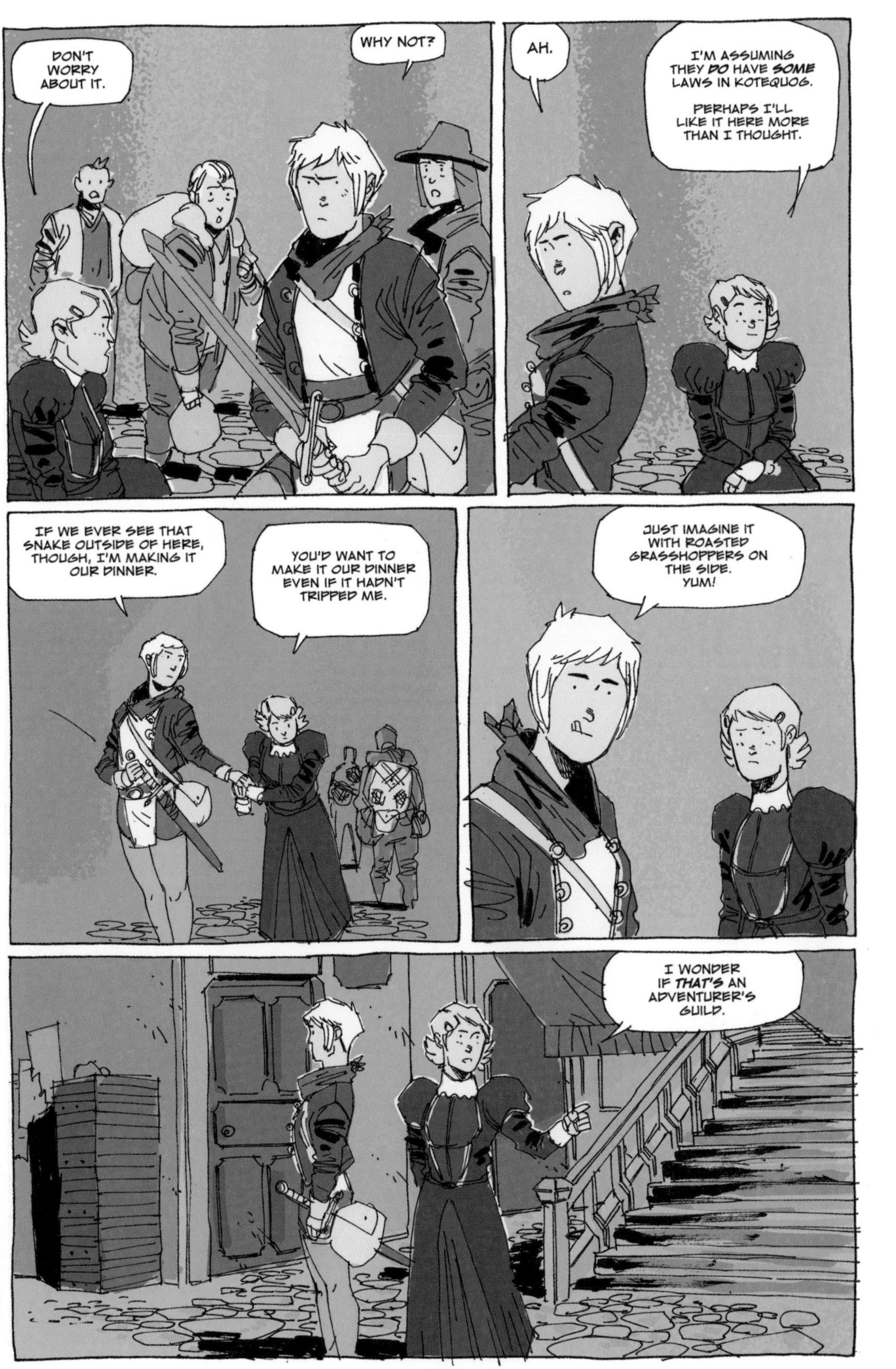
DON'T WORRY ABOUT IT.
WHY NOT?
AH.
I'M ASSUMING THEY *DO* HAVE *SOME* LAWS IN KOTEQUOG.
PERHAPS I'LL LIKE IT HERE MORE THAN I THOUGHT.
IF WE EVER SEE THAT SNAKE OUTSIDE OF HERE, THOUGH, I'M MAKING IT OUR DINNER.
YOU'D WANT TO MAKE IT OUR DINNER EVEN IF IT HADN'T TRIPPED ME.
JUST IMAGINE IT WITH ROASTED GRASSHOPPERS ON THE SIDE. YUM!
I WONDER IF *THAT'S* AN ADVENTURER'S GUILD.

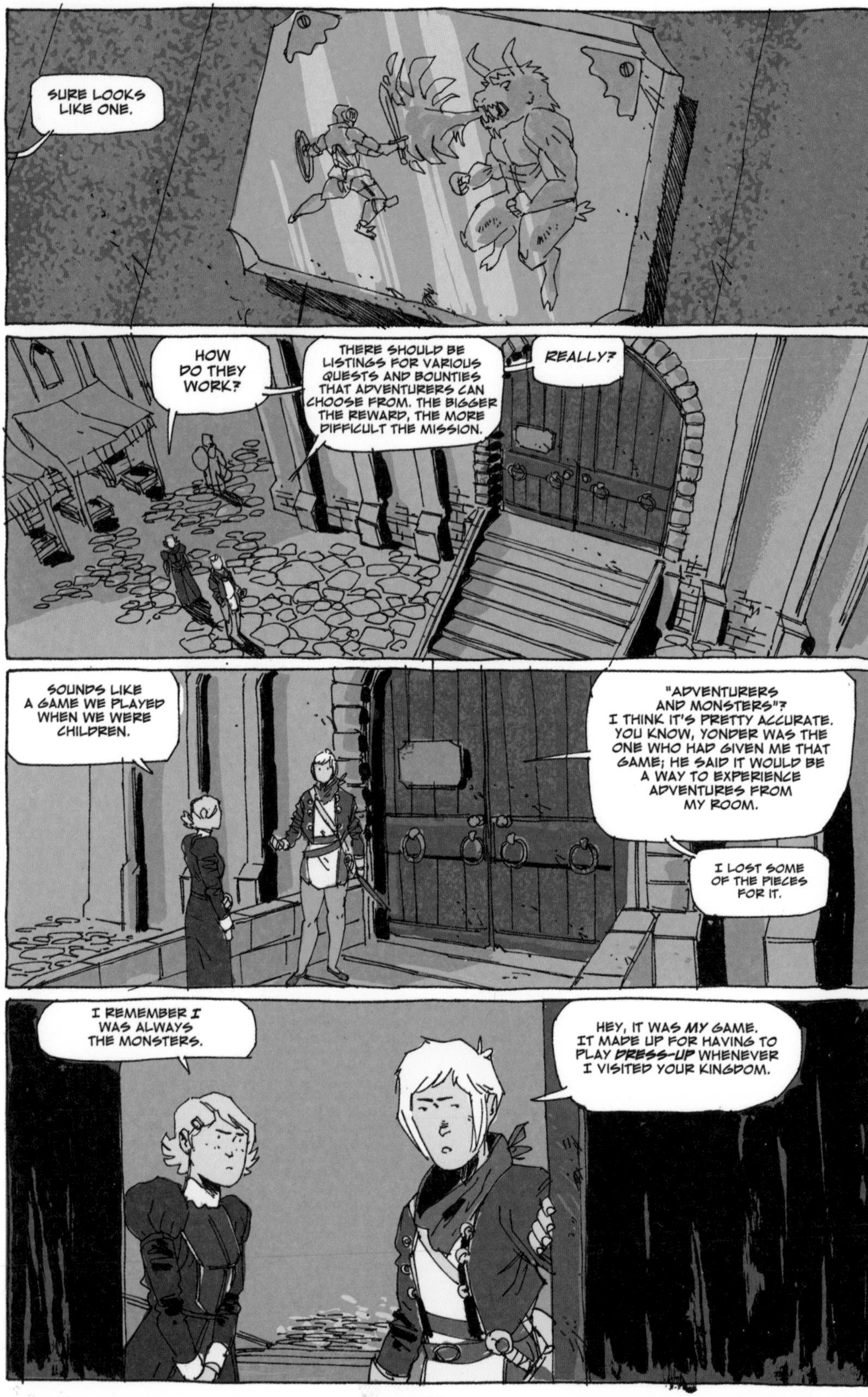
SURE LOOKS LIKE ONE.
HOW DO THEY WORK?
THERE SHOULD BE LISTINGS FOR VARIOUS QUESTS AND BOUNTIES THAT ADVENTURERS CAN CHOOSE FROM. THE BIGGER THE REWARD, THE MORE DIFFICULT THE MISSION.
REALLY?
SOUNDS LIKE A GAME WE PLAYED WHEN WE WERE CHILDREN.
"ADVENTURERS AND MONSTERS"? I THINK IT'S PRETTY ACCURATE. YOU KNOW, YONDER WAS THE ONE WHO HAD GIVEN ME THAT GAME; HE SAID IT WOULD BE A WAY TO EXPERIENCE ADVENTURES FROM MY ROOM.
I LOST SOME OF THE PIECES FOR IT.
I REMEMBER I WAS ALWAYS THE MONSTERS.
HEY, IT WAS MY GAME. IT MADE UP FOR HAVING TO PLAY DRESS-UP WHENEVER I VISITED YOUR KINGDOM.

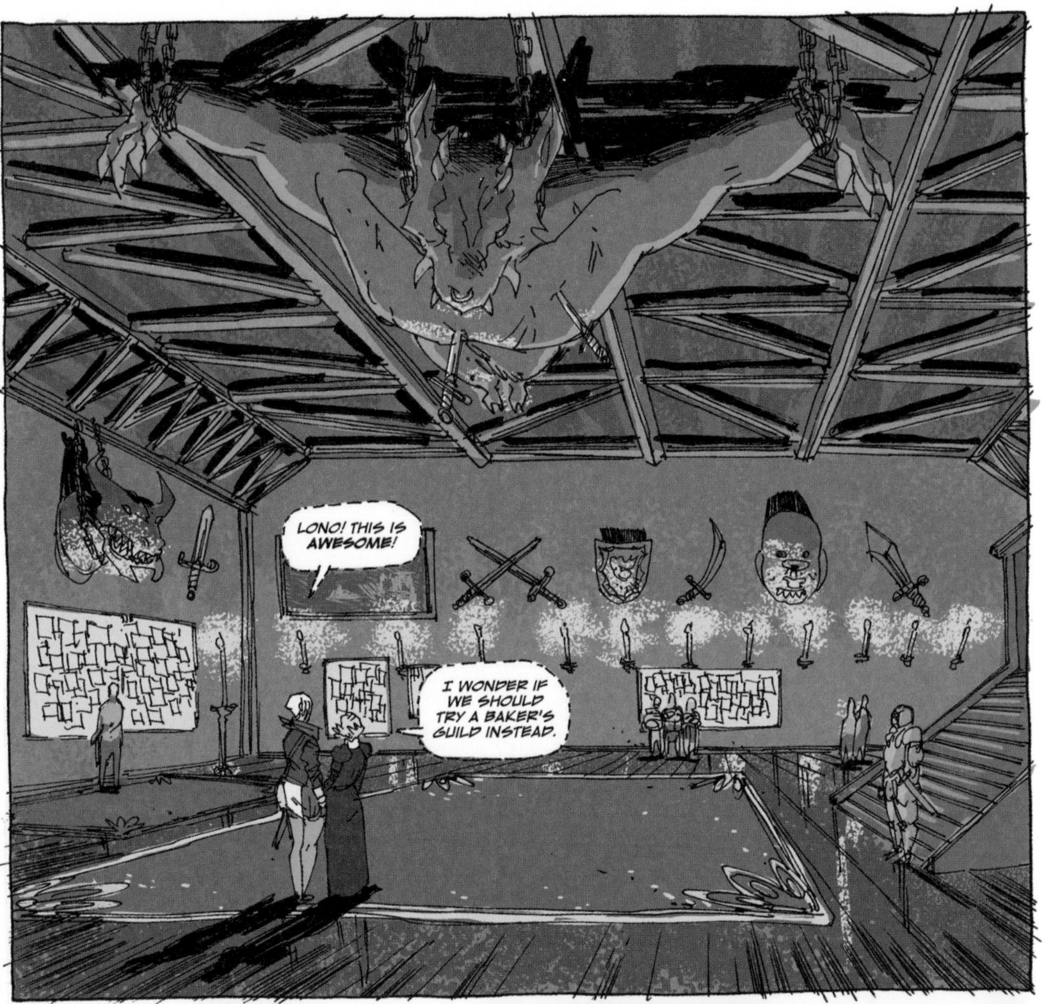
LONO! THIS IS **AWESOME!**
I WONDER IF WE SHOULD TRY A BAKER'S GUILD INSTEAD.

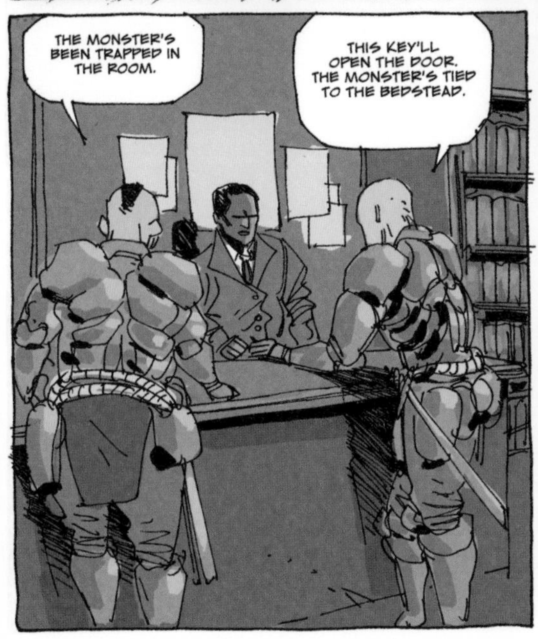
THE MONSTER'S BEEN TRAPPED IN THE ROOM.
THIS KEY'LL OPEN THE DOOR. THE MONSTER'S TIED TO THE BEDSTEAD.

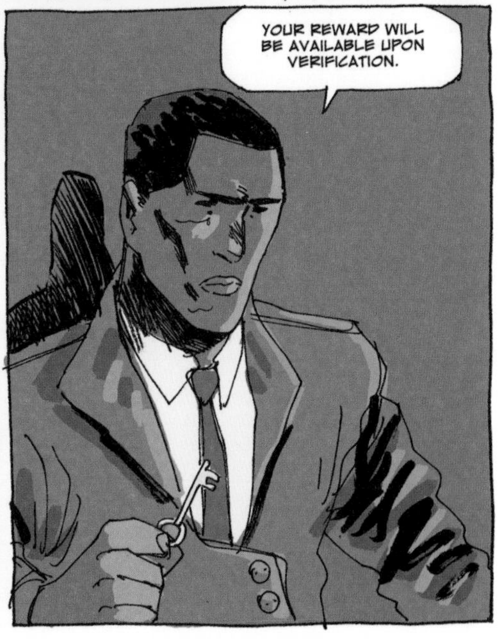
YOUR REWARD WILL BE AVAILABLE UPON VERIFICATION.

COME ON -- LET'S GO ASK ABOUT JOINING.

HELLO, SIR! MY FRIEND AND I ARE LOOKING TO EARN SOME EXTRA GOLD. WE WERE WONDERING IF YOU HAVE ANY ASSIGNMENTS AVAILABLE.

SOMETHING KIND OF *GIRL-FRIENDLY*.

DO EITHER OF YOU HAVE ANY EXPERIENCE DOING *ANYTHING*?

MORE THAN *YOU KNOW*, SIR.

...

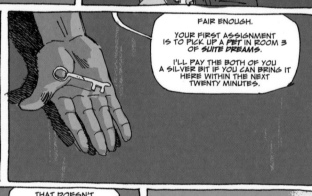

FAIR ENOUGH.

YOUR FIRST ASSIGNMENT IS TO PICK UP A *PET* IN ROOM 3 OF *SUITE DREAMS*.

I'LL PAY THE BOTH OF YOU A SILVER BIT IF YOU CAN BRING IT HERE WITHIN THE NEXT TWENTY MINUTES.

AWESOME! WE'LL DO THE BEST JOB YOU'VE EVER SEEN!

THAT DOESN'T SOUND BAD AT ALL!

To be Continued...

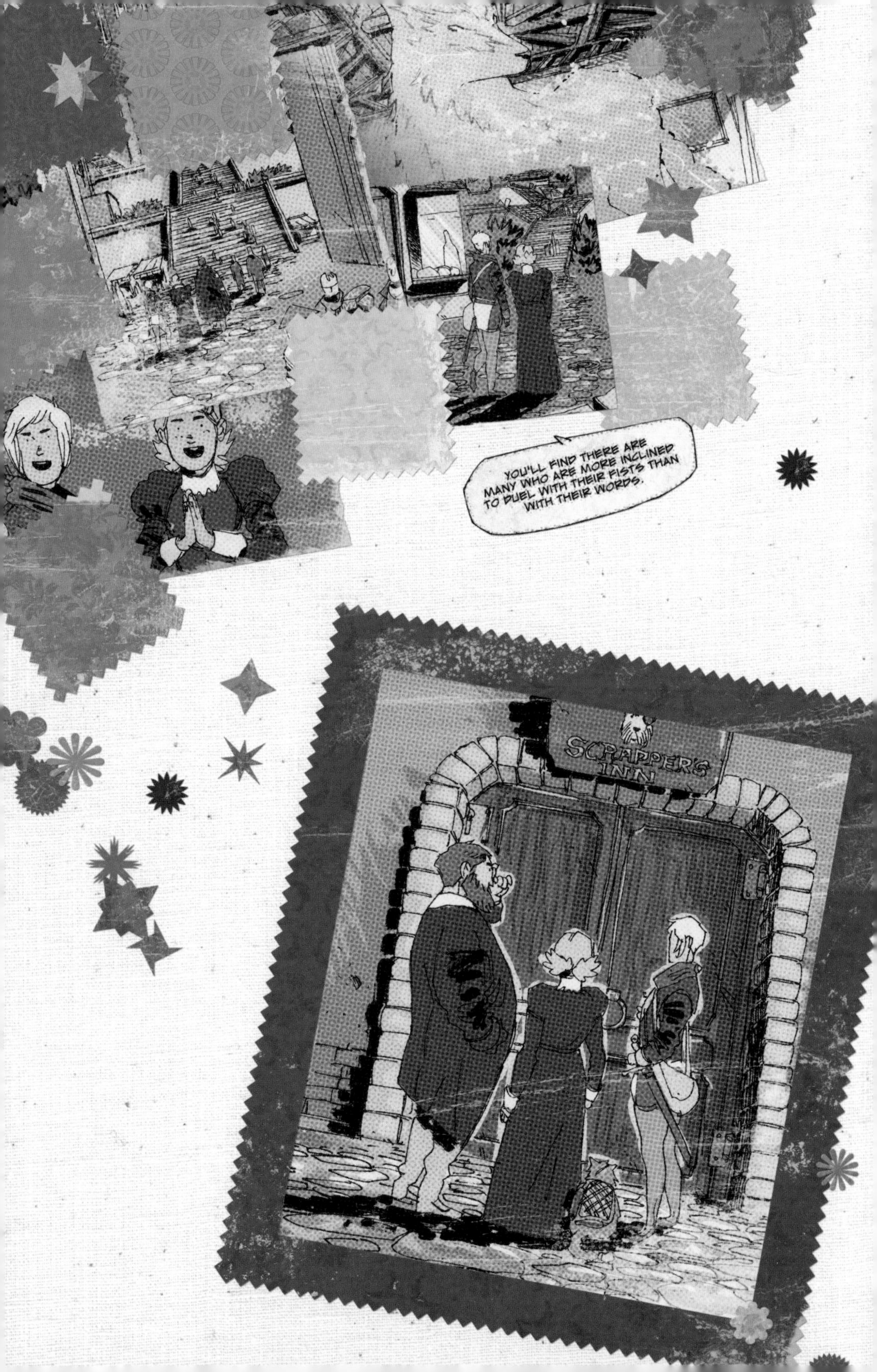
YOU'LL FIND THERE ARE MANY WHO ARE MORE INCLINED TO DUEL WITH THEIR FISTS THAN WITH THEIR WORDS.
SCRAPPER'S INN

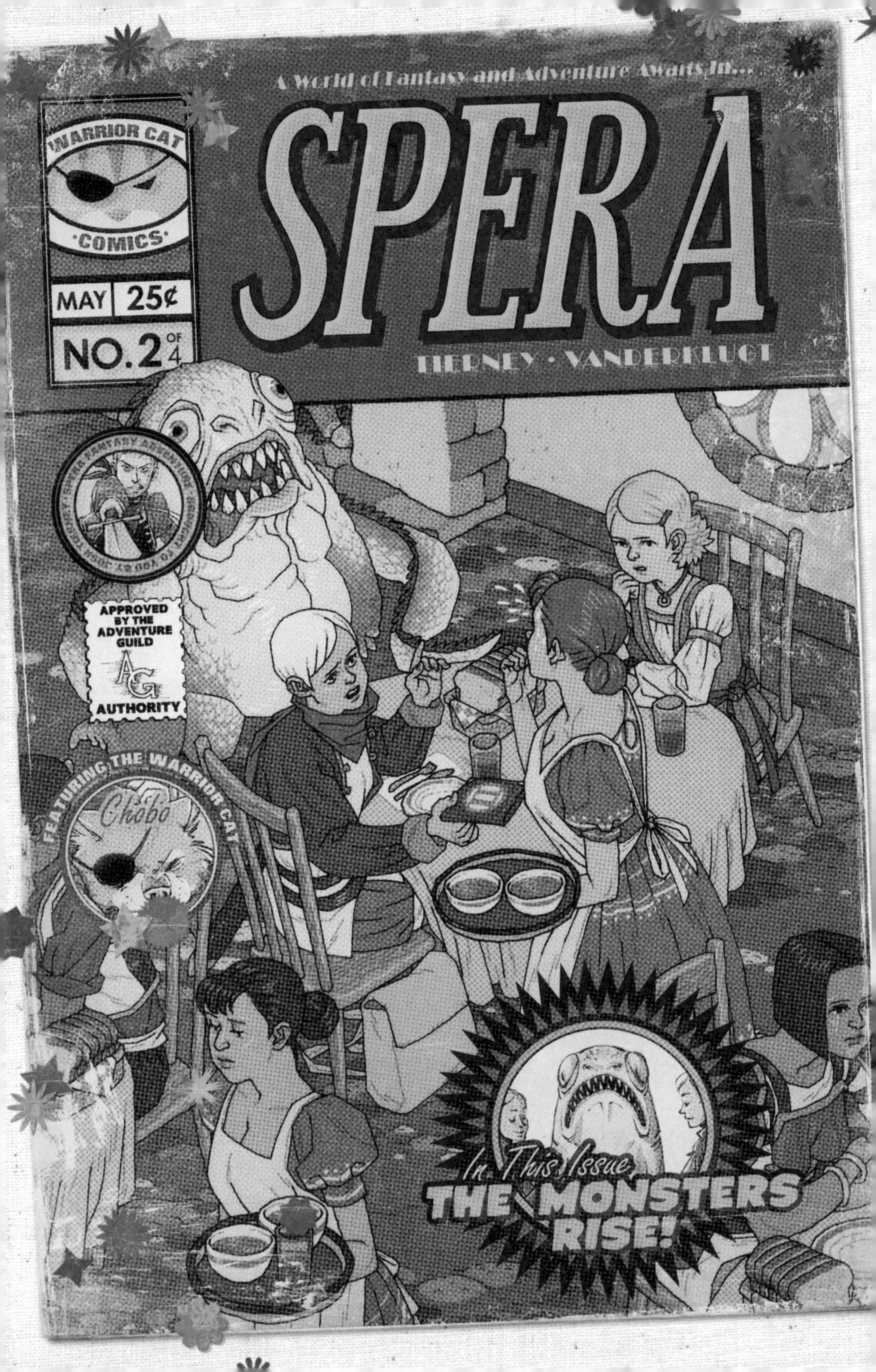
A World of Fantasy and Adventure Awaits In...
SPERA
WARRIOR CAT COMICS
MAY 25¢
NO. 2 OF 4
TIERNEY · VANDERKLUGT
APPROVED BY THE ADVENTURE GUILD
AG
AUTHORITY
FEATURING THE WARRIOR CAT
Chobo
In This Issue
THE MONSTERS RISE!

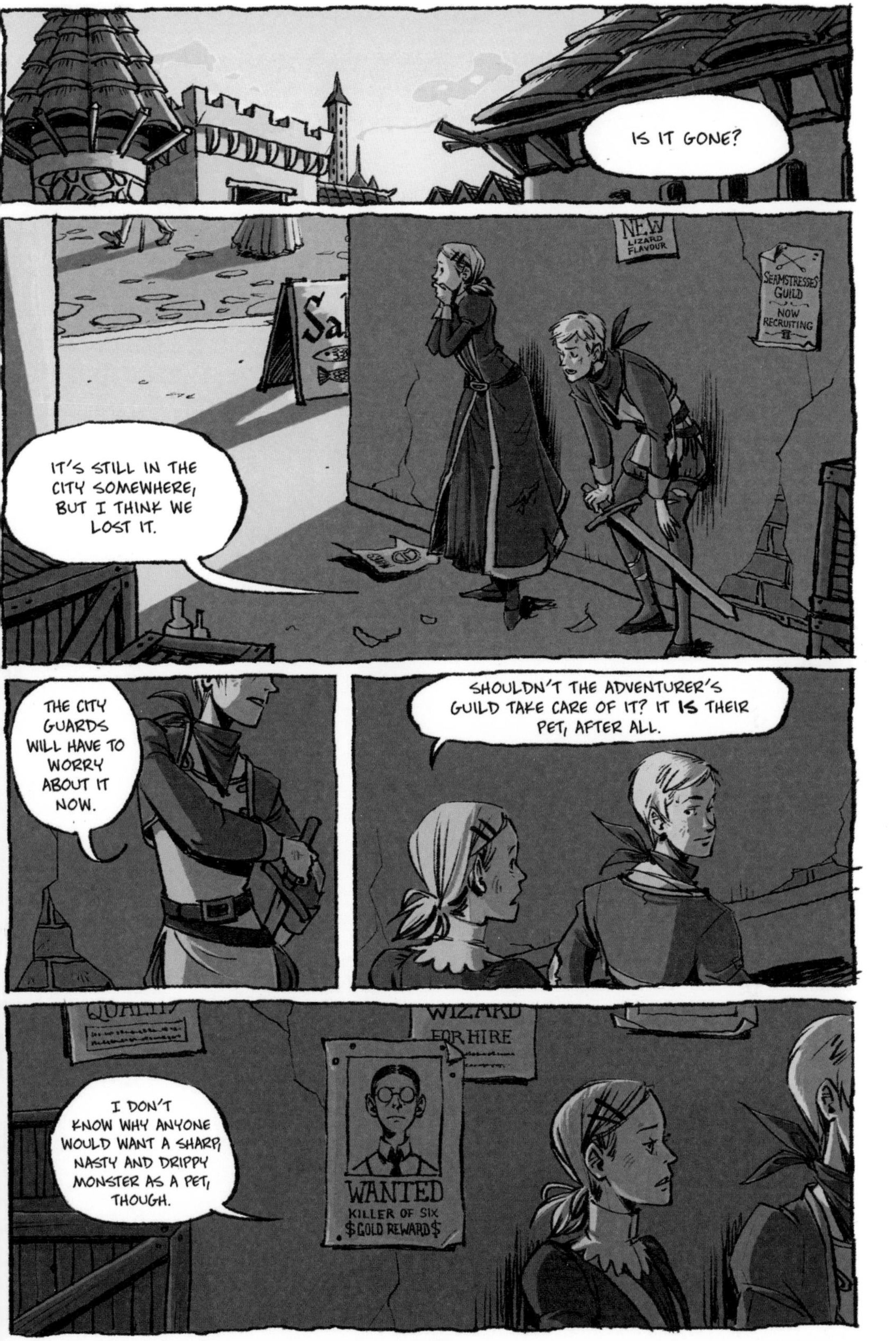
IS IT GONE?
NEW LIZARD FLAVOUR
SEAMSTRESSES' GUILD NOW RECRUITING
IT'S STILL IN THE CITY SOMEWHERE, BUT I THINK WE LOST IT.
THE CITY GUARDS WILL HAVE TO WORRY ABOUT IT NOW.
SHOULDN'T THE ADVENTURER'S GUILD TAKE CARE OF IT? IT **IS** THEIR PET, AFTER ALL.
WIZARD FOR HIRE
WANTED KILLER OF SIX $GOLD REWARD$
I DON'T KNOW WHY ANYONE WOULD WANT A SHARP, NASTY AND DRIPPY MONSTER AS A PET, THOUGH.

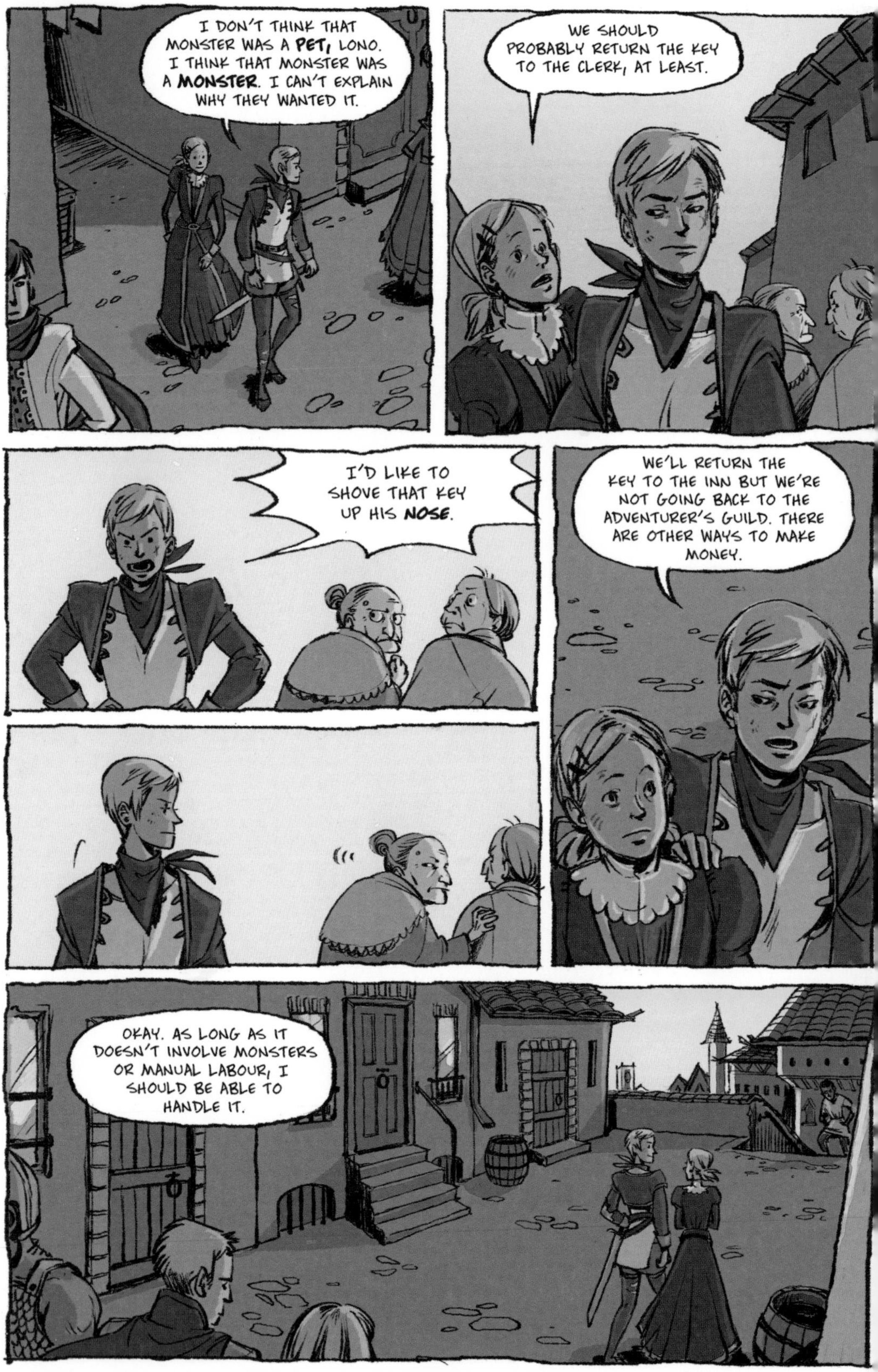
I DON'T THINK THAT MONSTER WAS A PET, LONO. I THINK THAT MONSTER WAS A MONSTER. I CAN'T EXPLAIN WHY THEY WANTED IT.
WE SHOULD PROBABLY RETURN THE KEY TO THE CLERK, AT LEAST.
I'D LIKE TO SHOVE THAT KEY UP HIS NOSE.
WE'LL RETURN THE KEY TO THE INN BUT WE'RE NOT GOING BACK TO THE ADVENTURER'S GUILD. THERE ARE OTHER WAYS TO MAKE MONEY.
OKAY. AS LONG AS IT DOESN'T INVOLVE MONSTERS OR MANUAL LABOUR, I SHOULD BE ABLE TO HANDLE IT.

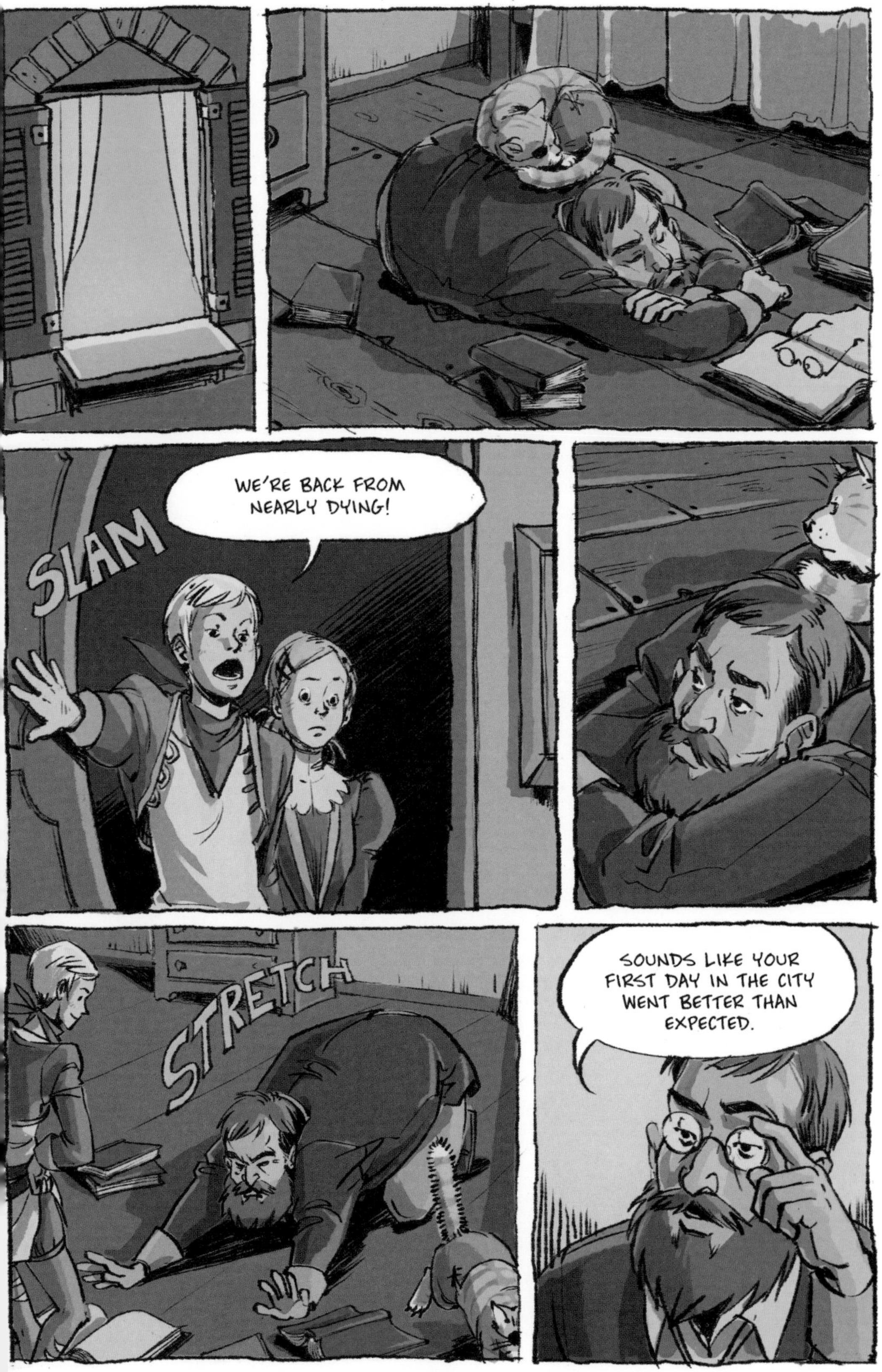
WE'RE BACK FROM NEARLY DYING!
SLAM
STRETCH
SOUNDS LIKE YOUR FIRST DAY IN THE CITY WENT BETTER THAN EXPECTED.

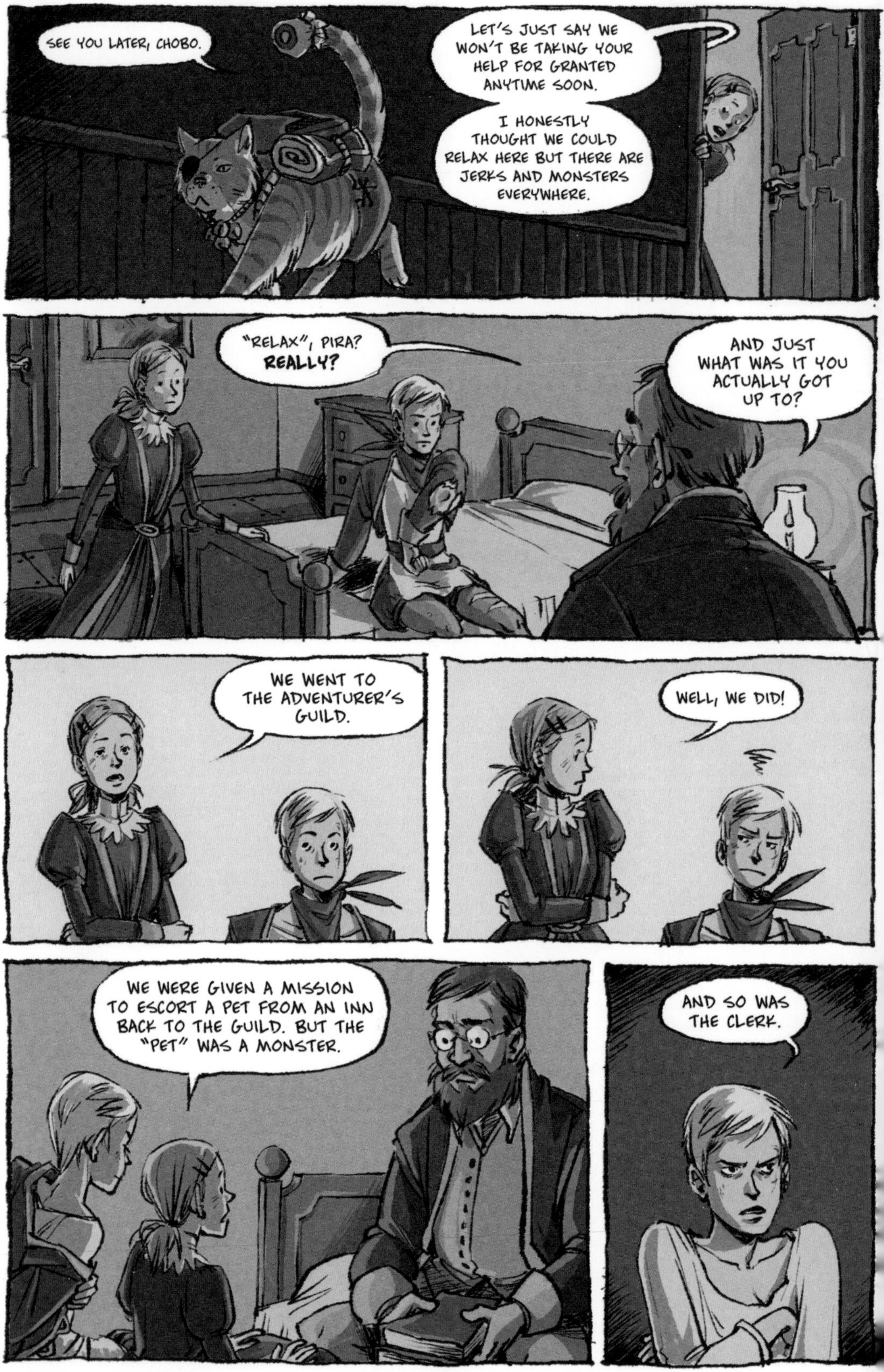
SEE YOU LATER, CHOBO.
LET'S JUST SAY WE WON'T BE TAKING YOUR HELP FOR GRANTED ANYTIME SOON.
I HONESTLY THOUGHT WE COULD RELAX HERE BUT THERE ARE JERKS AND MONSTERS EVERYWHERE.
"RELAX", PIRA? REALLY?
AND JUST WHAT WAS IT YOU ACTUALLY GOT UP TO?
WE WENT TO THE ADVENTURER'S GUILD.
WELL, WE DID!
WE WERE GIVEN A MISSION TO ESCORT A PET FROM AN INN BACK TO THE GUILD. BUT THE "PET" WAS A MONSTER.
AND SO WAS THE CLERK.

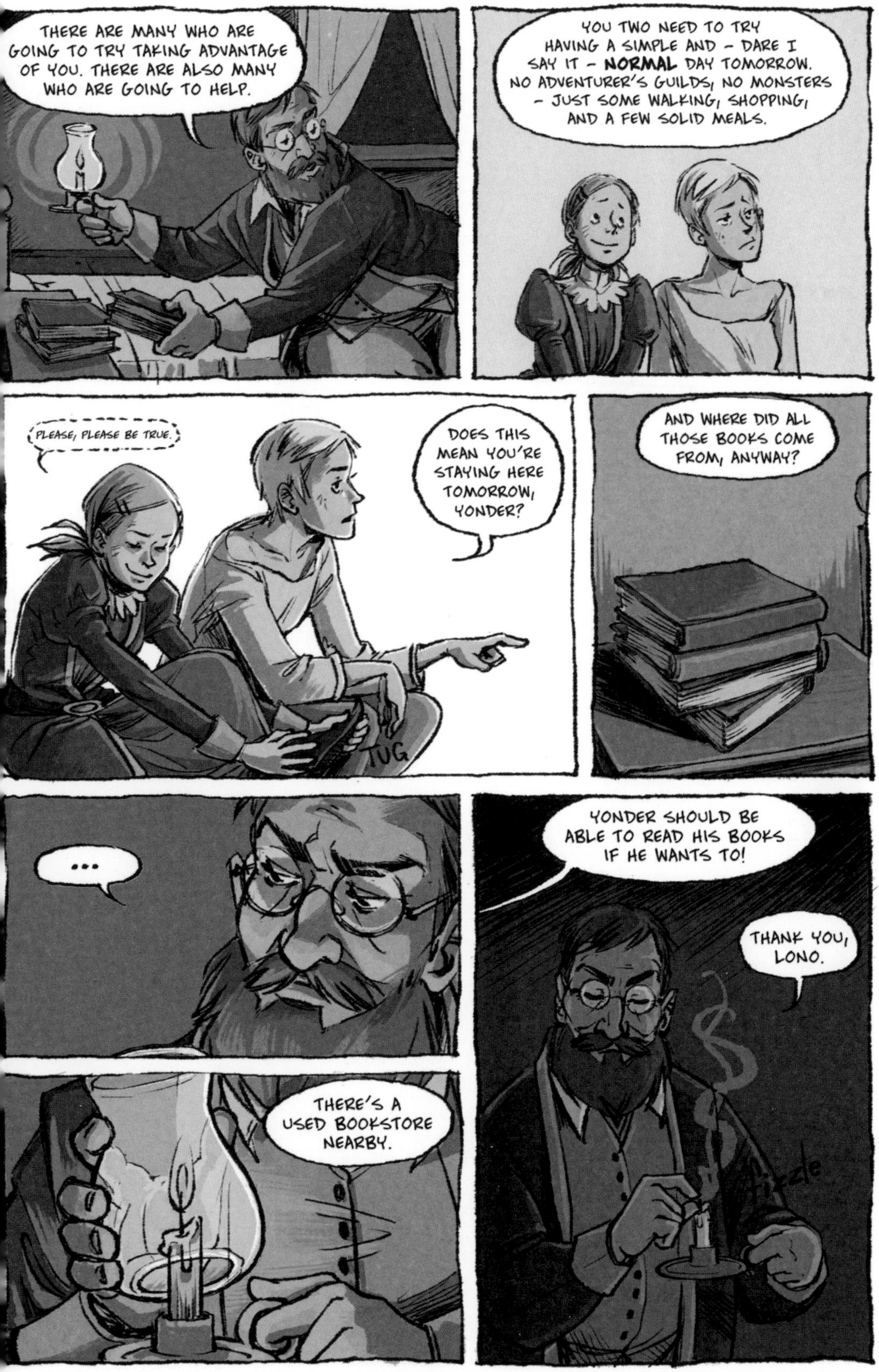
THERE ARE MANY WHO ARE GOING TO TRY TAKING ADVANTAGE OF YOU. THERE ARE ALSO MANY WHO ARE GOING TO HELP.
YOU TWO NEED TO TRY HAVING A SIMPLE AND – DARE I SAY IT – NORMAL DAY TOMORROW. NO ADVENTURER'S GUILDS, NO MONSTERS – JUST SOME WALKING, SHOPPING, AND A FEW SOLID MEALS.
PLEASE, PLEASE BE TRUE.
DOES THIS MEAN YOU'RE STAYING HERE TOMORROW, YONDER?
TUG
AND WHERE DID ALL THOSE BOOKS COME FROM, ANYWAY?
...
THERE'S A USED BOOKSTORE NEARBY.
YONDER SHOULD BE ABLE TO READ HIS BOOKS IF HE WANTS TO!
THANK YOU, LONO.
fizzle

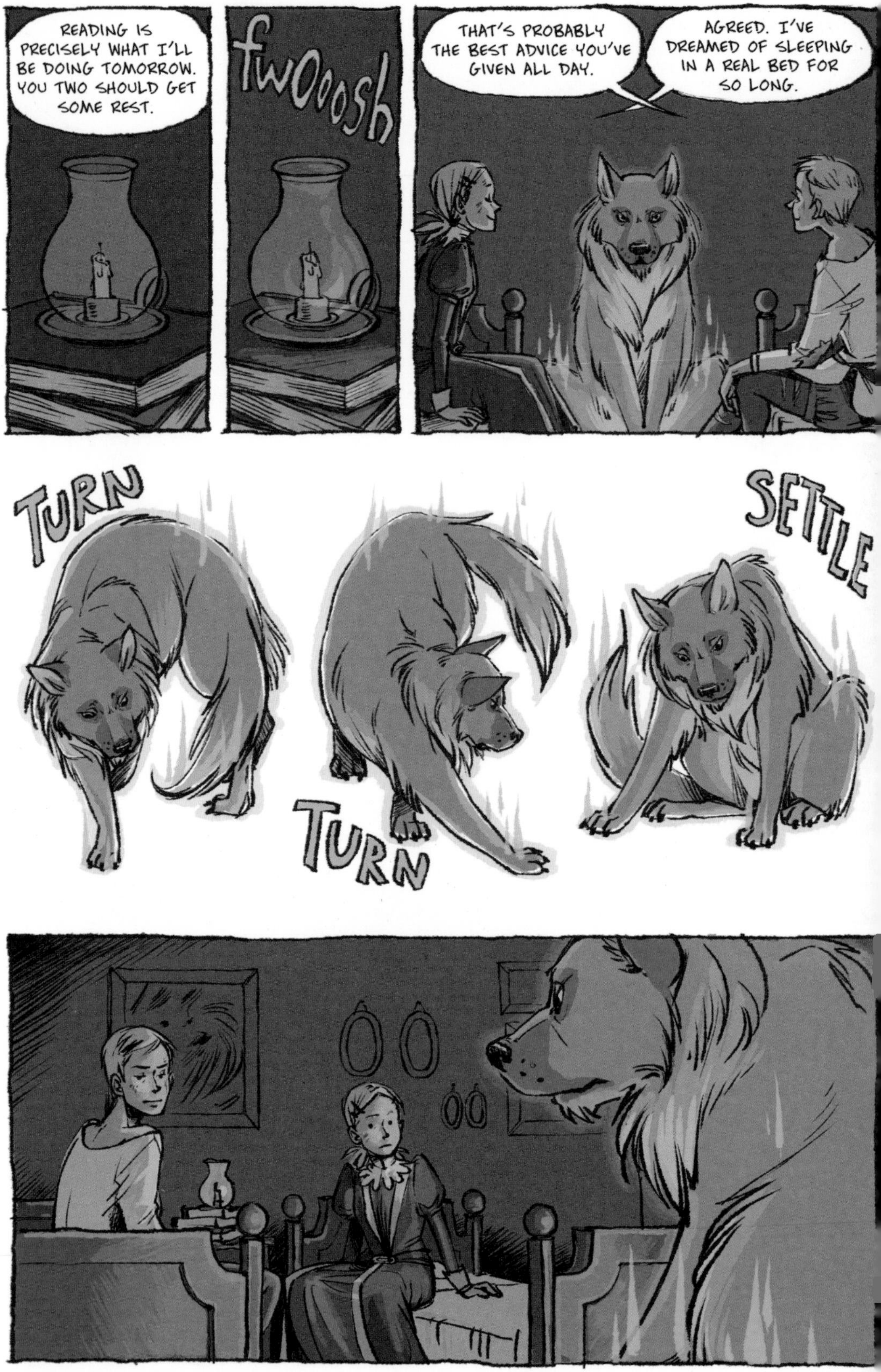
READING IS PRECISELY WHAT I'LL BE DOING TOMORROW. YOU TWO SHOULD GET SOME REST.
fwOooosh
THAT'S PROBABLY THE BEST ADVICE YOU'VE GIVEN ALL DAY.
AGREED. I'VE DREAMED OF SLEEPING IN A REAL BED FOR SO LONG.
TURN
TURN
SETTLE

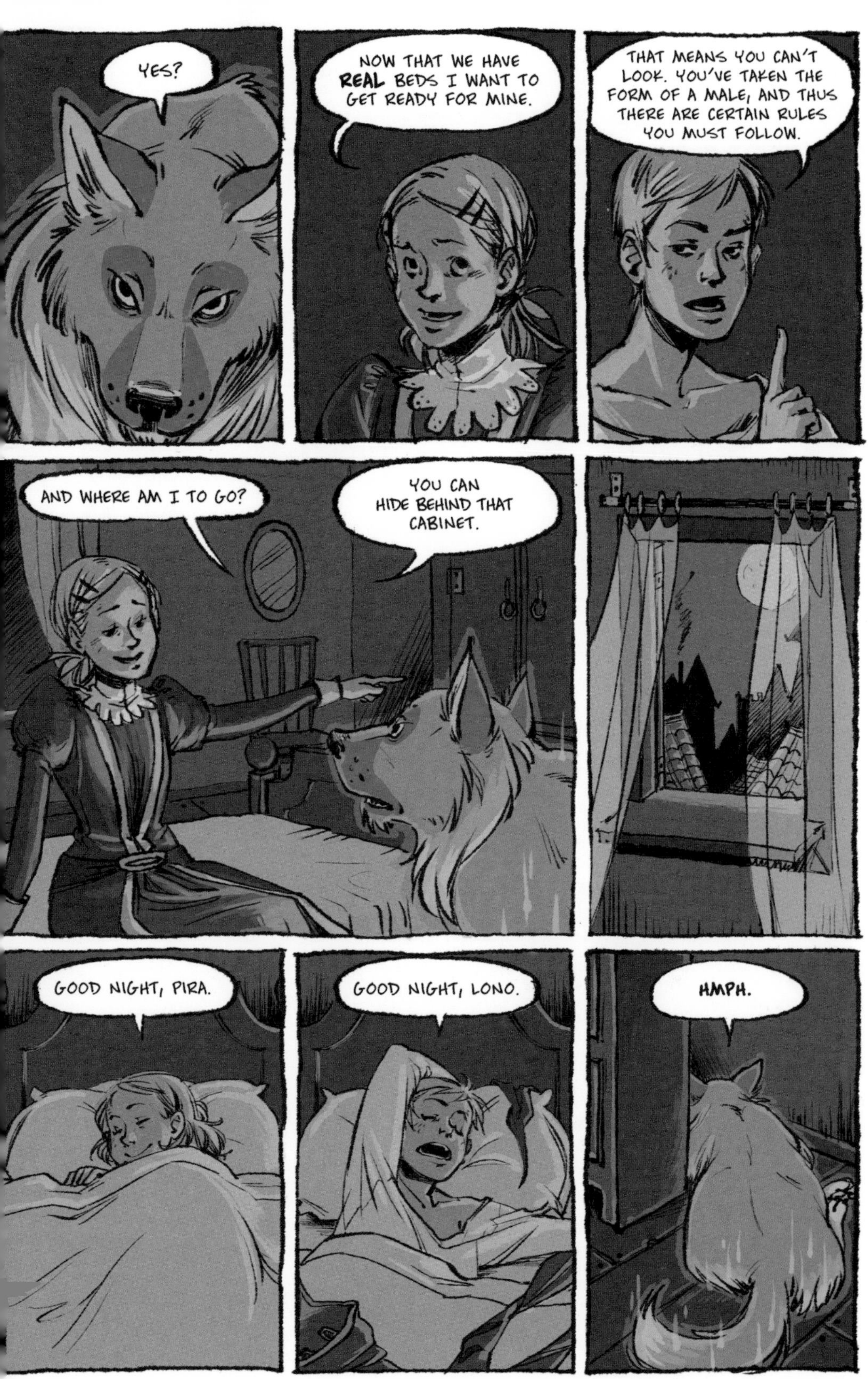
YES?
NOW THAT WE HAVE REAL BEDS I WANT TO GET READY FOR MINE.
THAT MEANS YOU CAN'T LOOK. YOU'VE TAKEN THE FORM OF A MALE, AND THUS THERE ARE CERTAIN RULES YOU MUST FOLLOW.
AND WHERE AM I TO GO?
YOU CAN HIDE BEHIND THAT CABINET.
GOOD NIGHT, PIRA.
GOOD NIGHT, LONO.
HMPH.

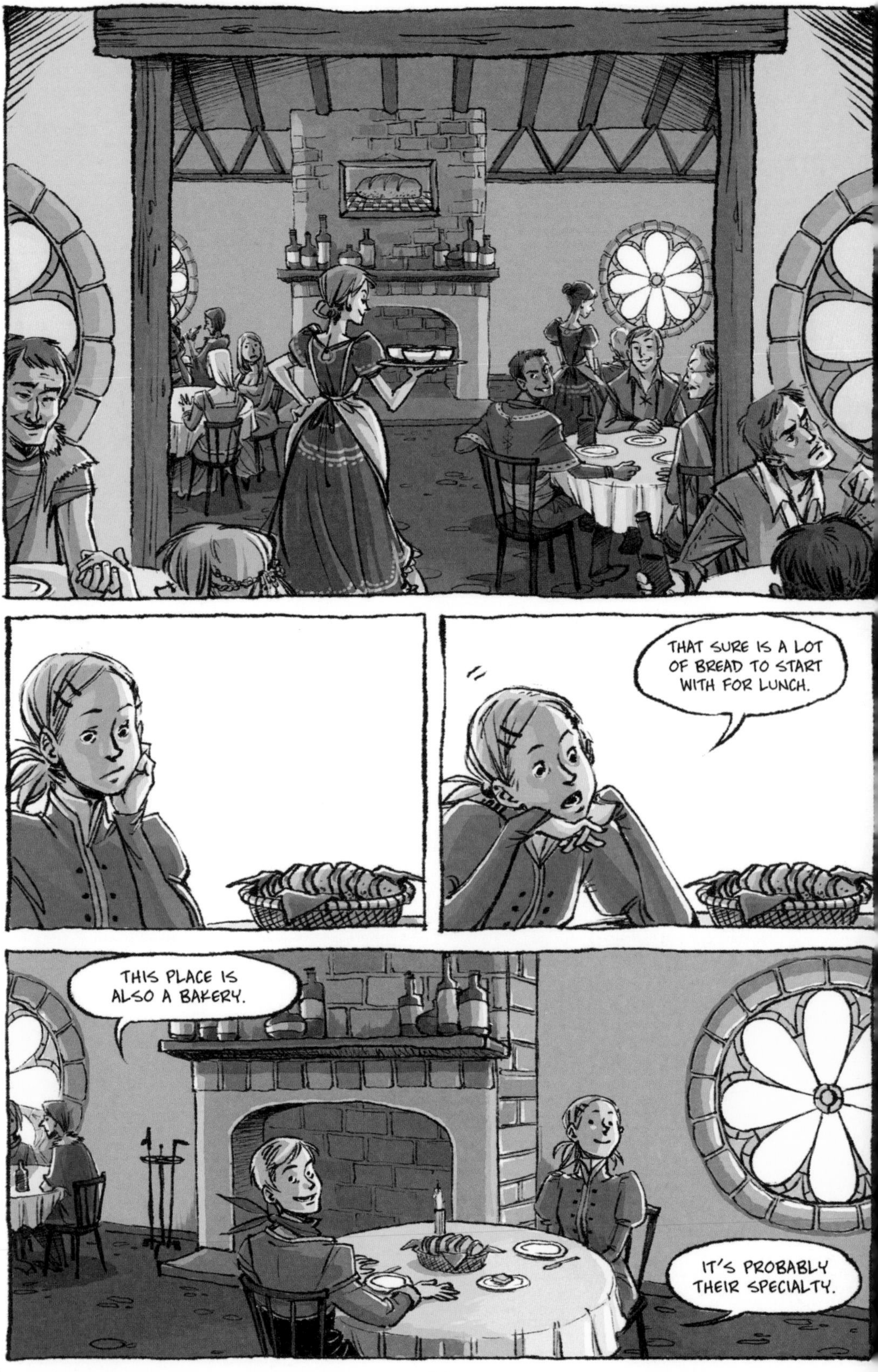
THAT SURE IS A LOT OF BREAD TO START WITH FOR LUNCH.
THIS PLACE IS ALSO A BAKERY.
IT'S PROBABLY THEIR SPECIALTY.

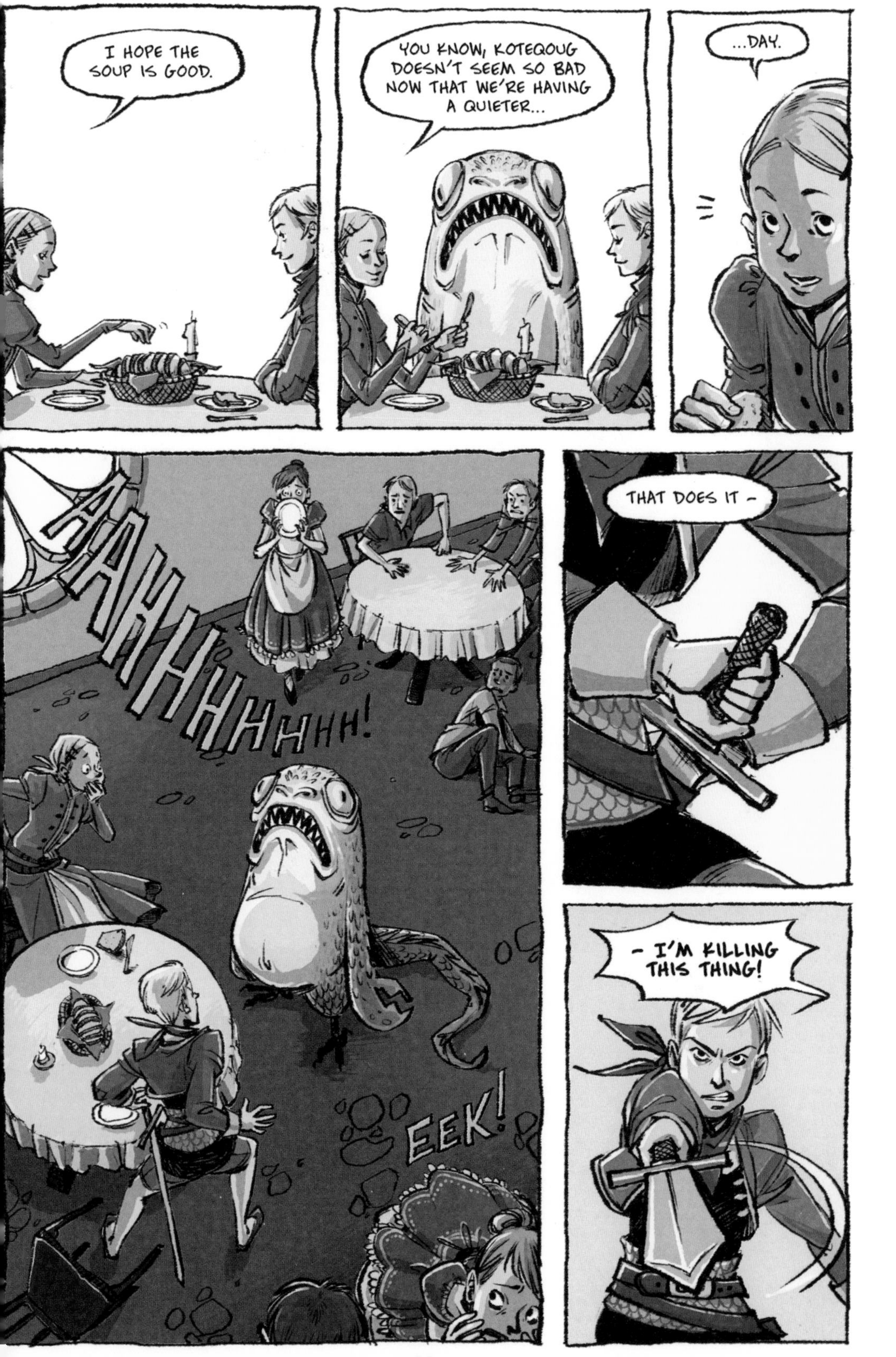
I HOPE THE SOUP IS GOOD.
YOU KNOW, KOTEQOUG DOESN'T SEEM SO BAD NOW THAT WE'RE HAVING A QUIETER...
...DAY.
AAHHHHHHHH!
EEK!
THAT DOES IT -
- I'M KILLING THIS THING!

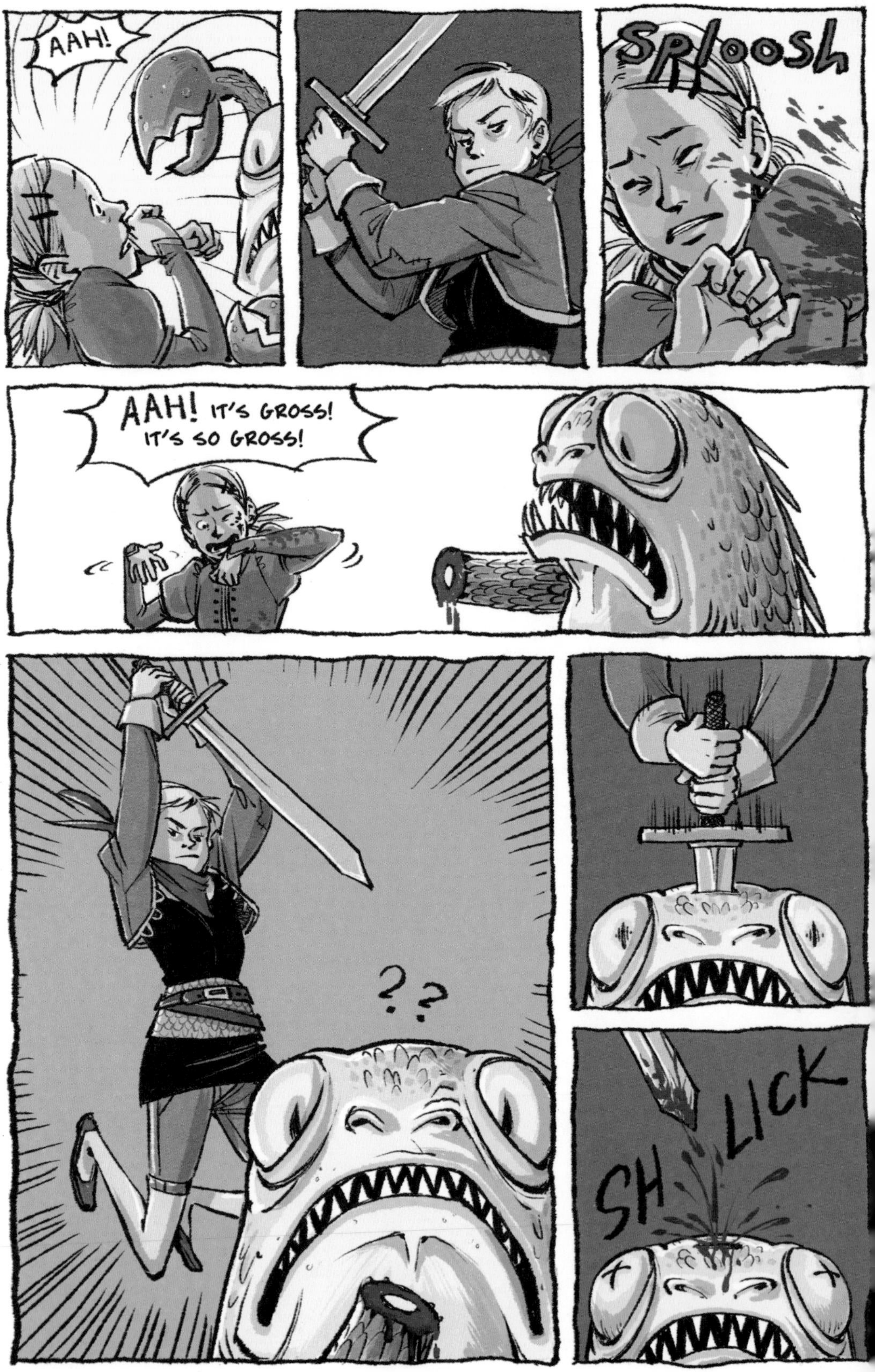
AAH!
SPLOOSH
AAH! IT'S GROSS! IT'S SO GROSS!
??
SH LICK

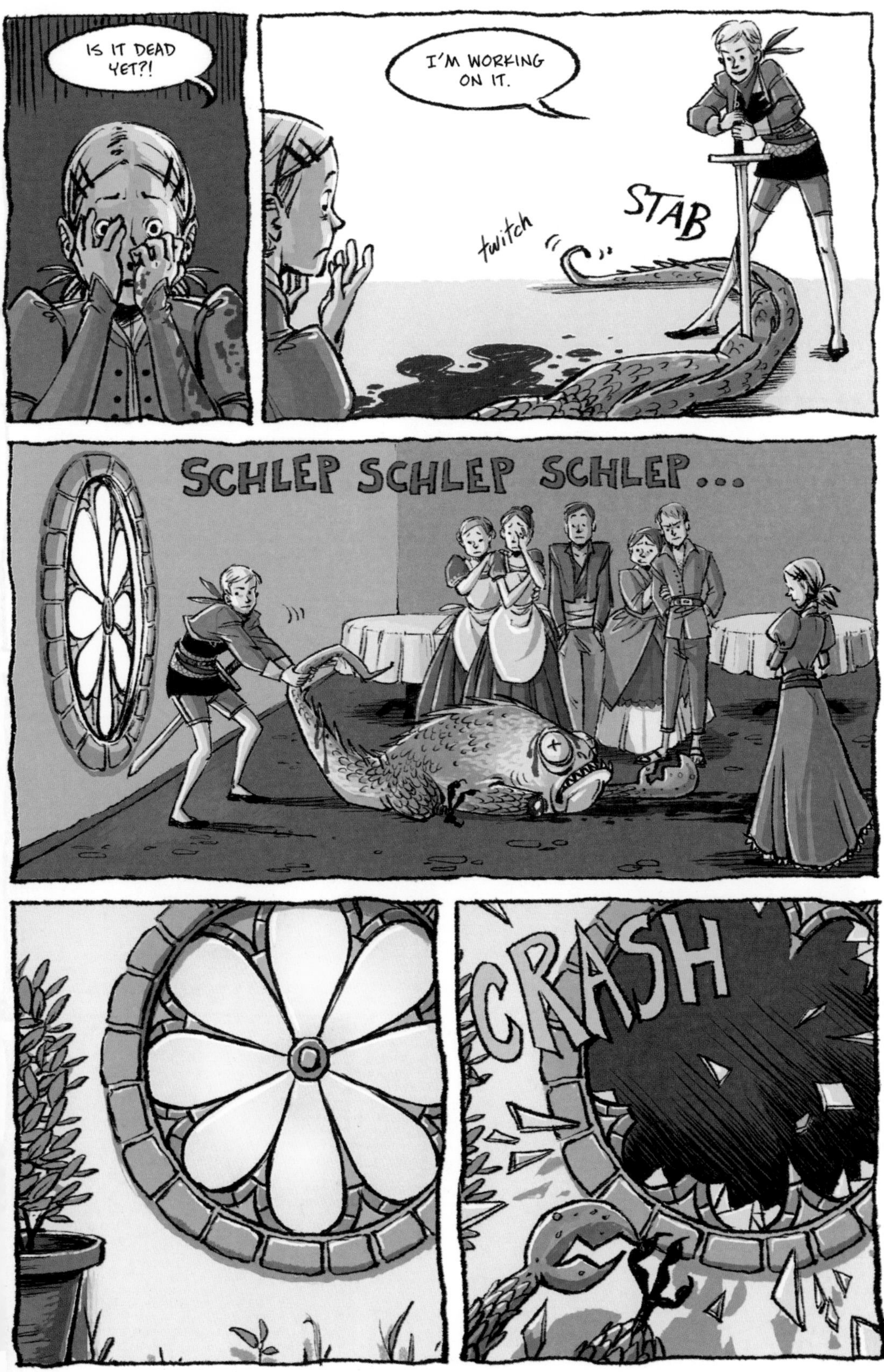
IS IT DEAD YET?!
I'M WORKING ON IT.
twitch
STAB
SCHLEP SCHLEP SCHLEP...
CRASH

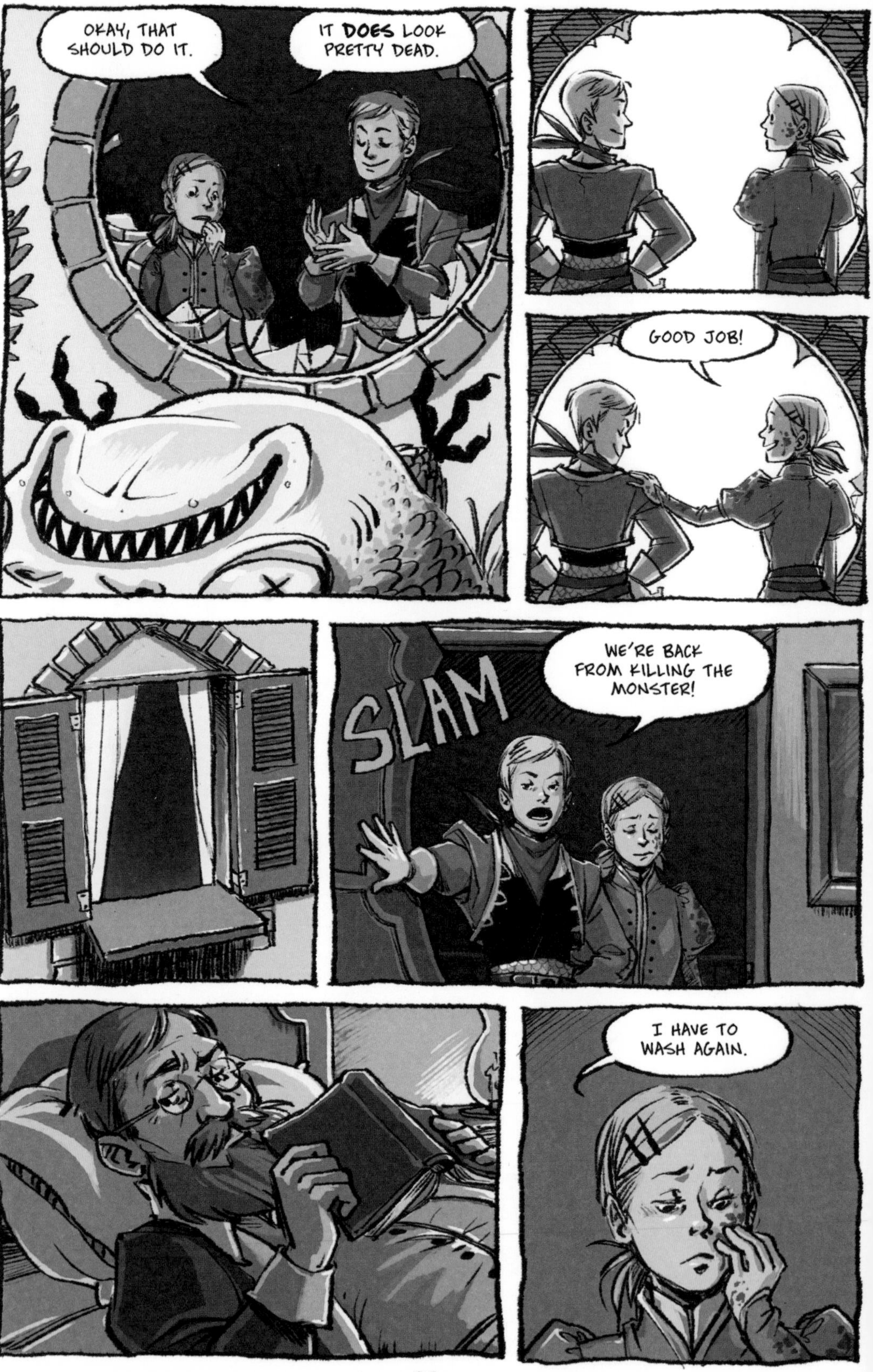
OKAY, THAT SHOULD DO IT.
IT DOES LOOK PRETTY DEAD.
GOOD JOB!
SLAM
WE'RE BACK FROM KILLING THE MONSTER!
I HAVE TO WASH AGAIN.

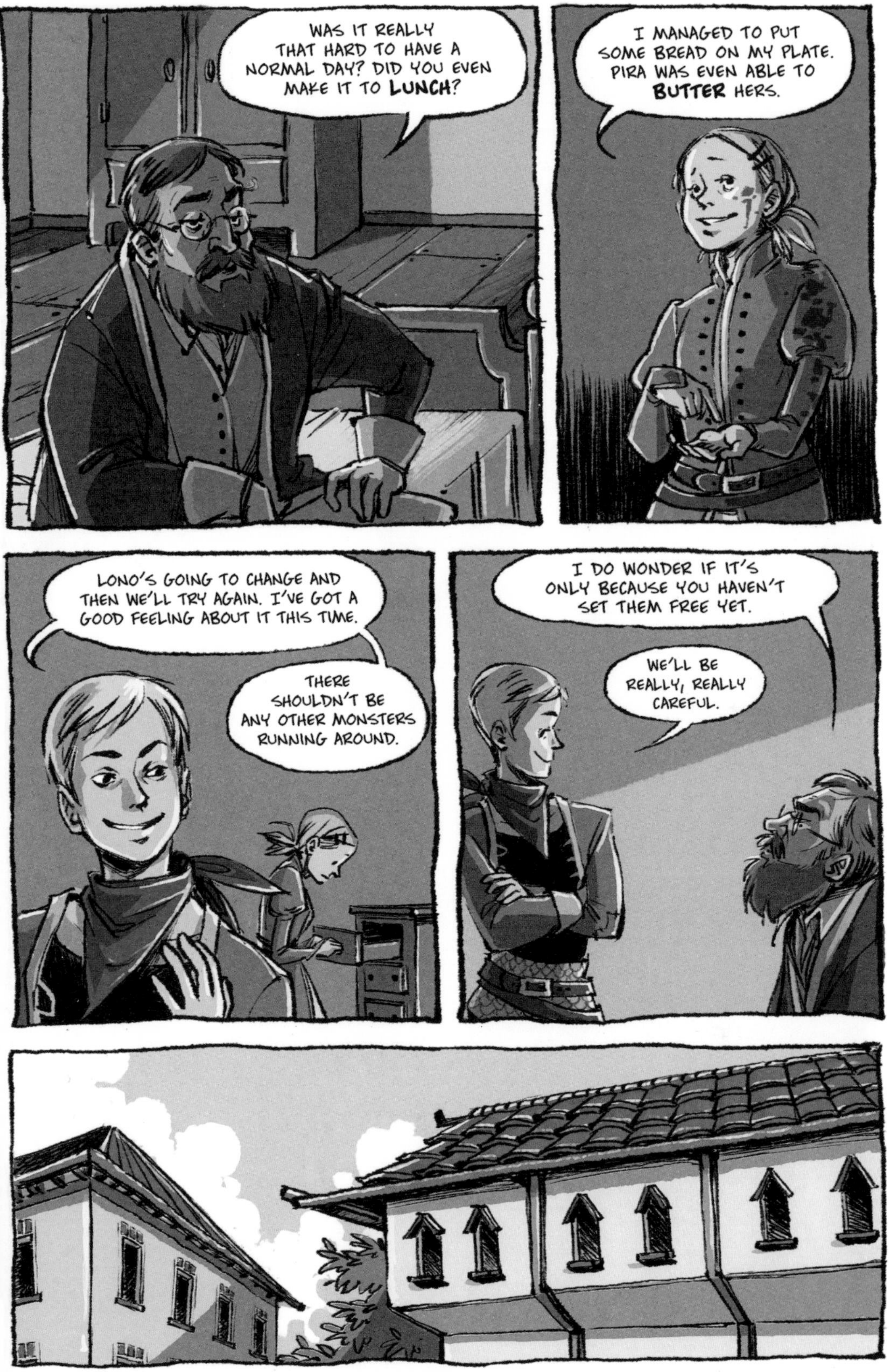
WAS IT REALLY THAT HARD TO HAVE A NORMAL DAY? DID YOU EVEN MAKE IT TO **LUNCH**?
I MANAGED TO PUT SOME BREAD ON MY PLATE. PIRA WAS EVEN ABLE TO **BUTTER** HERS.
LONO'S GOING TO CHANGE AND THEN WE'LL TRY AGAIN. I'VE GOT A GOOD FEELING ABOUT IT THIS TIME.
THERE SHOULDN'T BE ANY OTHER MONSTERS RUNNING AROUND.
I DO WONDER IF IT'S ONLY BECAUSE YOU HAVEN'T SET THEM FREE YET.
WE'LL BE REALLY, REALLY CAREFUL.

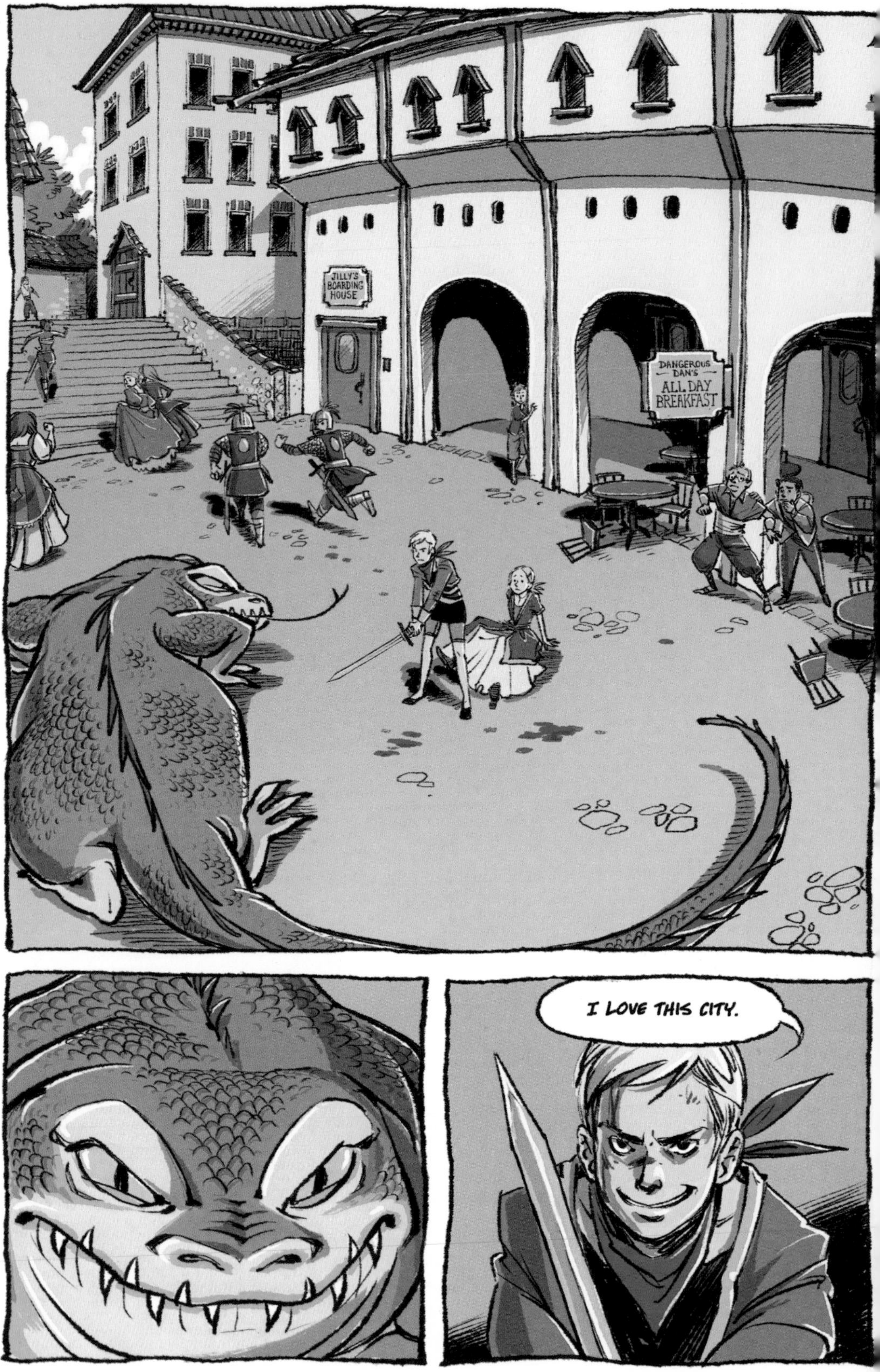
JILLY'S BOARDING HOUSE
DANGEROUS DAN'S ALL DAY BREAKFAST
I LOVE THIS CITY.

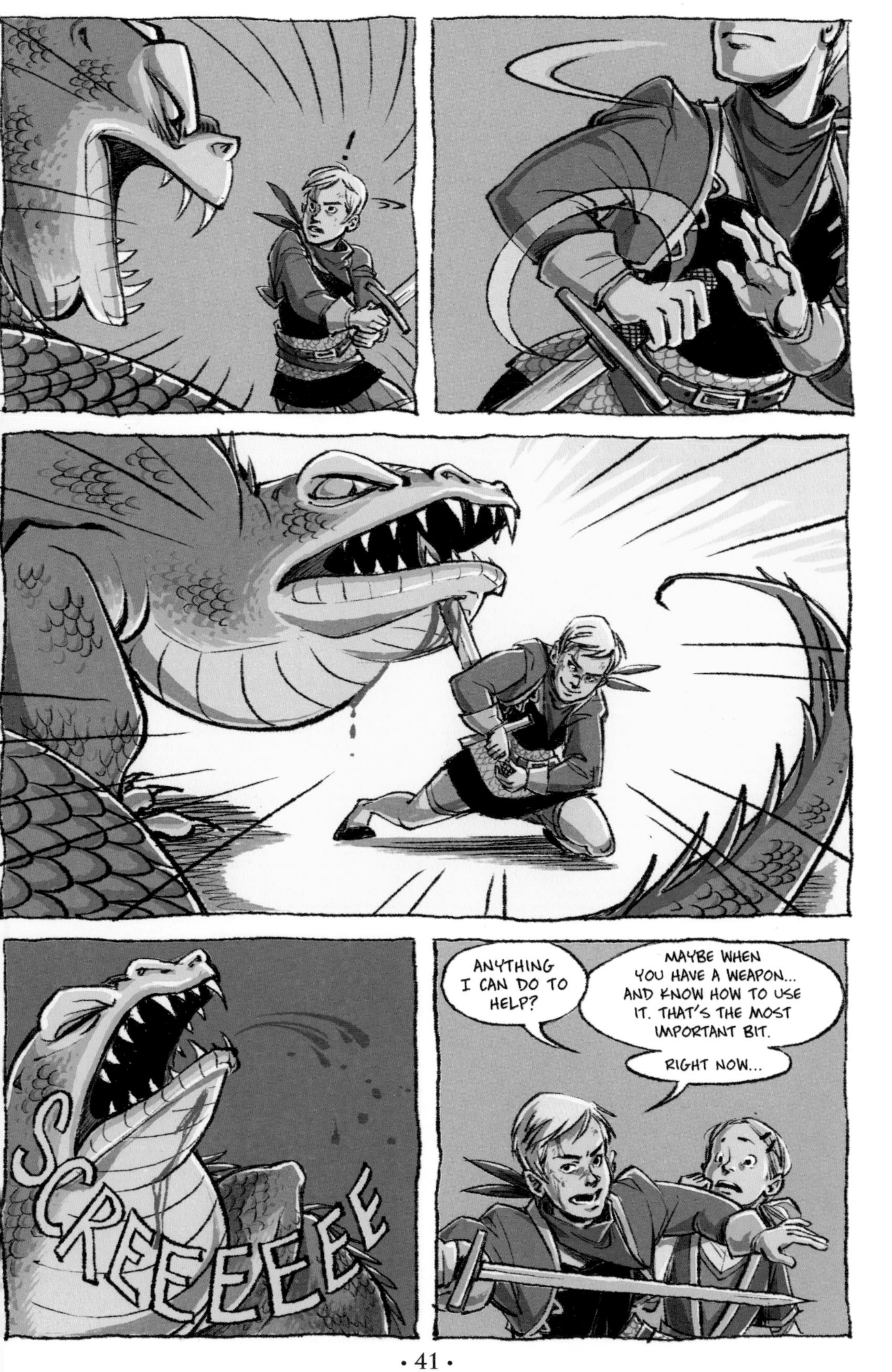
!
SCREEEEEE
ANYTHING I CAN DO TO HELP?
MAYBE WHEN YOU HAVE A WEAPON... AND KNOW HOW TO USE IT. THAT'S THE MOST IMPORTANT BIT.
RIGHT NOW...

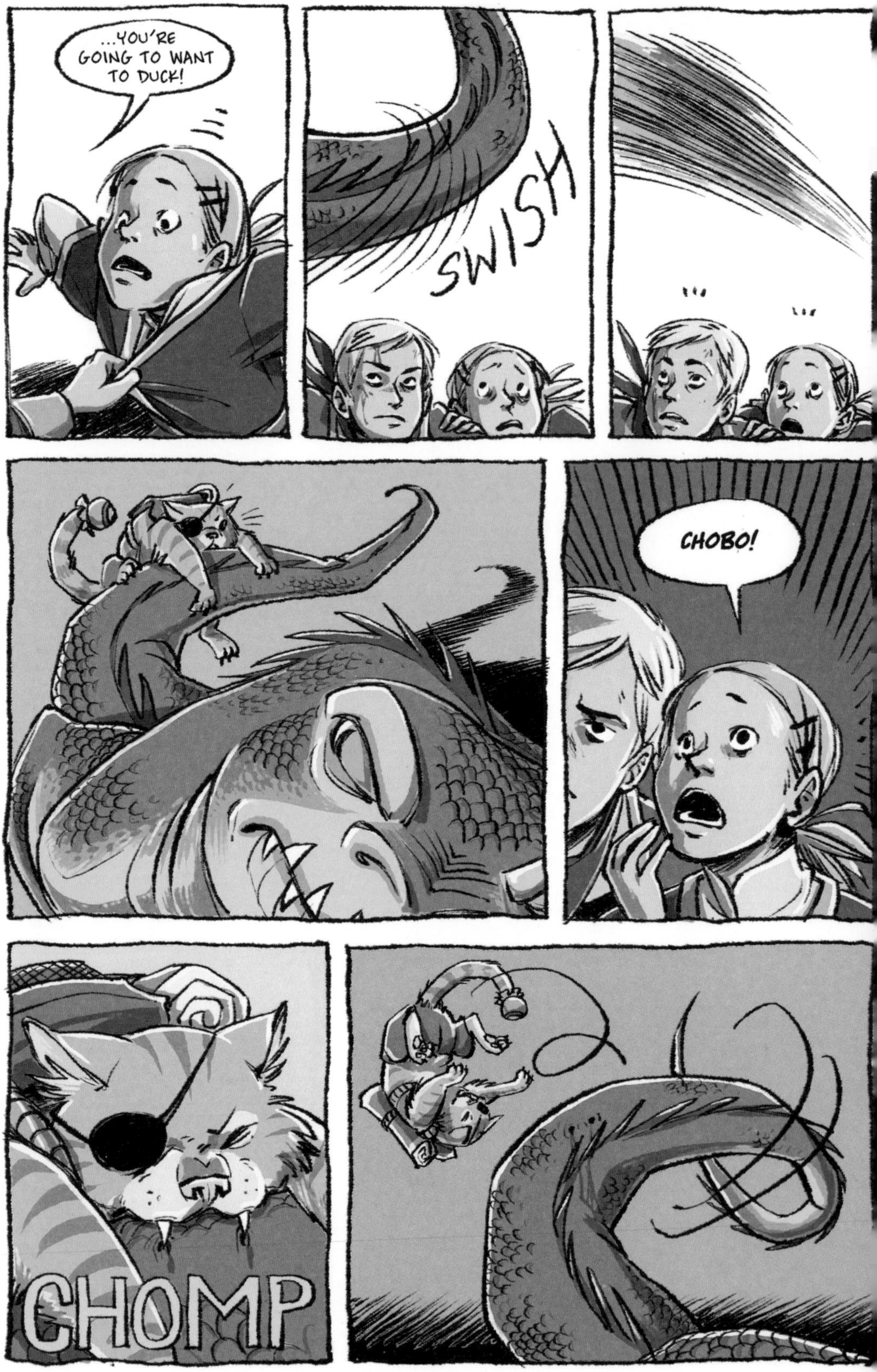
...YOU'RE GOING TO WANT TO DUCK!
SWISH
CHOBO!
CHOMP

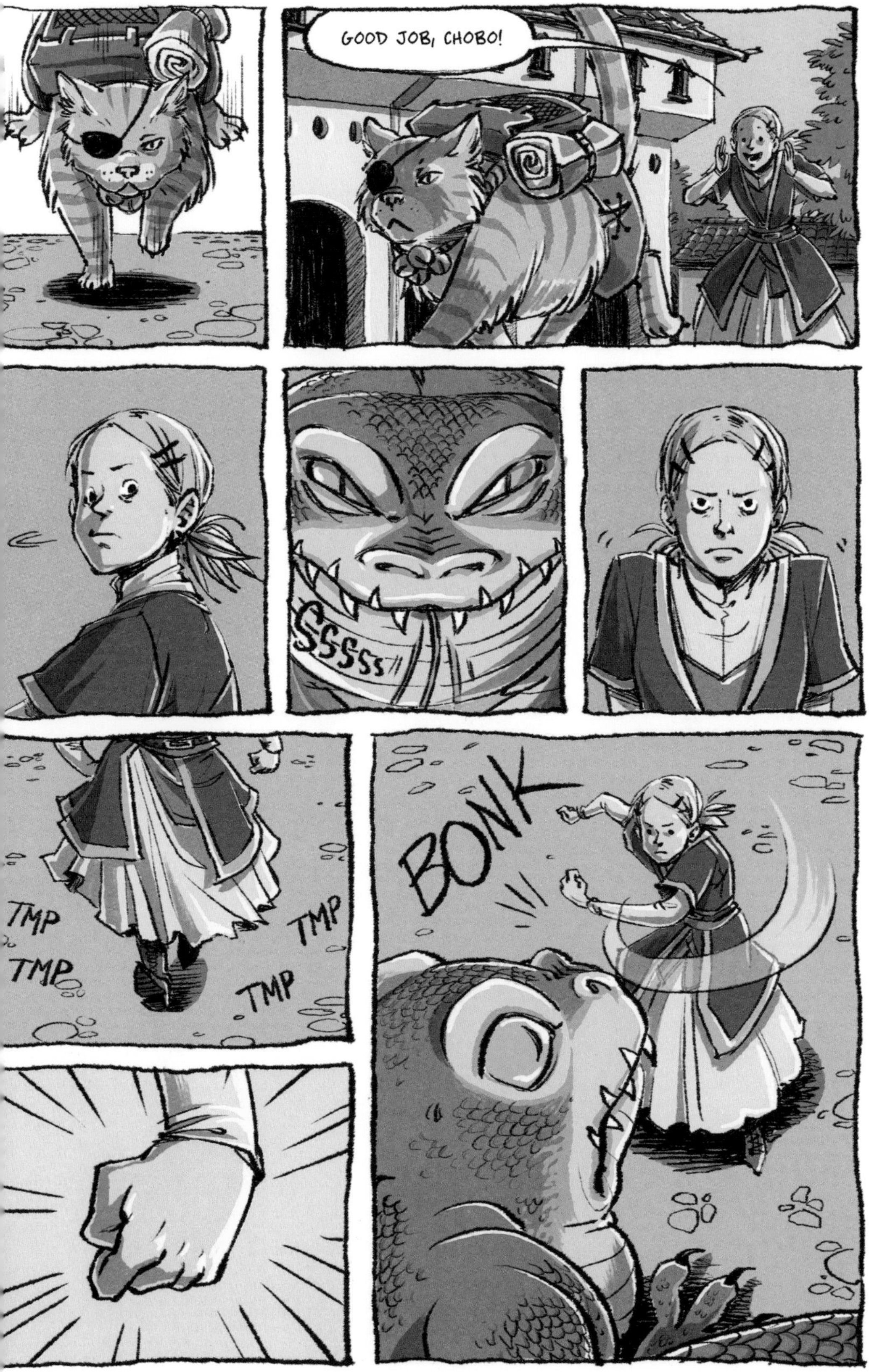
GOOD JOB, CHOBO!
SSSSSS
TMP
TMP
TMP
TMP
BONK

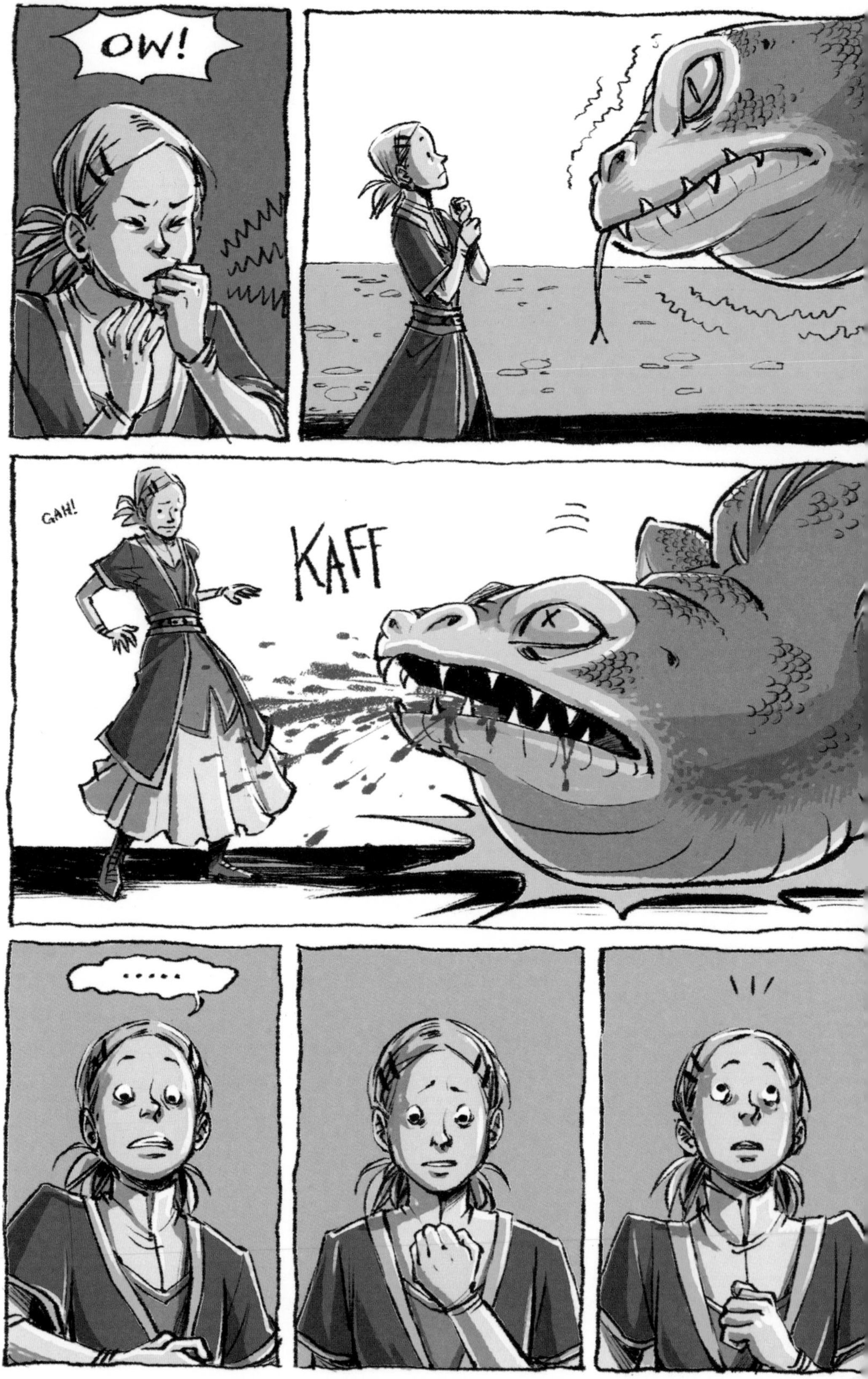
OW!
GAH!
KAFF
.....

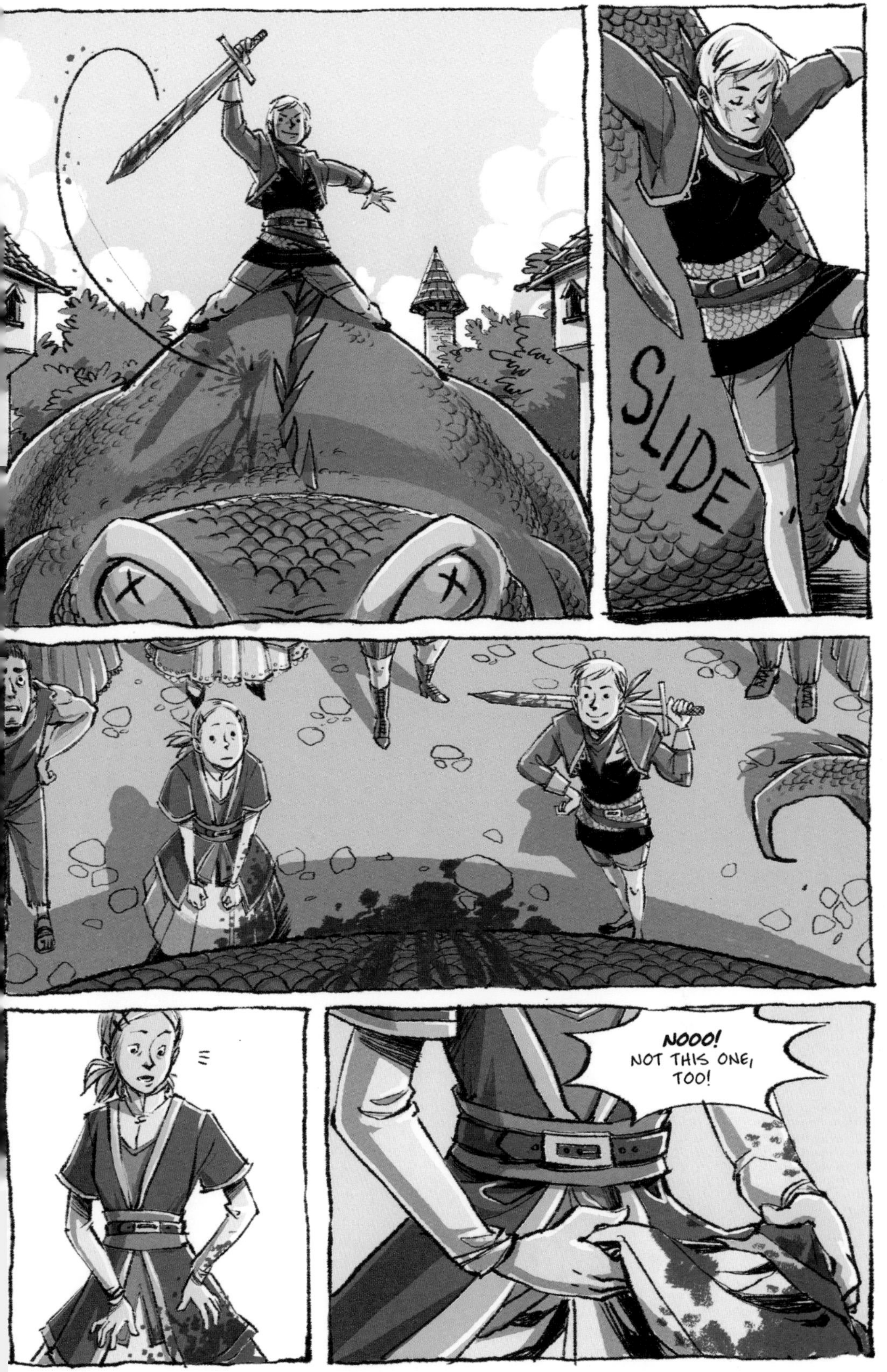
SLIDE
NOOO!
NOT THIS ONE,
TOO!

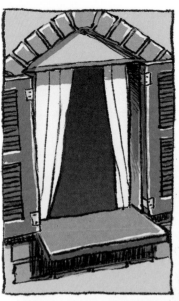

SNORT

NEXT:
PIRA & LONO
TRY AGAIN

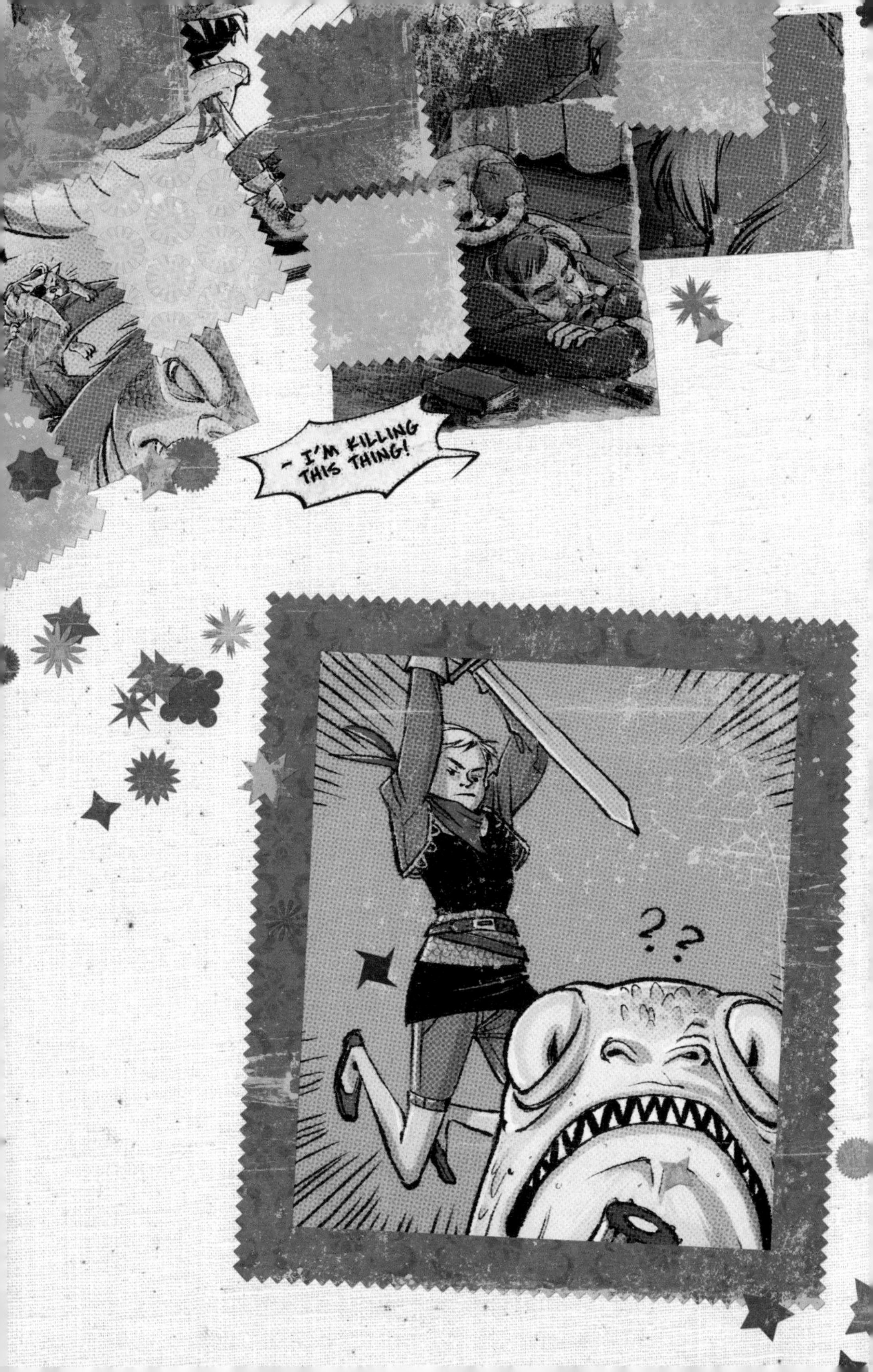
– I'M KILLING THIS THING!
??

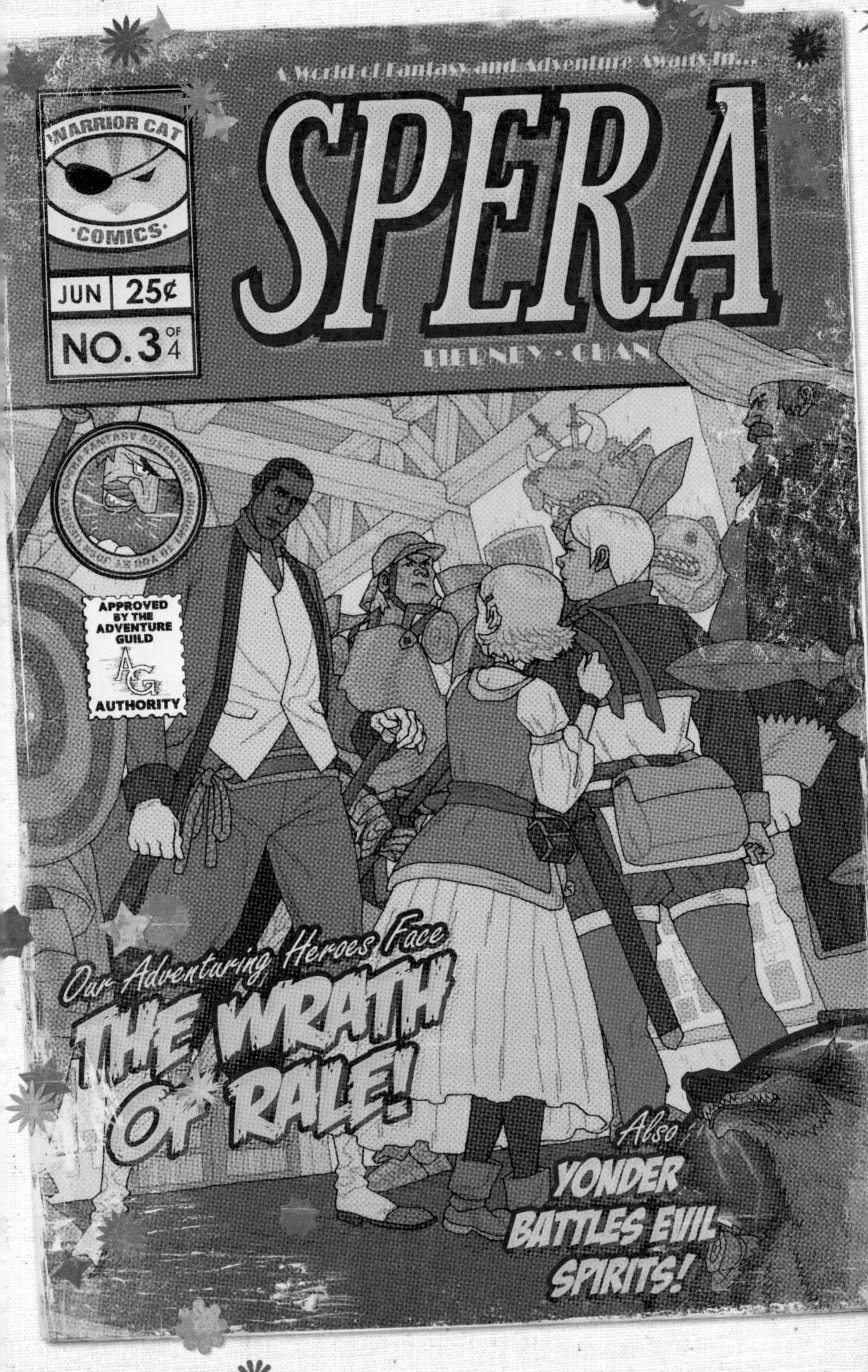

A World of Fantasy and Adventure Awaits In...
WARRIOR CAT
COMICS
JUN
25¢
NO. 3 OF 4
SPERA
TIERNEY · CHAN
APPROVED BY THE ADVENTURE GUILD
AG
AUTHORITY
Our Adventuring Heroes Face
THE WRATH OF RALE!
Also
YONDER BATTLES EVIL SPIRITS!

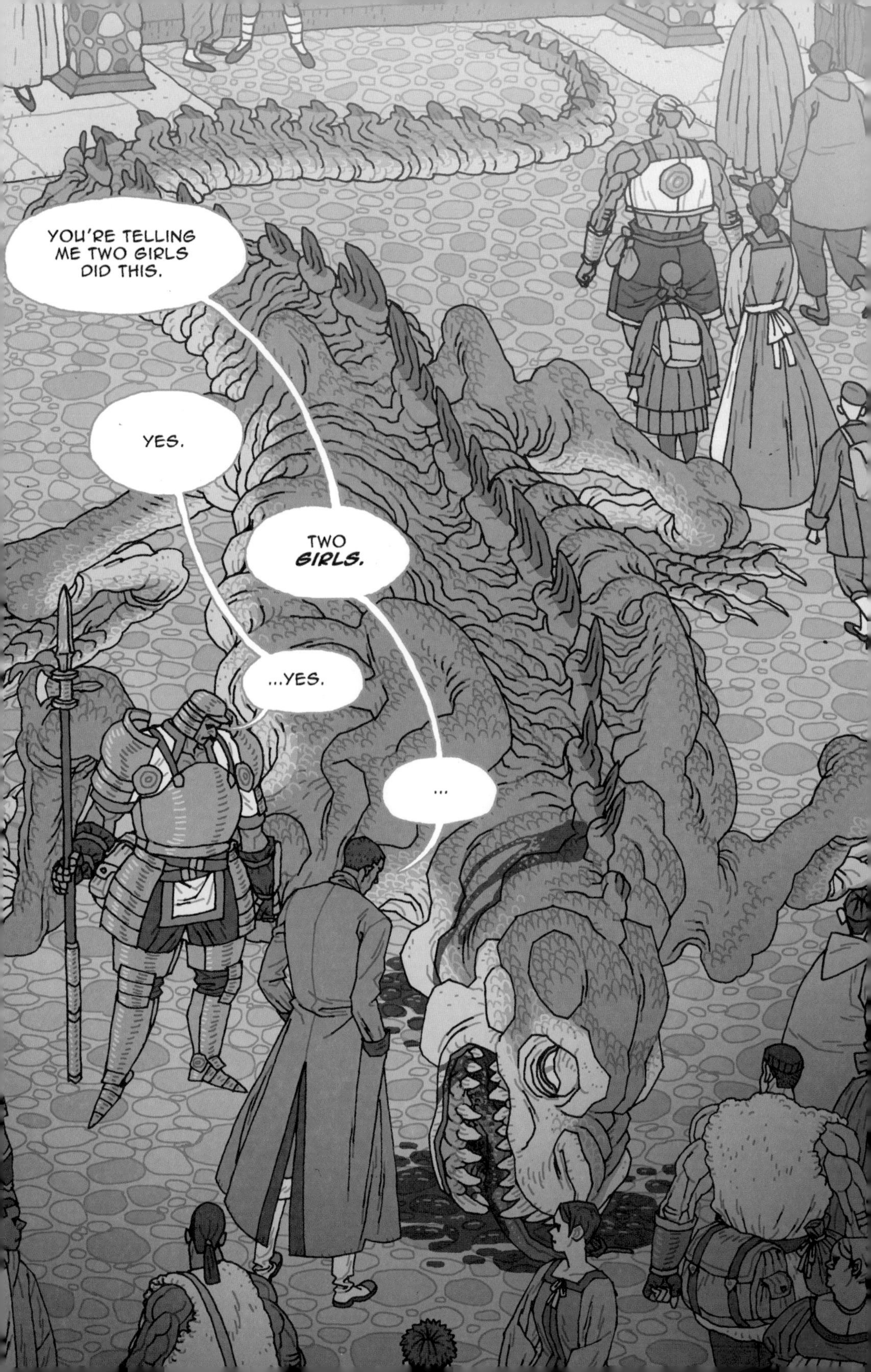
YOU'RE TELLING ME TWO GIRLS DID THIS.
YES.
TWO *GIRLS.*
...YES.
...

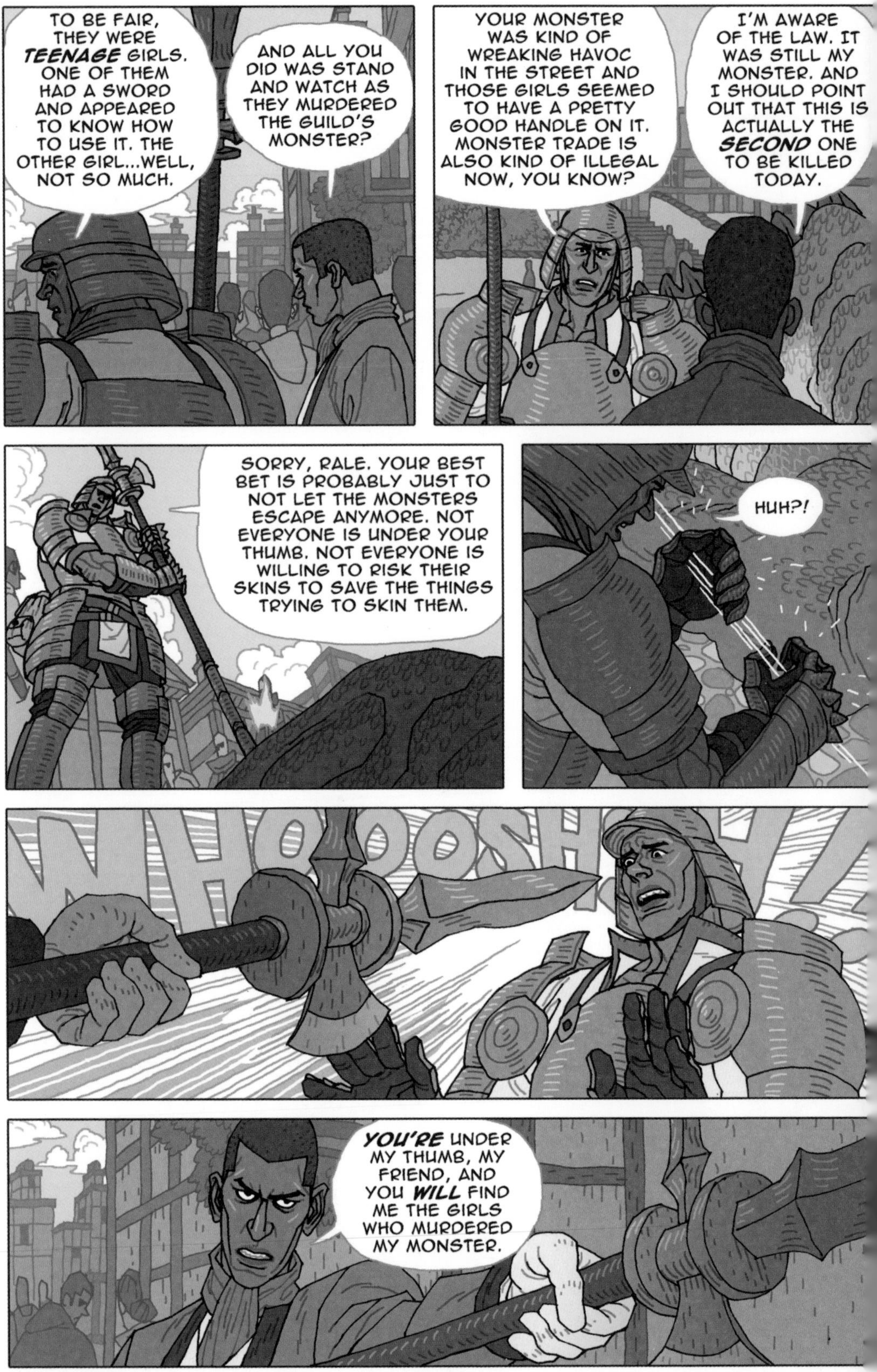
TO BE FAIR, THEY WERE TEENAGE GIRLS. ONE OF THEM HAD A SWORD AND APPEARED TO KNOW HOW TO USE IT. THE OTHER GIRL...WELL, NOT SO MUCH.
AND ALL YOU DID WAS STAND AND WATCH AS THEY MURDERED THE GUILD'S MONSTER?
YOUR MONSTER WAS KIND OF WREAKING HAVOC IN THE STREET AND THOSE GIRLS SEEMED TO HAVE A PRETTY GOOD HANDLE ON IT. MONSTER TRADE IS ALSO KIND OF ILLEGAL NOW, YOU KNOW?
I'M AWARE OF THE LAW. IT WAS STILL MY MONSTER. AND I SHOULD POINT OUT THAT THIS IS ACTUALLY THE SECOND ONE TO BE KILLED TODAY.
SORRY, RALE. YOUR BEST BET IS PROBABLY JUST TO NOT LET THE MONSTERS ESCAPE ANYMORE. NOT EVERYONE IS UNDER YOUR THUMB. NOT EVERYONE IS WILLING TO RISK THEIR SKINS TO SAVE THE THINGS TRYING TO SKIN THEM.
HUH?!
WHOOOSH
YOU'RE UNDER MY THUMB, MY FRIEND, AND YOU WILL FIND ME THE GIRLS WHO MURDERED MY MONSTER.

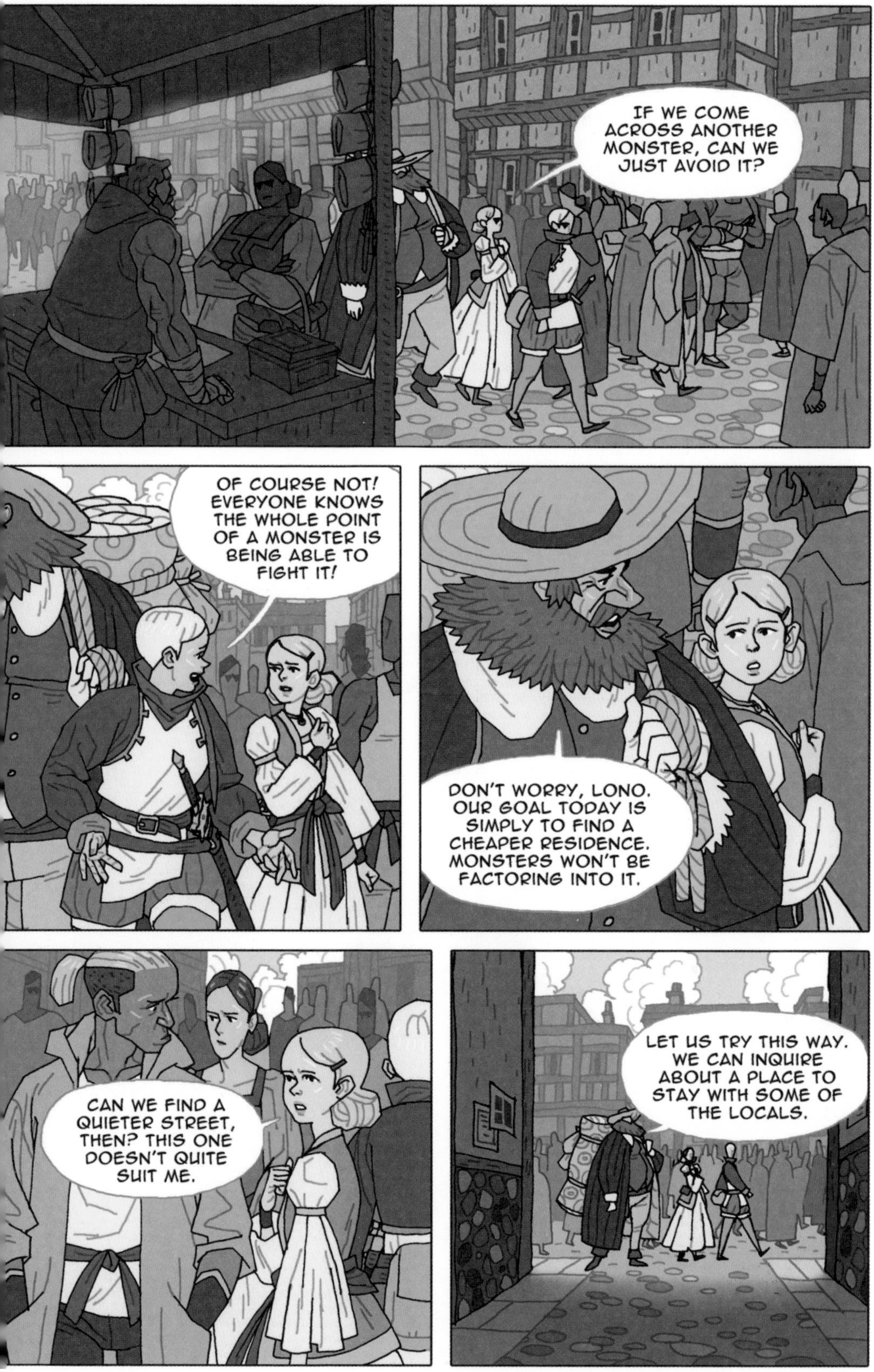
IF WE COME ACROSS ANOTHER MONSTER, CAN WE JUST AVOID IT?
OF COURSE NOT! EVERYONE KNOWS THE WHOLE POINT OF A MONSTER IS BEING ABLE TO FIGHT IT!
DON'T WORRY, LONO. OUR GOAL TODAY IS SIMPLY TO FIND A CHEAPER RESIDENCE. MONSTERS WON'T BE FACTORING INTO IT.
CAN WE FIND A QUIETER STREET, THEN? THIS ONE DOESN'T QUITE SUIT ME.
LET US TRY THIS WAY. WE CAN INQUIRE ABOUT A PLACE TO STAY WITH SOME OF THE LOCALS.

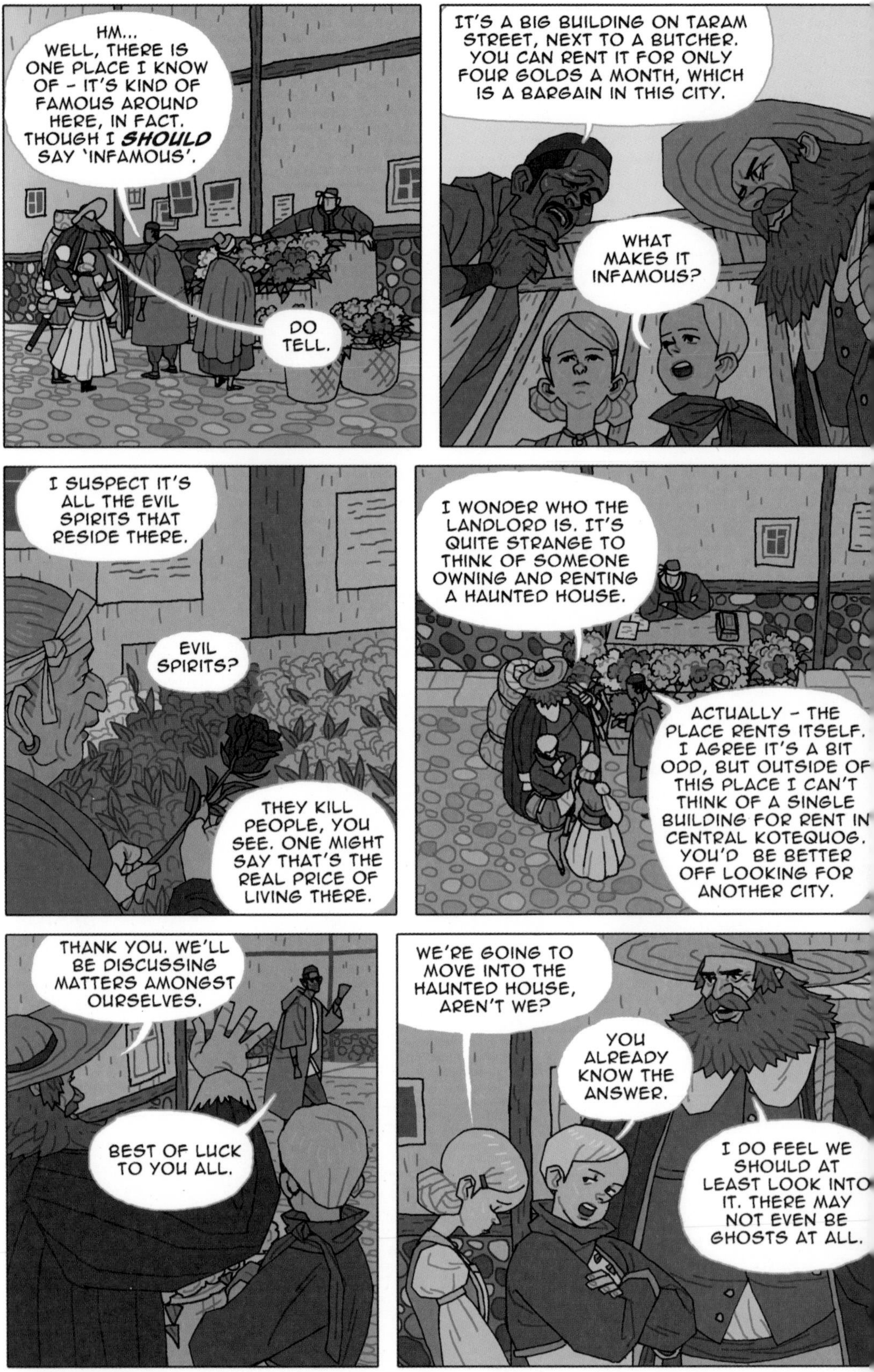
HM... WELL, THERE IS ONE PLACE I KNOW OF - IT'S KIND OF FAMOUS AROUND HERE, IN FACT. THOUGH I **SHOULD** SAY 'INFAMOUS'.
DO TELL.
IT'S A BIG BUILDING ON TARAM STREET, NEXT TO A BUTCHER. YOU CAN RENT IT FOR ONLY FOUR GOLDS A MONTH, WHICH IS A BARGAIN IN THIS CITY.
WHAT MAKES IT INFAMOUS?
I SUSPECT IT'S ALL THE EVIL SPIRITS THAT RESIDE THERE.
EVIL SPIRITS?
THEY KILL PEOPLE, YOU SEE. ONE MIGHT SAY THAT'S THE REAL PRICE OF LIVING THERE.
I WONDER WHO THE LANDLORD IS. IT'S QUITE STRANGE TO THINK OF SOMEONE OWNING AND RENTING A HAUNTED HOUSE.
ACTUALLY - THE PLACE RENTS ITSELF. I AGREE IT'S A BIT ODD, BUT OUTSIDE OF THIS PLACE I CAN'T THINK OF A SINGLE BUILDING FOR RENT IN CENTRAL KOTEQUOG. YOU'D BE BETTER OFF LOOKING FOR ANOTHER CITY.
THANK YOU. WE'LL BE DISCUSSING MATTERS AMONGST OURSELVES.
BEST OF LUCK TO YOU ALL.
WE'RE GOING TO MOVE INTO THE HAUNTED HOUSE, AREN'T WE?
YOU ALREADY KNOW THE ANSWER.
I DO FEEL WE SHOULD AT LEAST LOOK INTO IT. THERE MAY NOT EVEN BE GHOSTS AT ALL.

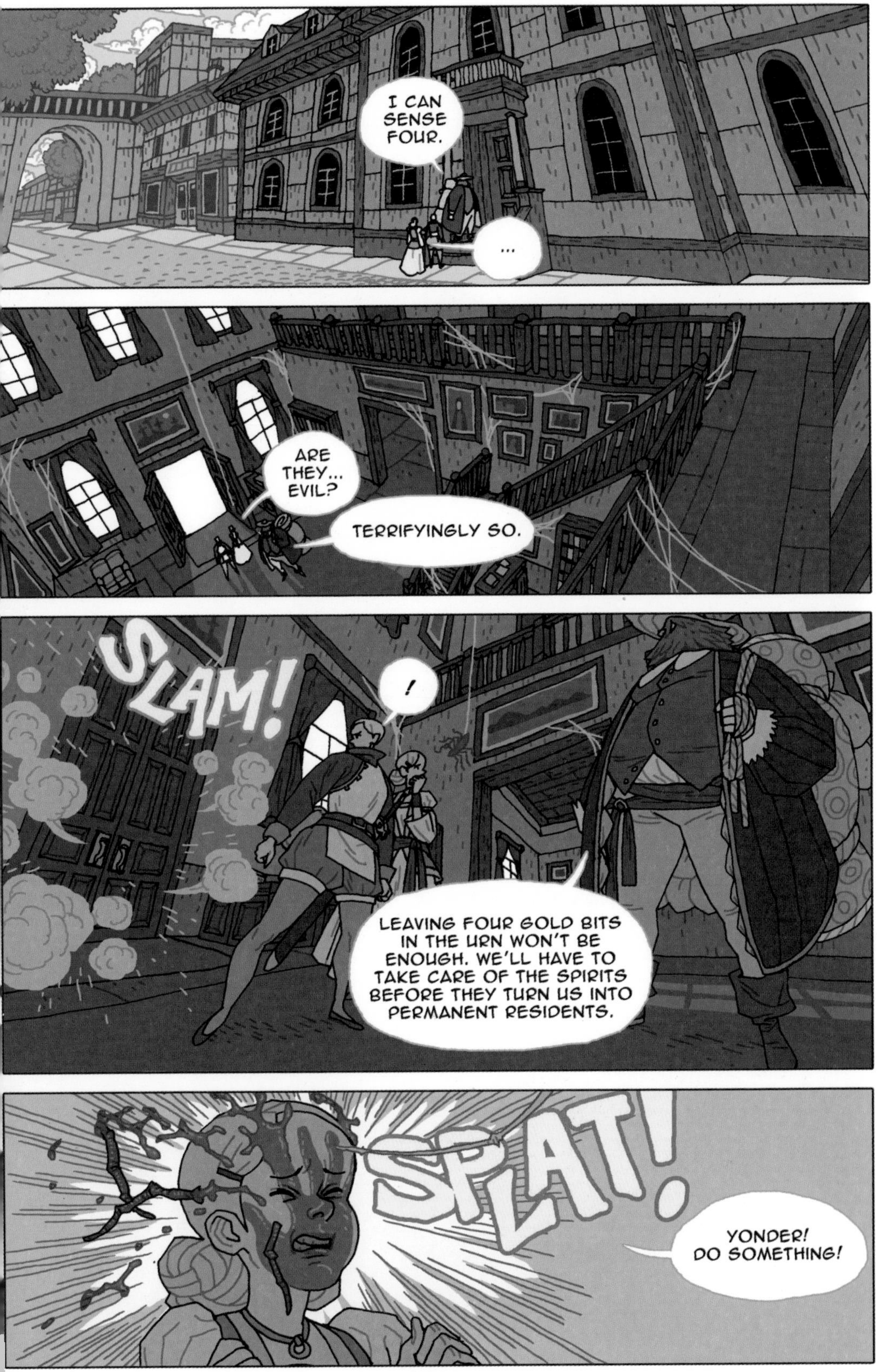
I CAN SENSE FOUR.
...
ARE THEY... EVIL?
TERRIFYINGLY SO.
SLAM!
!
LEAVING FOUR GOLD BITS IN THE URN WON'T BE ENOUGH. WE'LL HAVE TO TAKE CARE OF THE SPIRITS BEFORE THEY TURN US INTO PERMANENT RESIDENTS.
SPLAT!
YONDER! DO SOMETHING!

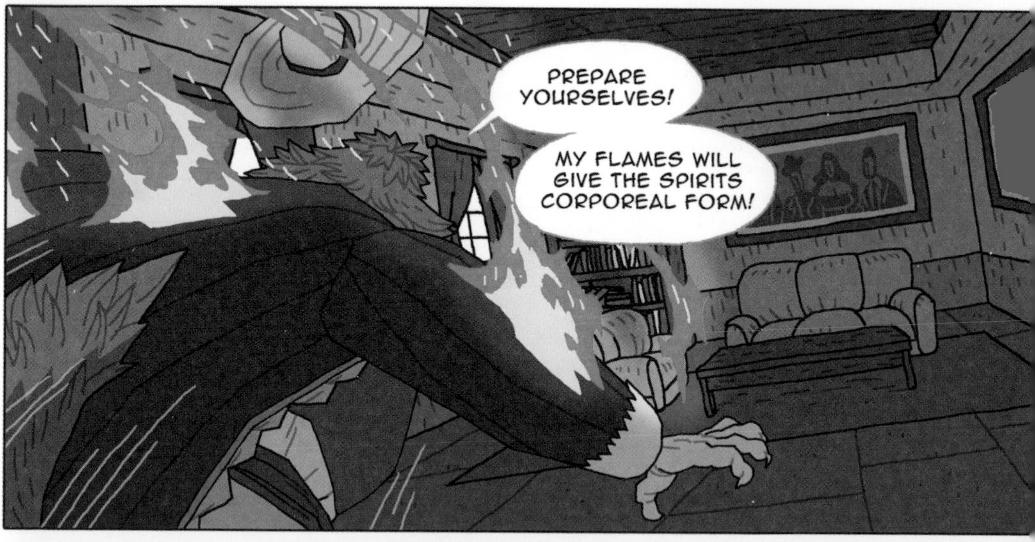
PREPARE YOURSELVES!
MY FLAMES WILL GIVE THE SPIRITS CORPOREAL FORM!

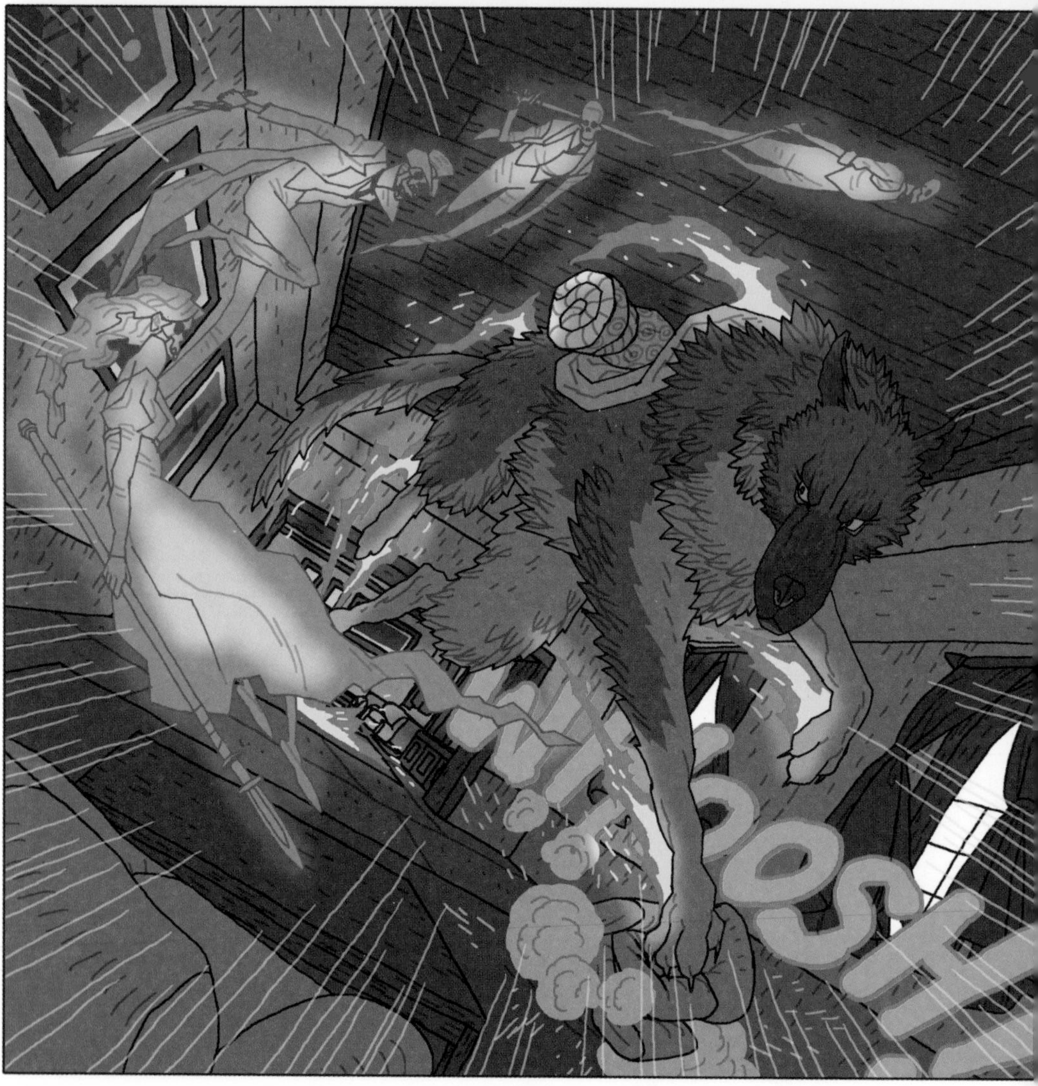
WHOOSH

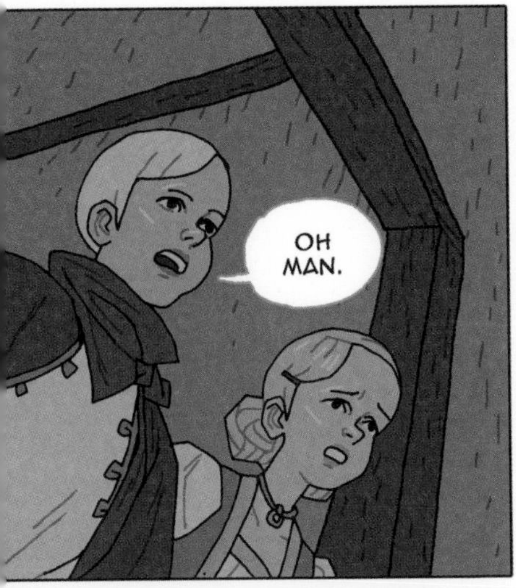
OH MAN.

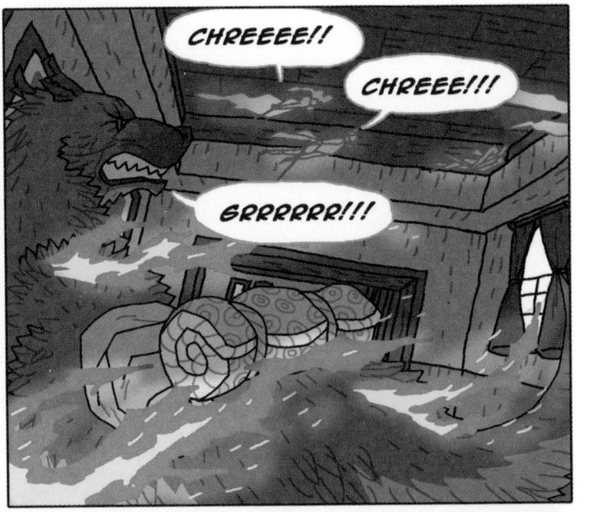
CHREEEE!!
CHREEE!!!
GRRRRRR!!!

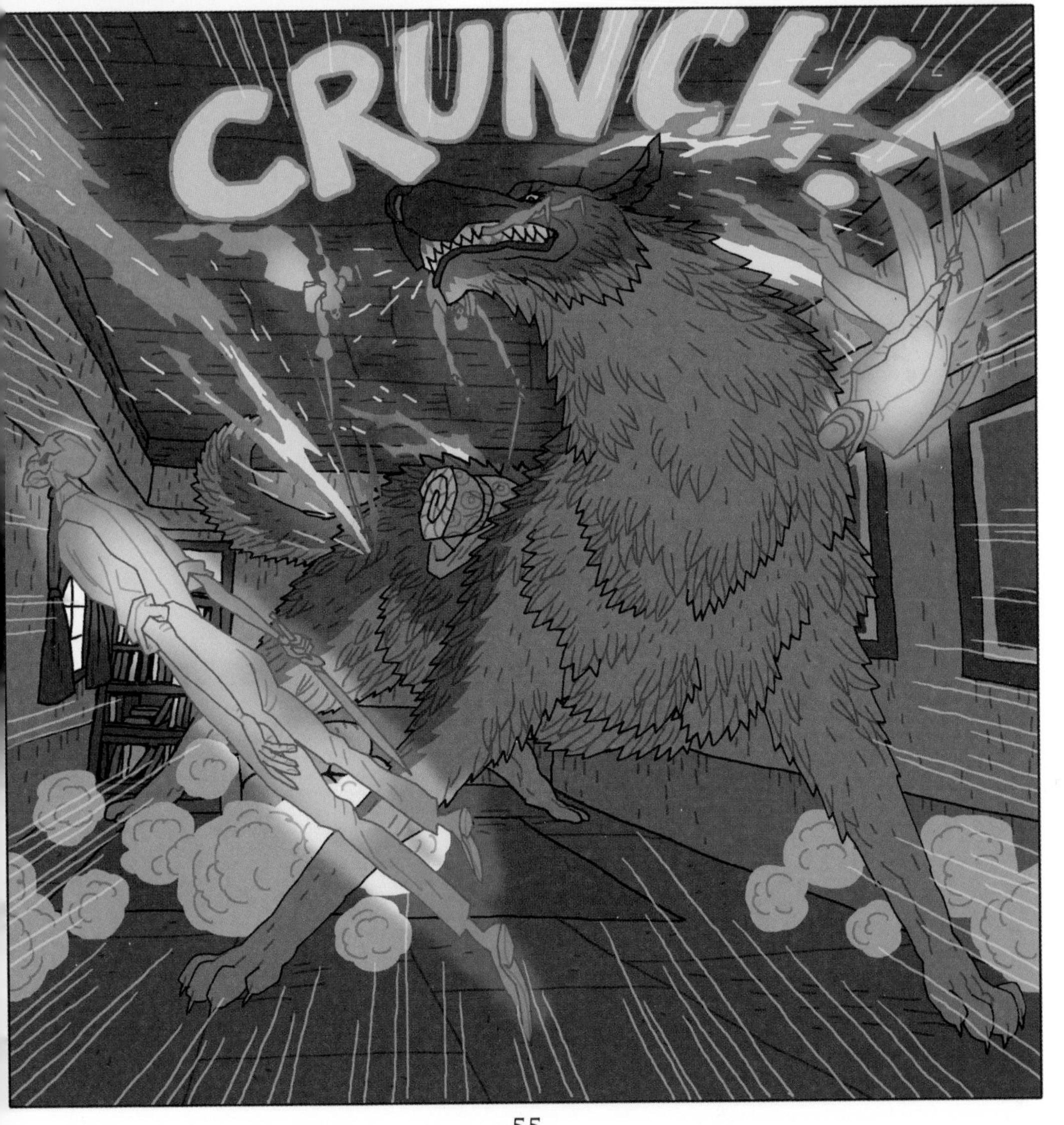
CRUNCH!!

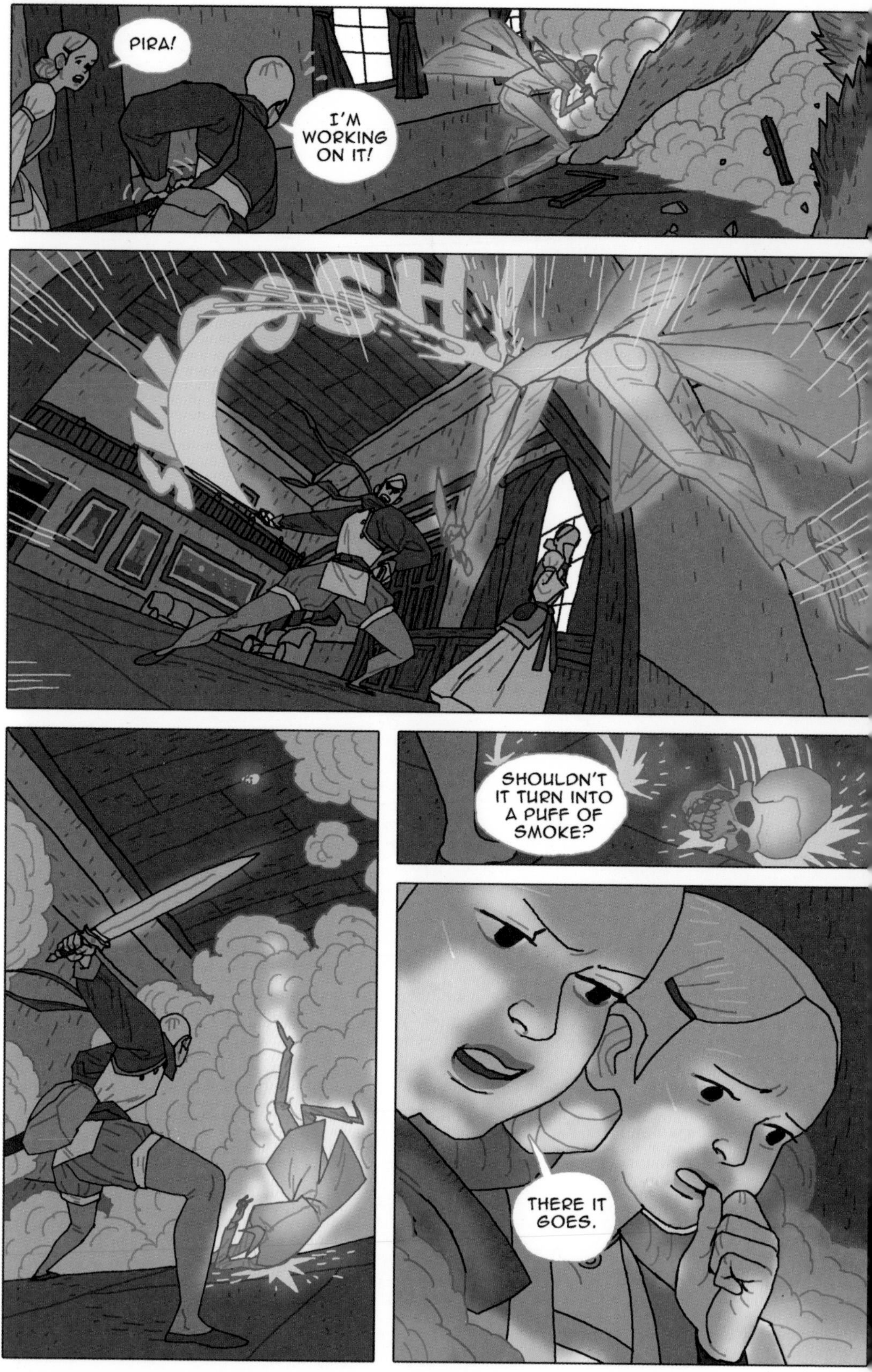
PIRA!
I'M WORKING ON IT!
SHOULDN'T IT TURN INTO A PUFF OF SMOKE?
THERE IT GOES.

KNOCK KNOCK KNOCK

I WONDER WHO THAT COULD BE.

YES?

AFTERNOON, YOUNG LADIES. WOULD YOU TWO HAPPEN TO BE THE ONES WHO KILLED THOSE MONSTERS THE OTHER DAY?

THAT WOULD BE US. IT WAS MOSTLY PIRA, THOUGH.

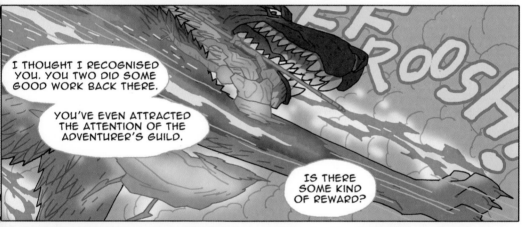

I THOUGHT I RECOGNISED YOU. YOU TWO DID SOME GOOD WORK BACK THERE.

YOU'VE EVEN ATTRACTED THE ATTENTION OF THE ADVENTURER'S GUILD.

IS THERE SOME KIND OF REWARD?

YOU'LL HAVE TO ASK RALE ABOUT THAT. HE'S THE ONE WHO WISHES TO SEE YOU.

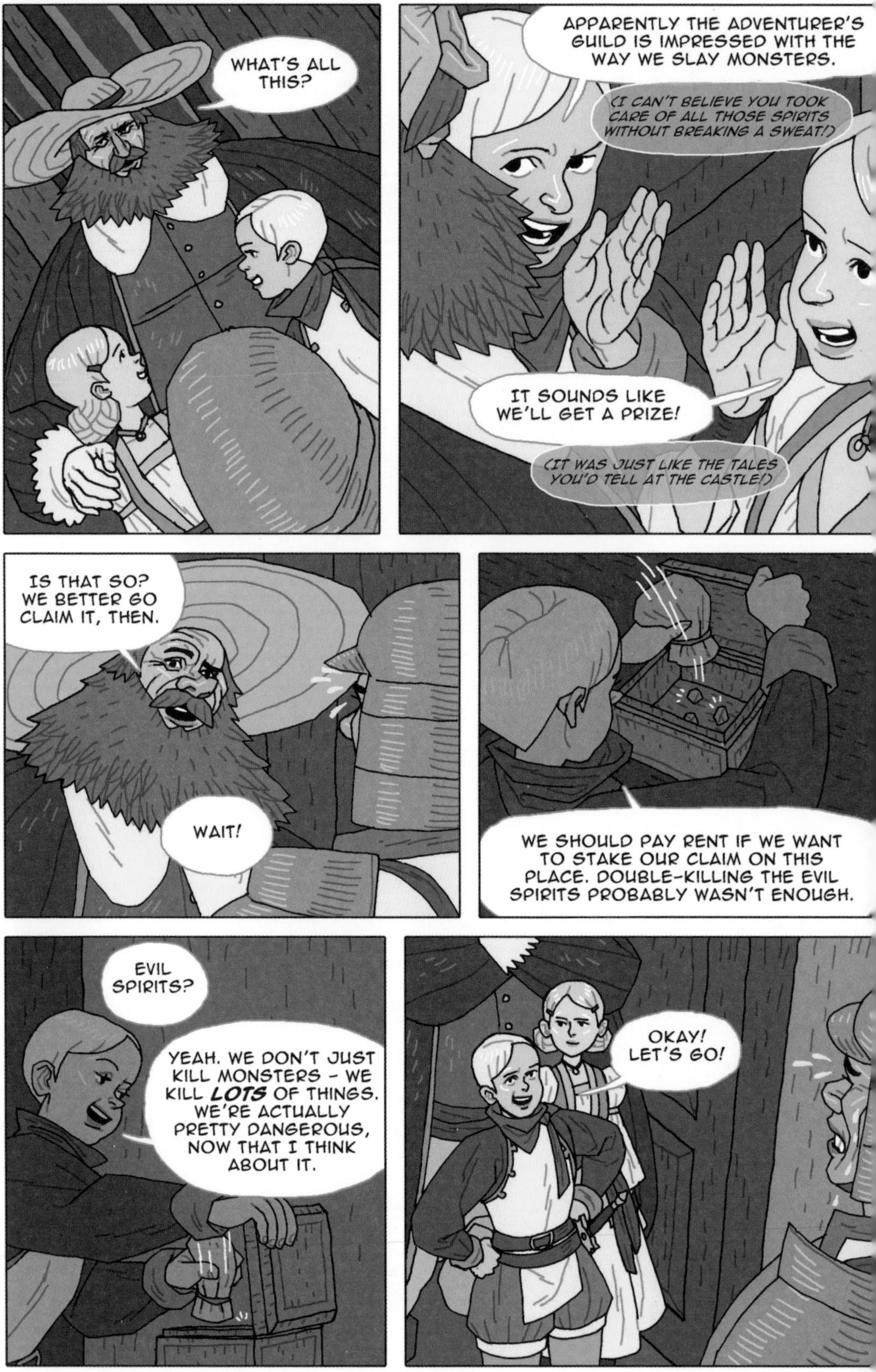
WHAT'S ALL THIS?
APPARENTLY THE ADVENTURER'S GUILD IS IMPRESSED WITH THE WAY WE SLAY MONSTERS.
(I CAN'T BELIEVE YOU TOOK CARE OF ALL THOSE SPIRITS WITHOUT BREAKING A SWEAT!)
IT SOUNDS LIKE WE'LL GET A PRIZE!
(IT WAS JUST LIKE THE TALES YOU'D TELL AT THE CASTLE!)
IS THAT SO? WE BETTER GO CLAIM IT, THEN.
WAIT!
WE SHOULD PAY RENT IF WE WANT TO STAKE OUR CLAIM ON THIS PLACE. DOUBLE-KILLING THE EVIL SPIRITS PROBABLY WASN'T ENOUGH.
EVIL SPIRITS?
YEAH. WE DON'T JUST KILL MONSTERS - WE KILL *LOTS* OF THINGS. WE'RE ACTUALLY PRETTY DANGEROUS, NOW THAT I THINK ABOUT IT.
OKAY! LET'S GO!

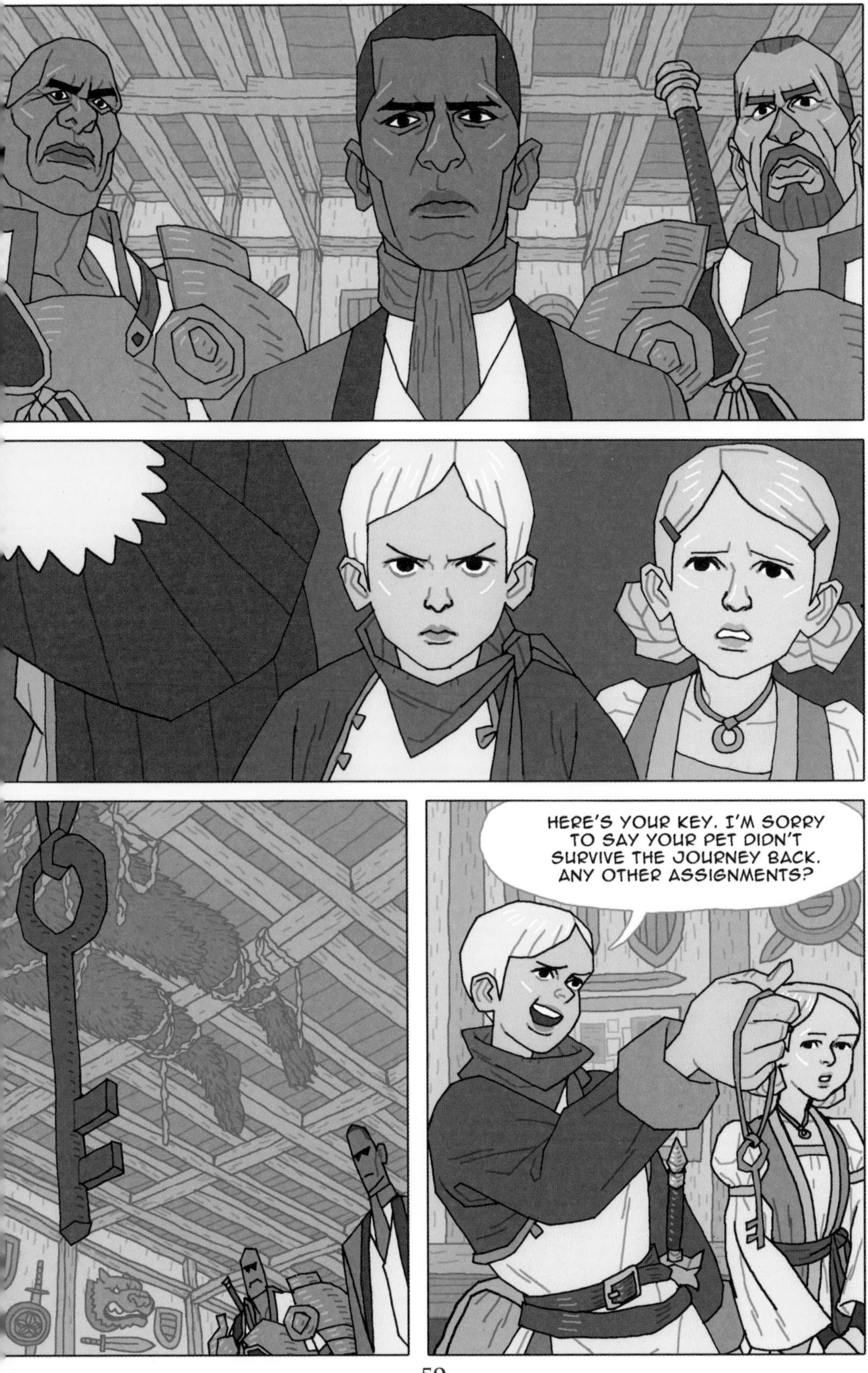
HERE'S YOUR KEY. I'M SORRY TO SAY YOUR PET DIDN'T SURVIVE THE JOURNEY BACK. ANY OTHER ASSIGNMENTS?

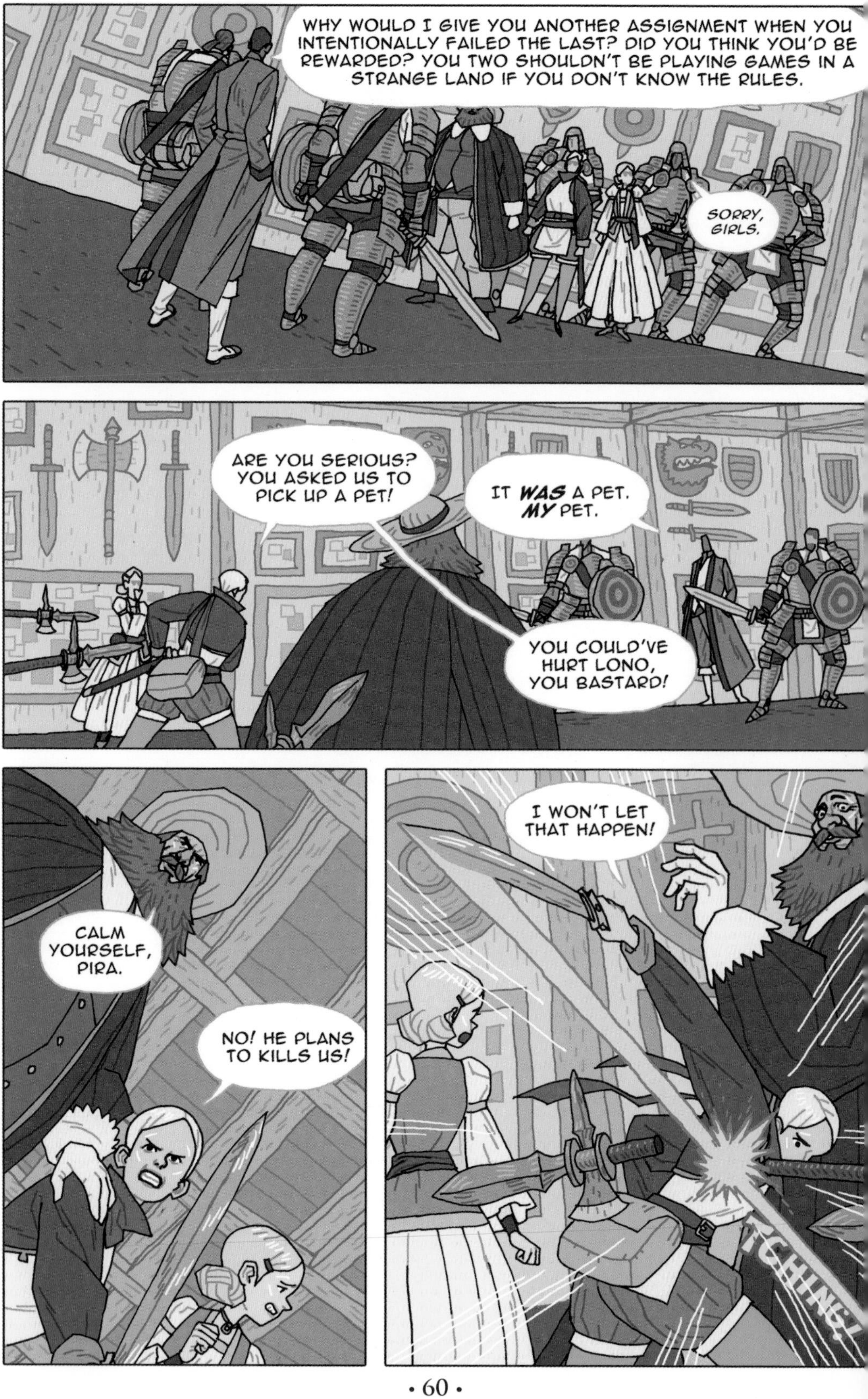
WHY WOULD I GIVE YOU ANOTHER ASSIGNMENT WHEN YOU INTENTIONALLY FAILED THE LAST? DID YOU THINK YOU'D BE REWARDED? YOU TWO SHOULDN'T BE PLAYING GAMES IN A STRANGE LAND IF YOU DON'T KNOW THE RULES.
SORRY, GIRLS.
ARE YOU SERIOUS? YOU ASKED US TO PICK UP A PET!
IT *WAS* A PET. *MY* PET.
YOU COULD'VE HURT LONO, YOU BASTARD!
CALM YOURSELF, PIRA.
NO! HE PLANS TO KILLS US!
I WON'T LET THAT HAPPEN!
TCHING!

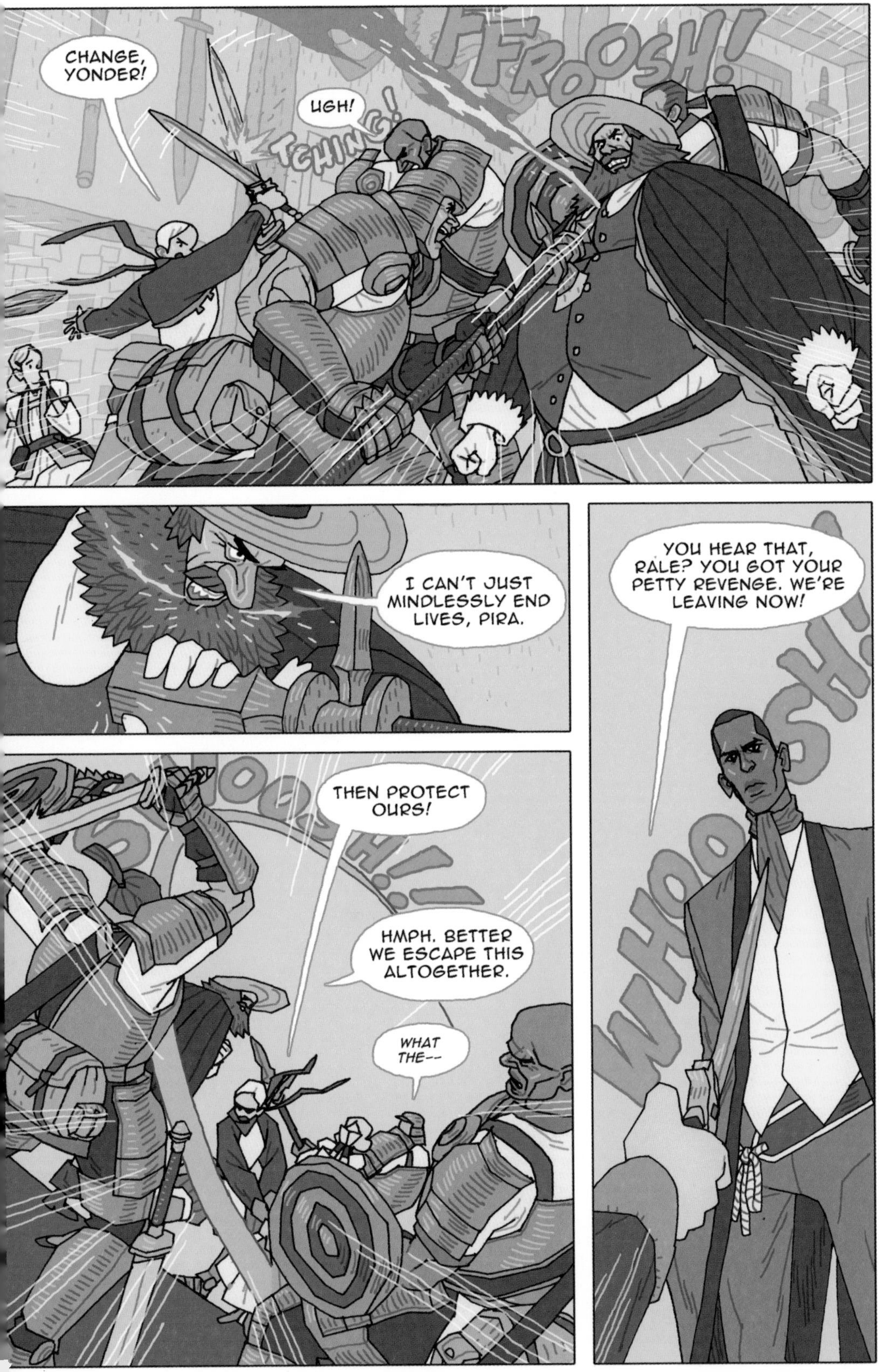

FFROOSH!
CHANGE, YONDER!
UGH!
TCHING!
I CAN'T JUST MINDLESSLY END LIVES, PIRA.
YOU HEAR THAT, RALE? YOU GOT YOUR PETTY REVENGE. WE'RE LEAVING NOW!
WHOOSH!
THEN PROTECT OURS!
SHOOSH!
HMPH. BETTER WE ESCAPE THIS ALTOGETHER.
WHAT THE--

THEY'VE PROVEN THEIR WORTH. I BELIEVE THESE GIRLS HAVE IT IN THEM TO BE ADVENTURERS AFTER ALL.

ARE WE LETTING THEM LEAVE?

AND THE MAN?

THEIR GUARDIAN SPIRIT. THAT MUCH IS CERTAIN.

A REAL SPIRIT? YOU CAN'T MEAN–

A LIVING, BREATHING MANIFESTATION OF AN ELEMENT. YES.

BUT THEY HATE PEOPLE!

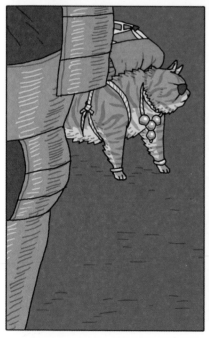

UH... HELLO.

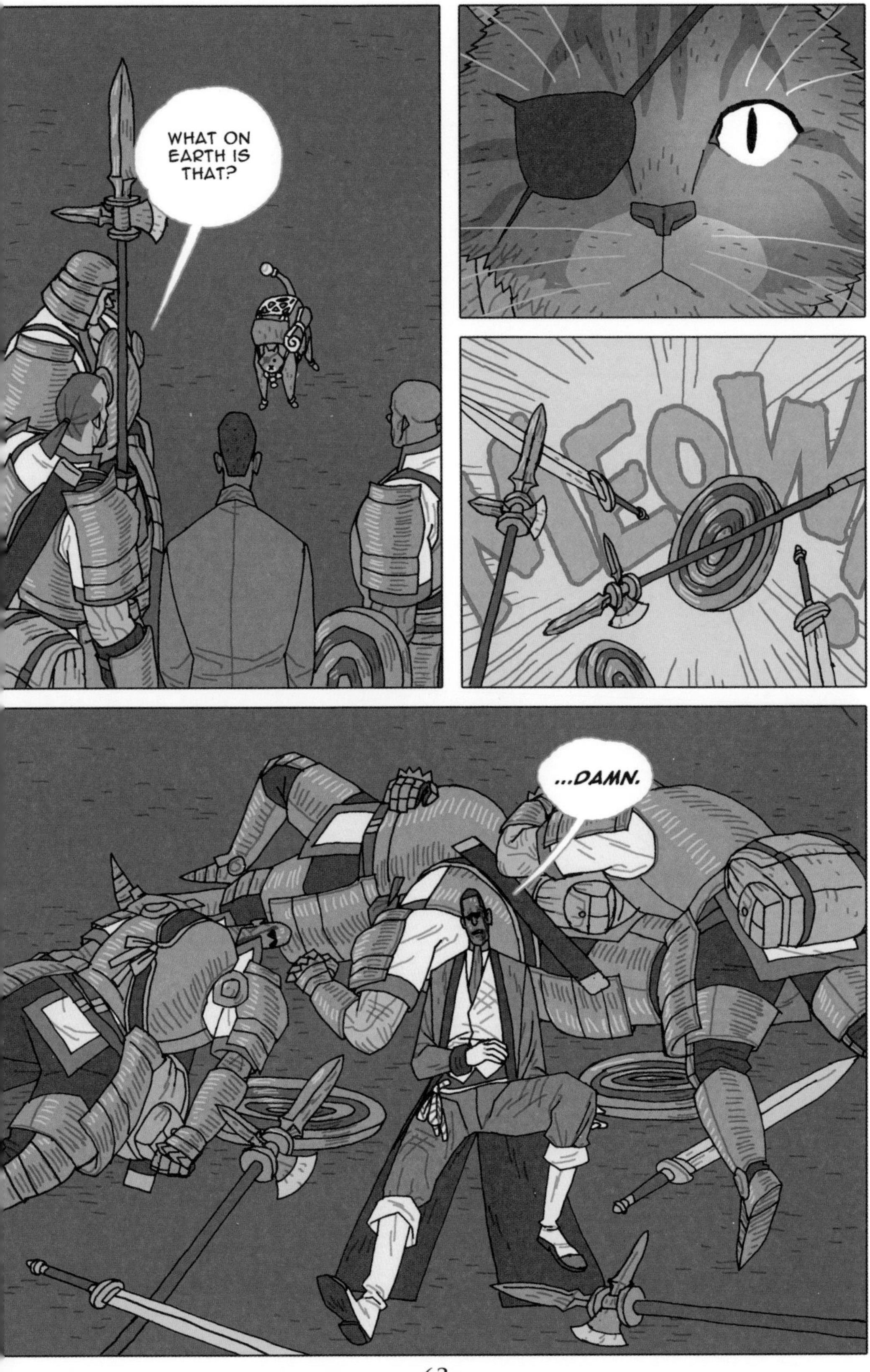
WHAT ON EARTH IS THAT?
MEOW!
...DAMN.

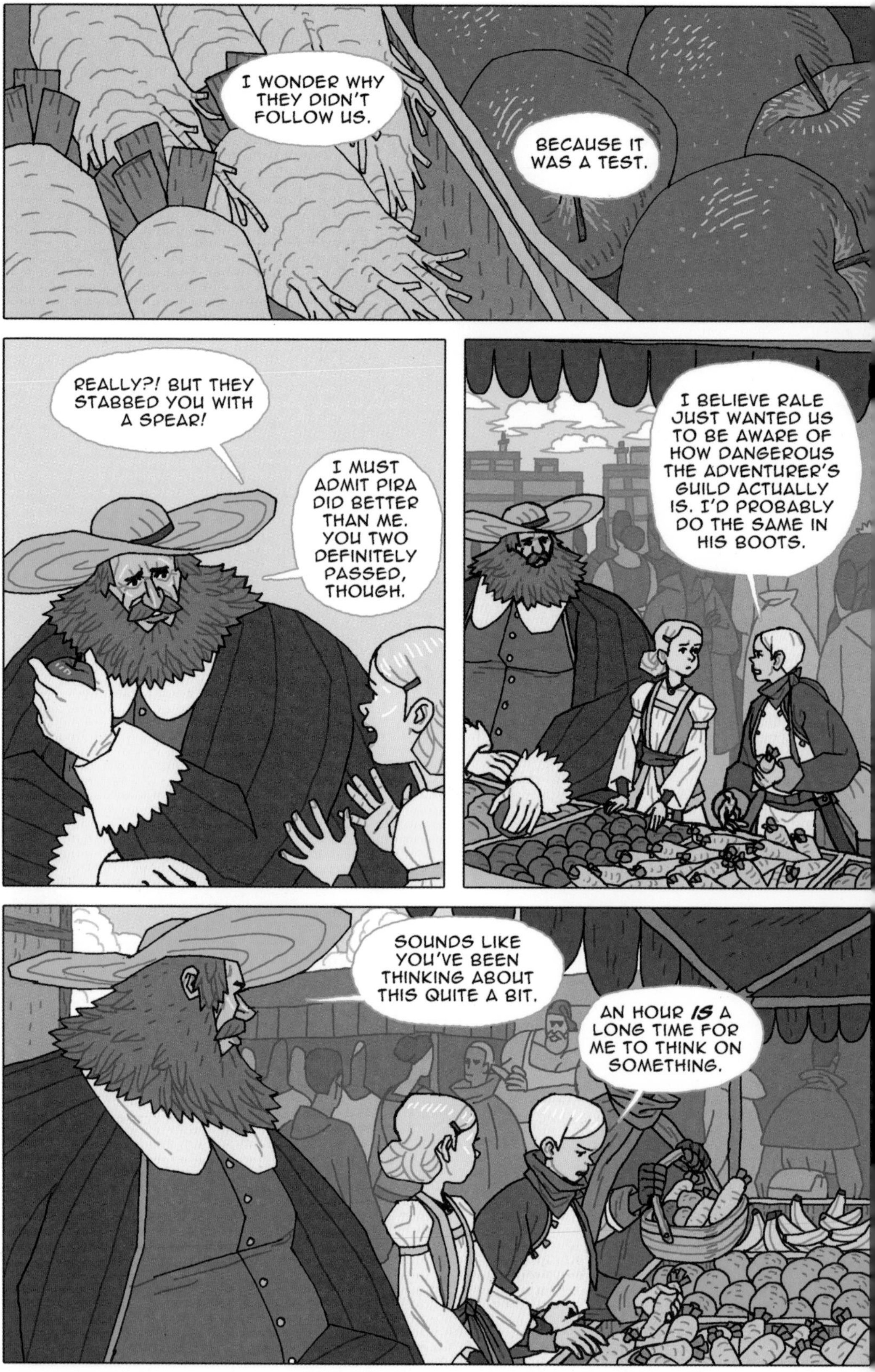
I WONDER WHY THEY DIDN'T FOLLOW US.
BECAUSE IT WAS A TEST.
REALLY?! BUT THEY STABBED YOU WITH A SPEAR!
I MUST ADMIT PIRA DID BETTER THAN ME. YOU TWO DEFINITELY PASSED, THOUGH.
I BELIEVE RALE JUST WANTED US TO BE AWARE OF HOW DANGEROUS THE ADVENTURER'S GUILD ACTUALLY IS. I'D PROBABLY DO THE SAME IN HIS BOOTS.
SOUNDS LIKE YOU'VE BEEN THINKING ABOUT THIS QUITE A BIT.
AN HOUR *IS* A LONG TIME FOR ME TO THINK ON SOMETHING.

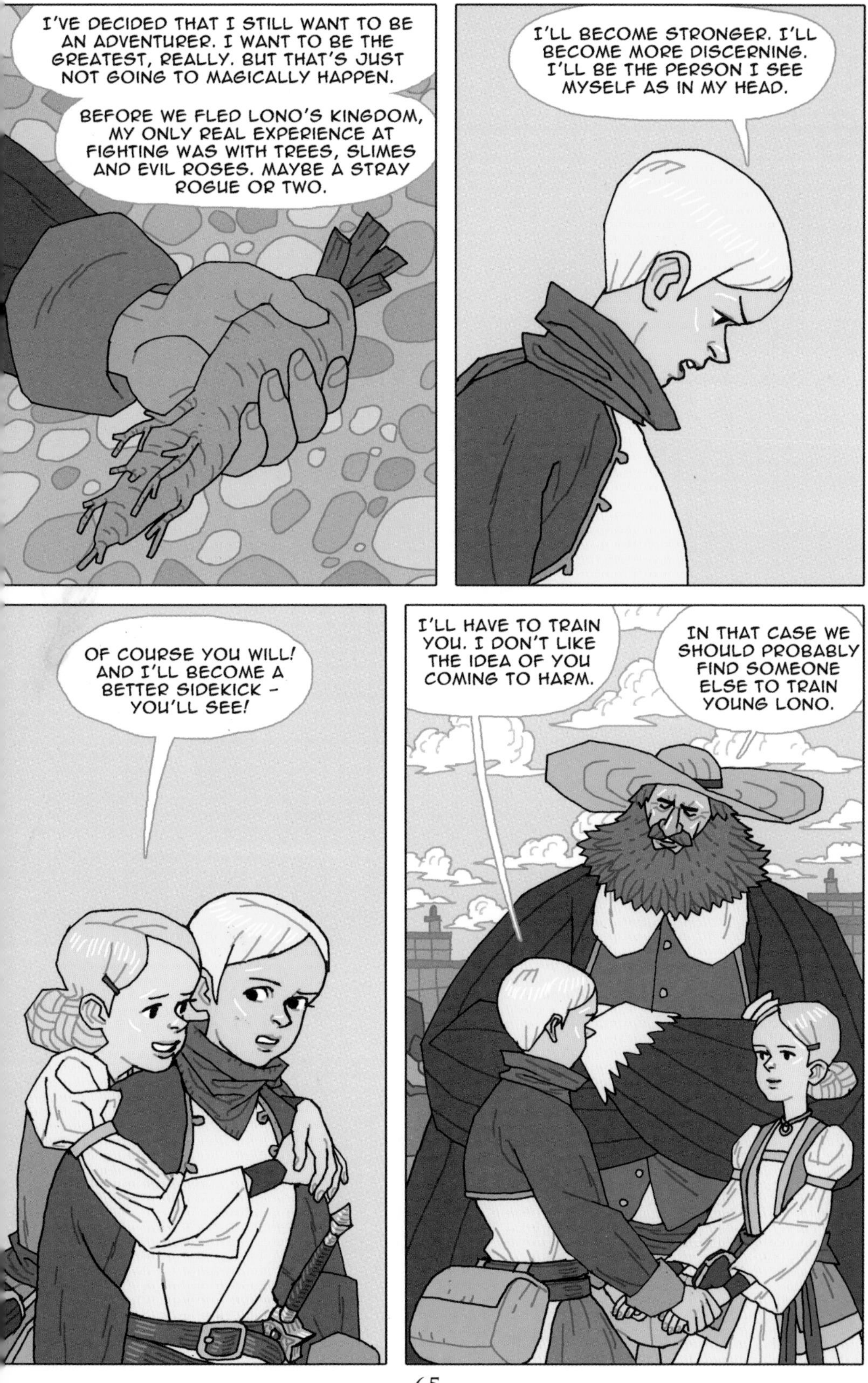
I'VE DECIDED THAT I STILL WANT TO BE AN ADVENTURER. I WANT TO BE THE GREATEST, REALLY. BUT THAT'S JUST NOT GOING TO MAGICALLY HAPPEN.
BEFORE WE FLED LONO'S KINGDOM, MY ONLY REAL EXPERIENCE AT FIGHTING WAS WITH TREES, SLIMES AND EVIL ROSES. MAYBE A STRAY ROGUE OR TWO.
I'LL BECOME STRONGER. I'LL BECOME MORE DISCERNING. I'LL BE THE PERSON I SEE MYSELF AS IN MY HEAD.
OF COURSE YOU WILL! AND I'LL BECOME A BETTER SIDEKICK - YOU'LL SEE!
I'LL HAVE TO TRAIN YOU. I DON'T LIKE THE IDEA OF YOU COMING TO HARM.
IN THAT CASE WE SHOULD PROBABLY FIND SOMEONE ELSE TO TRAIN YOUNG LONO.

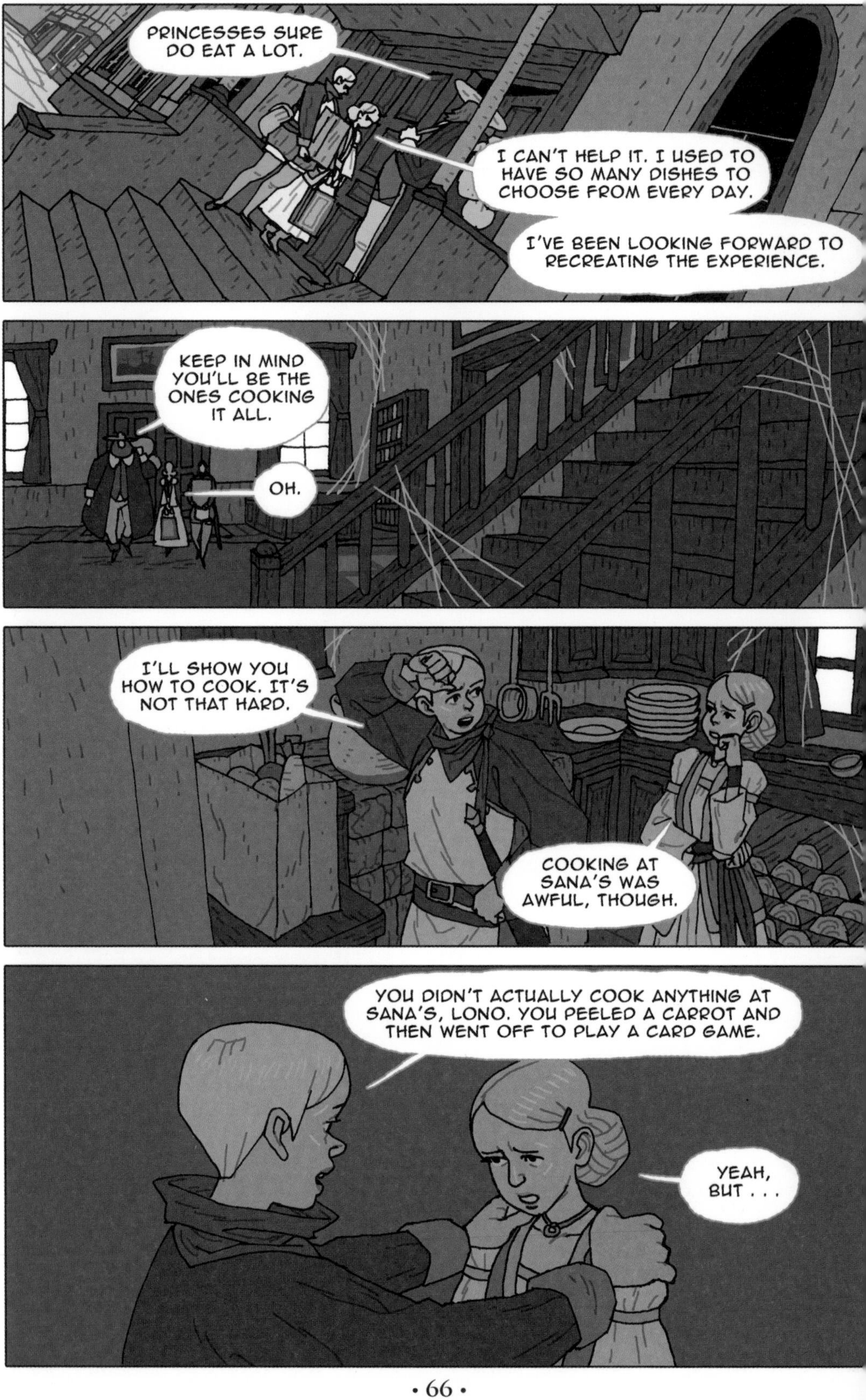
PRINCESSES SURE DO EAT A LOT.
I CAN'T HELP IT. I USED TO HAVE SO MANY DISHES TO CHOOSE FROM EVERY DAY.
I'VE BEEN LOOKING FORWARD TO RECREATING THE EXPERIENCE.
KEEP IN MIND YOU'LL BE THE ONES COOKING IT ALL.
OH.
I'LL SHOW YOU HOW TO COOK. IT'S NOT THAT HARD.
COOKING AT SANA'S WAS AWFUL, THOUGH.
YOU DIDN'T ACTUALLY COOK ANYTHING AT SANA'S, LONO. YOU PEELED A CARROT AND THEN WENT OFF TO PLAY A CARD GAME.
YEAH, BUT . . .

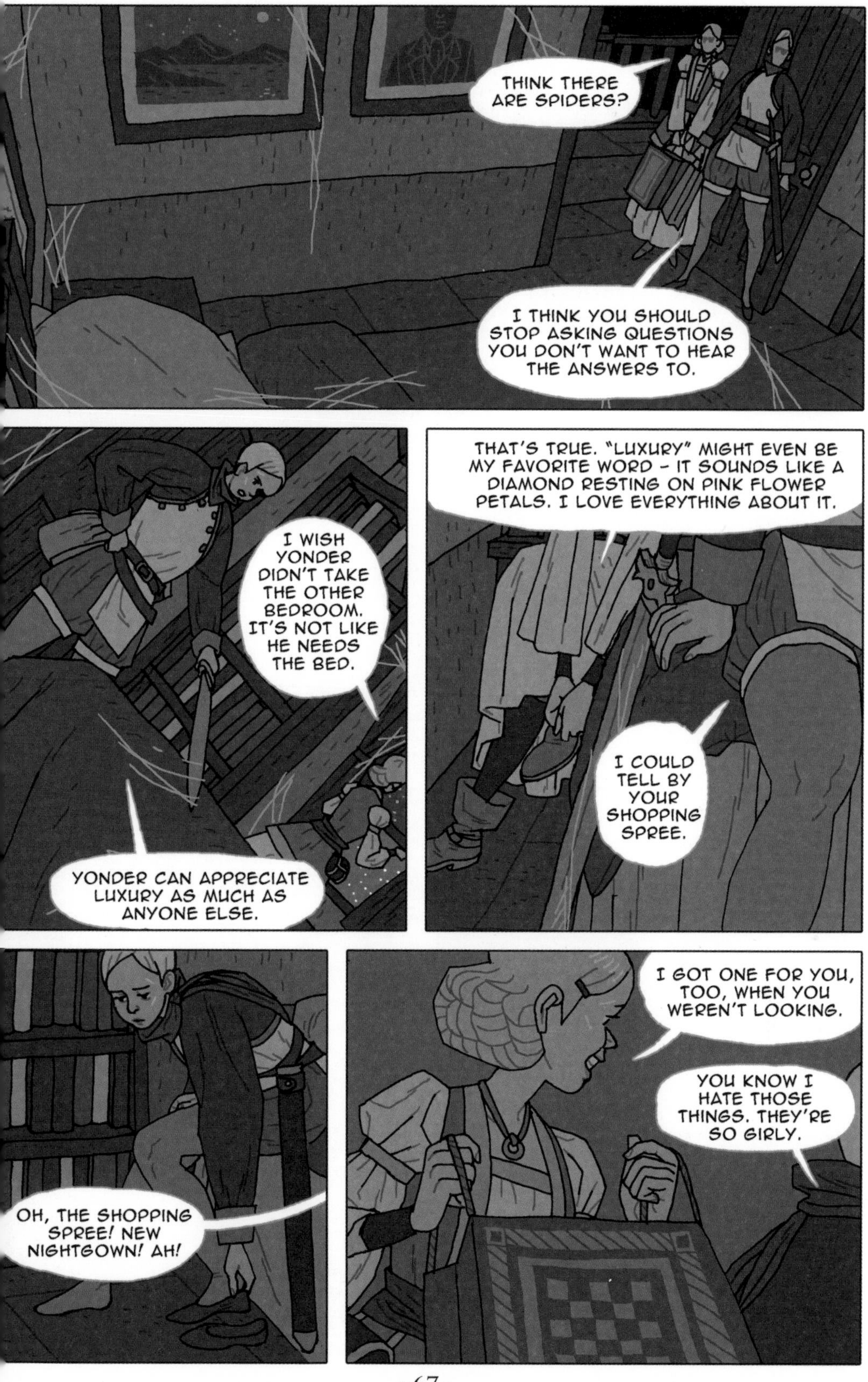
THINK THERE ARE SPIDERS?
I THINK YOU SHOULD STOP ASKING QUESTIONS YOU DON'T WANT TO HEAR THE ANSWERS TO.
I WISH YONDER DIDN'T TAKE THE OTHER BEDROOM. IT'S NOT LIKE HE NEEDS THE BED.
YONDER CAN APPRECIATE LUXURY AS MUCH AS ANYONE ELSE.
THAT'S TRUE. "LUXURY" MIGHT EVEN BE MY FAVORITE WORD - IT SOUNDS LIKE A DIAMOND RESTING ON PINK FLOWER PETALS. I LOVE EVERYTHING ABOUT IT.
I COULD TELL BY YOUR SHOPPING SPREE.
OH, THE SHOPPING SPREE! NEW NIGHTGOWN! AH!
I GOT ONE FOR YOU, TOO, WHEN YOU WEREN'T LOOKING.
YOU KNOW I HATE THOSE THINGS. THEY'RE SO GIRLY.

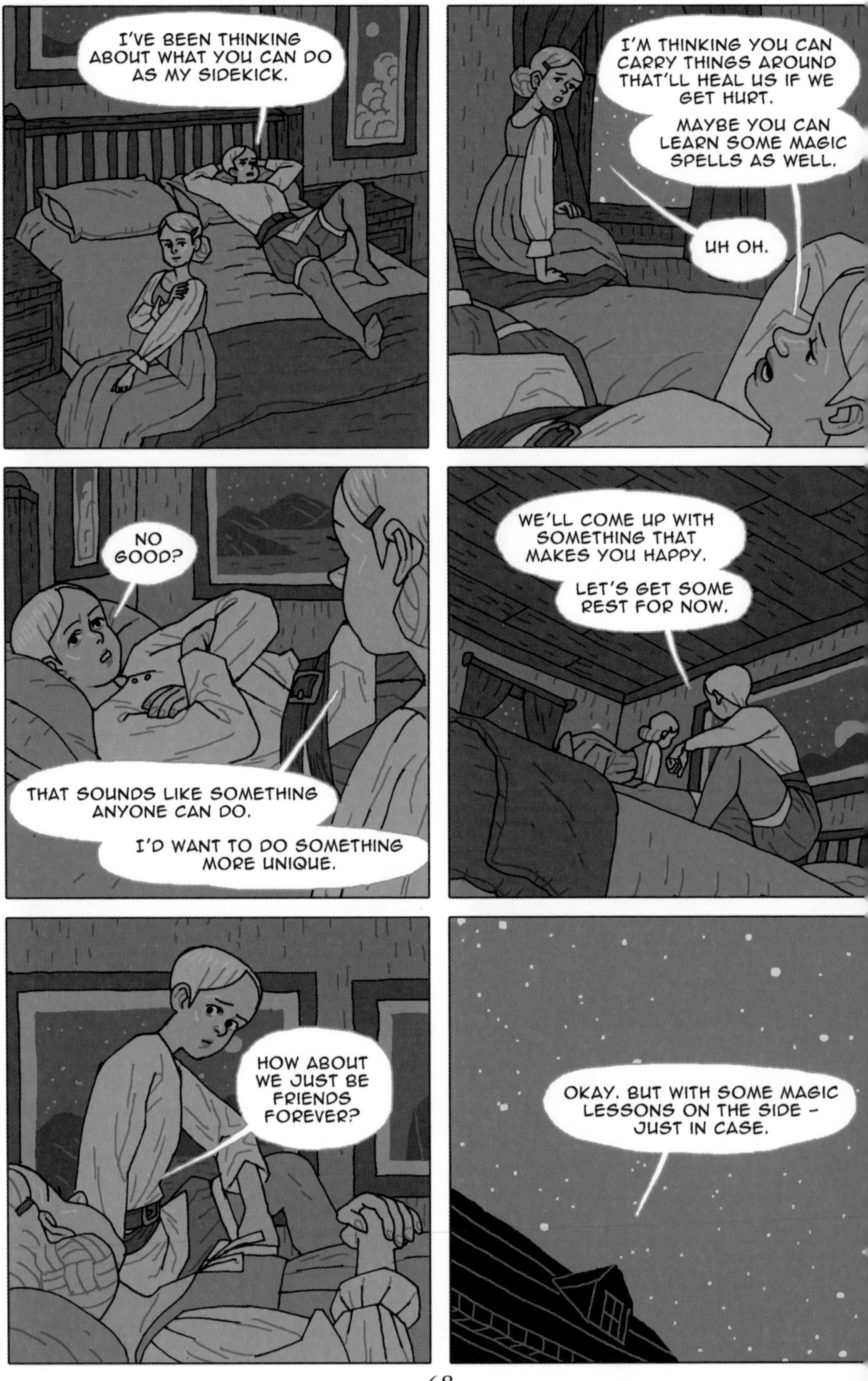
I'VE BEEN THINKING ABOUT WHAT YOU CAN DO AS MY SIDEKICK.
I'M THINKING YOU CAN CARRY THINGS AROUND THAT'LL HEAL US IF WE GET HURT.
MAYBE YOU CAN LEARN SOME MAGIC SPELLS AS WELL.
UH OH.
NO GOOD?
THAT SOUNDS LIKE SOMETHING ANYONE CAN DO.
I'D WANT TO DO SOMETHING MORE UNIQUE.
WE'LL COME UP WITH SOMETHING THAT MAKES YOU HAPPY.
LET'S GET SOME REST FOR NOW.
HOW ABOUT WE JUST BE FRIENDS FOREVER?
OKAY. BUT WITH SOME MAGIC LESSONS ON THE SIDE - JUST IN CASE.

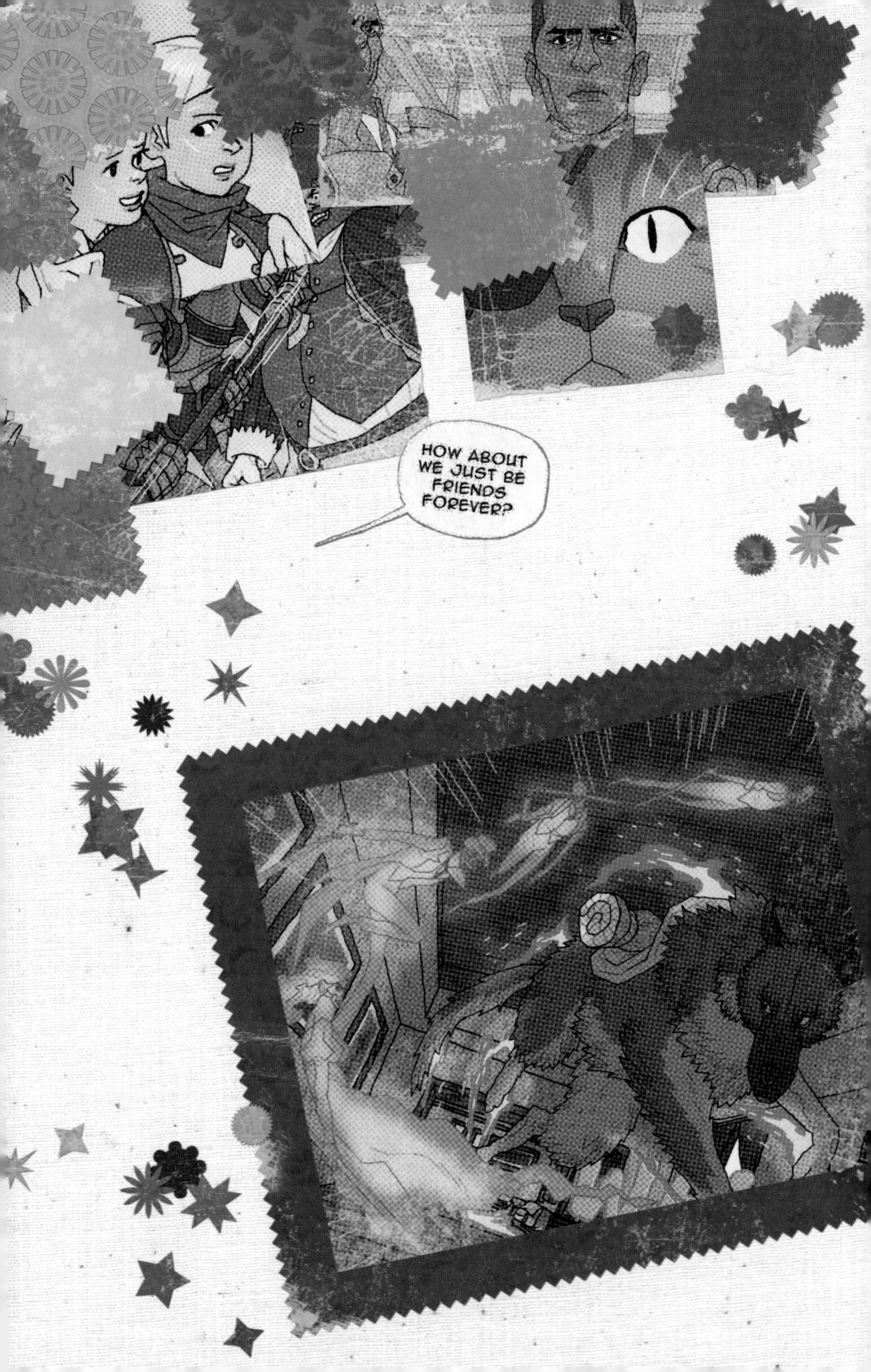
HOW ABOUT WE JUST BE FRIENDS FOREVER?

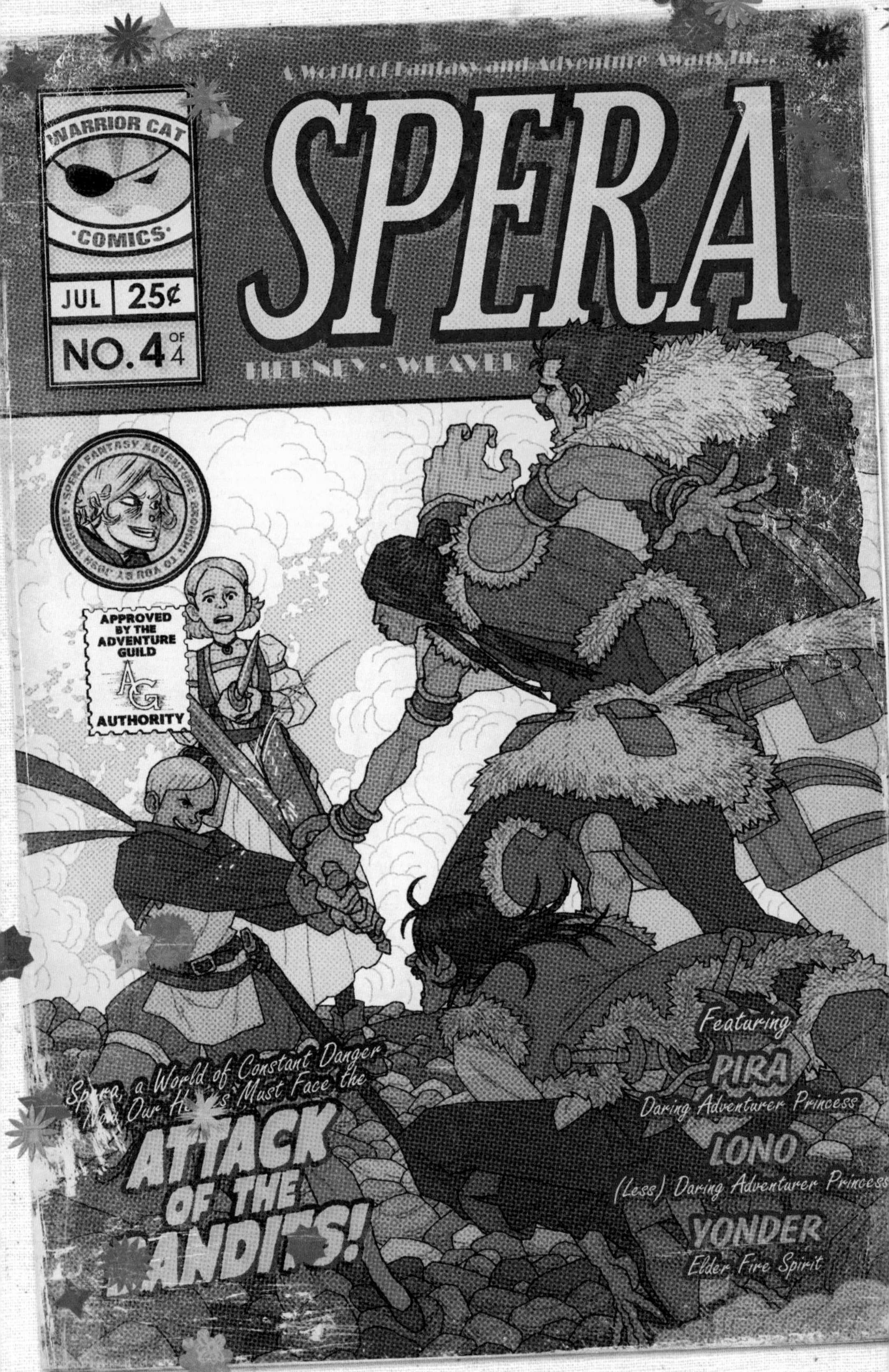

A World of Fantasy and Adventure Awaits In...

SPERA

WARRIOR CAT COMICS

JUL | 25¢

NO. 4 OF 4

HEUNEY · WEAVER

APPROVED BY THE ADVENTURE GUILD

AUTHORITY

Spera, a World of Constant Danger
And Our Heroes Must Face the

ATTACK OF THE BANDITS!

Featuring

PIRA
Daring Adventurer Princess

LONO
(Less) Daring Adventurer Princess

YONDER
Elder Fire Spirit

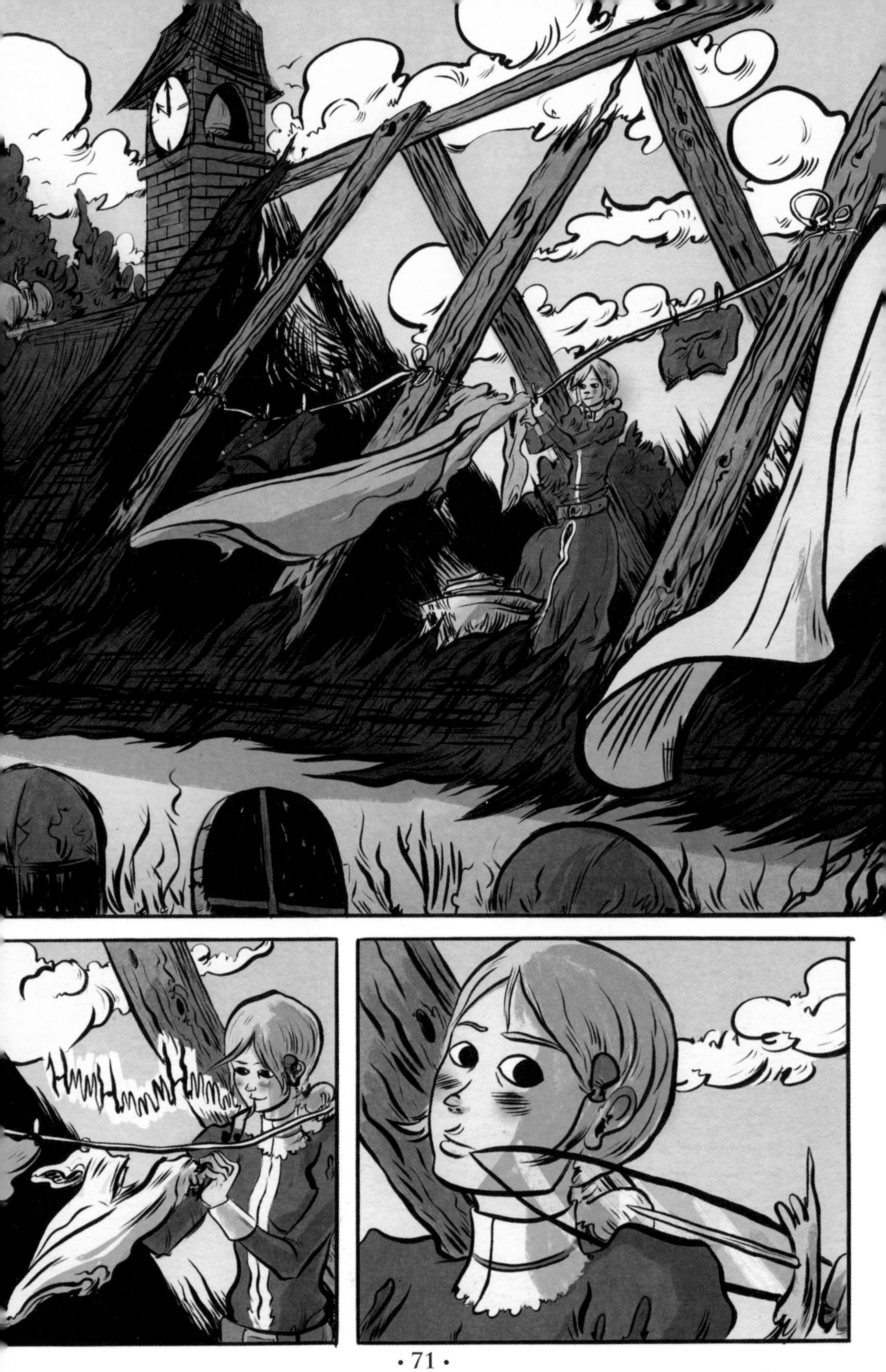
HmmHmmmHmm

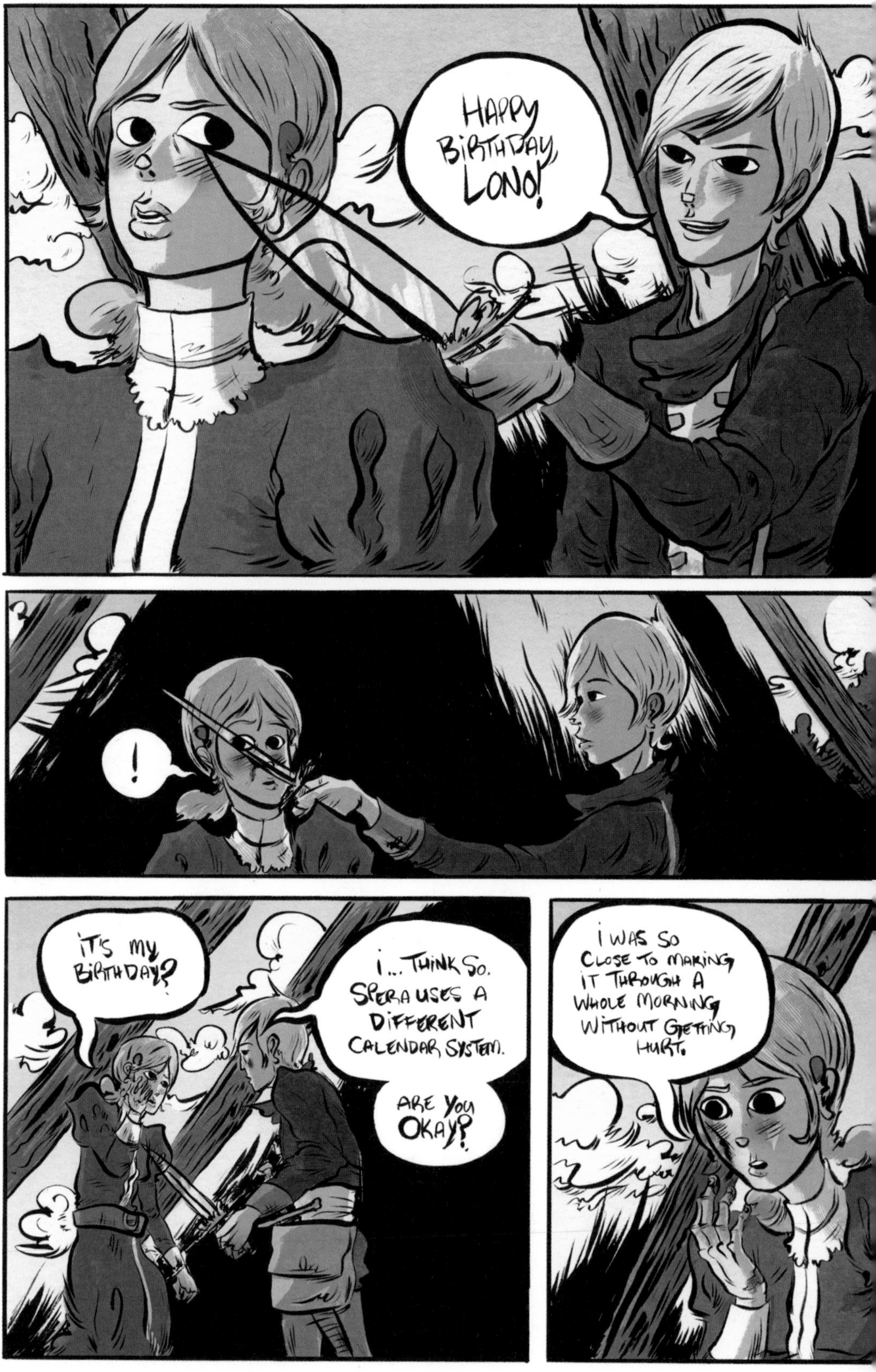
HAPPY BIRTHDAY, LONO!
!
IT'S MY BIRTHDAY?
I... THINK SO. SPERA USES A DIFFERENT CALENDAR SYSTEM.
ARE YOU OKAY?
I WAS SO CLOSE TO MAKING IT THROUGH A WHOLE MORNING WITHOUT GETTING HURT.

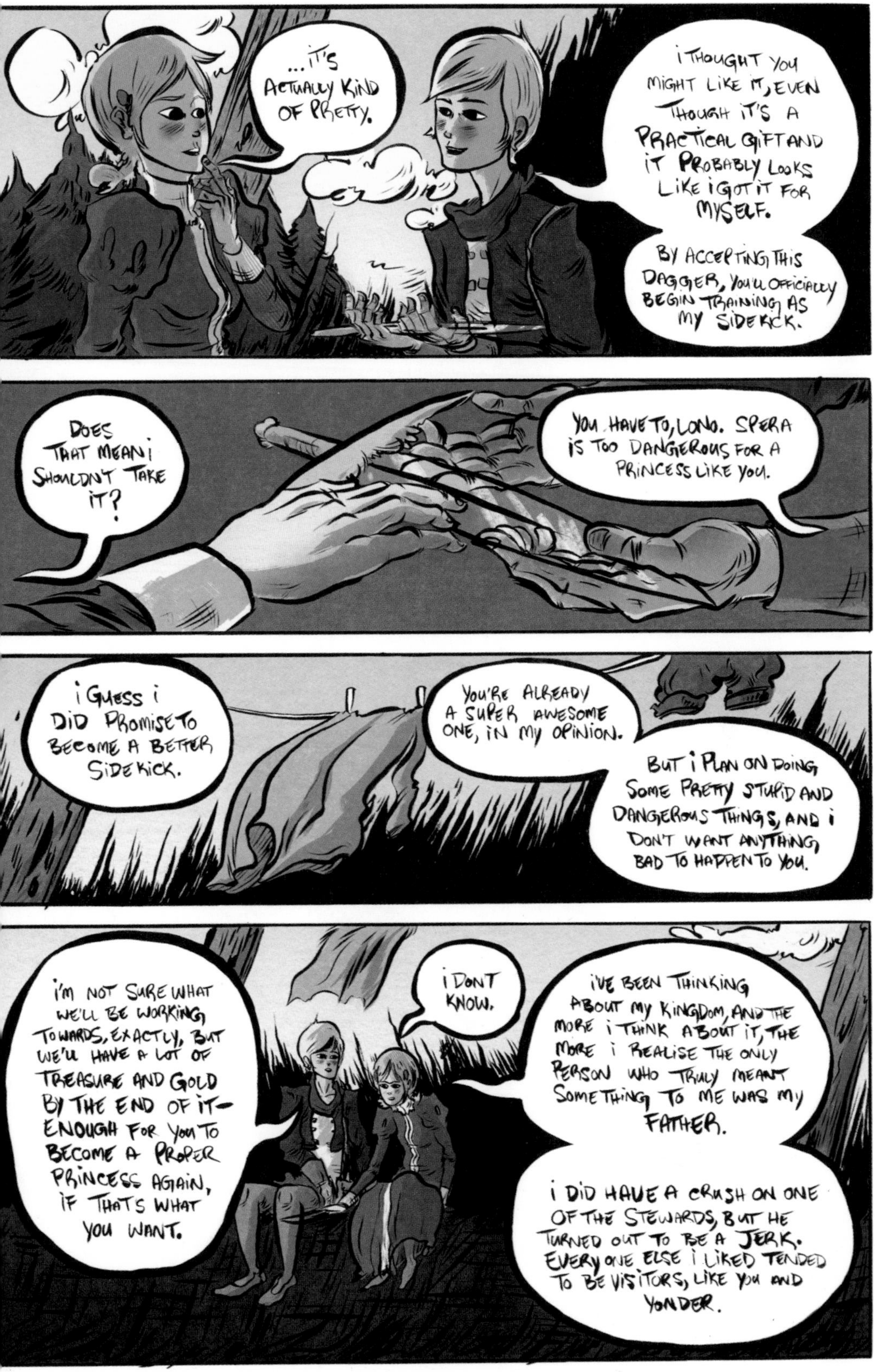
...IT'S ACTUALLY KIND OF PRETTY.
I THOUGHT YOU MIGHT LIKE IT, EVEN THOUGH IT'S A PRACTICAL GIFT AND IT PROBABLY LOOKS LIKE I GOT IT FOR MYSELF.
BY ACCEPTING THIS DAGGER, YOU'LL OFFICIALLY BEGIN TRAINING AS MY SIDEKICK.
DOES THAT MEAN I SHOULDN'T TAKE IT?
YOU HAVE TO, LONO. SPERA IS TOO DANGEROUS FOR A PRINCESS LIKE YOU.
I GUESS I DID PROMISE TO BECOME A BETTER SIDEKICK.
YOU'RE ALREADY A SUPER AWESOME ONE, IN MY OPINION.
BUT I PLAN ON DOING SOME PRETTY STUPID AND DANGEROUS THINGS, AND I DON'T WANT ANYTHING BAD TO HAPPEN TO YOU.
I'M NOT SURE WHAT WE'LL BE WORKING TOWARDS, EXACTLY, BUT WE'LL HAVE A LOT OF TREASURE AND GOLD BY THE END OF IT— ENOUGH FOR YOU TO BECOME A PROPER PRINCESS AGAIN, IF THAT'S WHAT YOU WANT.
I DONT KNOW.
I'VE BEEN THINKING ABOUT MY KINGDOM, AND THE MORE I THINK ABOUT IT, THE MORE I REALISE THE ONLY PERSON WHO TRULY MEANT SOMETHING TO ME WAS MY FATHER.
I DID HAVE A CRUSH ON ONE OF THE STEWARDS, BUT HE TURNED OUT TO BE A JERK. EVERYONE ELSE I LIKED TENDED TO BE VISITORS, LIKE YOU AND YONDER.

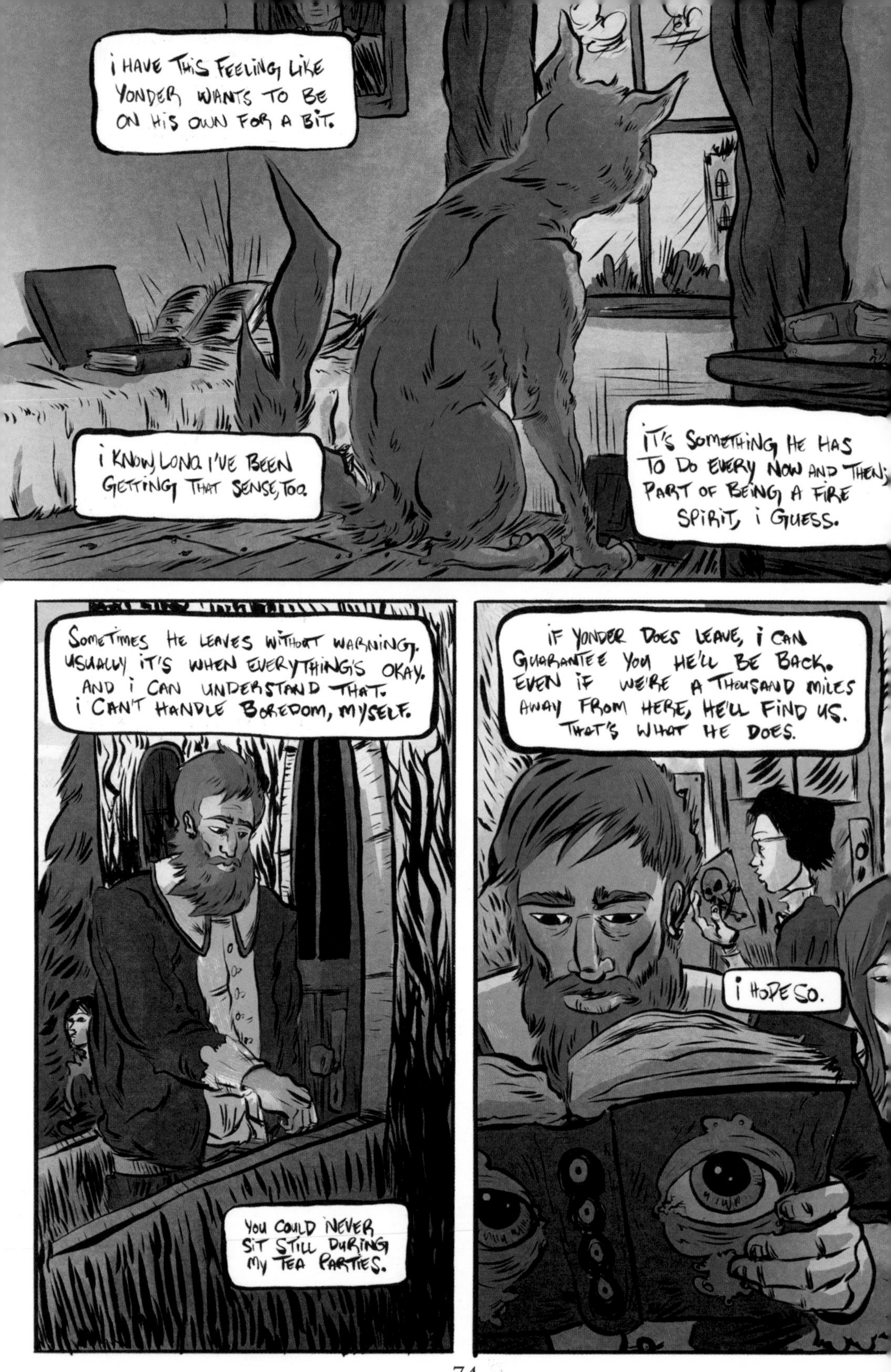
I HAVE THIS FEELING LIKE YONDER WANTS TO BE ON HIS OWN FOR A BIT.
I KNOW, LONG I'VE BEEN GETTING THAT SENSE, TOO.
IT'S SOMETHING HE HAS TO DO EVERY NOW AND THEN; PART OF BEING A FIRE SPIRIT, I GUESS.
SOMETIMES HE LEAVES WITHOUT WARNING. USUALLY IT'S WHEN EVERYTHING'S OKAY. AND I CAN UNDERSTAND THAT. I CAN'T HANDLE BOREDOM, MYSELF.
YOU COULD NEVER SIT STILL DURING MY TEA PARTIES.
IF YONDER DOES LEAVE, I CAN GUARANTEE YOU HE'LL BE BACK. EVEN IF WE'RE A THOUSAND MILES AWAY FROM HERE, HE'LL FIND US. THAT'S WHAT HE DOES.
I HOPE SO.

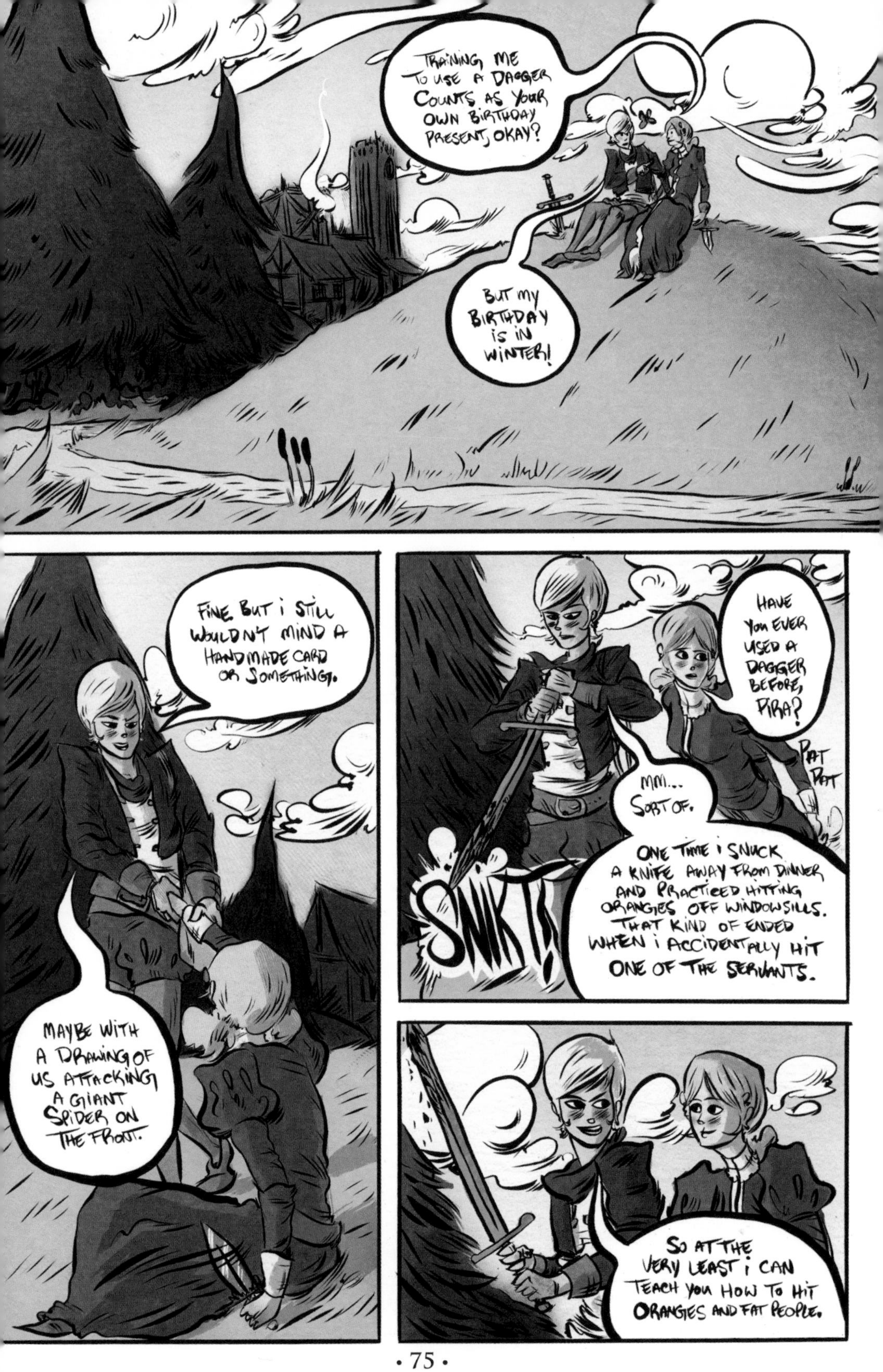
TRAINING ME TO USE A DAGGER COUNTS AS YOUR OWN BIRTHDAY PRESENT, OKAY?
BUT MY BIRTHDAY IS IN WINTER!
FINE. BUT I STILL WOULDN'T MIND A HANDMADE CARD OR SOMETHING.
MAYBE WITH A DRAWING OF US ATTACKING A GIANT SPIDER ON THE FRONT.
HAVE YOU EVER USED A DAGGER BEFORE, PIRA?
PAT PAT
SNIKT!
MM... SORT OF.
ONE TIME I SNUCK A KNIFE AWAY FROM DINNER AND PRACTICED HITTING ORANGES OFF WINDOWSILLS. THAT KIND OF ENDED WHEN I ACCIDENTALLY HIT ONE OF THE SERVANTS.
SO AT THE VERY LEAST I CAN TEACH YOU HOW TO HIT ORANGES AND FAT PEOPLE.

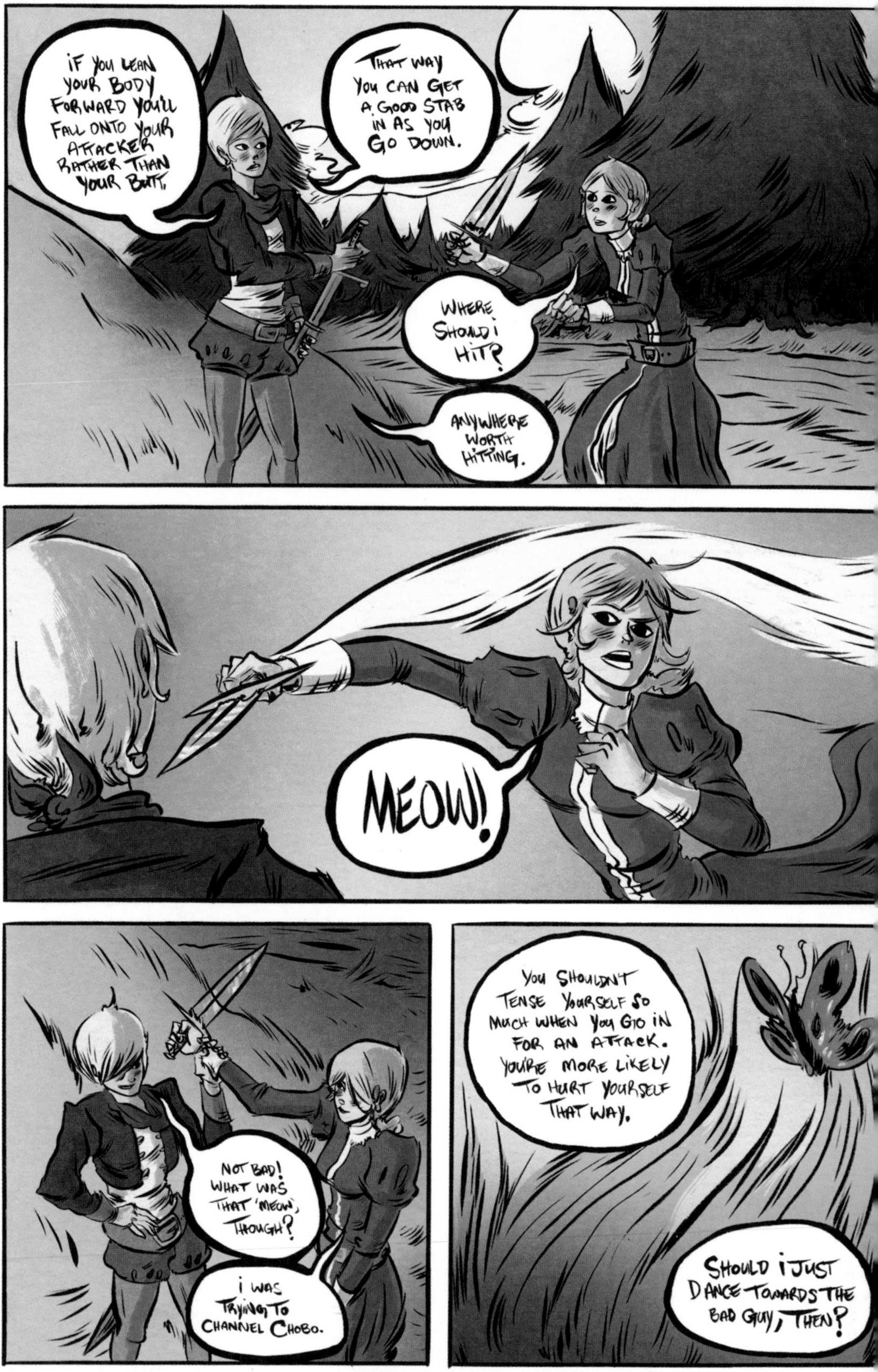
iF YOU LEAN YOUR BODY FORWARD YOU'LL FALL ONTO YOUR ATTACKER RATHER THAN YOUR BUTT.
THAT WAY YOU CAN GET A GOOD STAB IN AS YOU GO DOWN.
WHERE SHOULD i HIT?
ANYWHERE WORTH HITTING.
MEOW!
NOT BAD! WHAT WAS THAT 'MEOW', THOUGH?
i WAS TRYING TO CHANNEL CHOBO.
YOU SHOULDN'T TENSE YOURSELF SO MUCH WHEN YOU GO IN FOR AN ATTACK. YOU'RE MORE LIKELY TO HURT YOURSELF THAT WAY.
SHOULD i JUST DANCE TOWARDS THE BAD GUY, THEN?

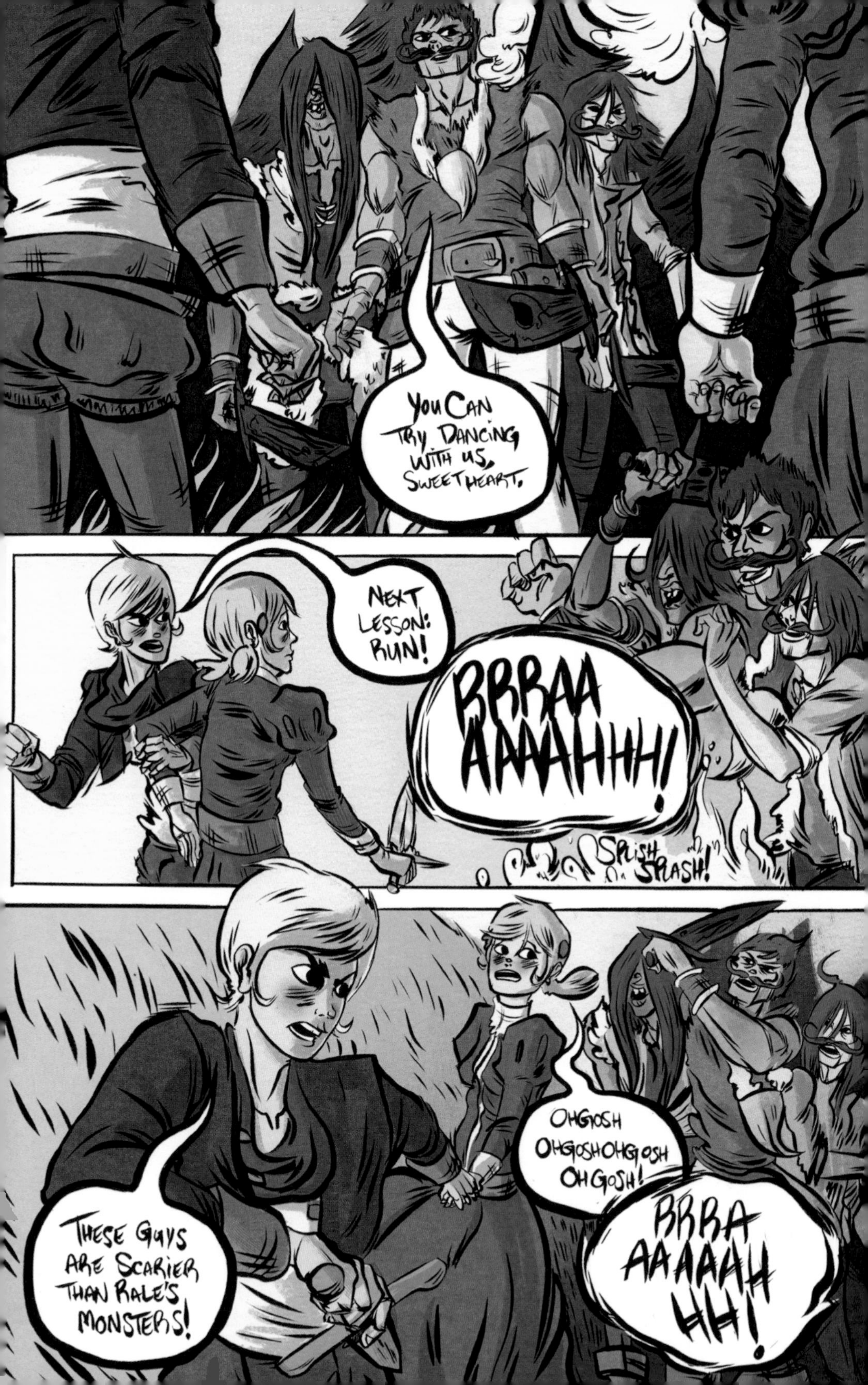
YOU CAN TRY DANCING WITH US, SWEETHEART.
NEXT LESSON: RUN!
BRRAAAAAHHH!
SPLISH SPLASH!
THESE GUYS ARE SCARIER THAN RALE'S MONSTERS!
OHGOSH OHGOSHOHGOSH OHGOSH!
BRRAAAAAHHH!

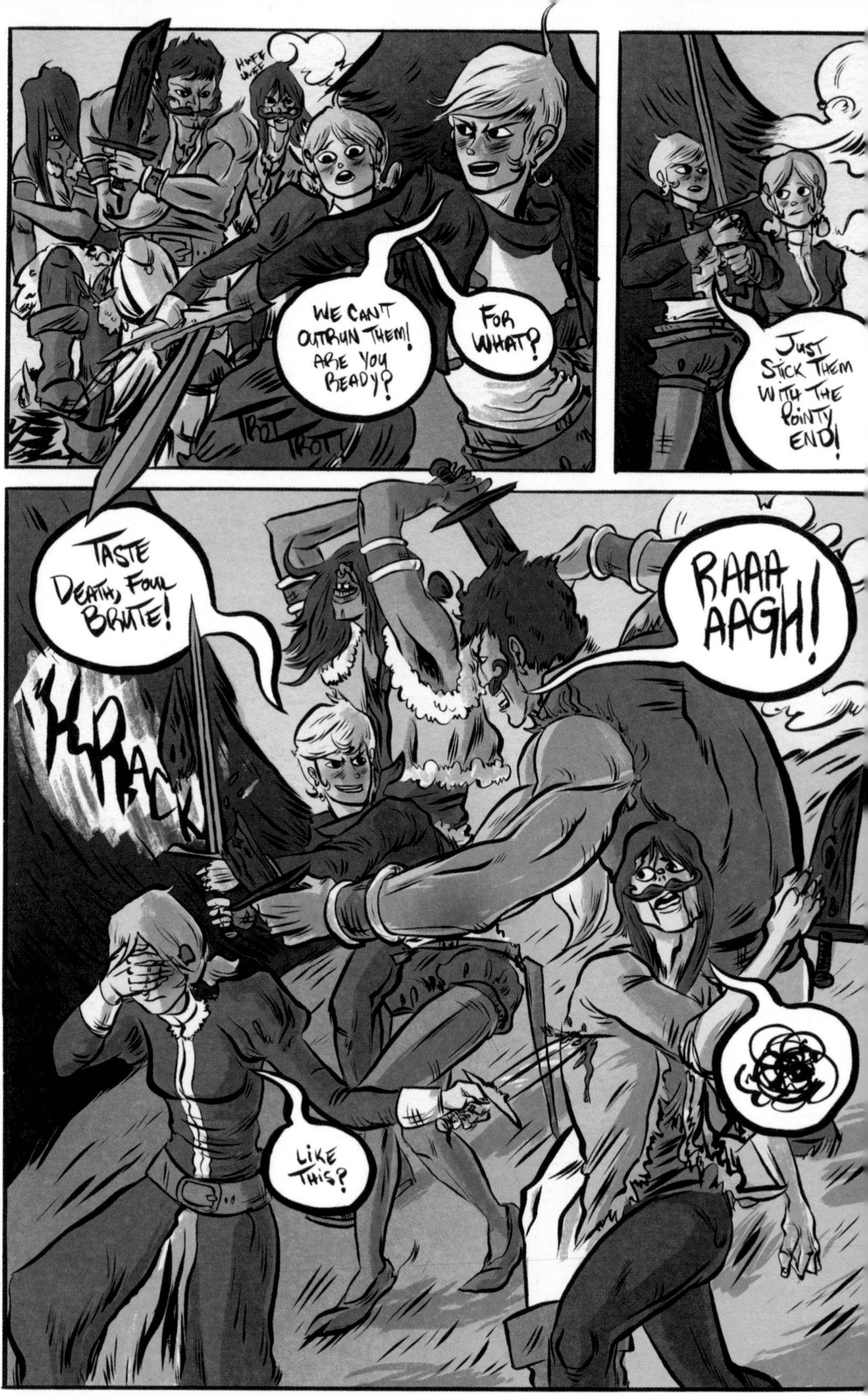

WE CAN'T OUTRUN THEM! ARE YOU READY?
FOR WHAT?
TROT TROT
JUST STICK THEM WITH THE POINTY END!
TASTE DEATH, FOUL BRUTE!
KRACK
RAAAAAGH!
LIKE THIS?

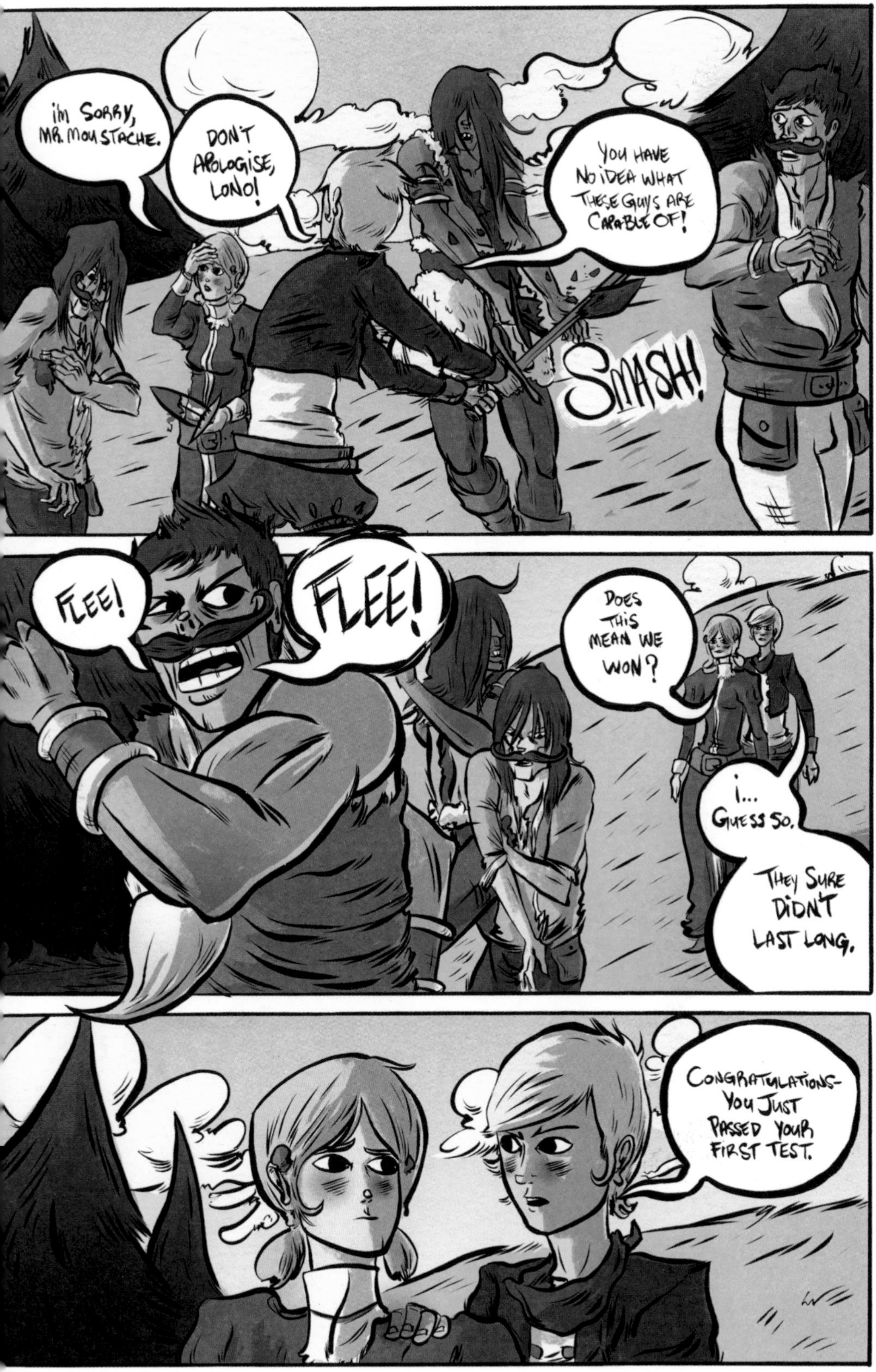
I'M SORRY, MR. MOUSTACHE.
DON'T APOLOGISE, LONO!
YOU HAVE NO IDEA WHAT THESE GUYS ARE CAPABLE OF!
SMASH!
FLEE!
FLEE!
DOES THIS MEAN WE WON?
I... GUESS SO.
THEY SURE DIDN'T LAST LONG.
CONGRATULATIONS- YOU JUST PASSED YOUR FIRST TEST.

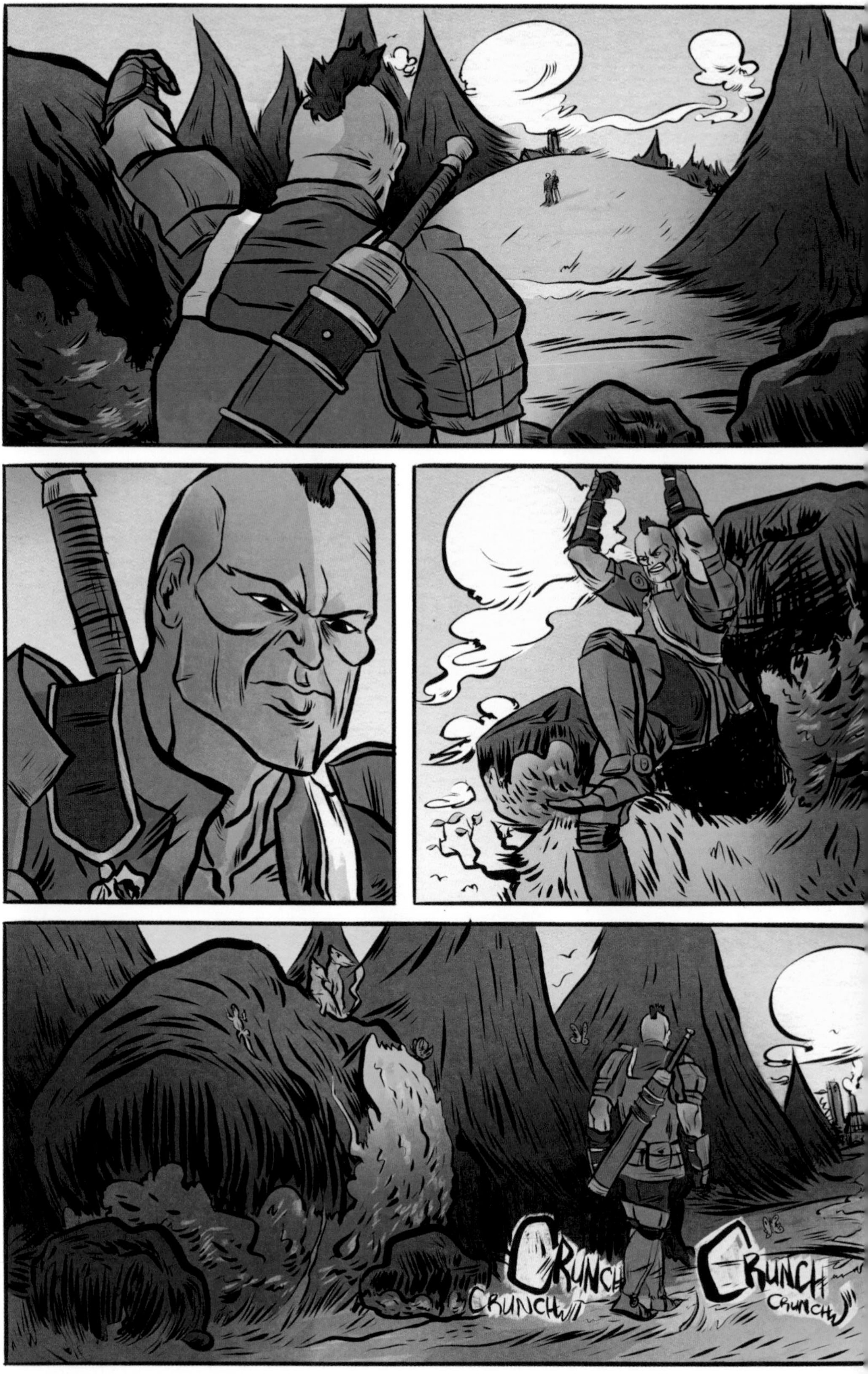
CRUNCH
CRUNCH
CRUNCH
CRUNCH

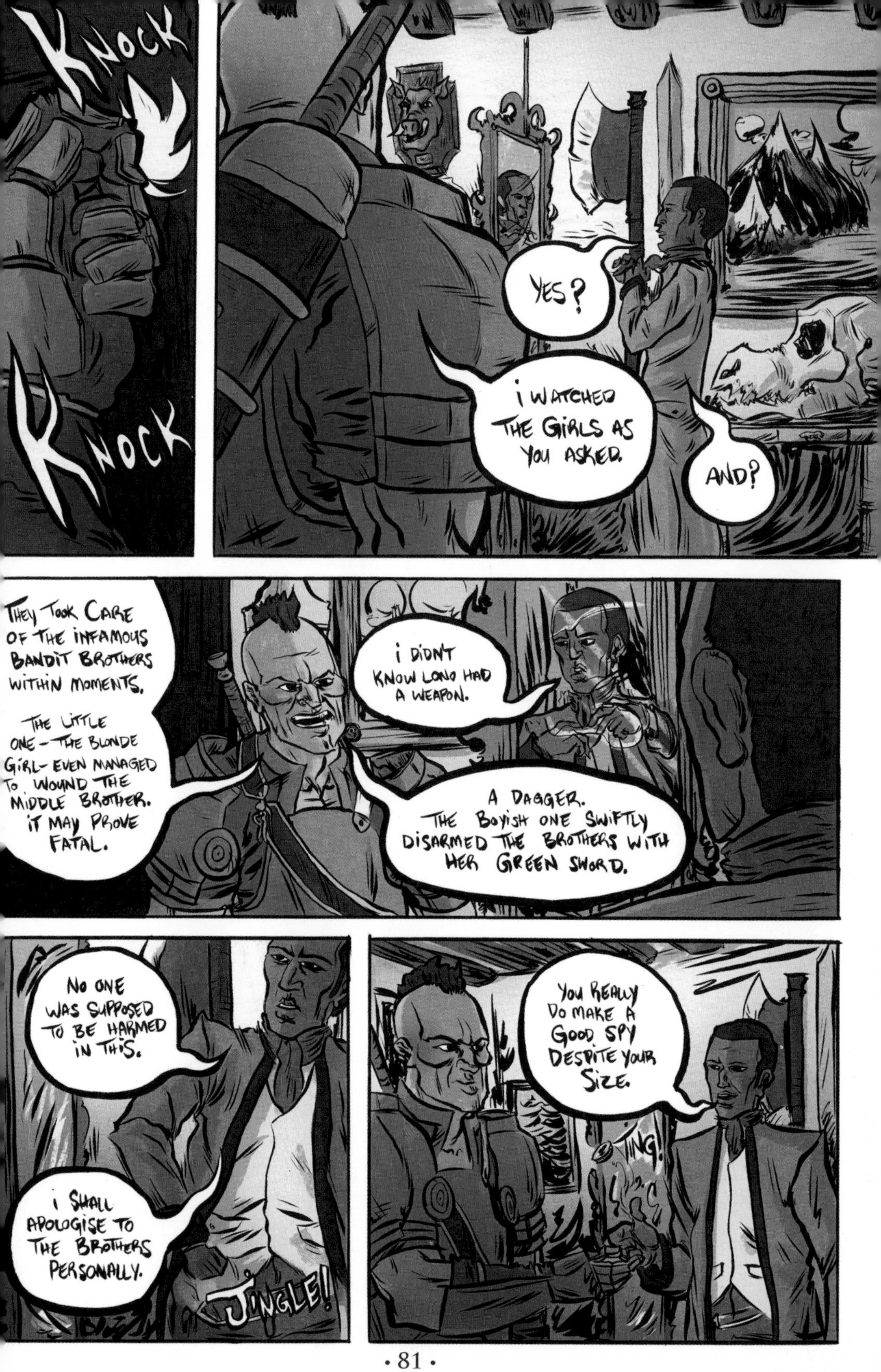
KNOCK
KNOCK
YES?
I WATCHED THE GIRLS AS YOU ASKED.
AND?
THEY TOOK CARE OF THE INFAMOUS BANDIT BROTHERS WITHIN MOMENTS.
THE LITTLE ONE - THE BLONDE GIRL - EVEN MANAGED TO WOUND THE MIDDLE BROTHER. IT MAY PROVE FATAL.
I DIDN'T KNOW LONO HAD A WEAPON.
A DAGGER. THE BOYISH ONE SWIFTLY DISARMED THE BROTHERS WITH HER GREEN SWORD.
NO ONE WAS SUPPOSED TO BE HARMED IN THIS.
I SHALL APOLOGISE TO THE BROTHERS PERSONALLY.
JINGLE!
YOU REALLY DO MAKE A GOOD SPY DESPITE YOUR SIZE.
TING!

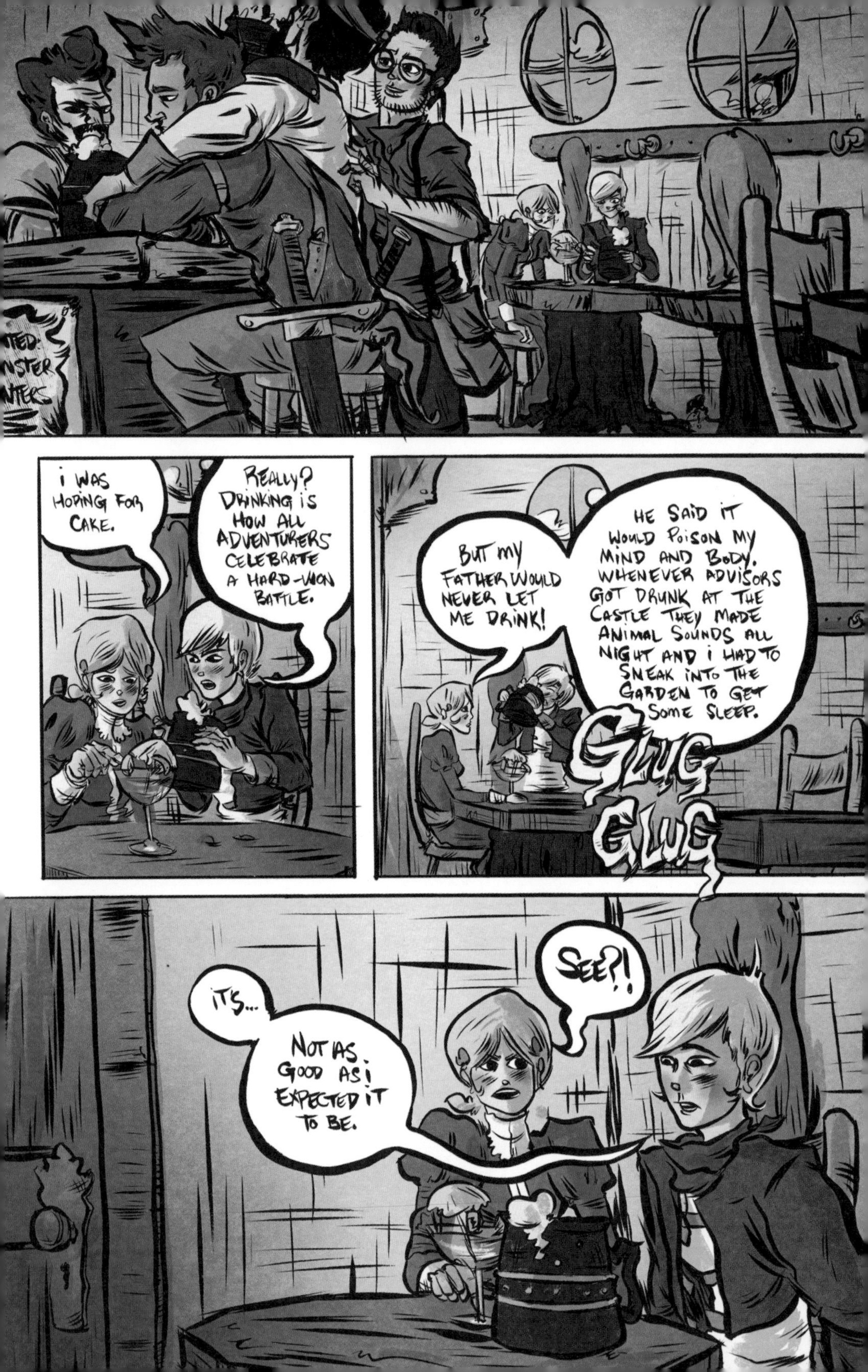

...TED: ...NSTER ...NTERS
i WAS HOPING FOR CAKE.
REALLY? DRINKING iS HOW ALL ADVENTURERS CELEBRATE A HARD-WON BATTLE.
BUT MY FATHER WOULD NEVER LET ME DRINK!
HE SAID IT WOULD POISON MY MIND AND BODY. WHENEVER ADVISORS GOT DRUNK AT THE CASTLE THEY MADE ANIMAL SOUNDS ALL NIGHT AND i HAD TO SNEAK INTO THE GARDEN TO GET SOME SLEEP.
GLUG GLUG
iT'S...
NOT AS GOOD AS i EXPECTED iT TO BE.
SEE?!

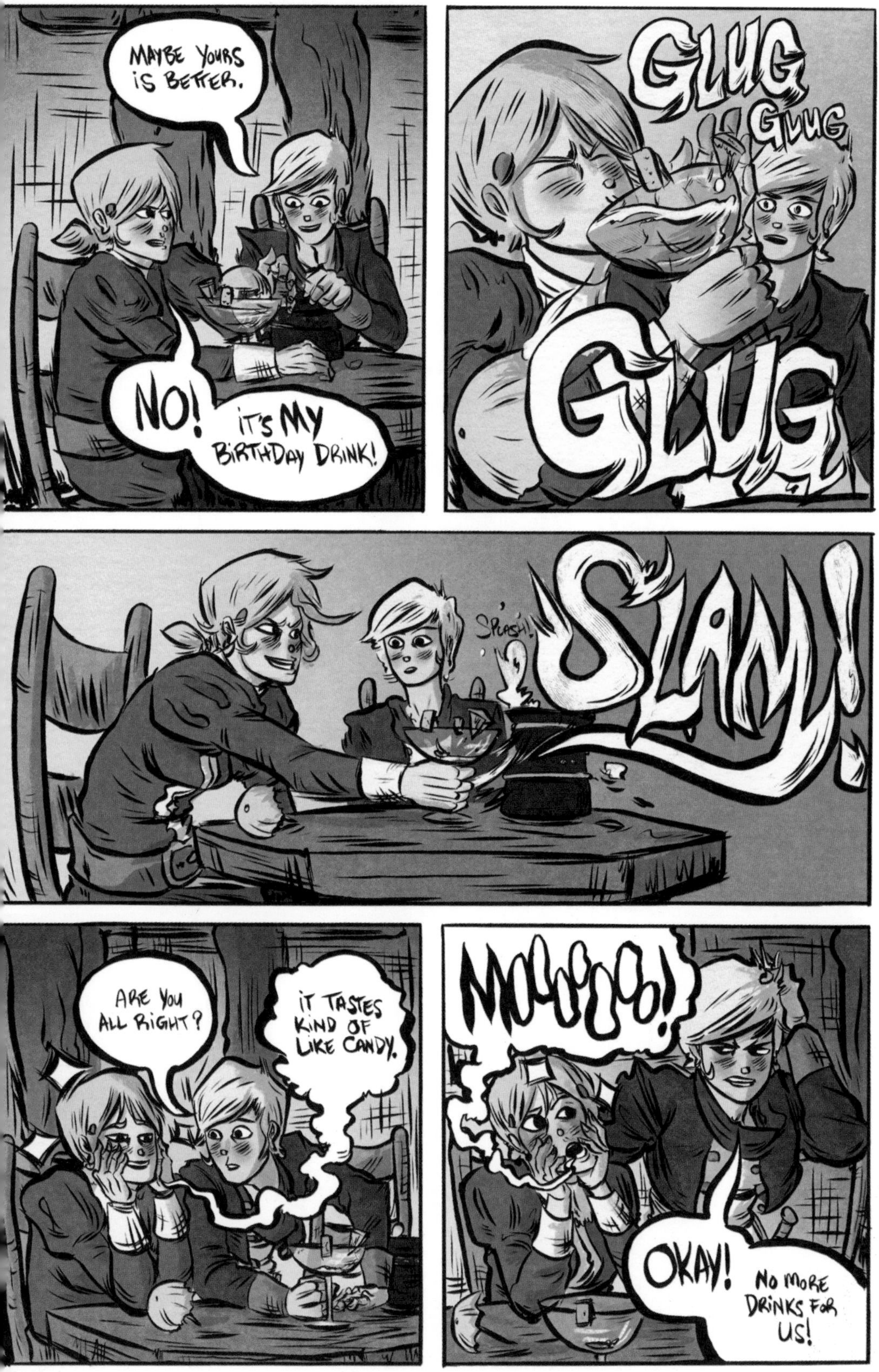
MAYBE YOURS IS BETTER.
NO! IT'S MY BIRTHDAY DRINK!
GLUG
GLUG
GLUG
SPLASH!
SLAM!
ARE YOU ALL RIGHT?
IT TASTES KIND OF LIKE CANDY.
MOOOOOOO!
OKAY! NO MORE DRINKS FOR US!

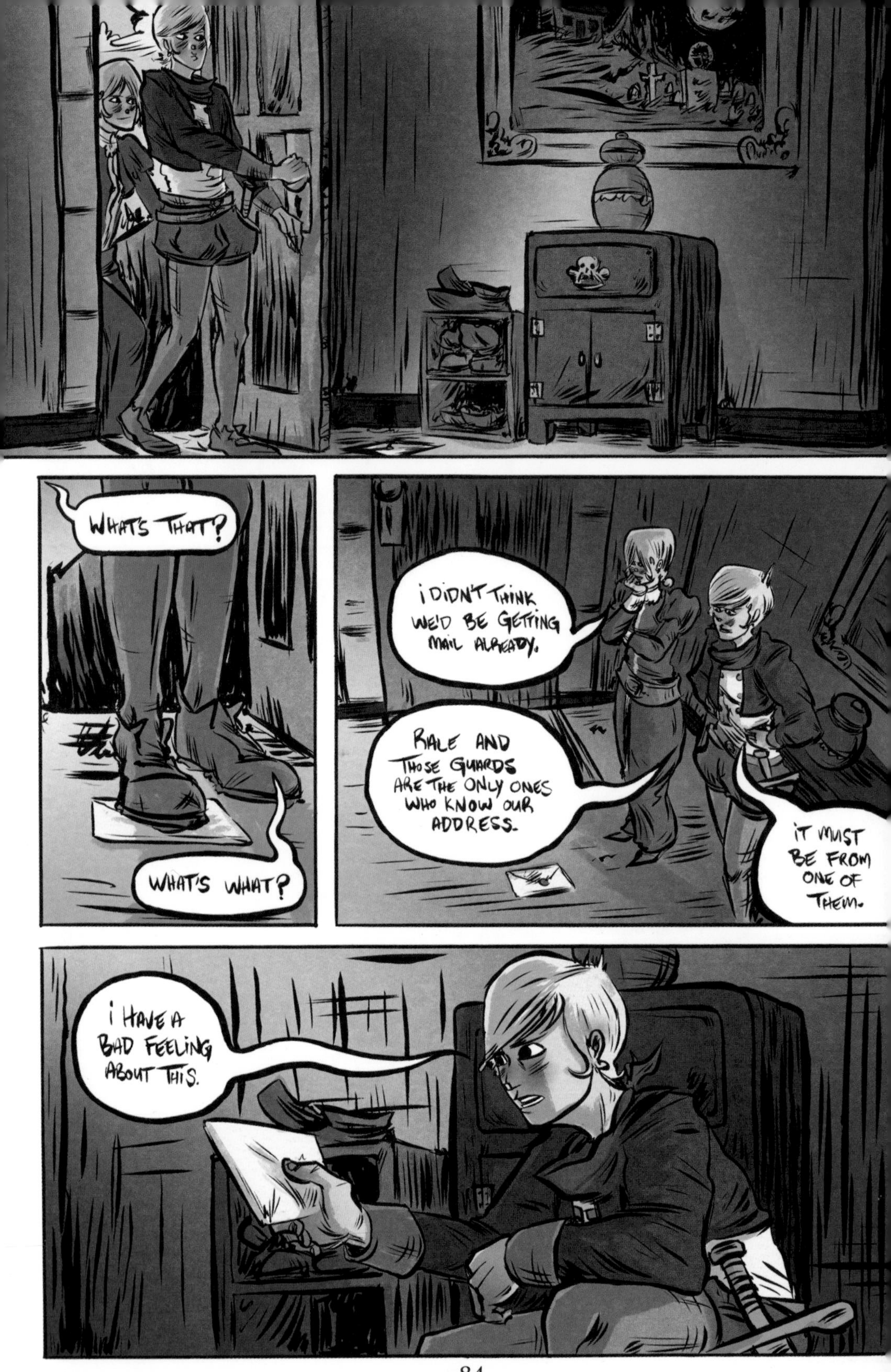
WHAT'S THAT?
WHAT'S WHAT?
I DIDN'T THINK WE'D BE GETTING MAIL ALREADY.
RIALE AND THOSE GUARDS ARE THE ONLY ONES WHO KNOW OUR ADDRESS.
IT MUST BE FROM ONE OF THEM.
I HAVE A BAD FEELING ABOUT THIS.

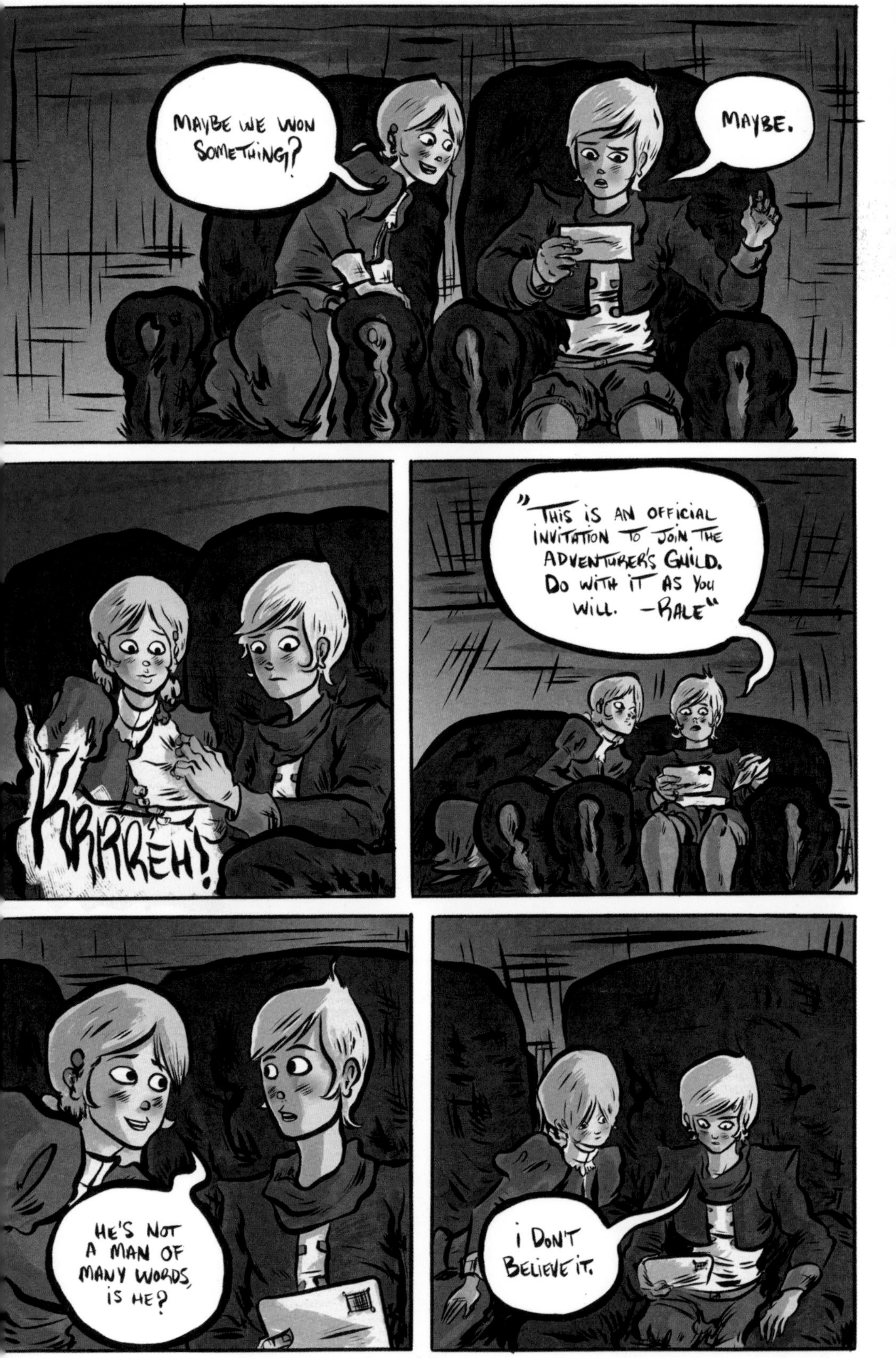
MAYBE WE WON SOMETHING?
MAYBE.
KRRREH!
"THIS IS AN OFFICIAL INVITATION TO JOIN THE ADVENTURER'S GUILD. DO WITH IT AS YOU WILL. -RALE"
HE'S NOT A MAN OF MANY WORDS, IS HE?
I DON'T BELIEVE IT.

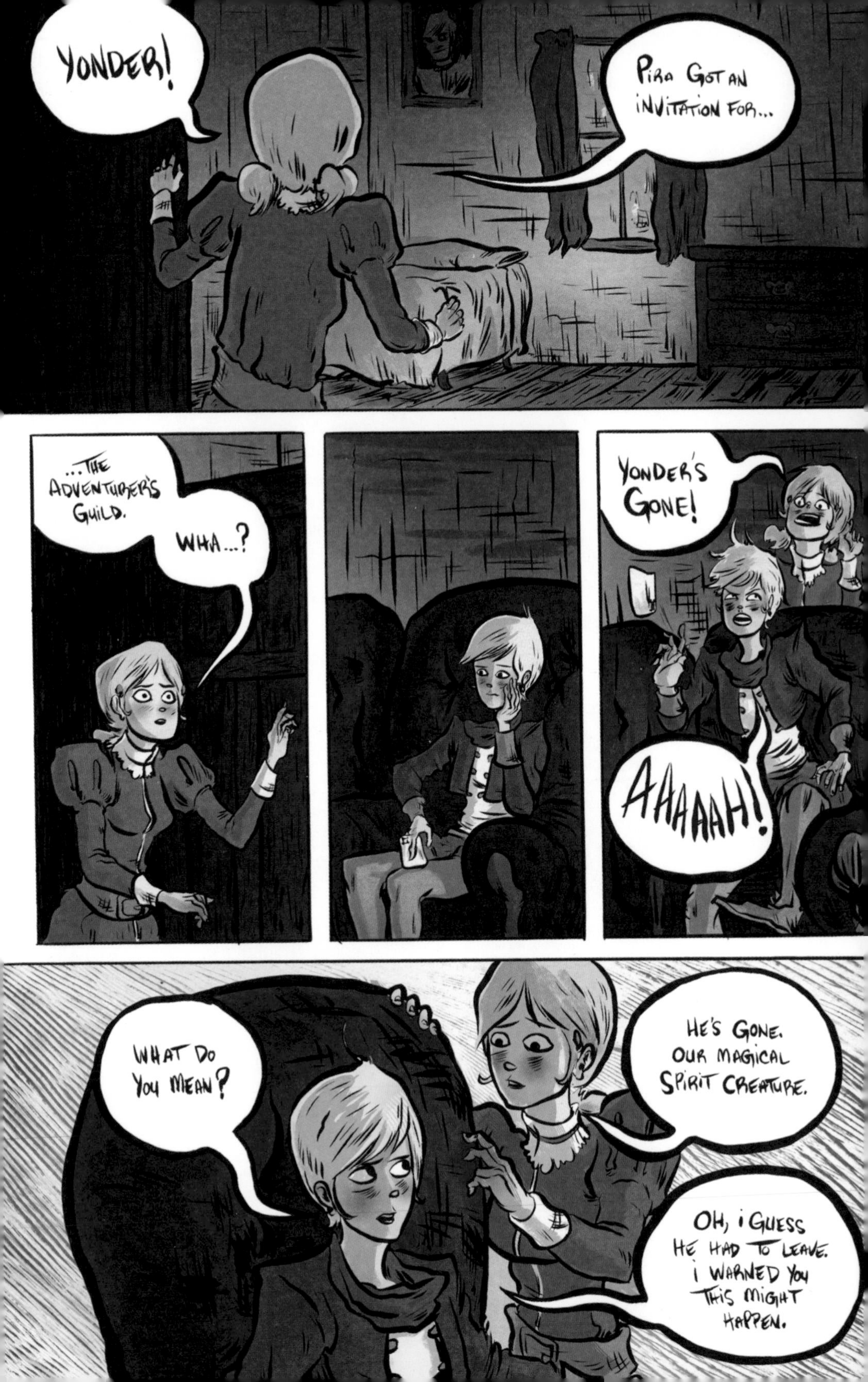
YONDER!
PIRA GOT AN INVITATION FOR...
...THE ADVENTURER'S GUILD.
WHA...?
YONDER'S GONE!
AAAAAH!
WHAT DO YOU MEAN?
HE'S GONE. OUR MAGICAL SPIRIT CREATURE.
OH, I GUESS HE HAD TO LEAVE. I WARNED YOU THIS MIGHT HAPPEN.

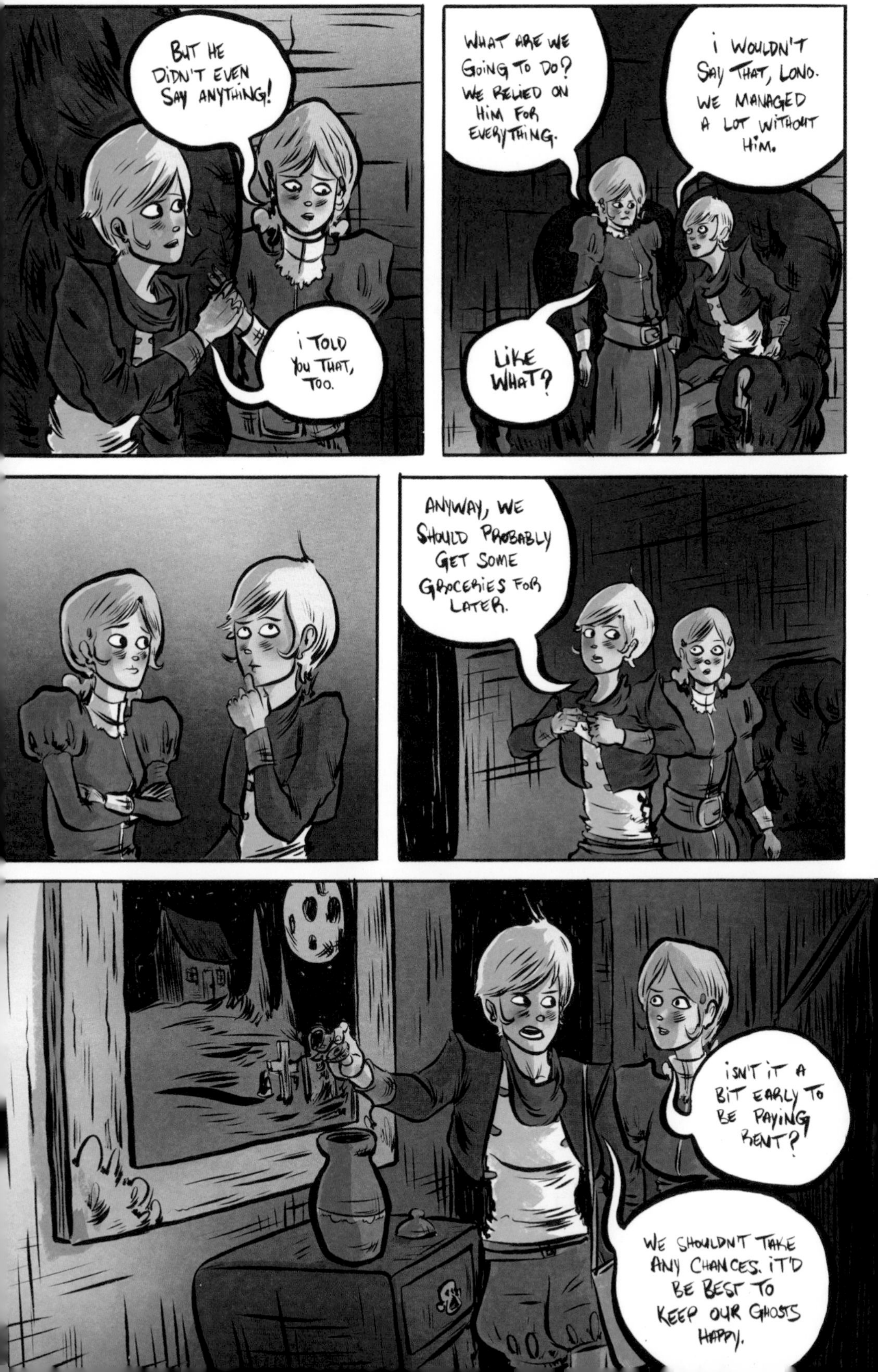
BUT HE DIDN'T EVEN SAY ANYTHING!
I TOLD YOU THAT, TOO.
WHAT ARE WE GOING TO DO? WE RELIED ON HIM FOR EVERYTHING.
I WOULDN'T SAY THAT, LONO. WE MANAGED A LOT WITHOUT HIM.
LIKE WHAT?
ANYWAY, WE SHOULD PROBABLY GET SOME GROCERIES FOR LATER.
ISN'T IT A BIT EARLY TO BE PAYING RENT?
WE SHOULDN'T TAKE ANY CHANCES. IT'D BE BEST TO KEEP OUR GHOSTS HAPPY.

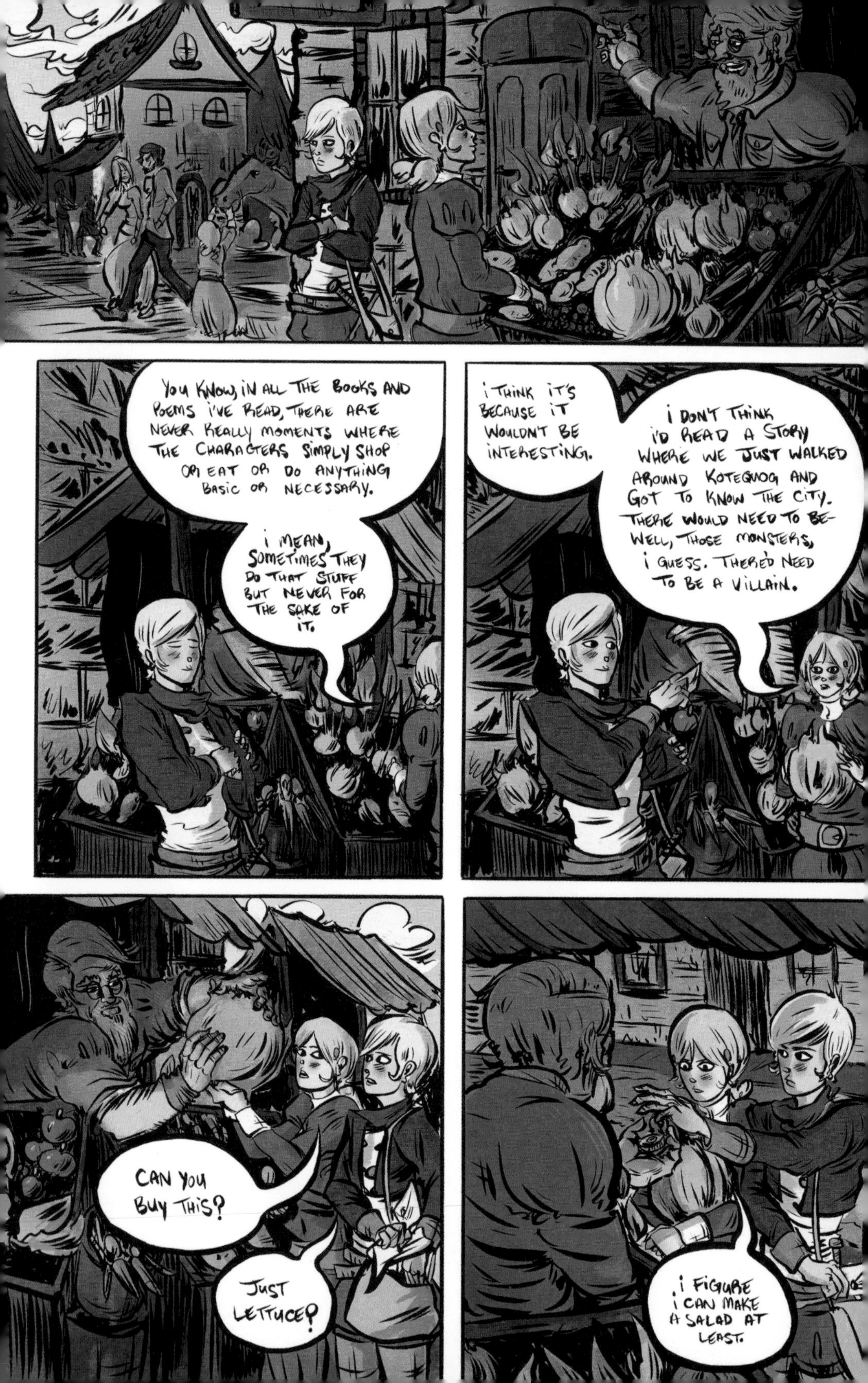
You know, in all the books and poems i've read, there are never really moments where the characters simply shop or eat or do anything basic or necessary.
i mean, sometimes they do that stuff but never for the sake of it.
i think it's because it wouldn't be interesting.
i don't think i'd read a story where we just walked around Kotequog and got to know the city. There would need to be- well, those monsters, i guess. There'd need to be a villain.
Can you buy this?
Just lettuce?
i figure i can make a salad at least.

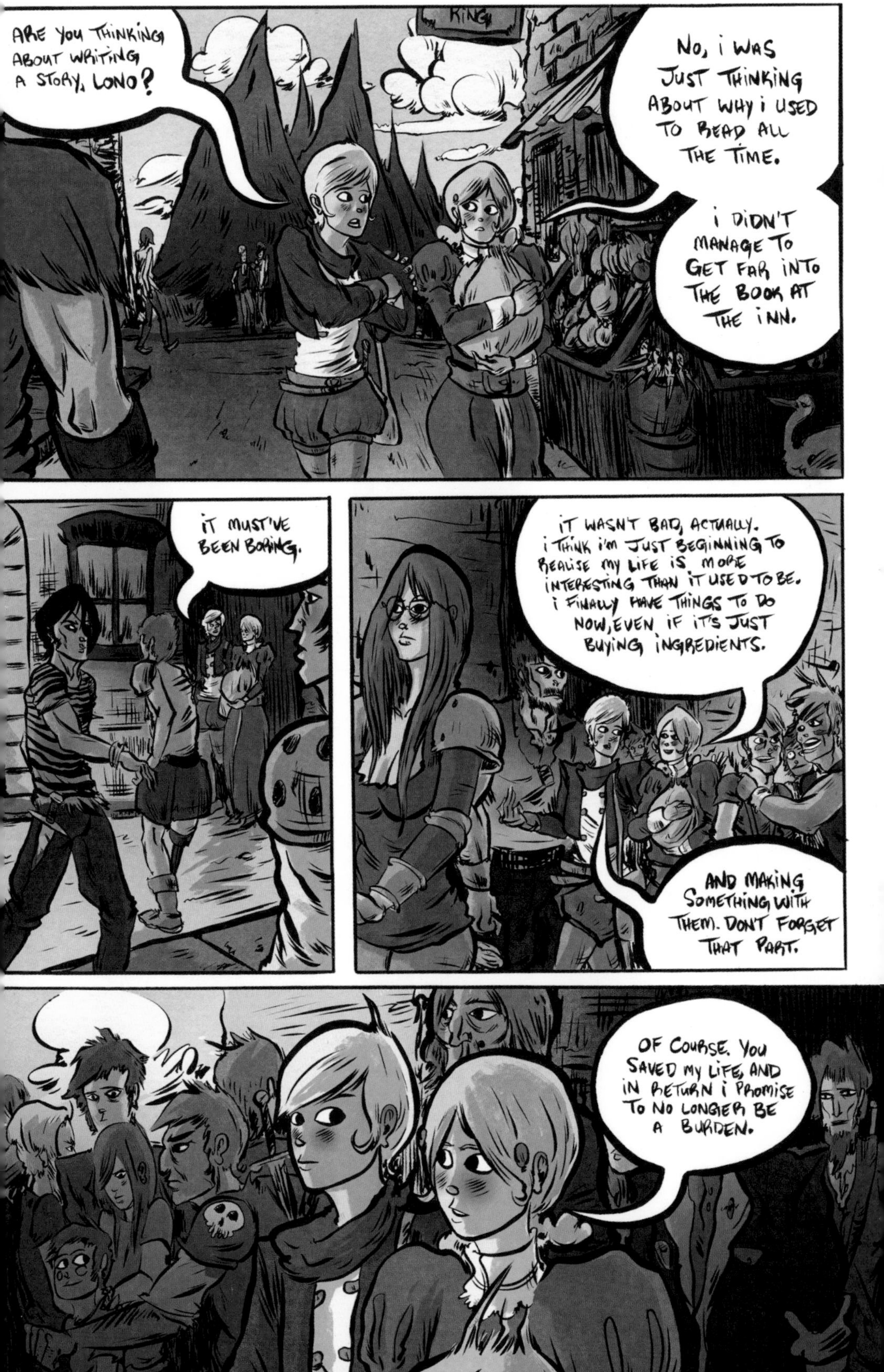
KING
ARE YOU THINKING ABOUT WRITING A STORY, LONO?
NO, I WAS JUST THINKING ABOUT WHY I USED TO READ ALL THE TIME.
I DIDN'T MANAGE TO GET FAR INTO THE BOOK AT THE INN.
IT MUST'VE BEEN BORING.
IT WASN'T BAD, ACTUALLY. I THINK I'M JUST BEGINNING TO REALISE MY LIFE IS MORE INTERESTING THAN IT USED TO BE. I FINALLY HAVE THINGS TO DO NOW, EVEN IF IT'S JUST BUYING INGREDIENTS.
AND MAKING SOMETHING WITH THEM. DON'T FORGET THAT PART.
OF COURSE. YOU SAVED MY LIFE, AND IN RETURN I PROMISE TO NO LONGER BE A BURDEN.

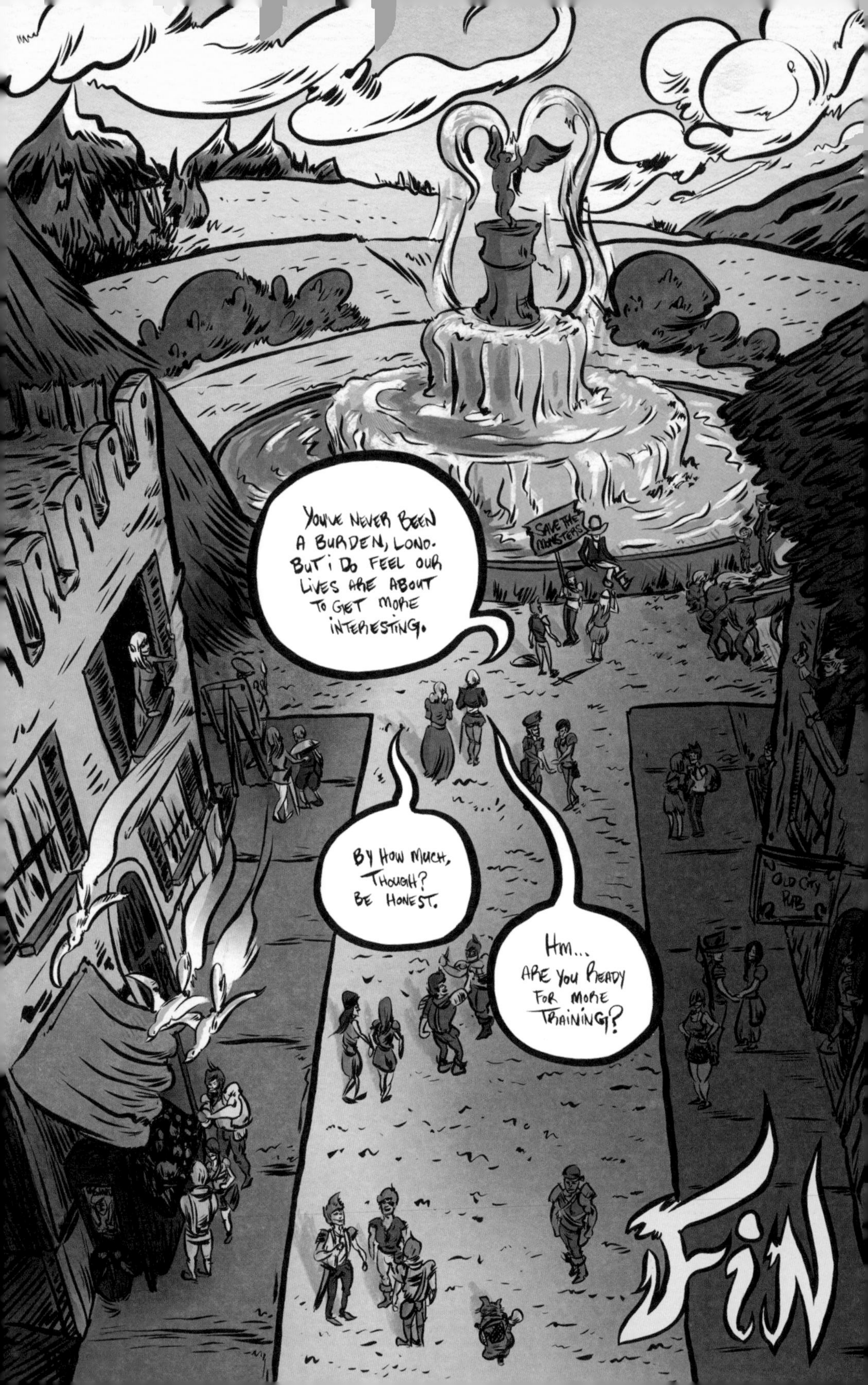
SAVE THE MONSTERS
YOU'VE NEVER BEEN A BURDEN, LONO. BUT I DO FEEL OUR LIVES ARE ABOUT TO GET MORE INTERESTING.
BY HOW MUCH, THOUGH? BE HONEST.
HM... ARE YOU READY FOR MORE TRAINING?
OLD CITY PUB
FIN

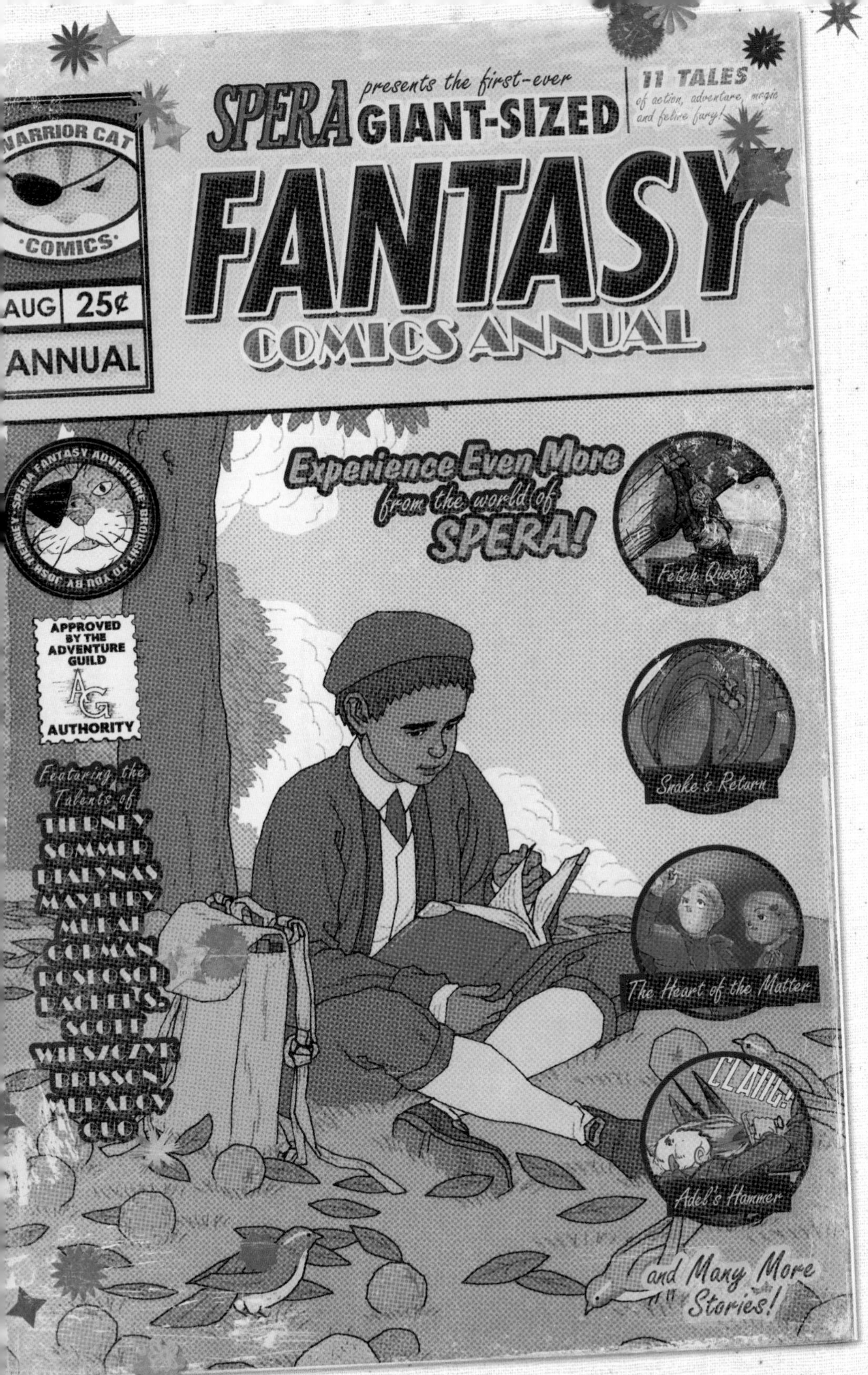
SPERA presents the first-ever
GIANT-SIZED
11 TALES
of action, adventure, magic and feline fury!
WARRIOR CAT
COMICS
AUG
25¢
ANNUAL
FANTASY
COMICS ANNUAL
SPERA FANTASY ADVENTURE BROUGHT TO YOU BY JOSH TIERNEY
APPROVED BY THE ADVENTURE GUILD
AG
AUTHORITY
Featuring the Talents of
TIERNEY
SOMMER
DIALYNAS
MAYBURY
MUKAI
GORMAN
ROSKOSCH
RACHEL S.
SCOTT
WIESZCZYK
BRISSON
MURADOV
GUO
Experience Even More from the world of SPERA!
Fetch Quest
Snake's Return
The Heart of the Matter
CLANG!
Adel's Hammer
and Many More Stories!

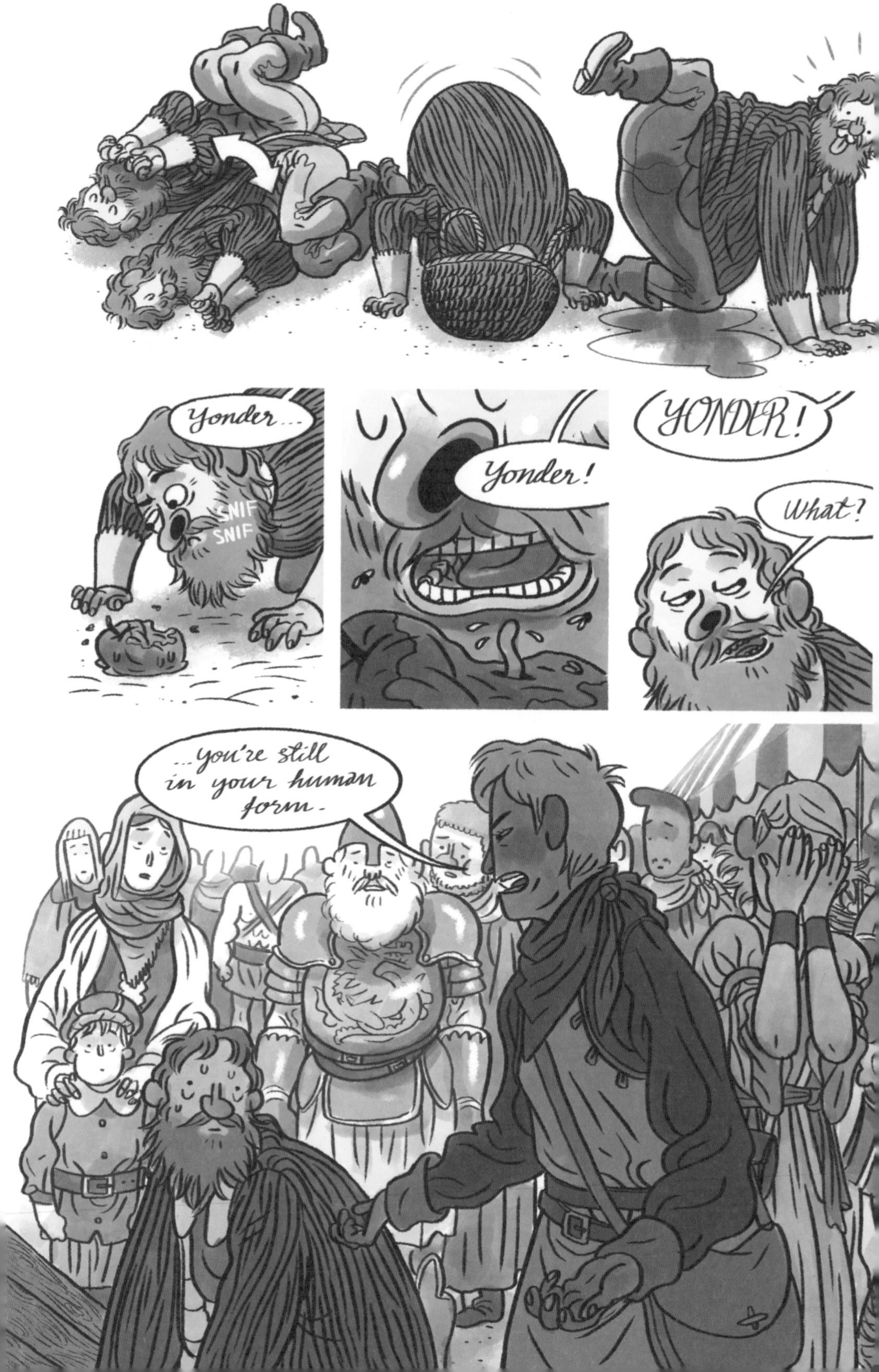
Yonder...
SNIF SNIF
Yonder!
YONDER!
What?
...you're still in your human form.

Fetch Quest.

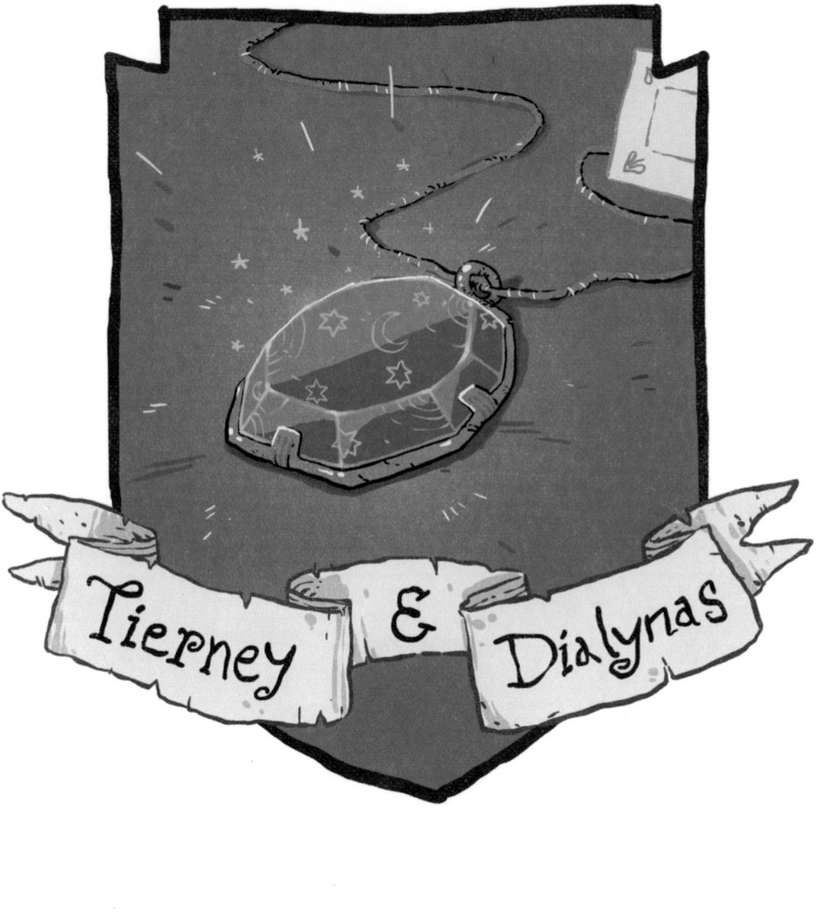
Tierney
&
Dialynas

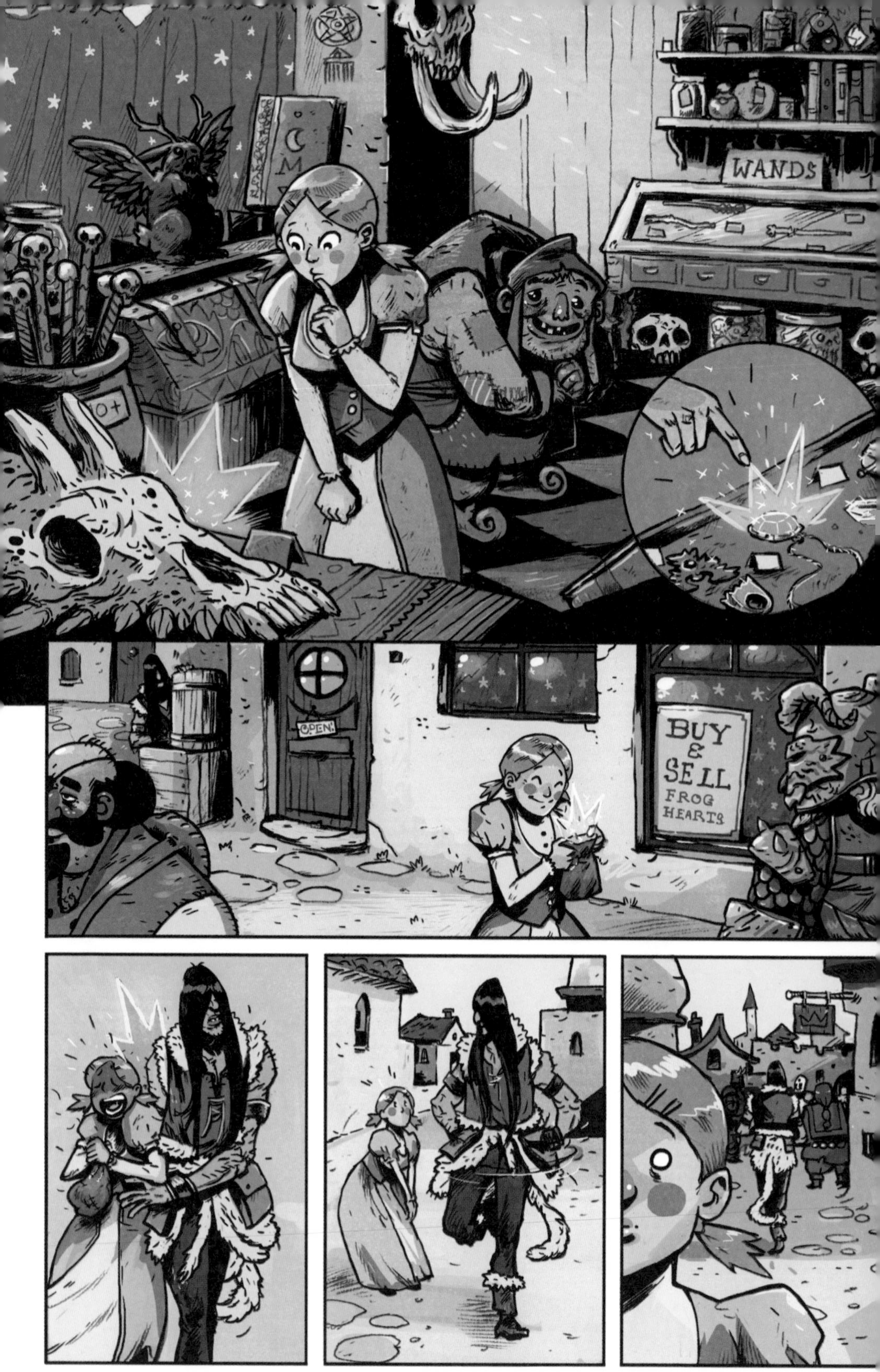

WANDS
OPEN
BUY & SELL FROG HEARTS

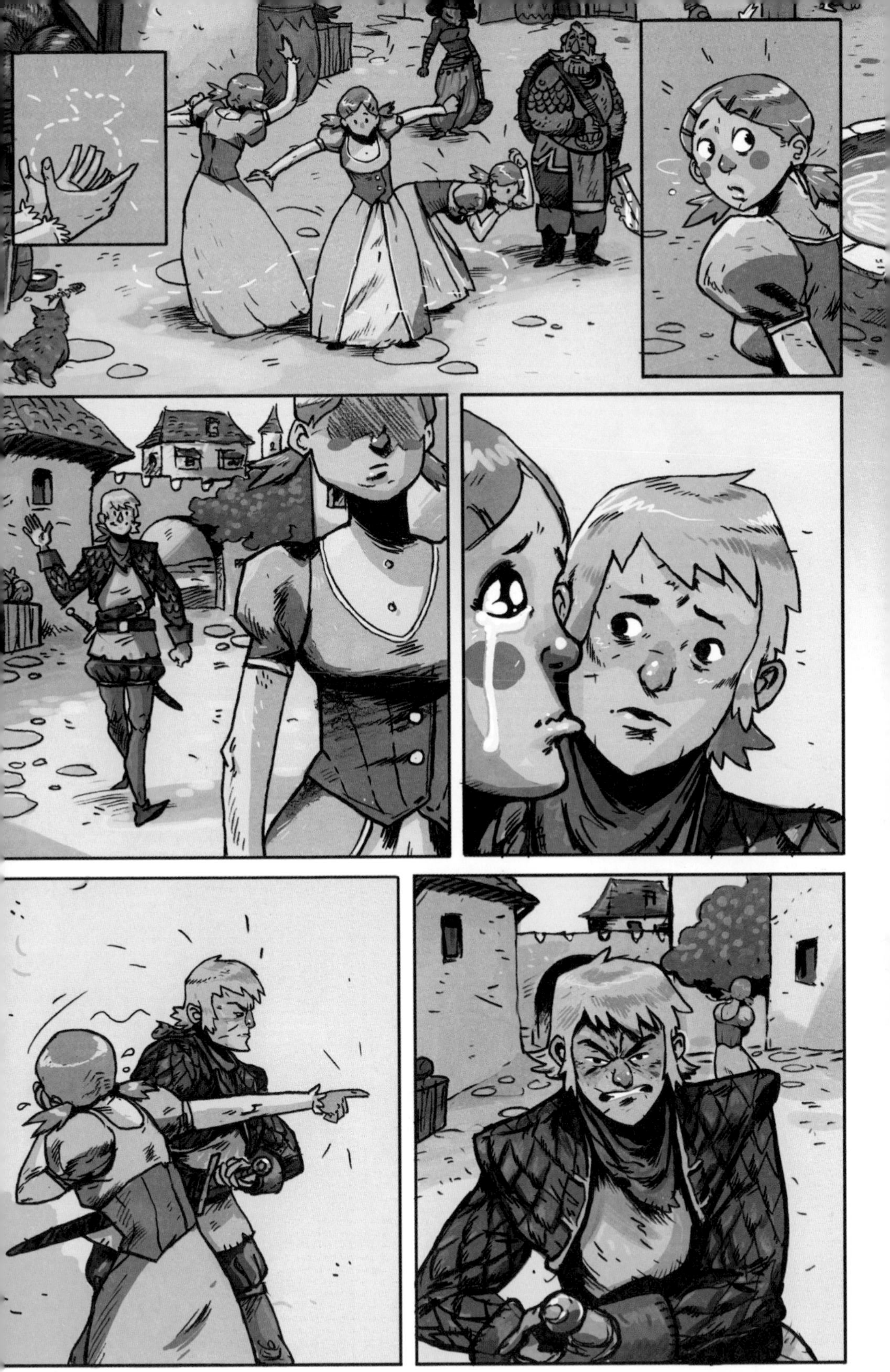

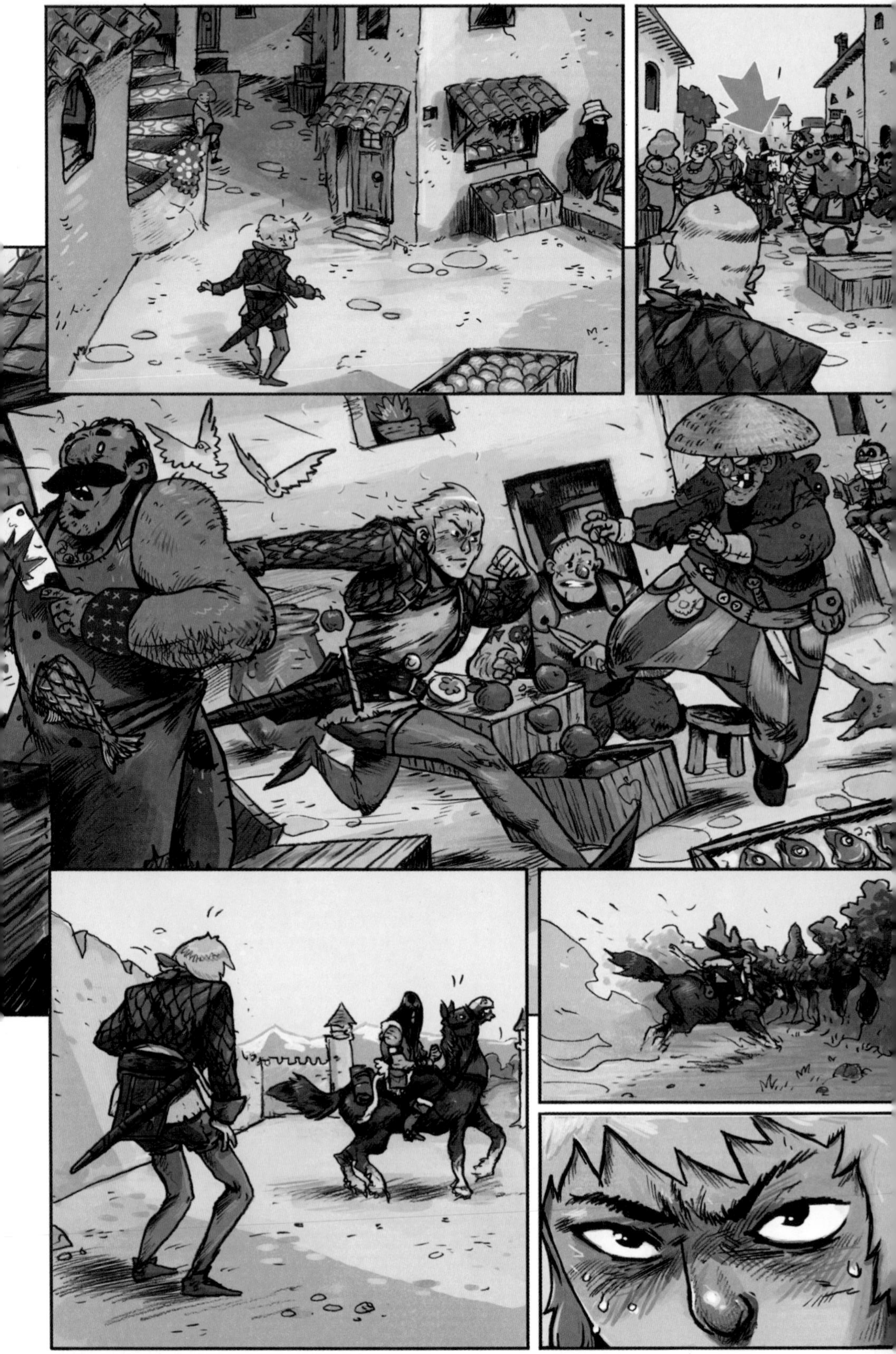

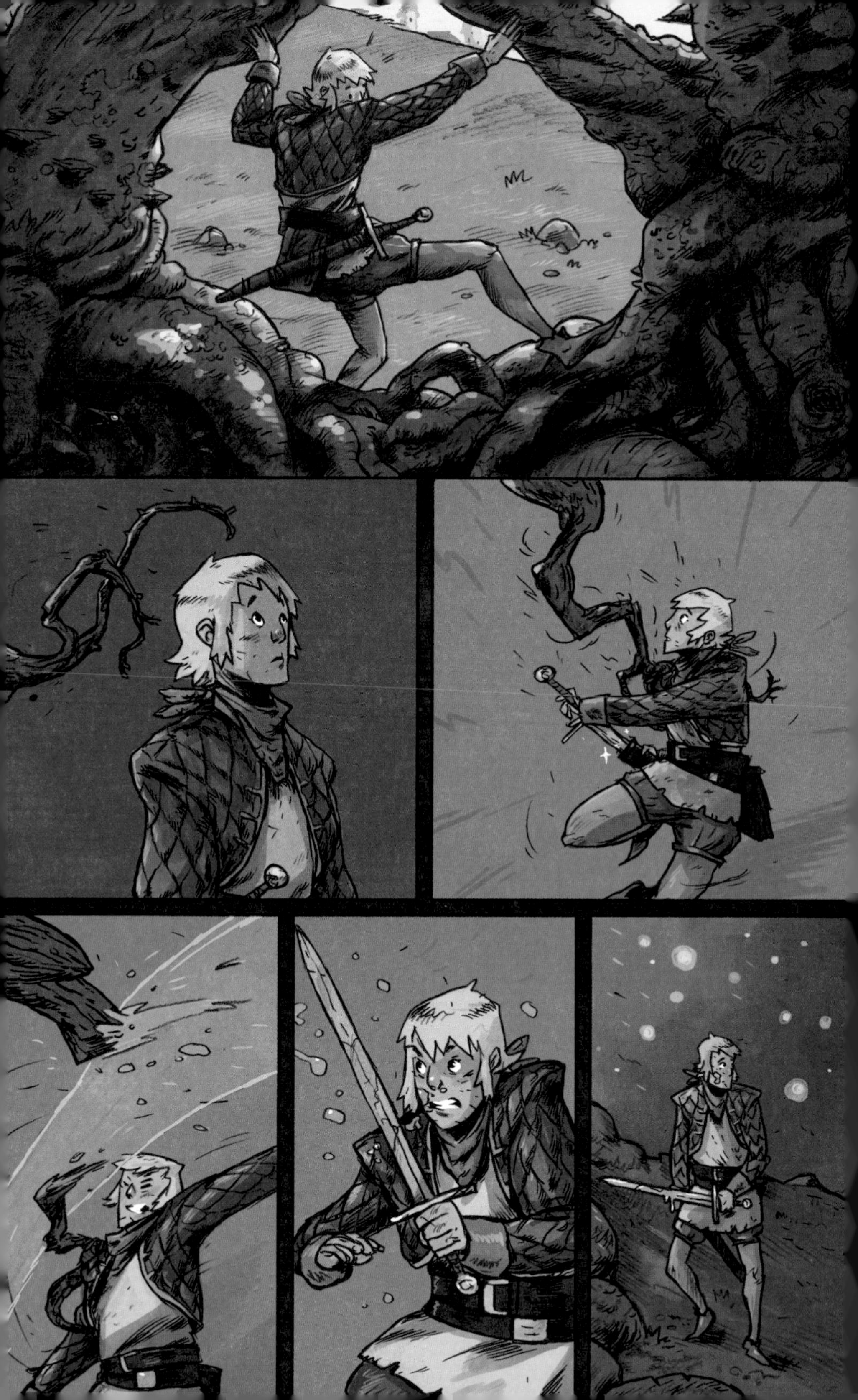

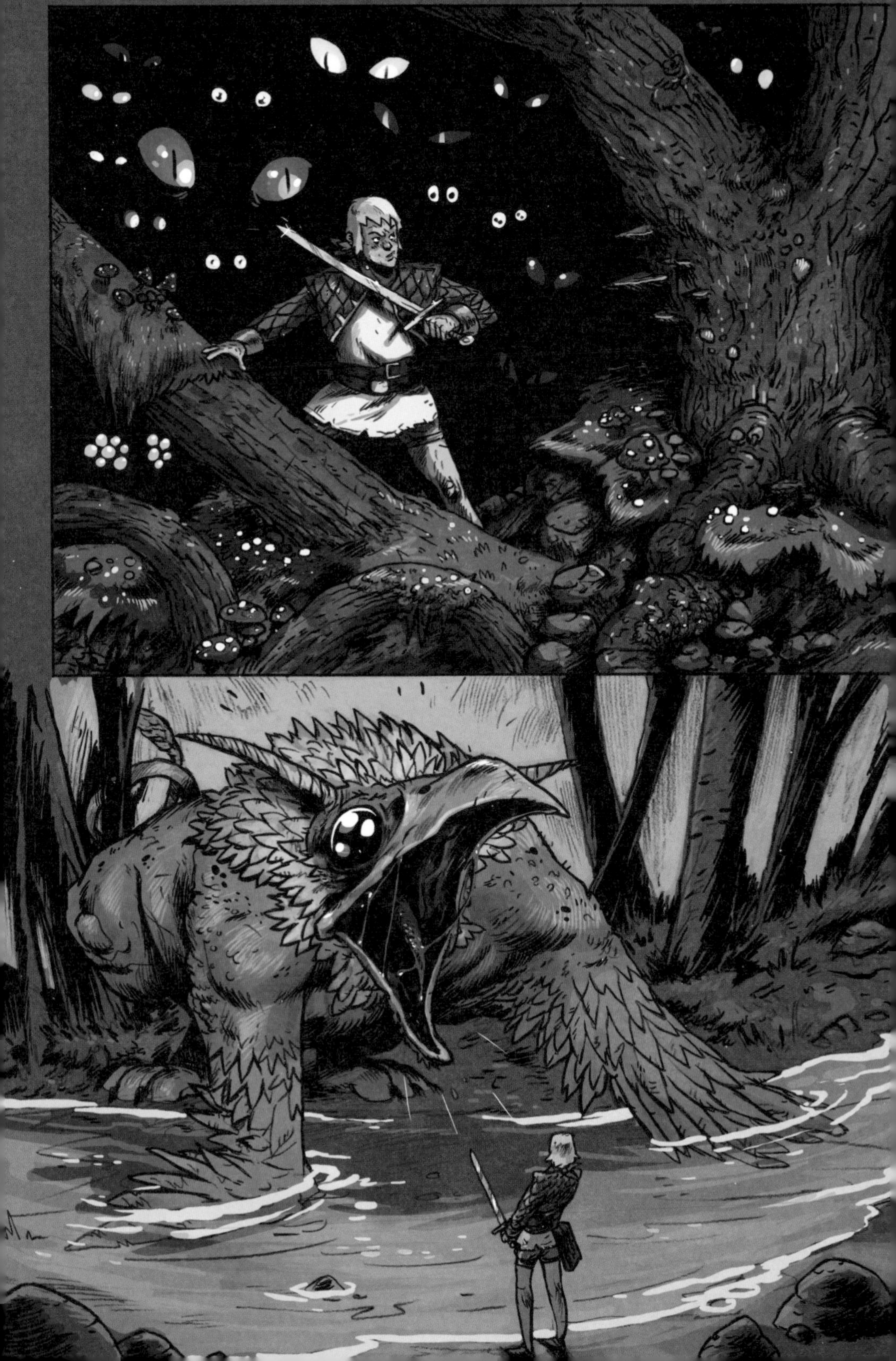

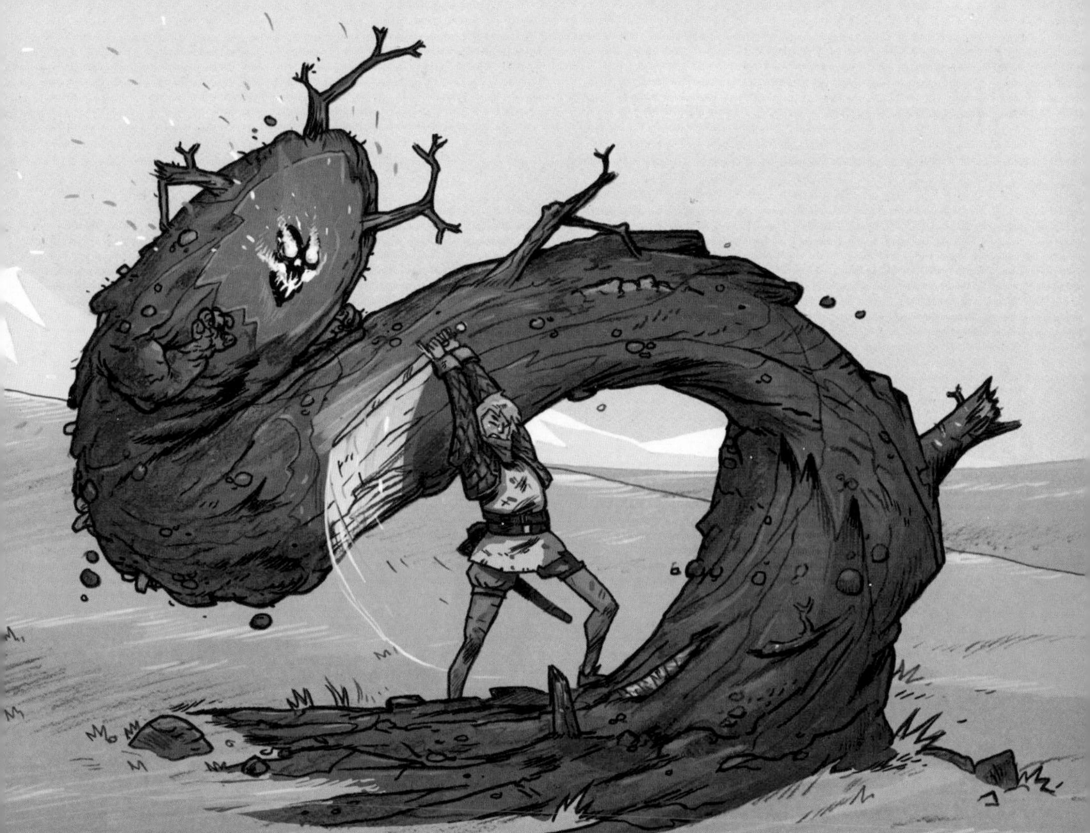

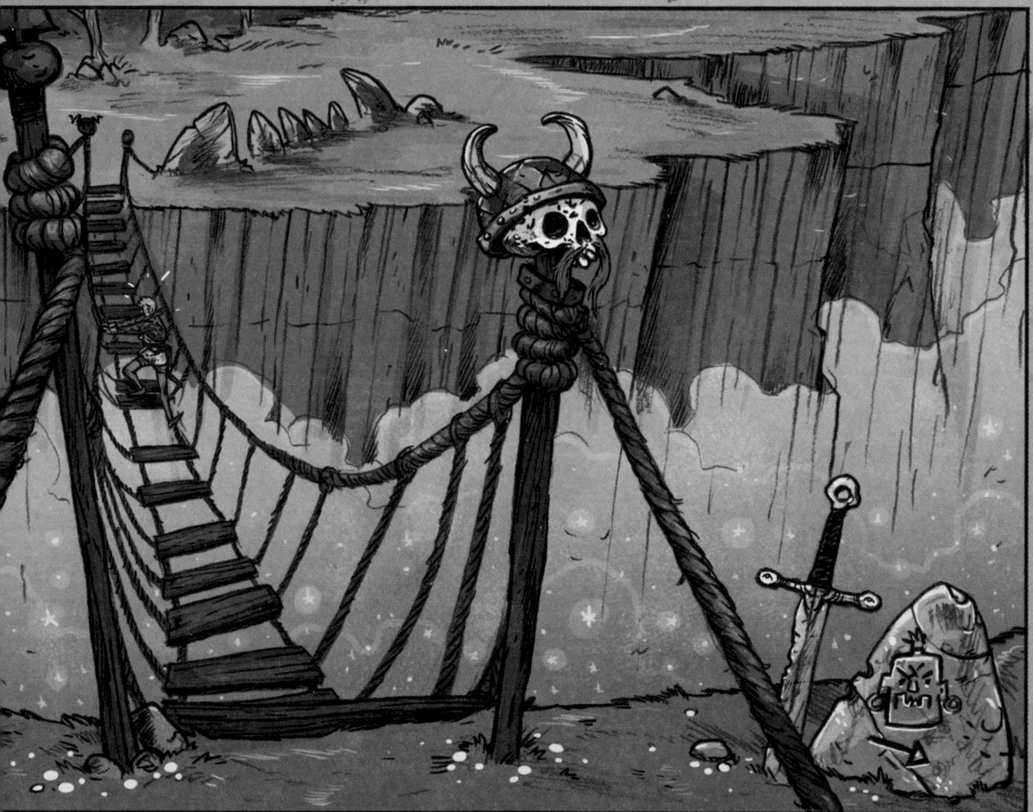

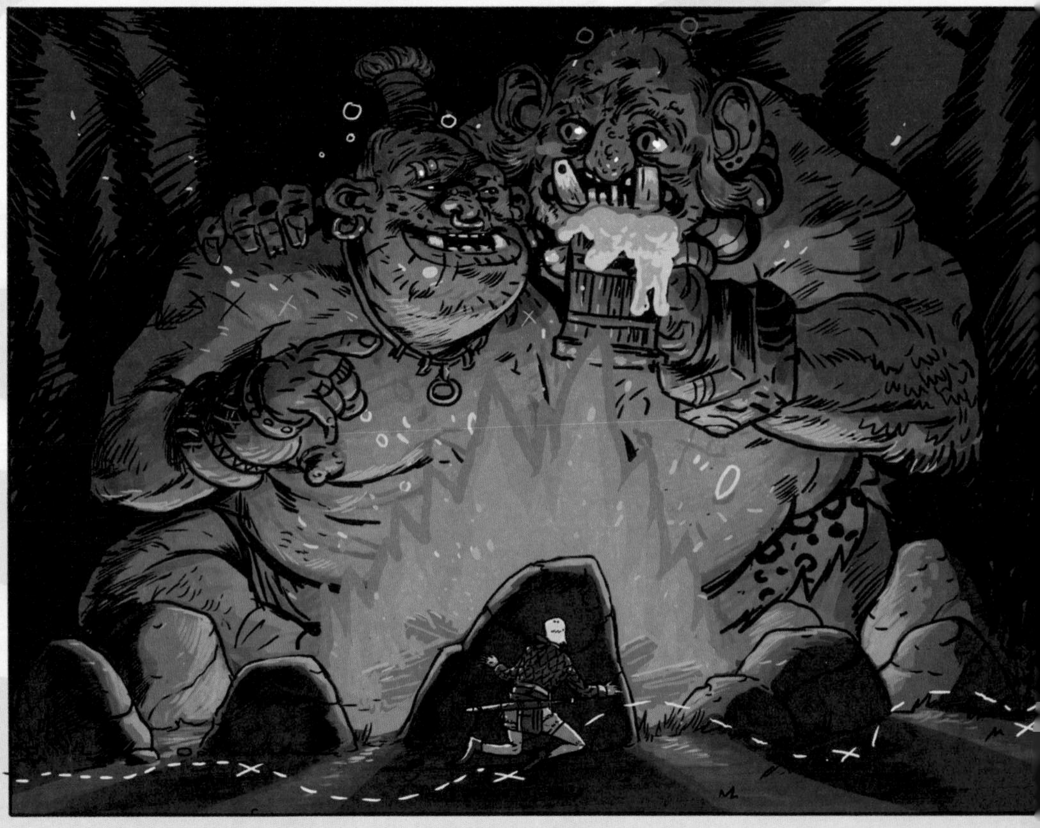
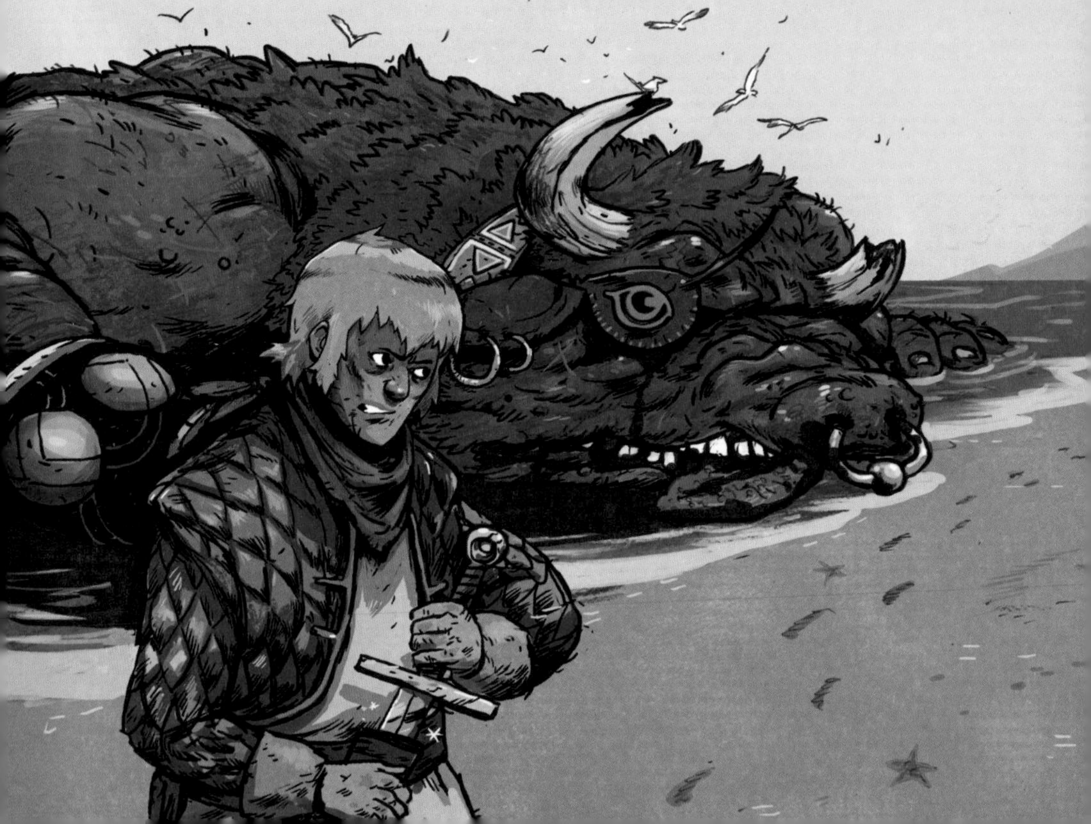

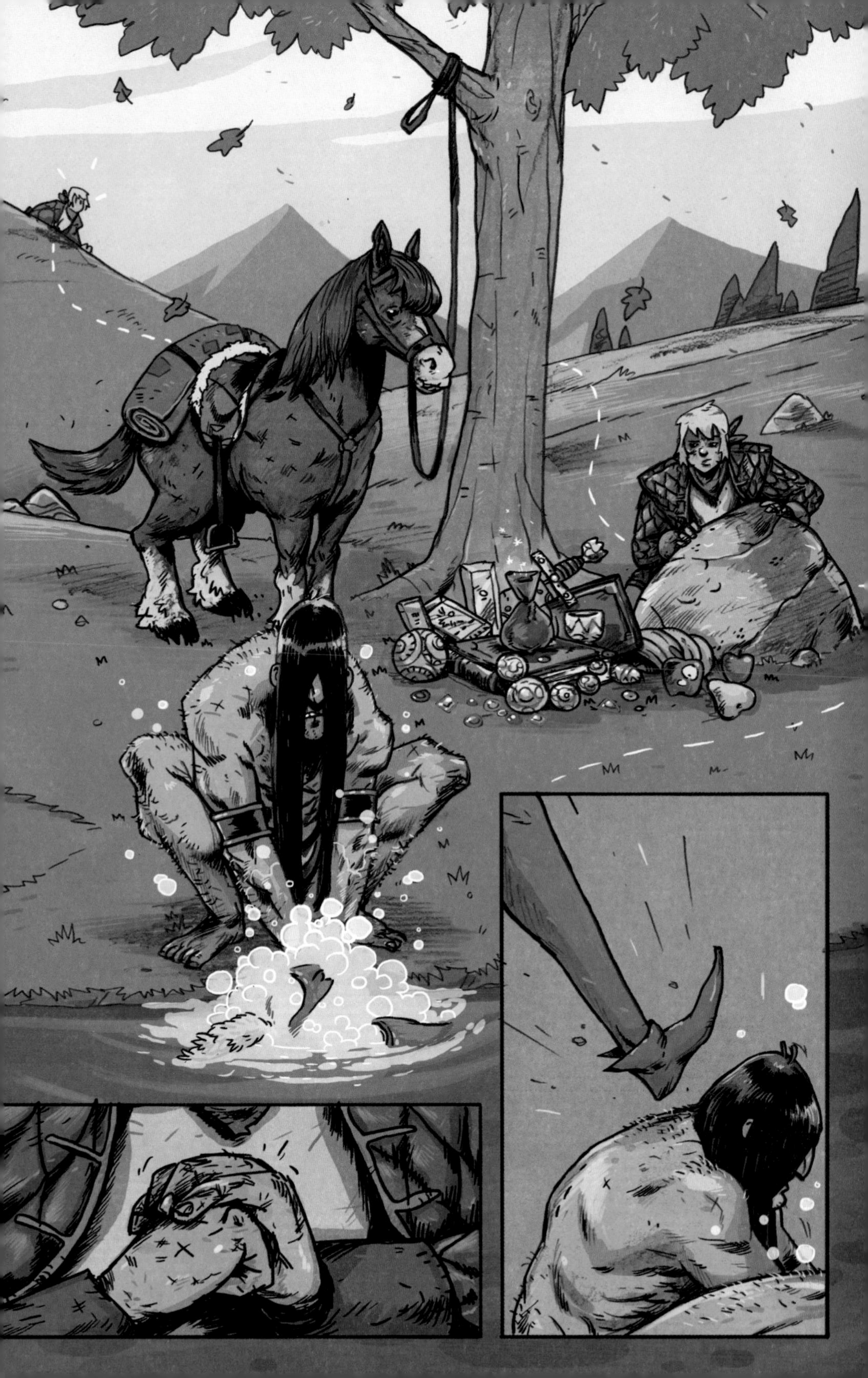

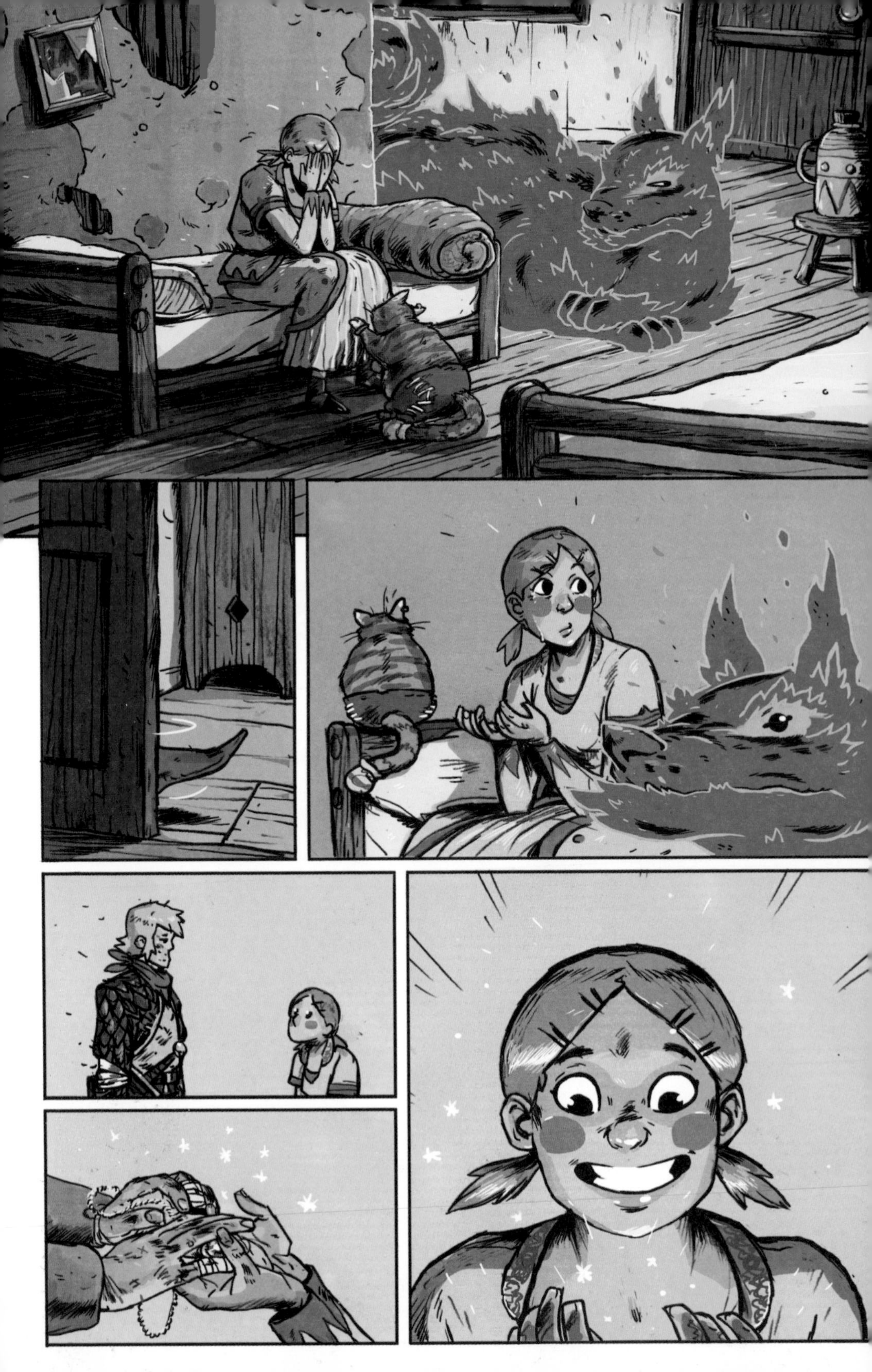

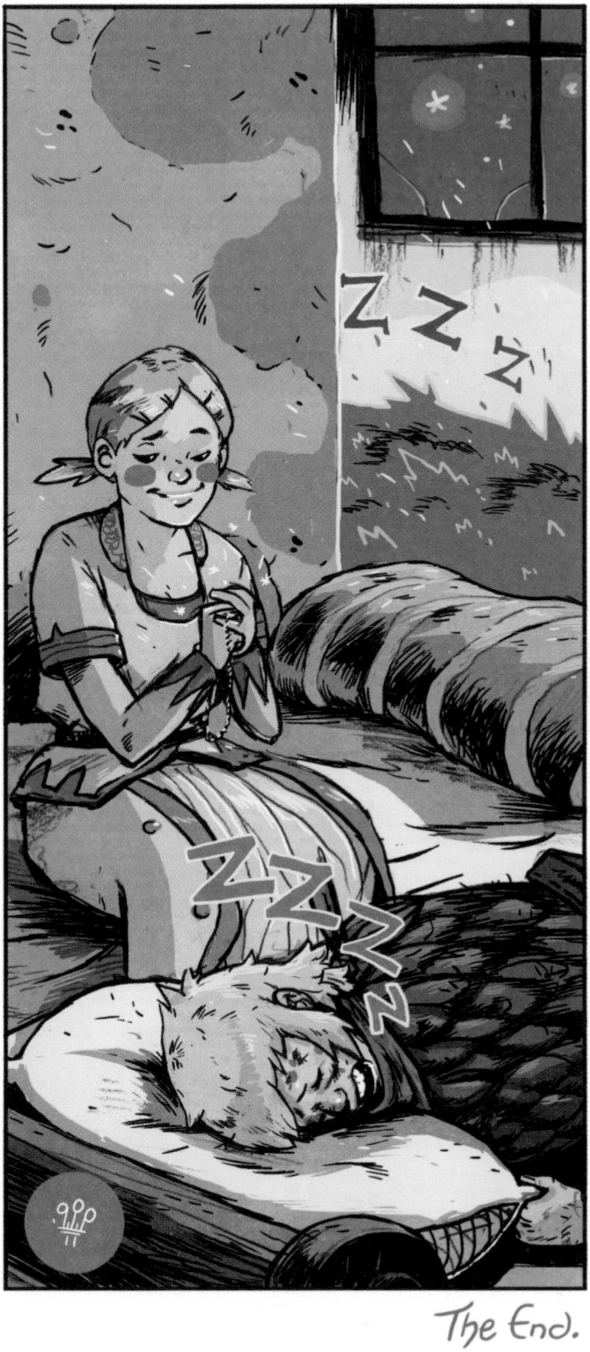
ZZZ
ZZZZ

The End.

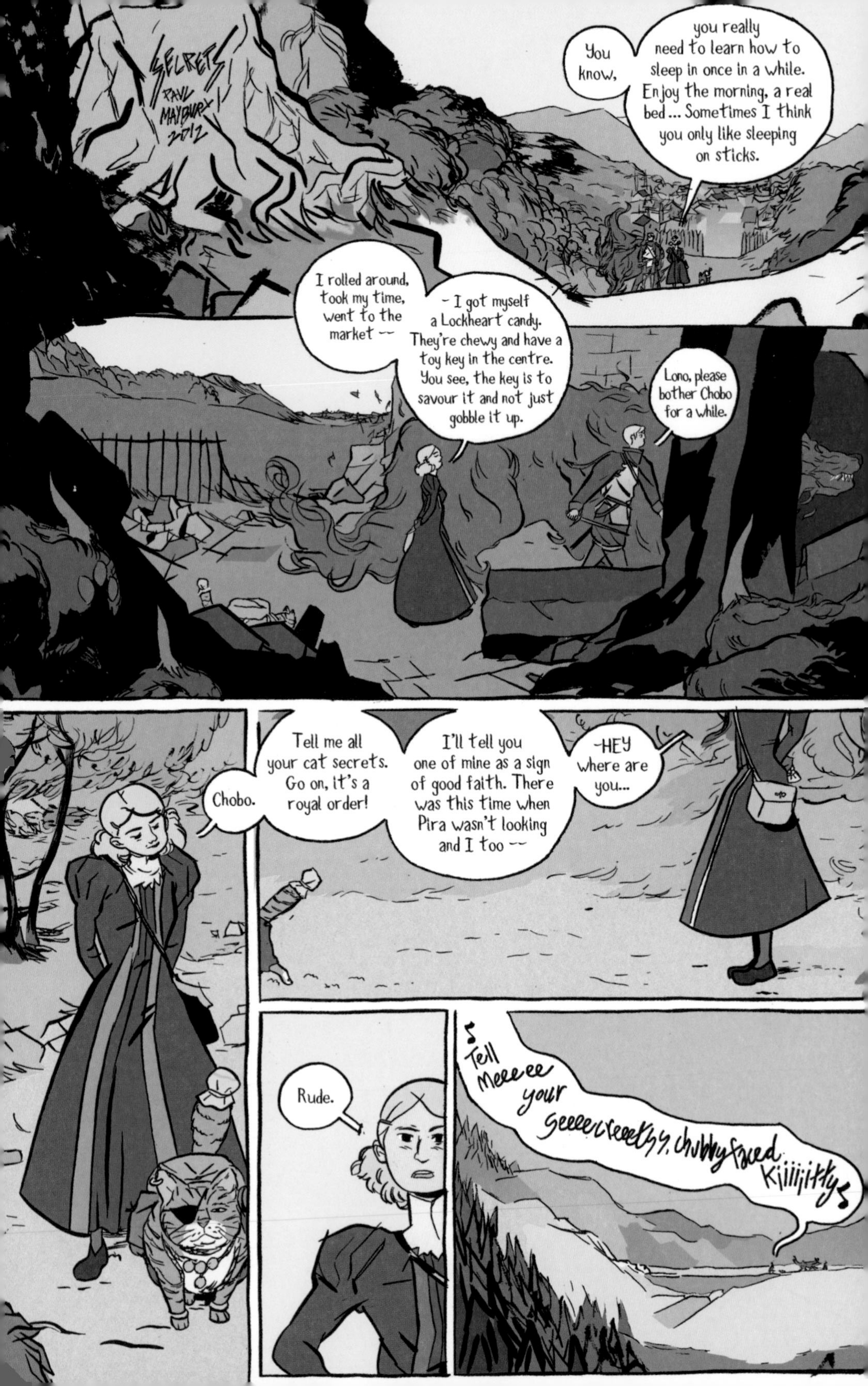
SECRETS
PAUL MAYBURY 2012
You know,
you really need to learn how to sleep in once in a while. Enjoy the morning, a real bed... Sometimes I think you only like sleeping on sticks.
I rolled around, took my time, went to the market ~
~ I got myself a Lockheart candy. They're chewy and have a toy key in the centre. You see, the key is to savour it and not just gobble it up.
Lono, please bother Chobo for a while.
Chobo.
Tell me all your cat secrets. Go on, it's a royal order!
I'll tell you one of mine as a sign of good faith. There was this time when Pira wasn't looking and I too ~~
-HEY where are you...
Rude.
Tell meeeee your seeeecreeetsss, chubbyfaced kiiiiittty

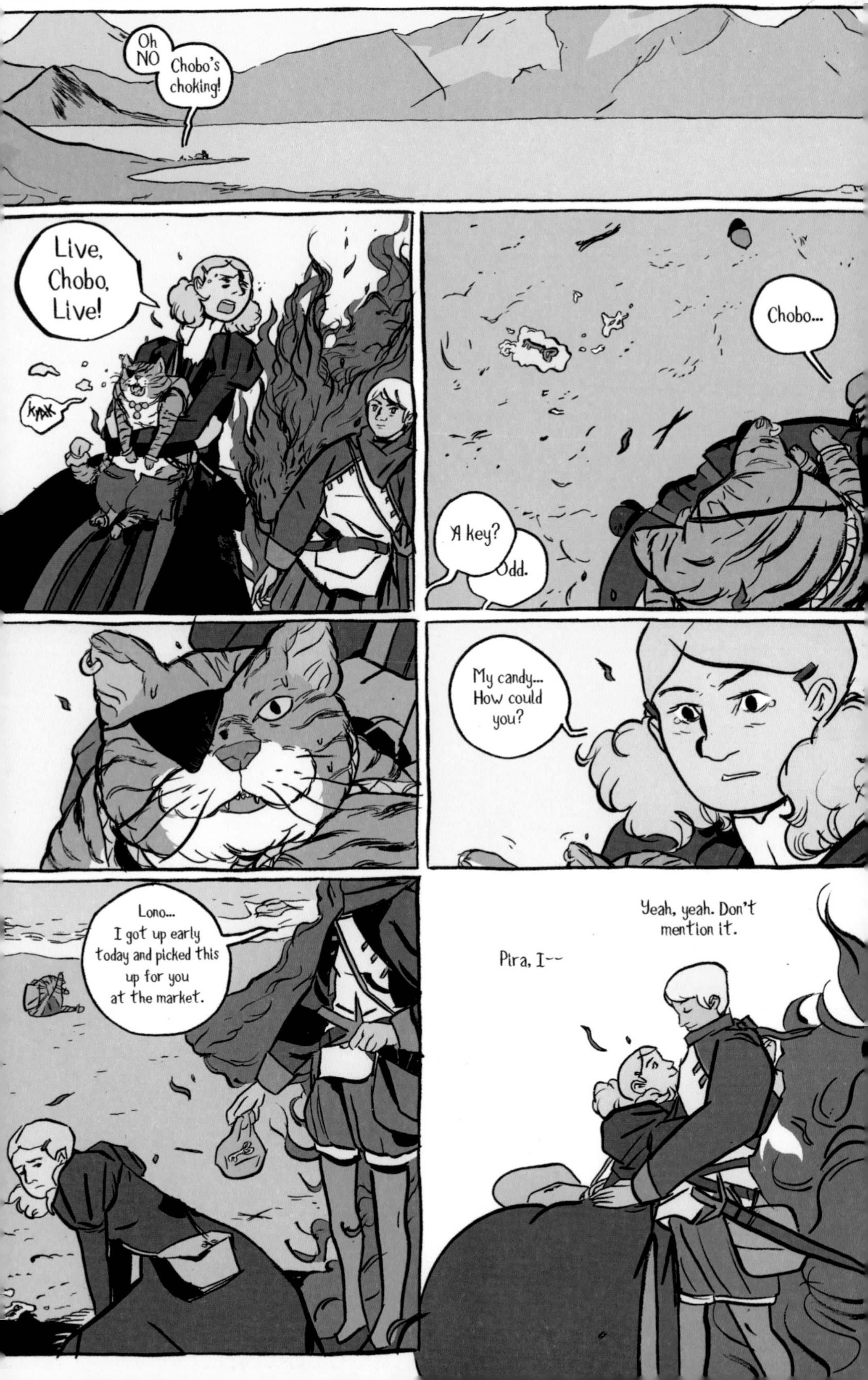
Oh NO
Chobo's choking!
Live, Chobo, Live!
KYAK
Chobo...
A key?
Odd.
My candy... How could you?
Lono... I got up early today and picked this up for you at the market.
Pira, I--
Yeah, yeah. Don't mention it.

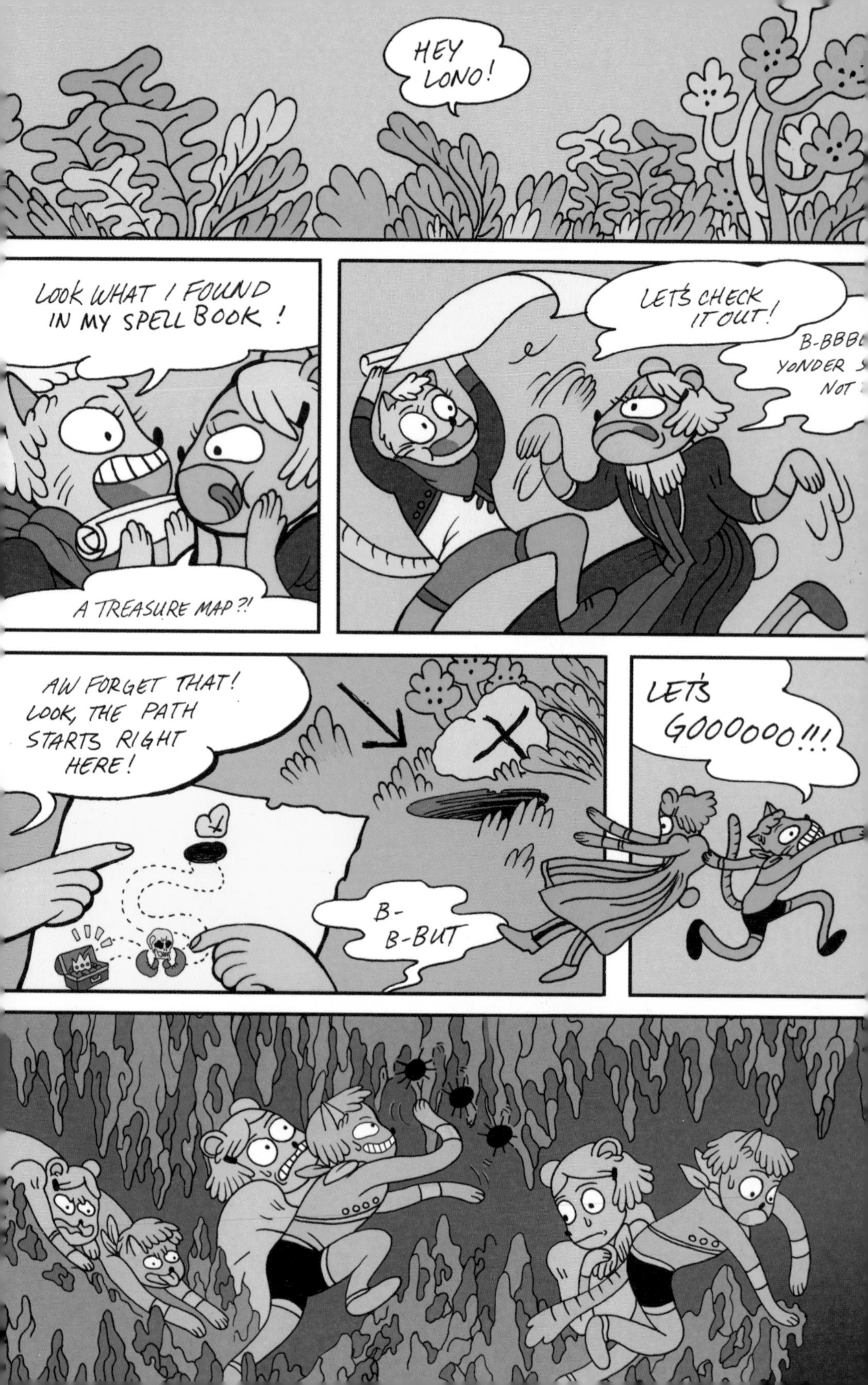
HEY LONO!
LOOK WHAT I FOUND IN MY SPELL BOOK!
A TREASURE MAP?!
LET'S CHECK IT OUT!
YONDER
NOT
AW FORGET THAT! LOOK, THE PATH STARTS RIGHT HERE!
B- B-BUT
LET'S GOOOOOO!!!

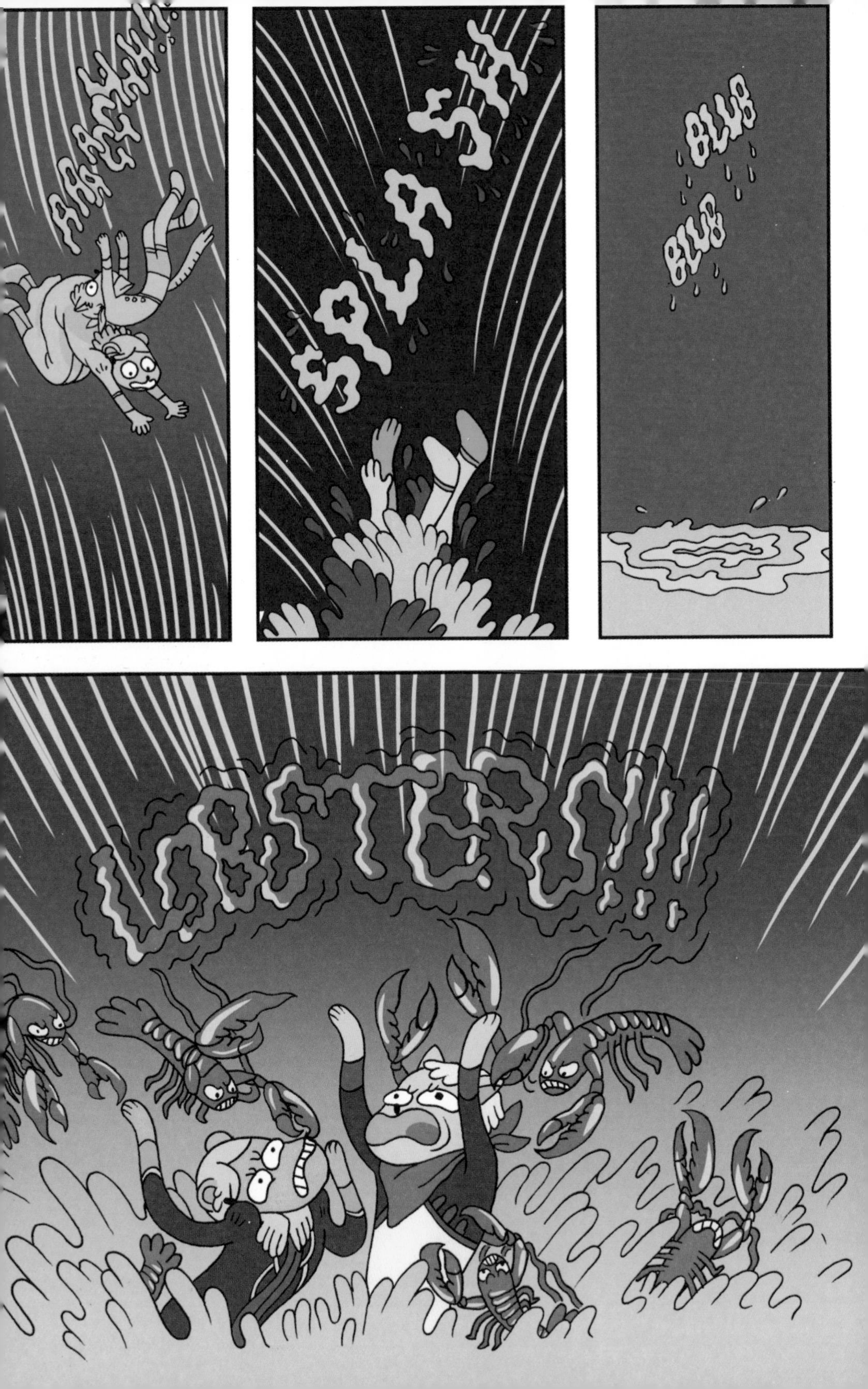
AAAGYYHH!!
SPLASH
BLUB
BLUB
LOBSTERS!!!

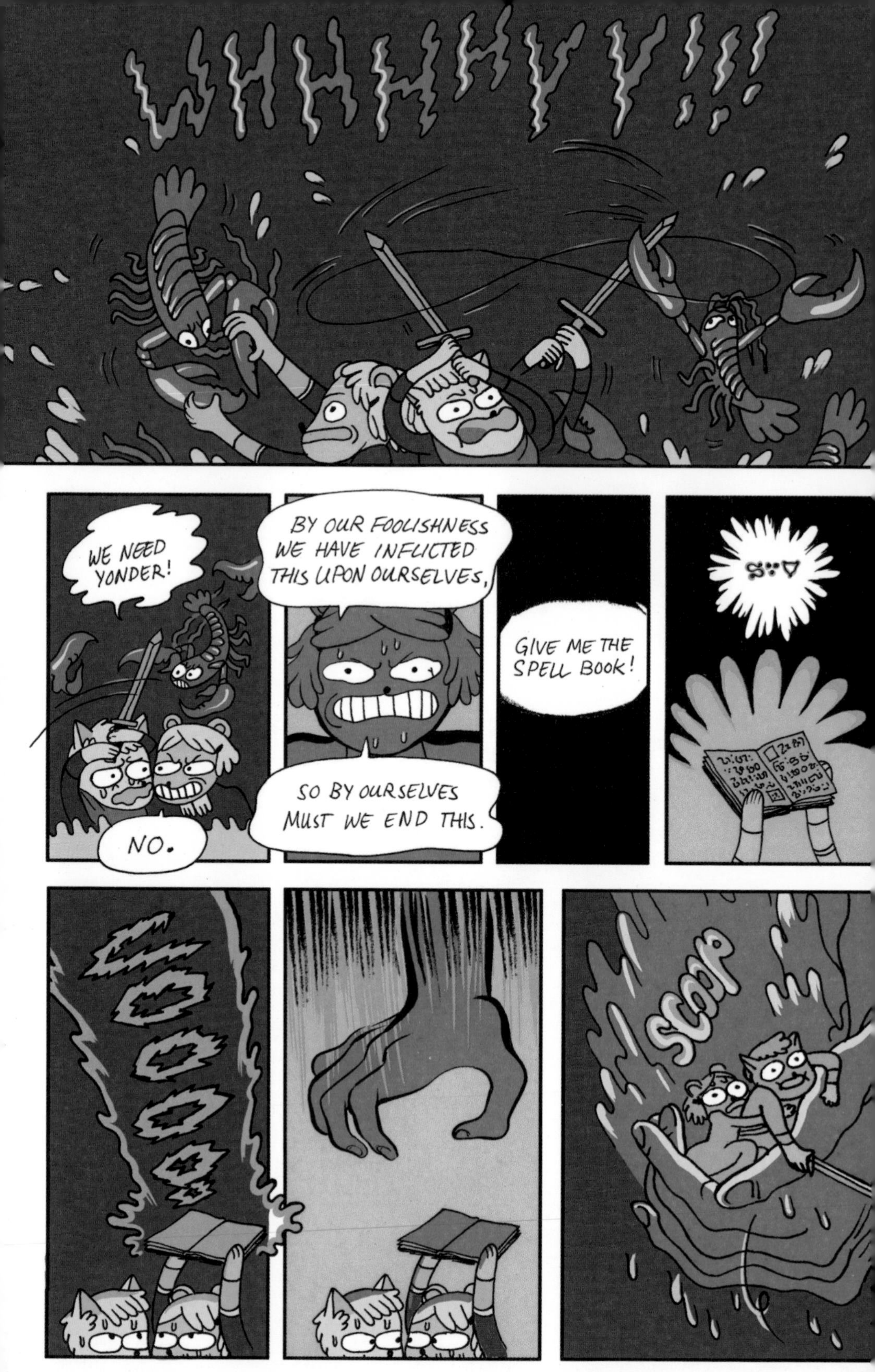
WHHHHYY!!!
WE NEED YONDER!
NO.
BY OUR FOOLISHNESS WE HAVE INFLICTED THIS UPON OURSELVES,
SO BY OURSELVES MUST WE END THIS.
GIVE ME THE SPELL BOOK!
SCOOP

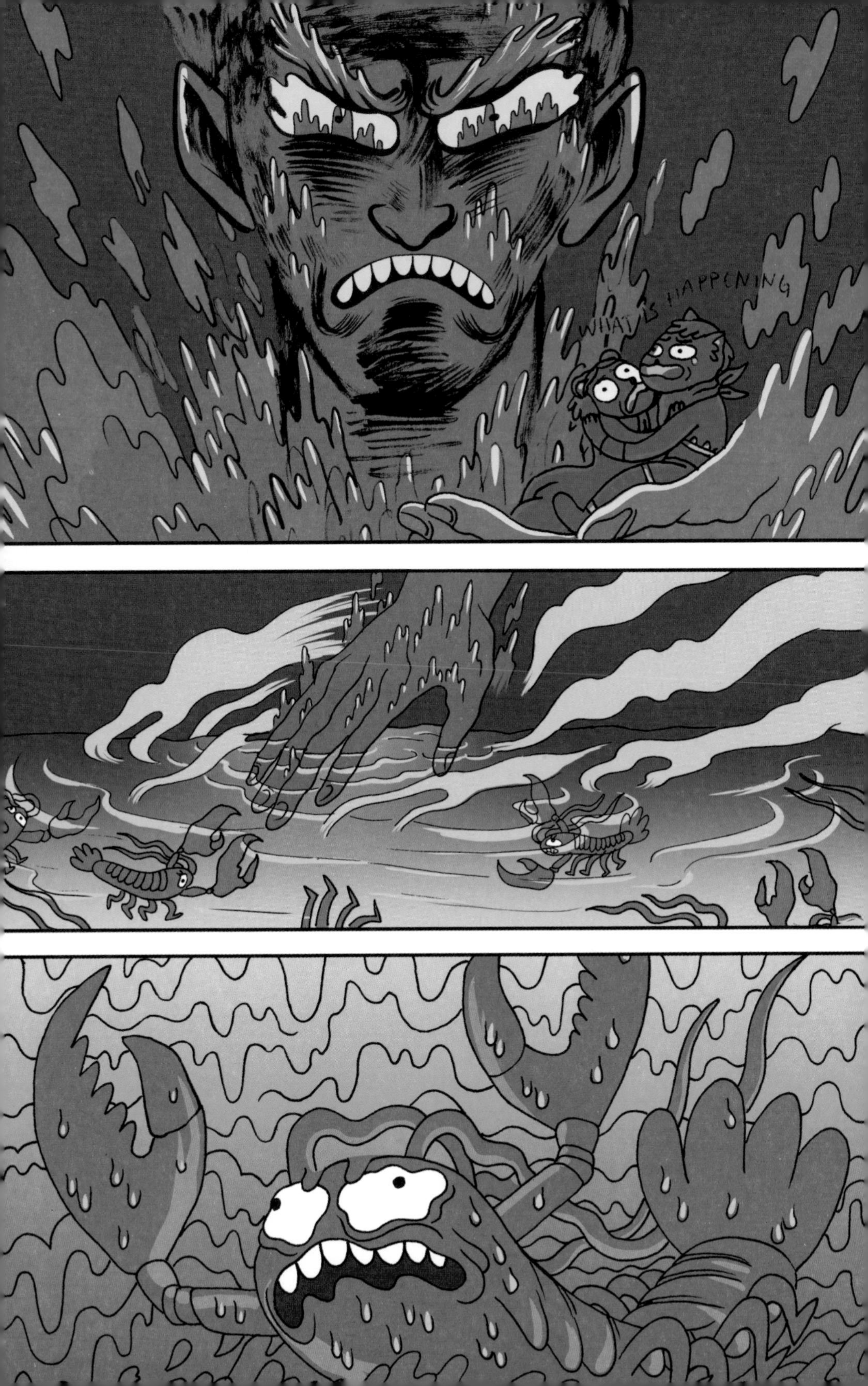
WHAT IS HAPPENING

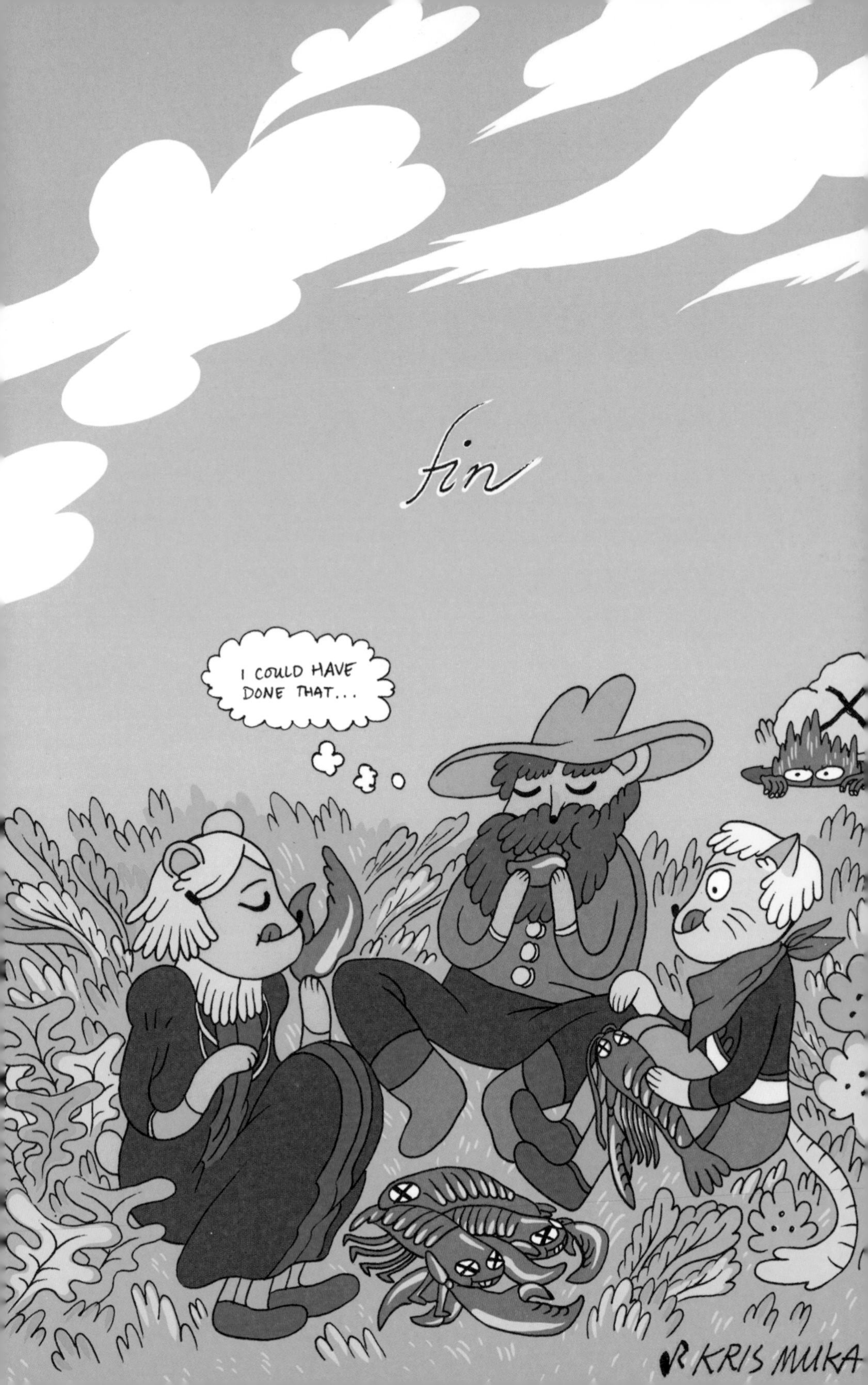
fin
I COULD HAVE DONE THAT...
KRIS MUKAI

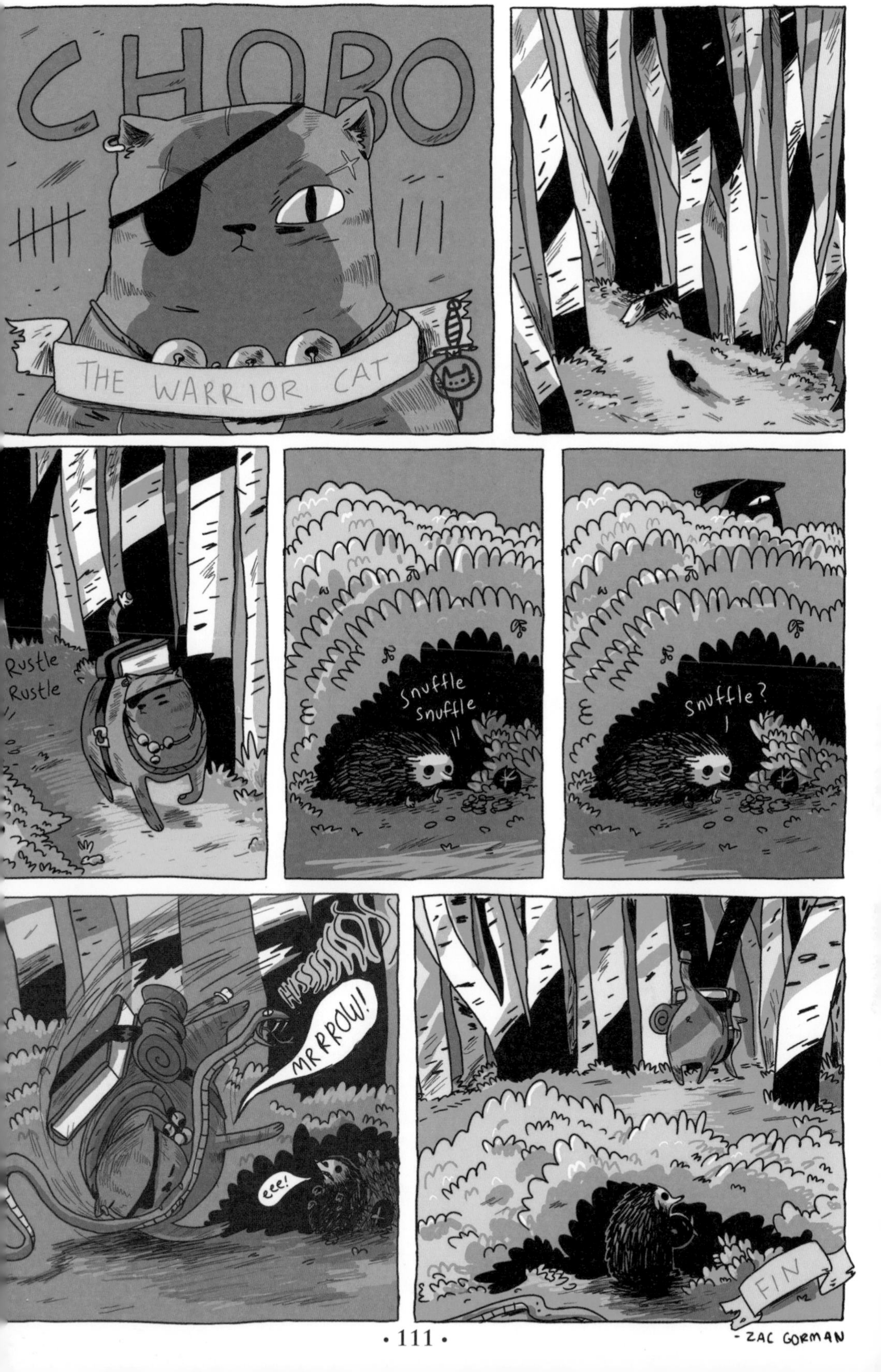
CHOBO
THE WARRIOR CAT
Rustle
Rustle
snuffle
snuffle
snuffle?
HSSSSSSS
MRRROW!
eee!
FIN
- ZAC GORMAN

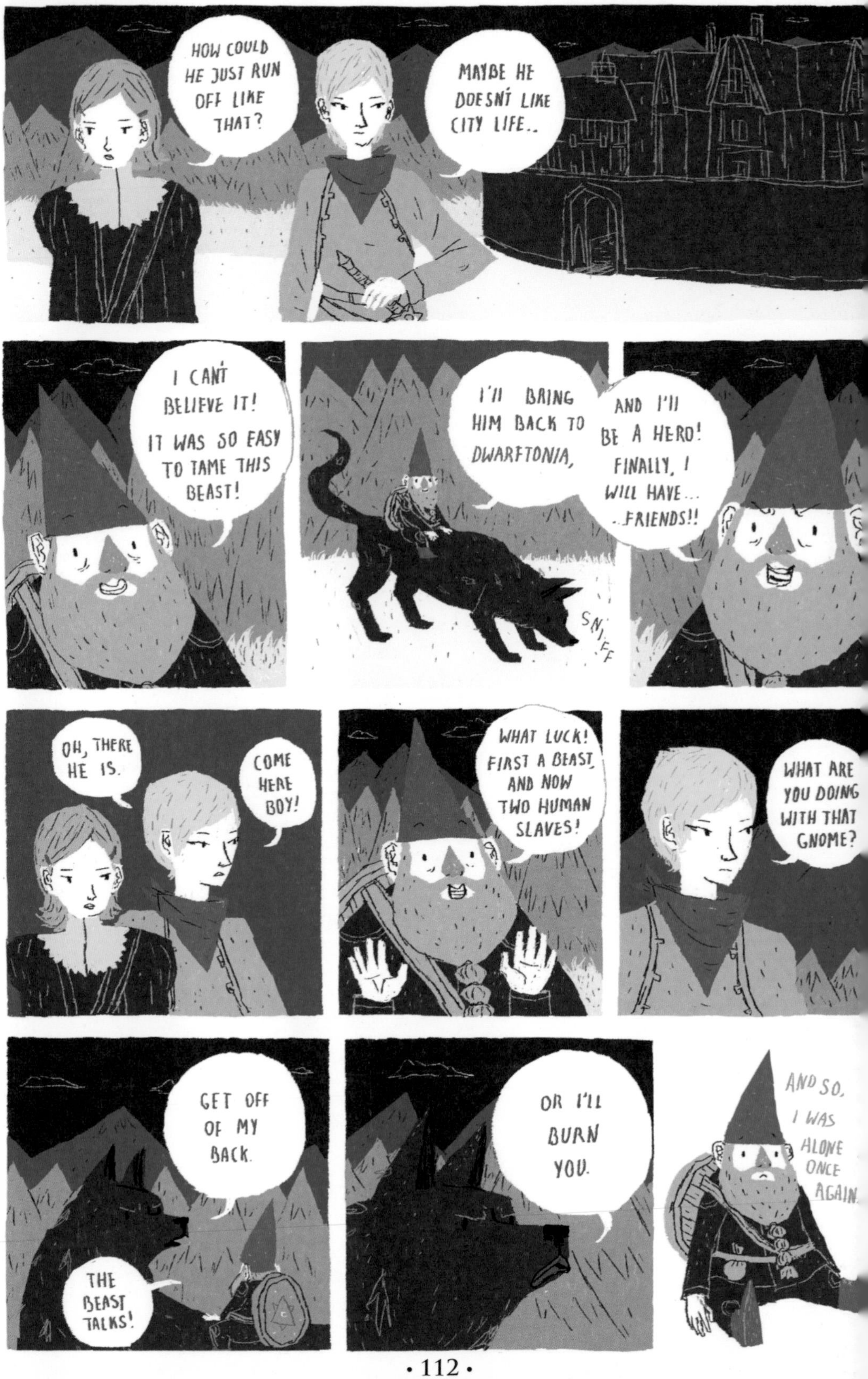
HOW COULD HE JUST RUN OFF LIKE THAT?
MAYBE HE DOESN'T LIKE CITY LIFE..
I CAN'T BELIEVE IT!
IT WAS SO EASY TO TAME THIS BEAST!
I'LL BRING HIM BACK TO DWARFTONIA,
SNIFF
AND I'LL BE A HERO! FINALLY, I WILL HAVE... ...FRIENDS!!
OH, THERE HE IS.
COME HERE BOY!
WHAT LUCK! FIRST A BEAST, AND NOW TWO HUMAN SLAVES!
WHAT ARE YOU DOING WITH THAT GNOME?
GET OFF OF MY BACK.
THE BEAST TALKS!
OR I'LL BURN YOU.
AND SO, I WAS ALONE ONCE AGAIN.

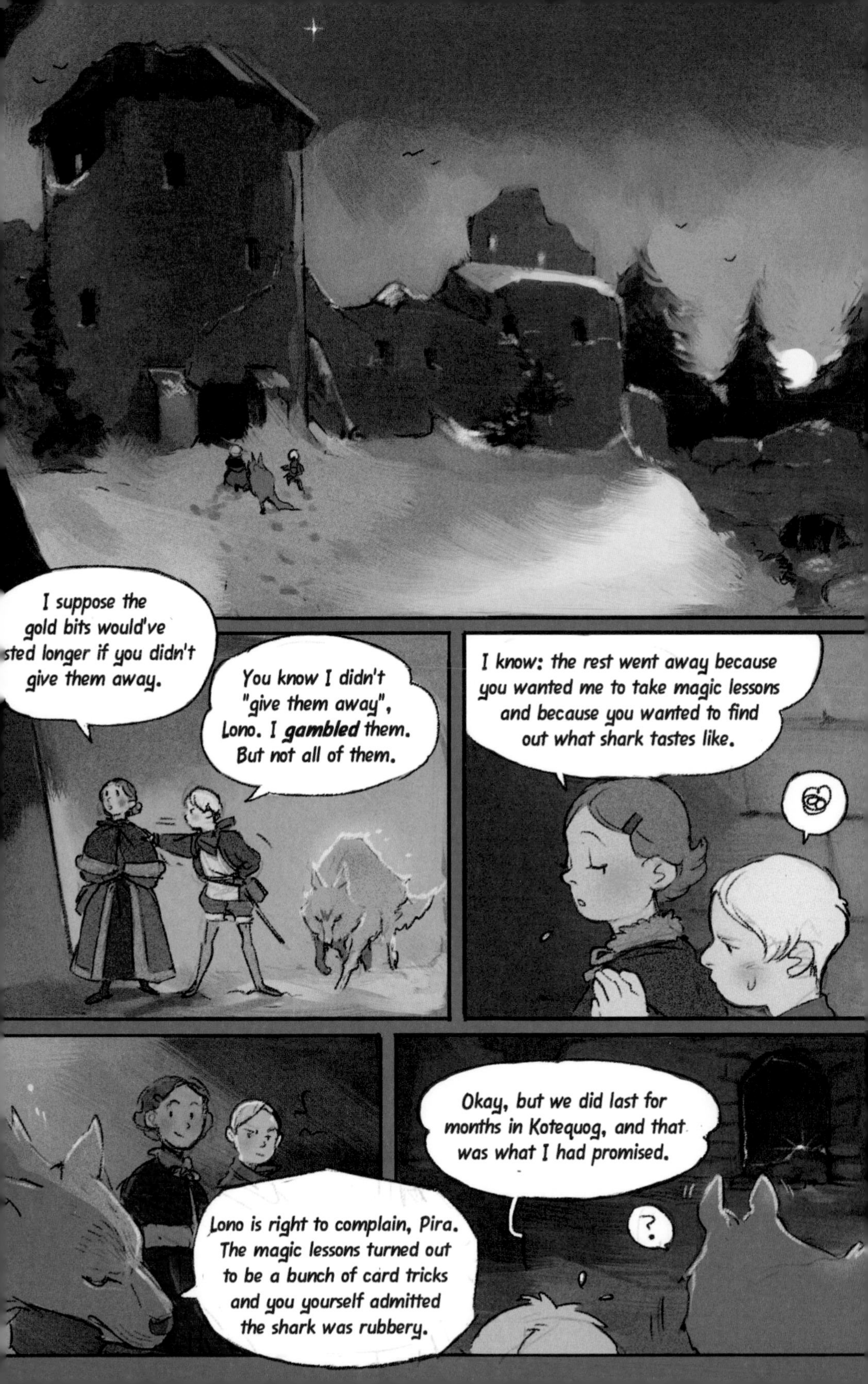
I suppose the gold bits would've sted longer if you didn't give them away.
You know I didn't "give them away", Lono. I **gambled** them. But not all of them.
I know: the rest went away because you wanted me to take magic lessons and because you wanted to find out what shark tastes like.
Okay, but we did last for months in Kotequog, and that was what I had promised.
?
Lono is right to complain, Pira. The magic lessons turned out to be a bunch of card tricks and you yourself admitted the shark was rubbery.

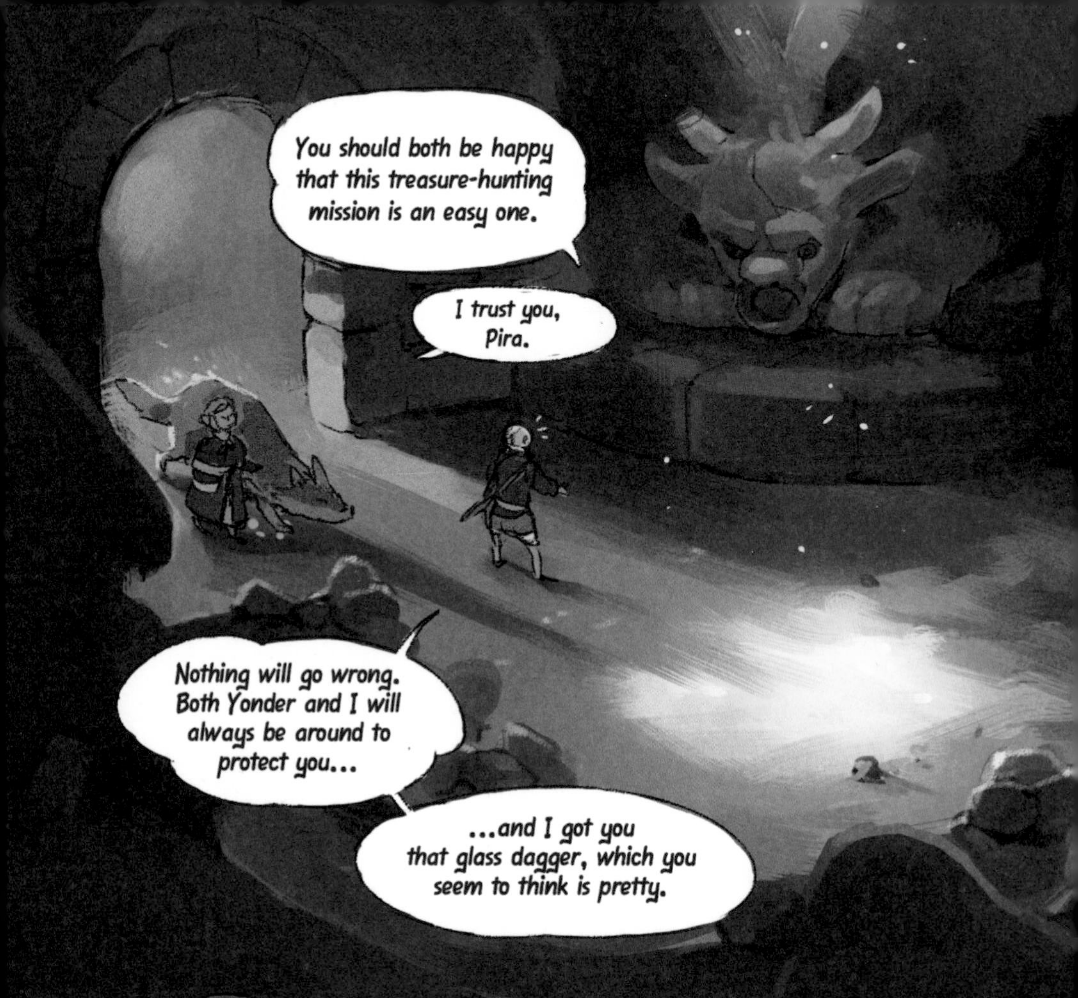
You should both be happy that this treasure-hunting mission is an easy one.
I trust you, Pira.
Nothing will go wrong. Both Yonder and I will always be around to protect you...
...and I got you that glass dagger, which you seem to think is pretty.

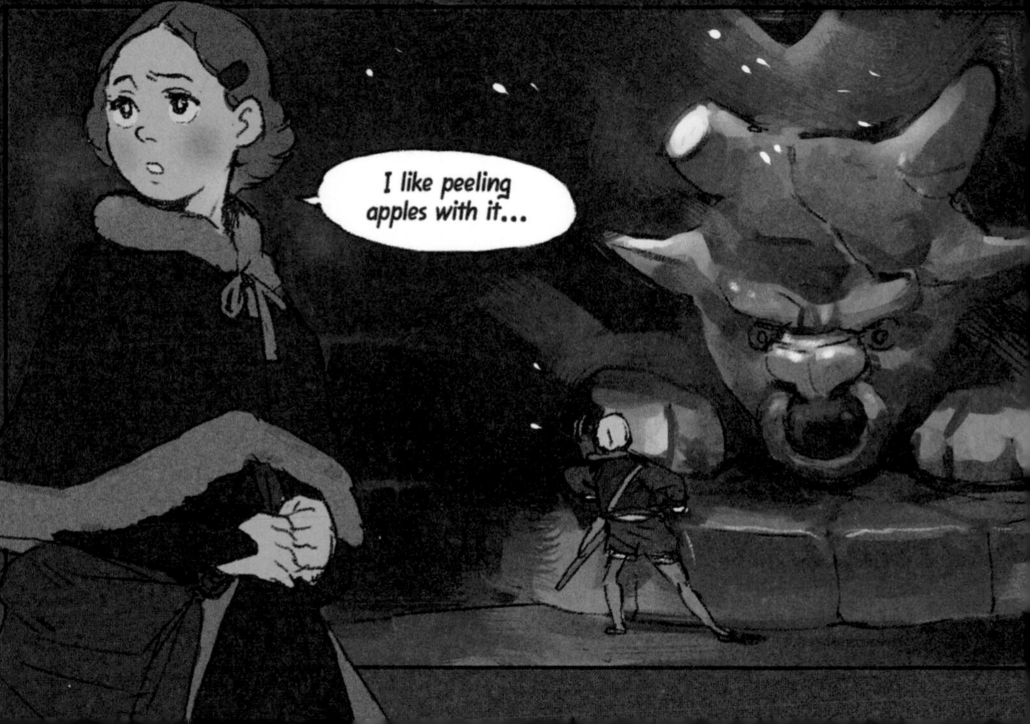
I like peeling apples with it...

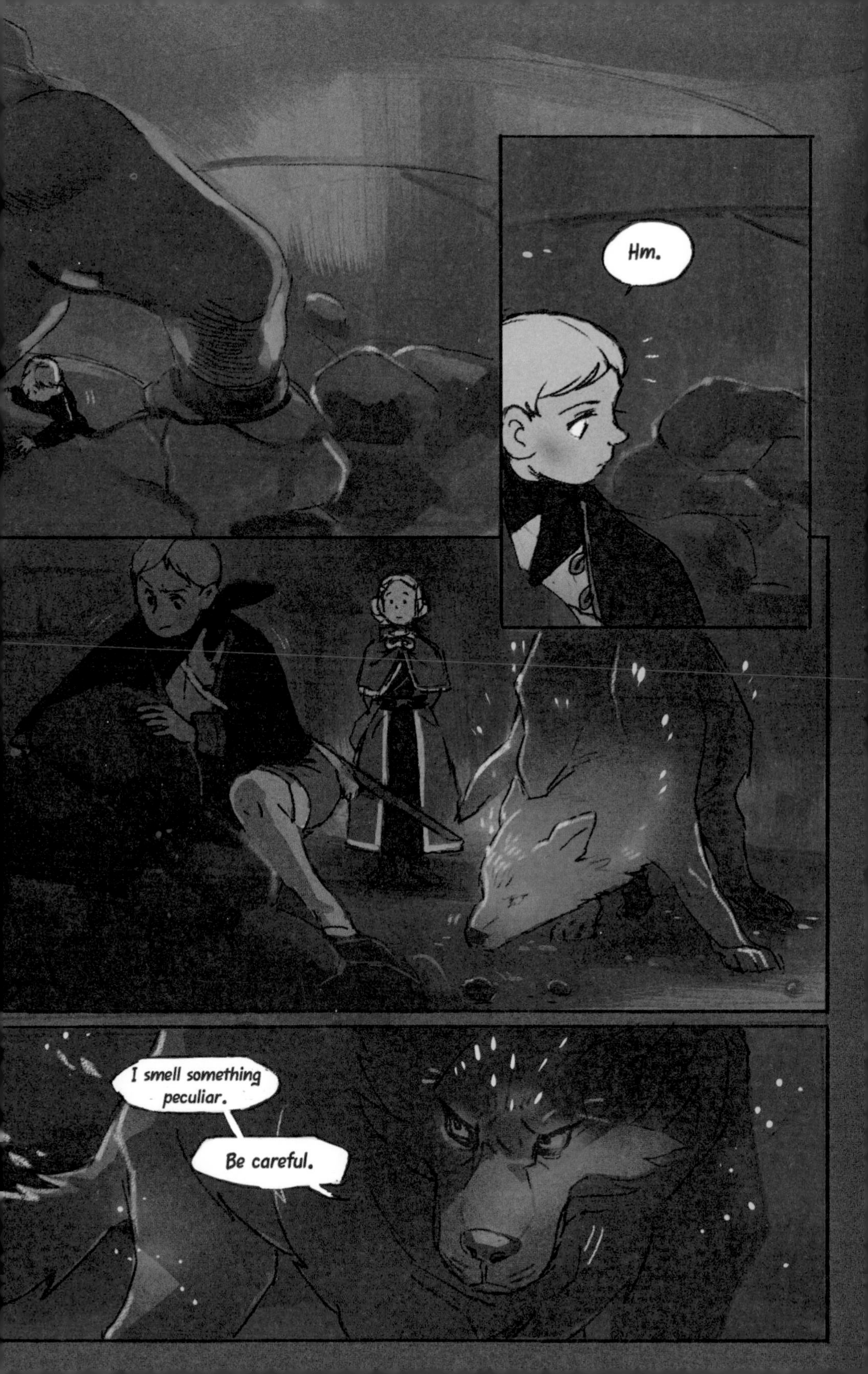
Hm.
I smell something peculiar.
Be careful.

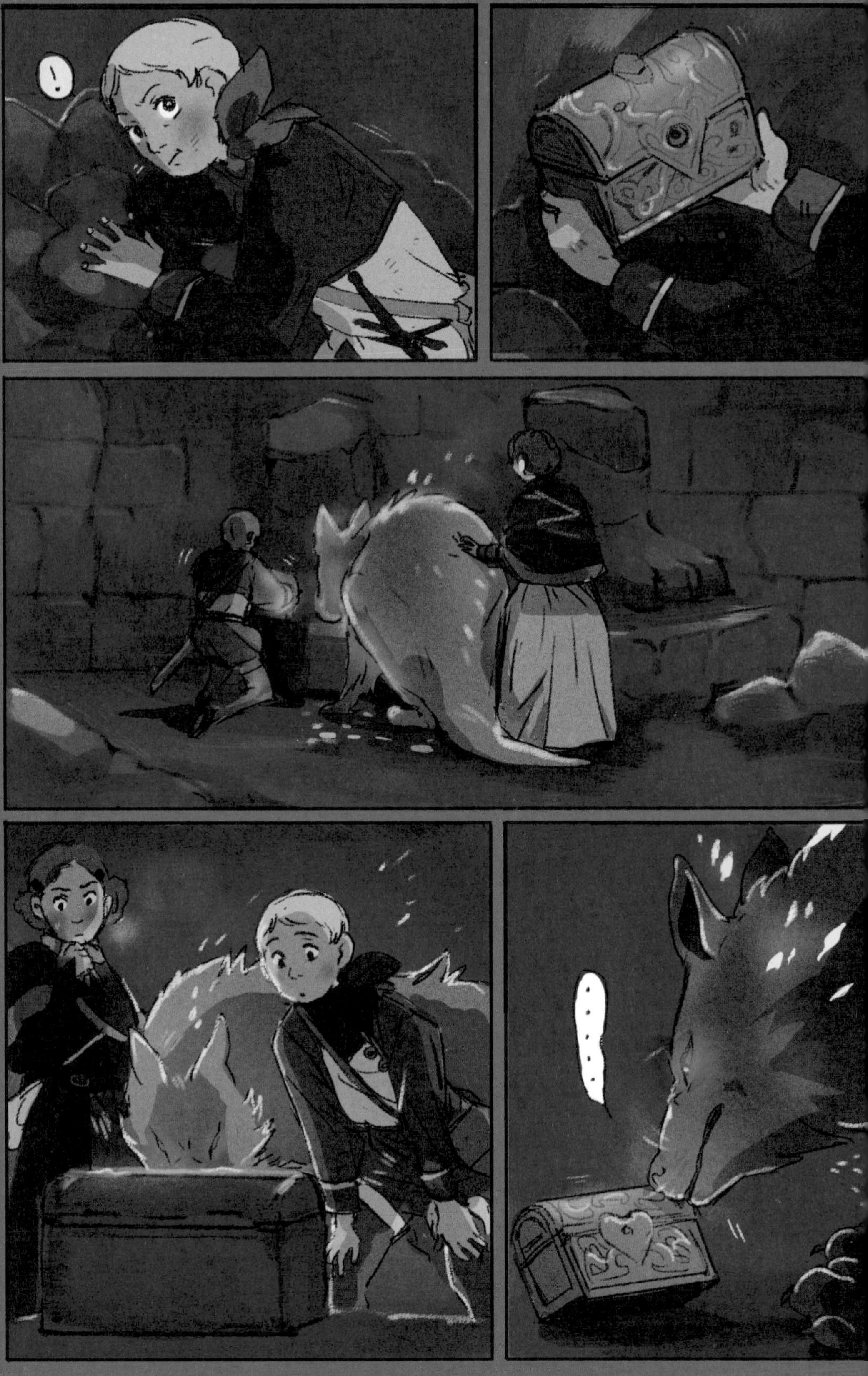
!
. . . . .

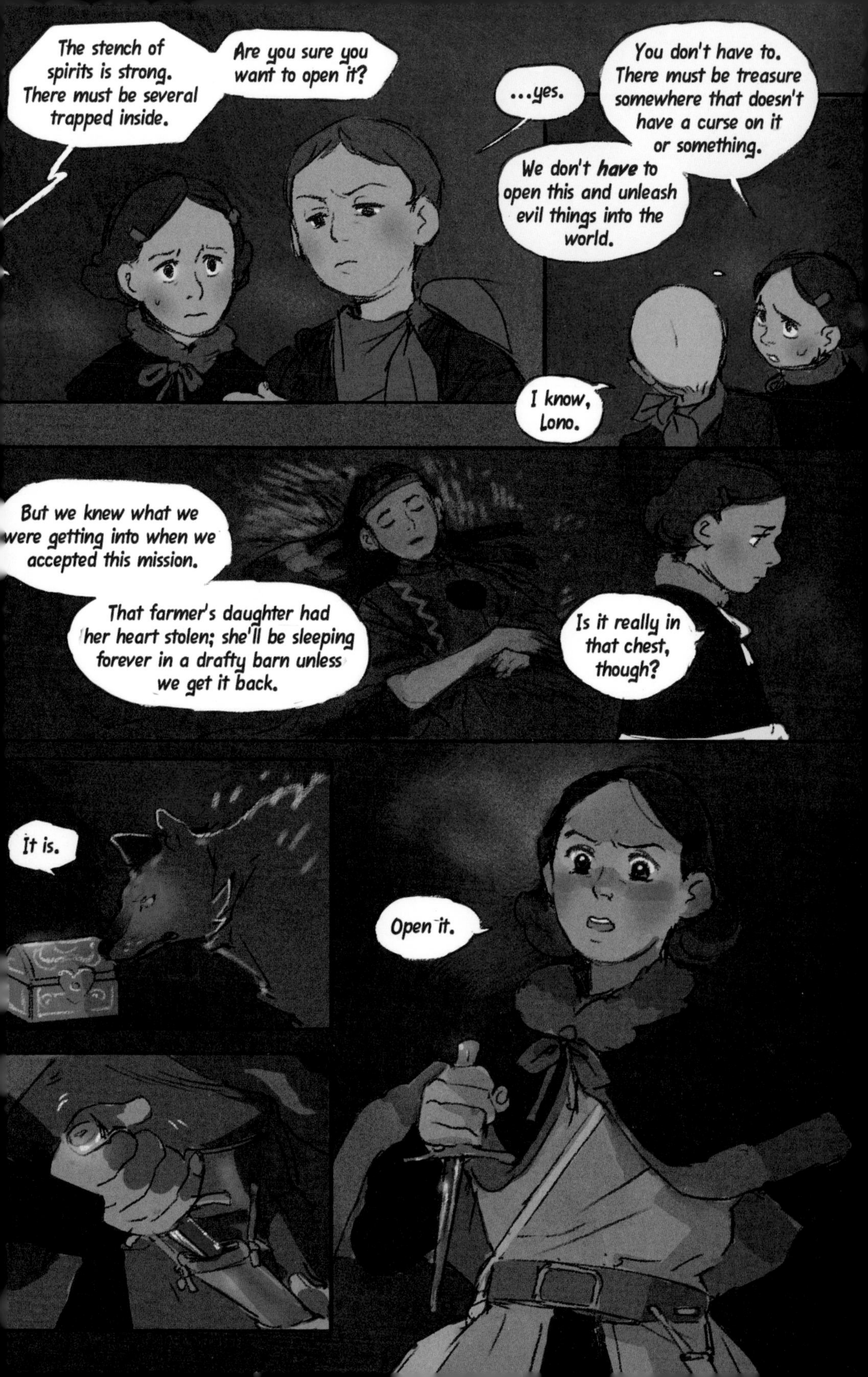
The stench of spirits is strong. There must be several trapped inside.
Are you sure you want to open it?
...yes.
You don't have to. There must be treasure somewhere that doesn't have a curse on it or something.
We don't *have* to open this and unleash evil things into the world.
I know, Lono.
But we knew what we were getting into when we accepted this mission.
That farmer's daughter had her heart stolen; she'll be sleeping forever in a drafty barn unless we get it back.
Is it really in that chest, though?
It is.
Open it.

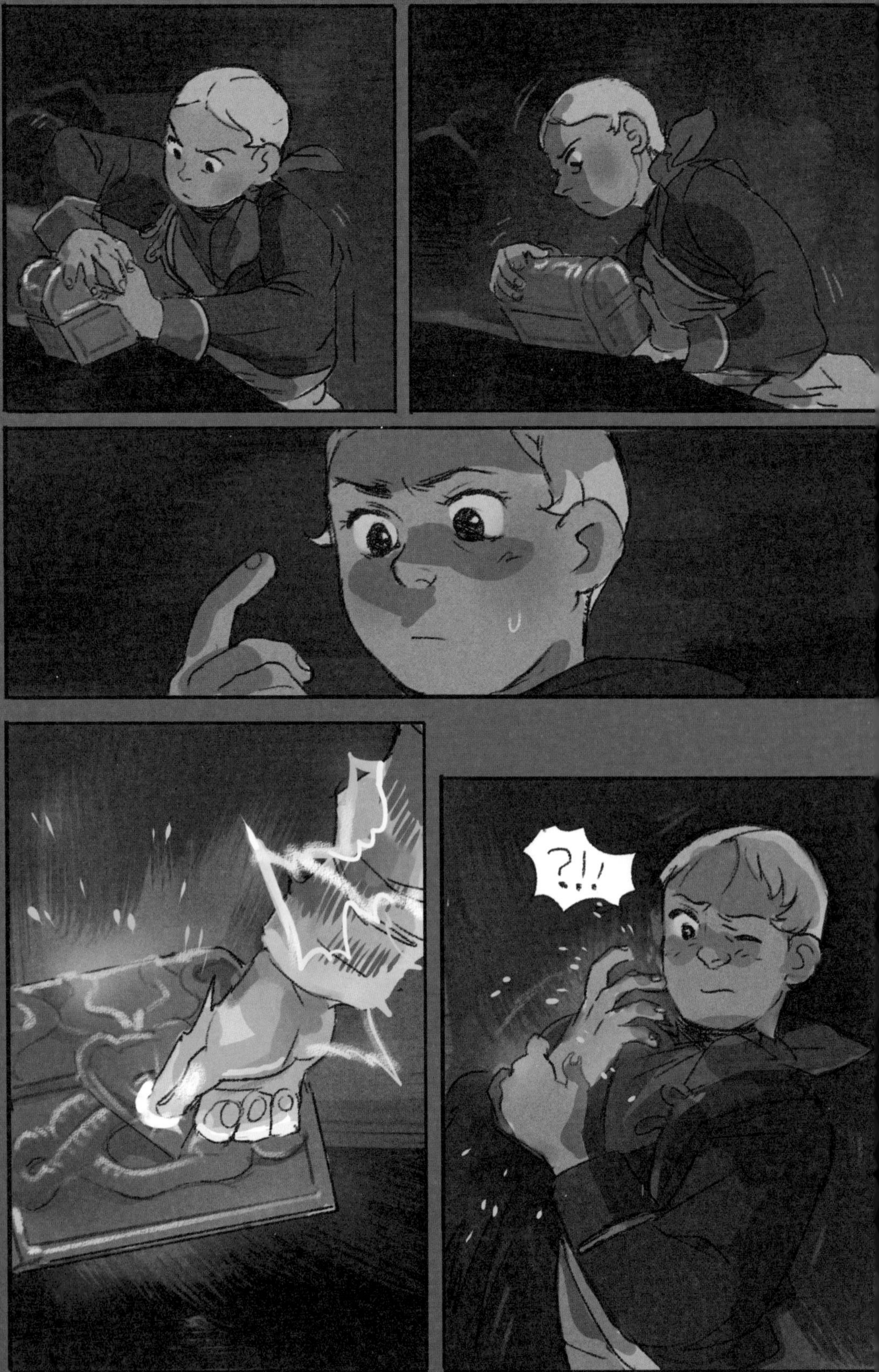
?!!

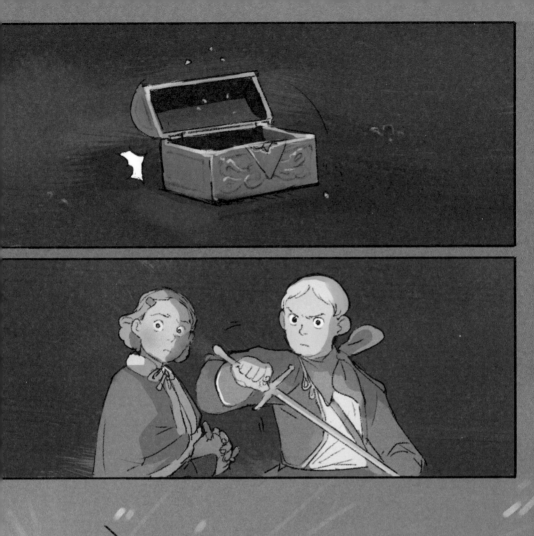

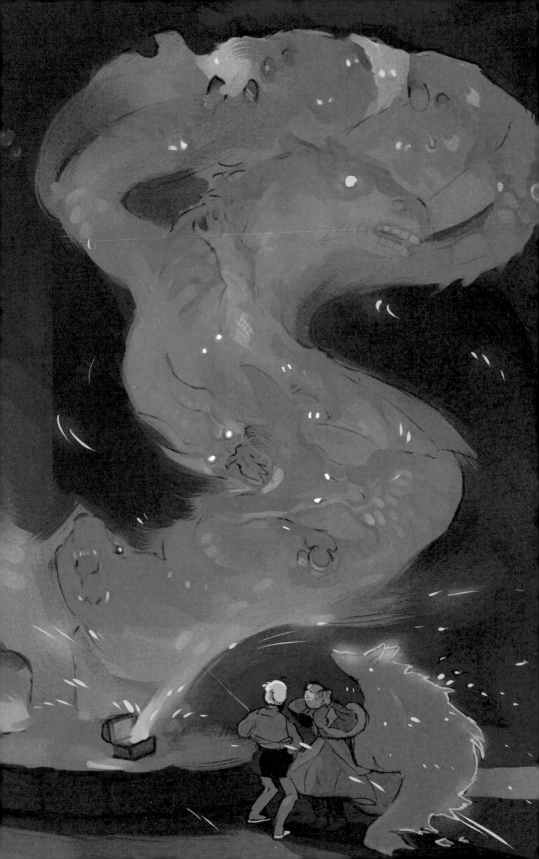

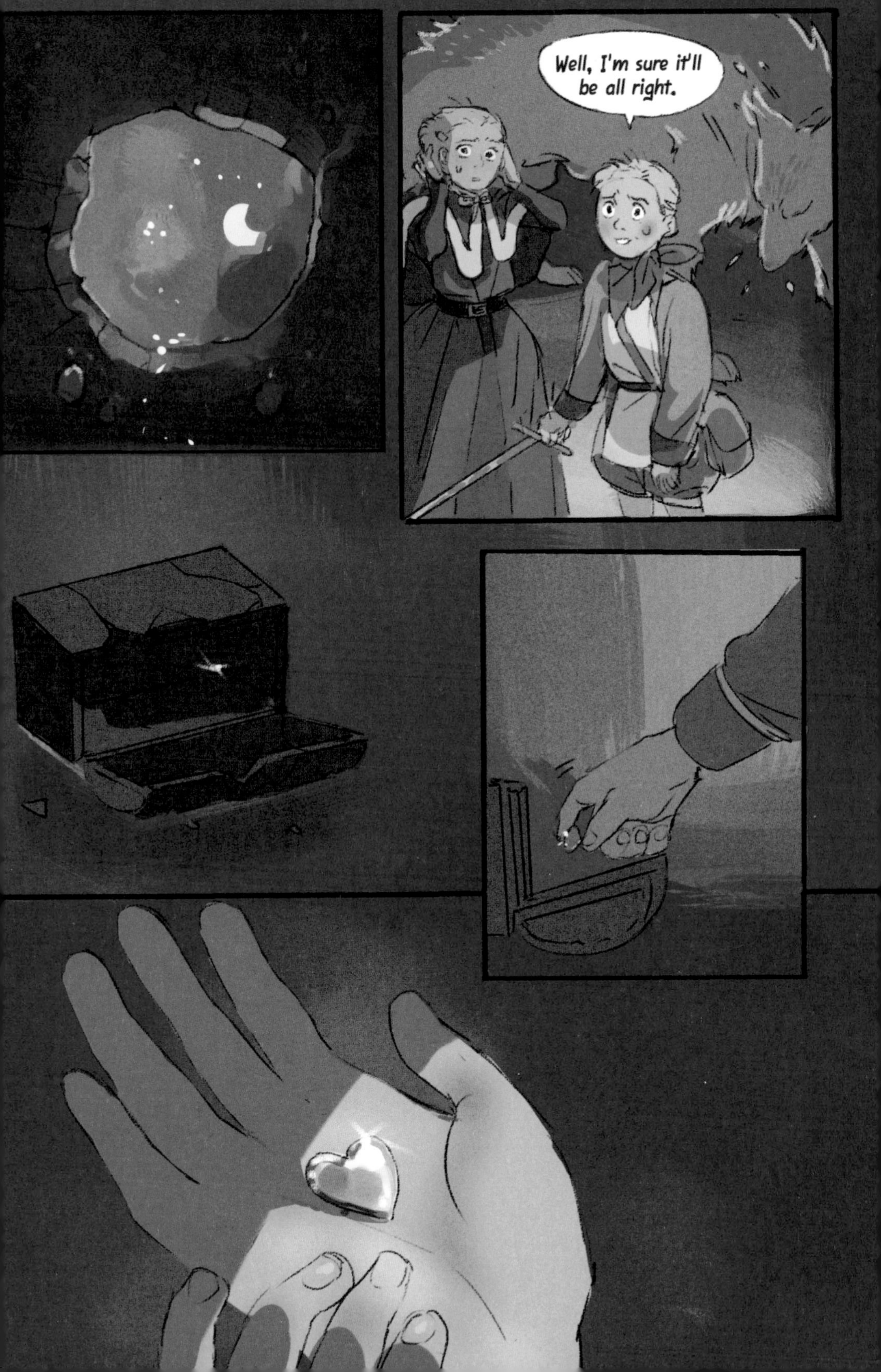
Well, I'm sure it'll be all right.

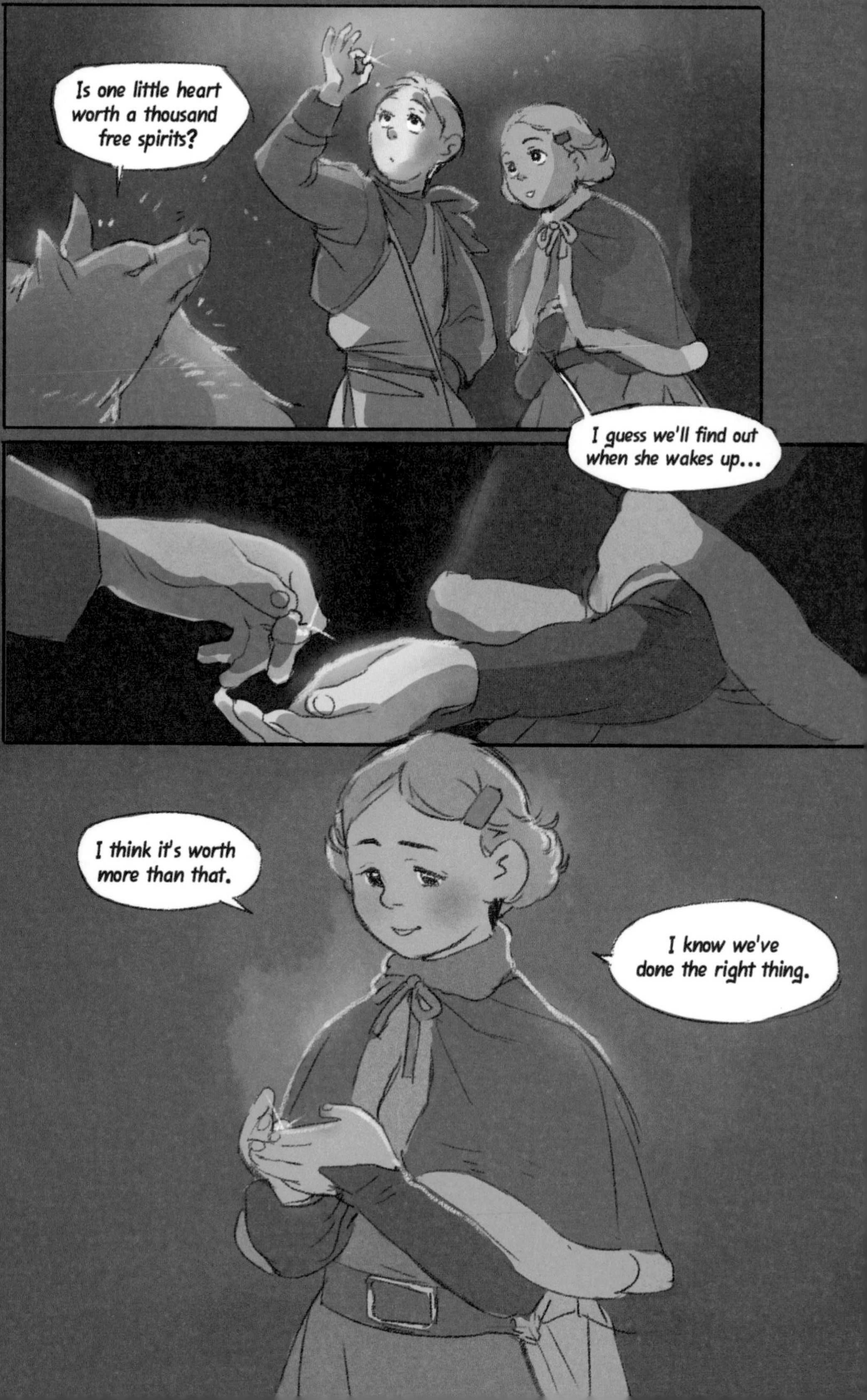
Is one little heart worth a thousand free spirits?
I guess we'll find out when she wakes up...
I think it's worth more than that.
I know we've done the right thing.

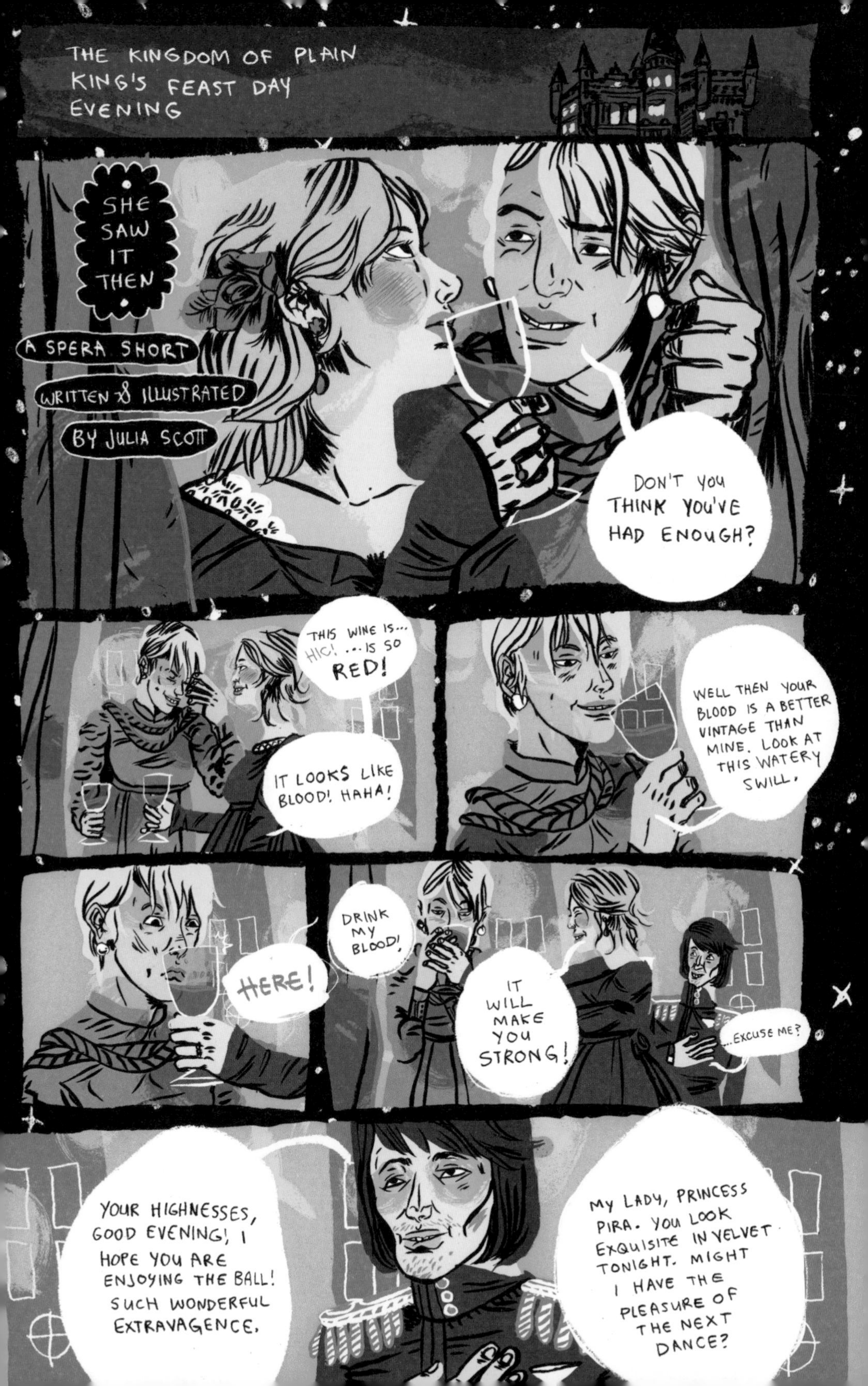
THE KINGDOM OF PLAIN
KING'S FEAST DAY
EVENING
SHE SAW IT THEN
A SPERA SHORT
WRITTEN & ILLUSTRATED
BY JULIA SCOTT
DON'T YOU THINK YOU'VE HAD ENOUGH?
THIS WINE IS... HIC! ...IS SO RED!
IT LOOKS LIKE BLOOD! HAHA!
WELL THEN YOUR BLOOD IS A BETTER VINTAGE THAN MINE. LOOK AT THIS WATERY SWILL.
HERE!
DRINK MY BLOOD!
IT WILL MAKE YOU STRONG!
...EXCUSE ME?
YOUR HIGHNESSES, GOOD EVENING! I HOPE YOU ARE ENJOYING THE BALL! SUCH WONDERFUL EXTRAVAGENCE.
MY LADY, PRINCESS PIRA. YOU LOOK EXQUISITE IN VELVET TONIGHT. MIGHT I HAVE THE PLEASURE OF THE NEXT DANCE?

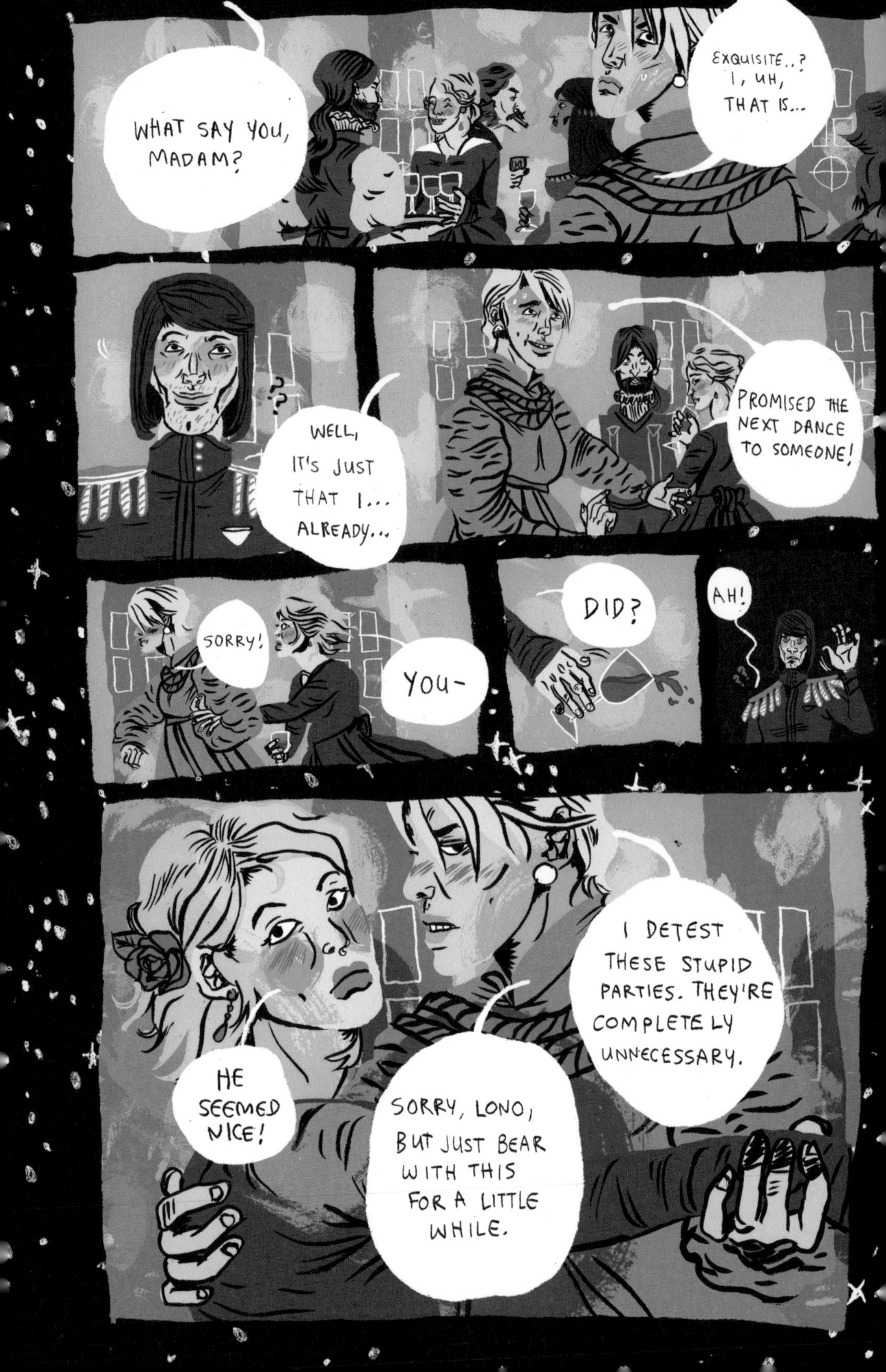
WHAT SAY YOU, MADAM?
EXQUISITE..? I, UH, THAT IS...
WELL, IT'S JUST THAT I... ALREADY...
PROMISED THE NEXT DANCE TO SOMEONE!
SORRY!
YOU-
DID?
AH!
I DETEST THESE STUPID PARTIES. THEY'RE COMPLETELY UNNECESSARY.
HE SEEMED NICE!
SORRY, LONO, BUT JUST BEAR WITH THIS FOR A LITTLE WHILE.

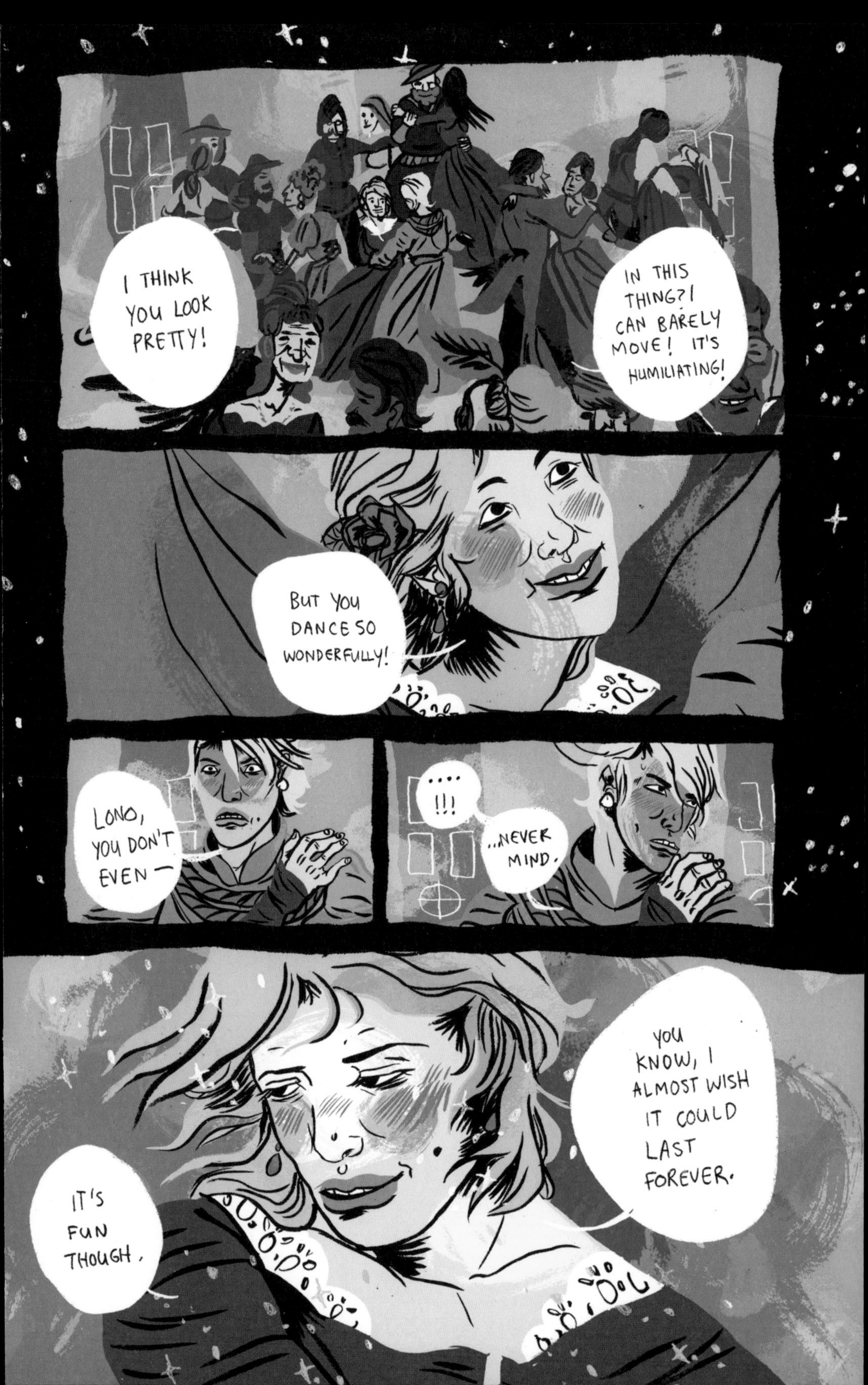
I THINK YOU LOOK PRETTY!
IN THIS THING?! CAN BARELY MOVE! IT'S HUMILIATING!
BUT YOU DANCE SO WONDERFULLY!
LONO, YOU DON'T EVEN—
....
!!!
...NEVER MIND.
YOU KNOW, I ALMOST WISH IT COULD LAST FOREVER.
IT'S FUN THOUGH.

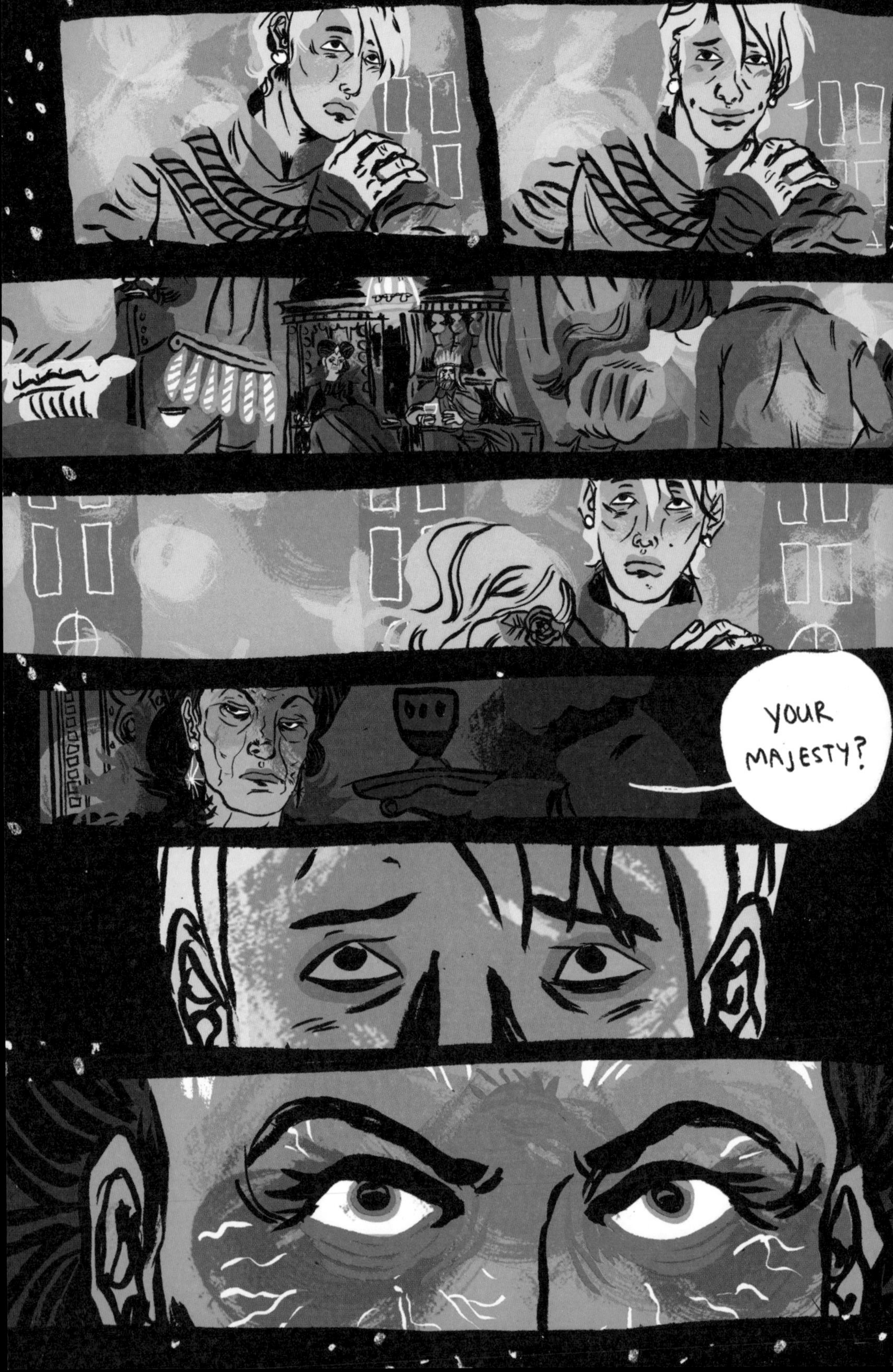
YOUR MAJESTY?

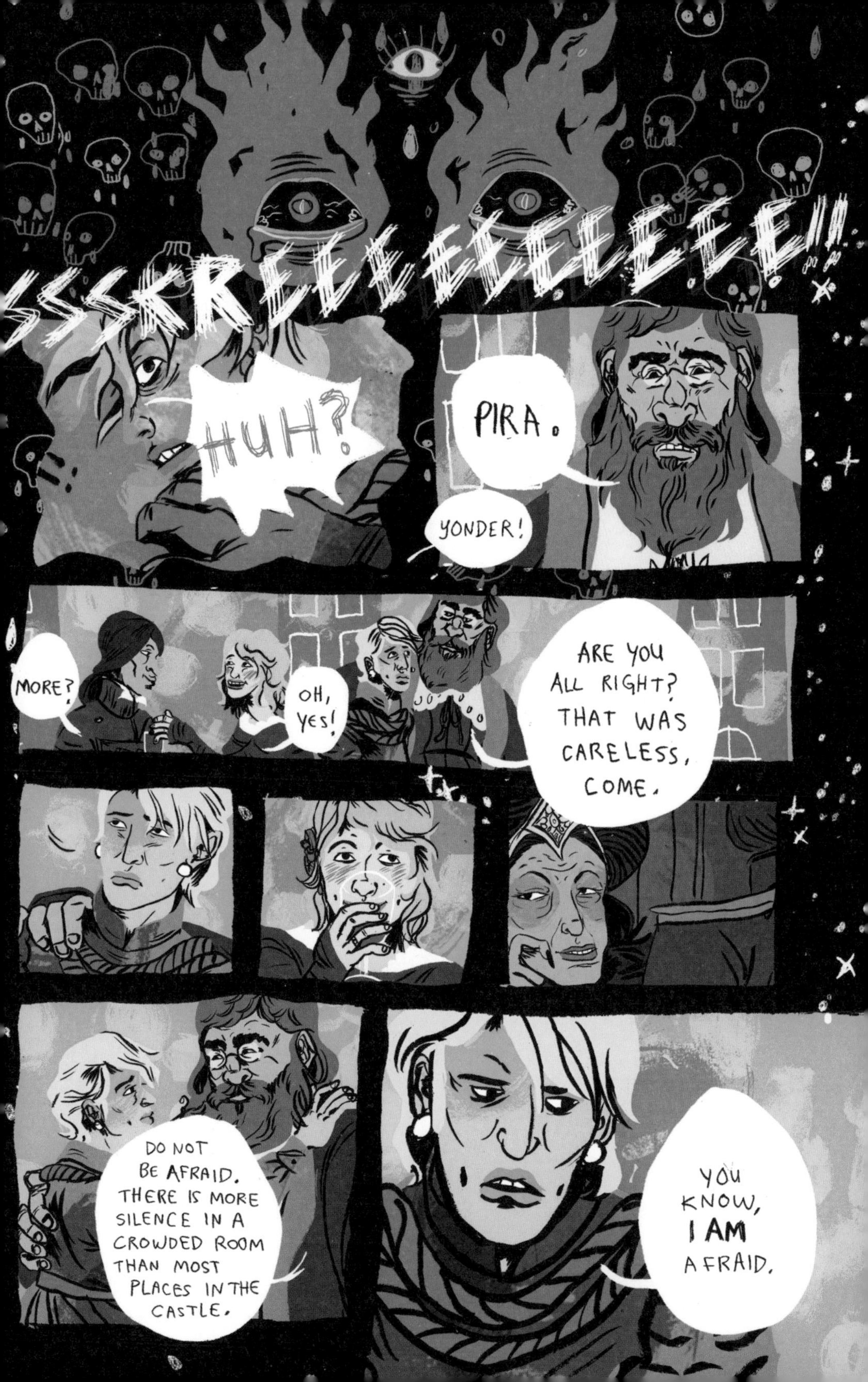
SSSKREEEEEEEEE!!
HUH?
PIRA.
YONDER!
MORE?
OH, YES!
ARE YOU ALL RIGHT? THAT WAS CARELESS, COME.
DO NOT BE AFRAID. THERE IS MORE SILENCE IN A CROWDED ROOM THAN MOST PLACES IN THE CASTLE.
YOU KNOW, **I AM** AFRAID.

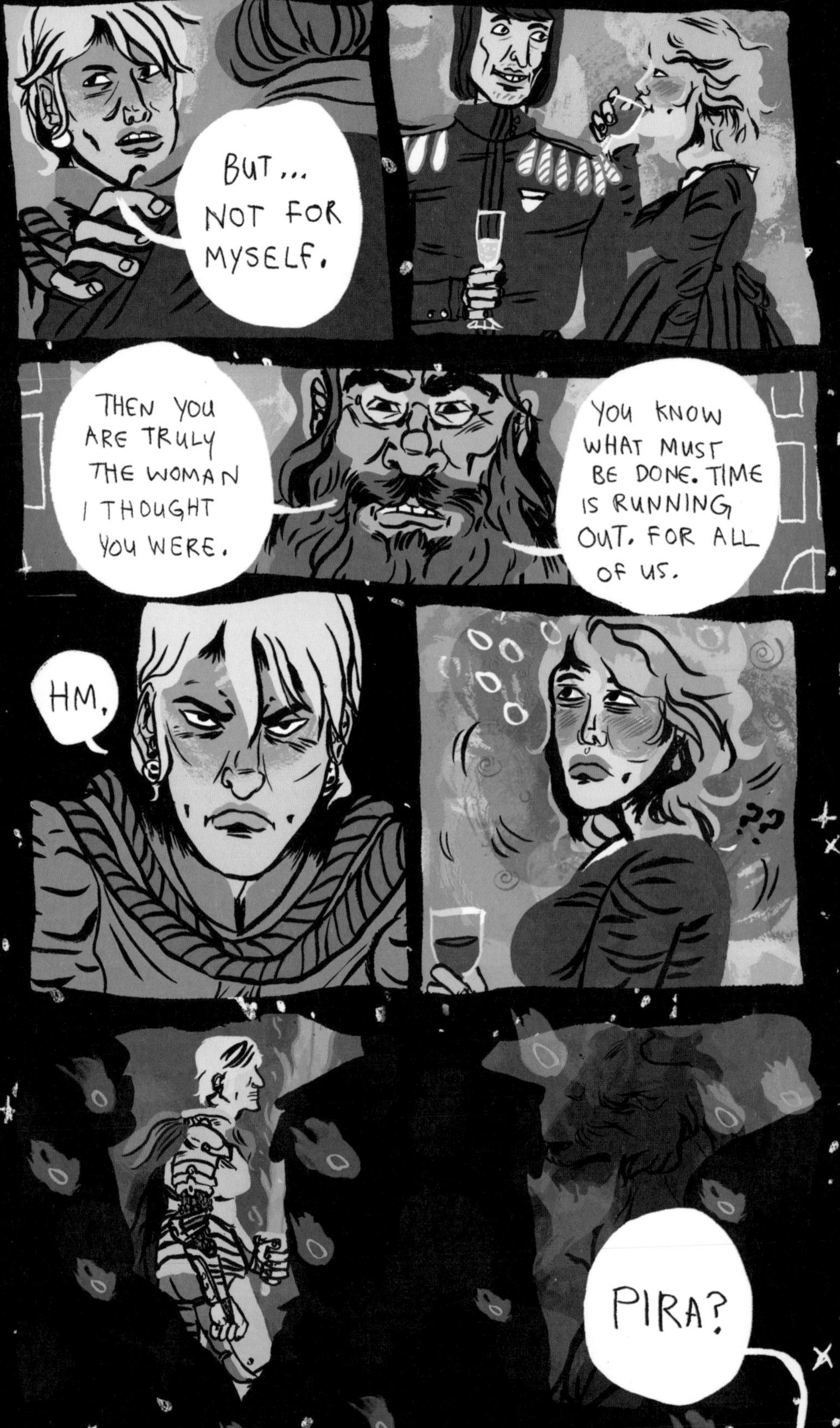
BUT... NOT FOR MYSELF.
THEN YOU ARE TRULY THE WOMAN I THOUGHT YOU WERE.
YOU KNOW WHAT MUST BE DONE. TIME IS RUNNING OUT. FOR ALL OF US.
HM.
??
PIRA?

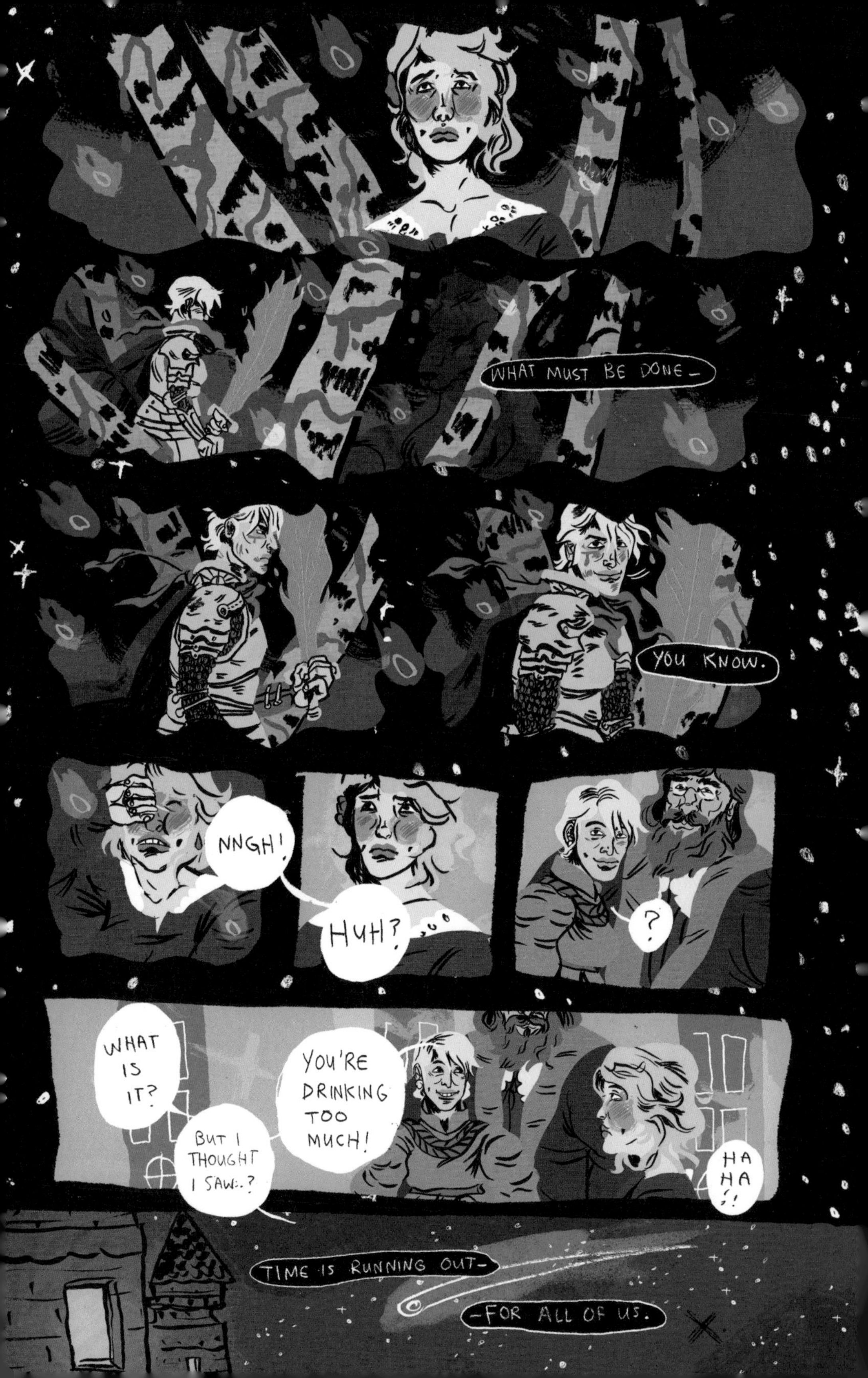
WHAT MUST BE DONE—
YOU KNOW.
NNGH!
HUH?
?
WHAT IS IT?
BUT I THOUGHT I SAW...?
YOU'RE DRINKING TOO MUCH!
HA HA ;!
TIME IS RUNNING OUT—
—FOR ALL OF US.

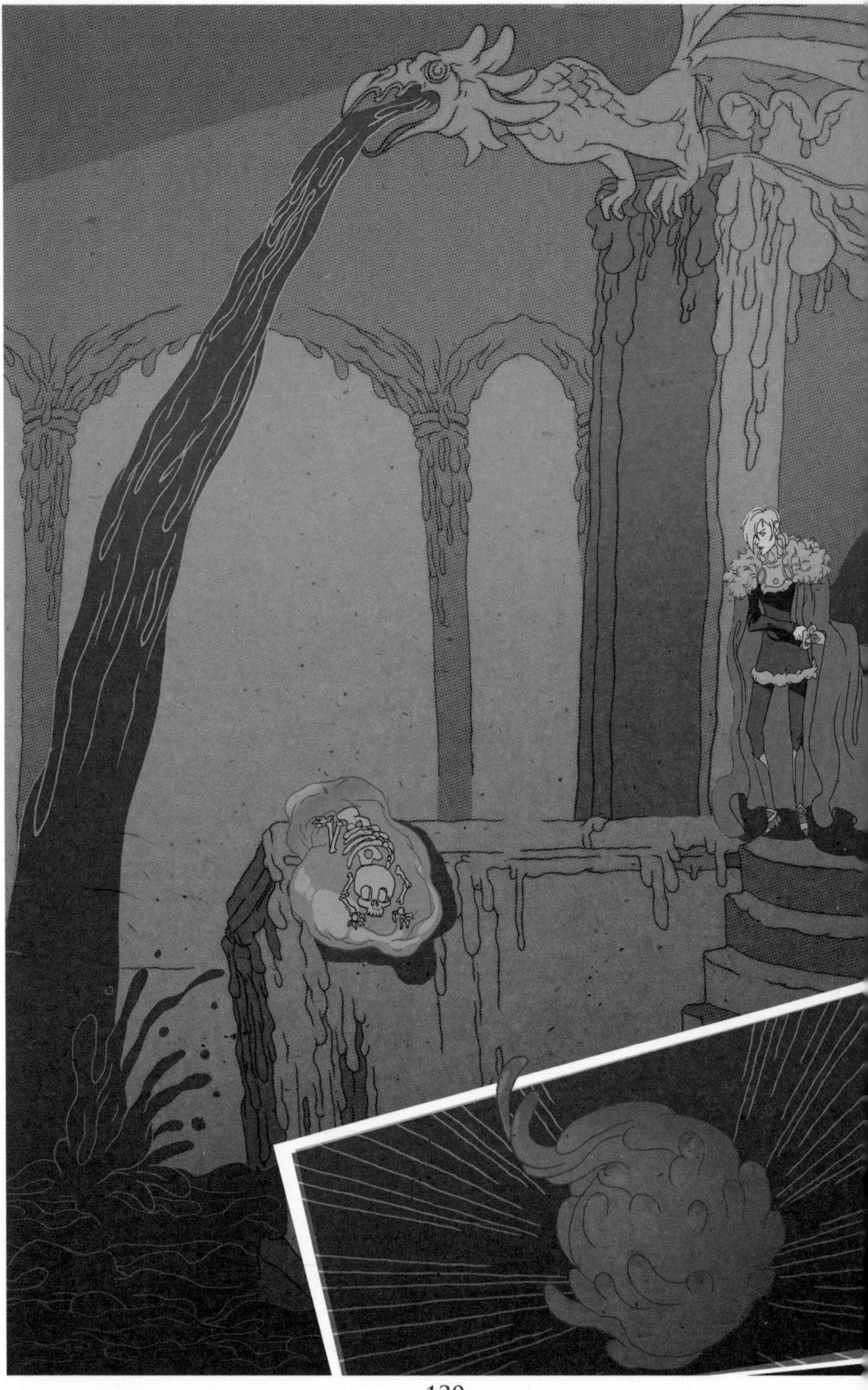

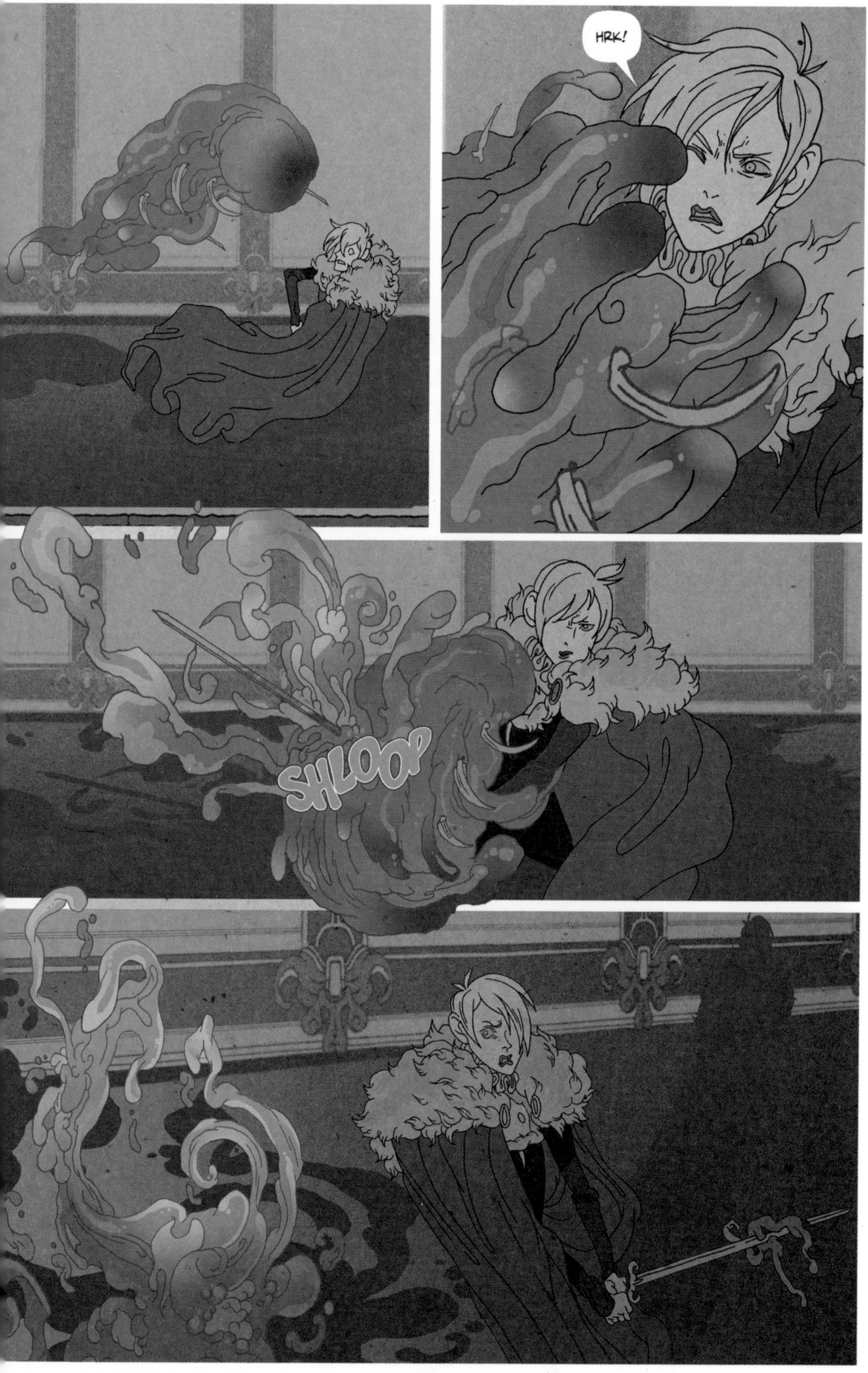
HRK!
SHLOOP

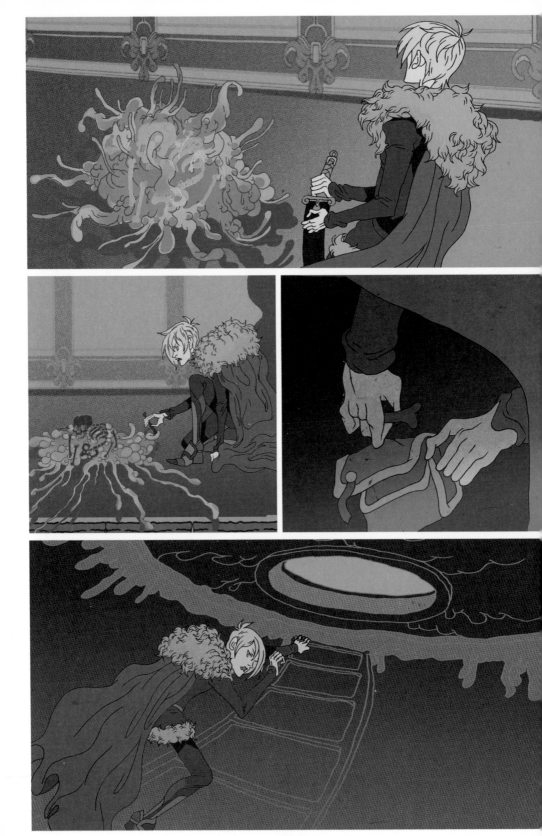

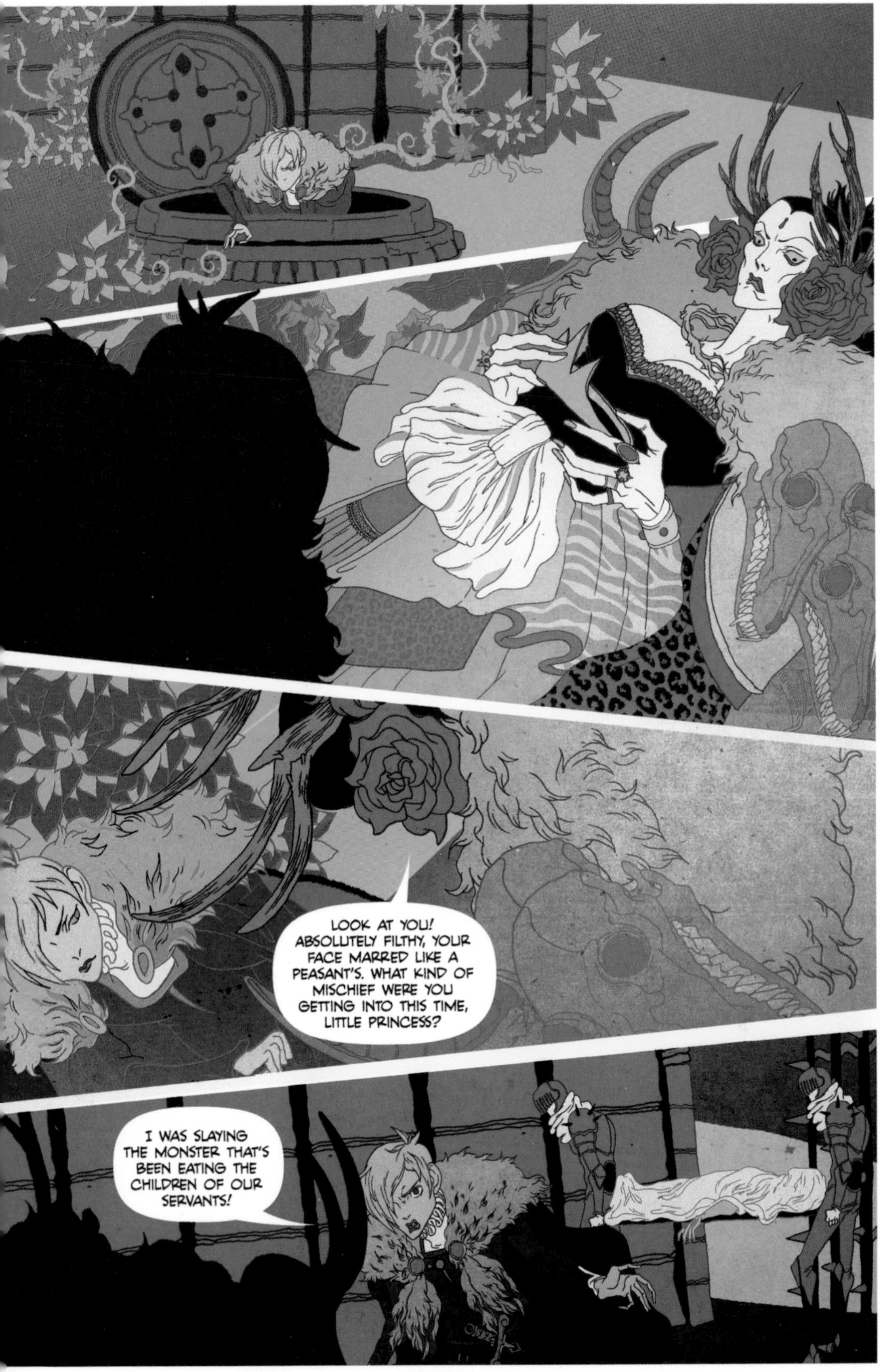

LOOK AT YOU! ABSOLUTELY FILTHY, YOUR FACE MARRED LIKE A PEASANT'S. WHAT KIND OF MISCHIEF WERE YOU GETTING INTO THIS TIME, LITTLE PRINCESS?
I WAS SLAYING THE MONSTER THAT'S BEEN EATING THE CHILDREN OF OUR SERVANTS!

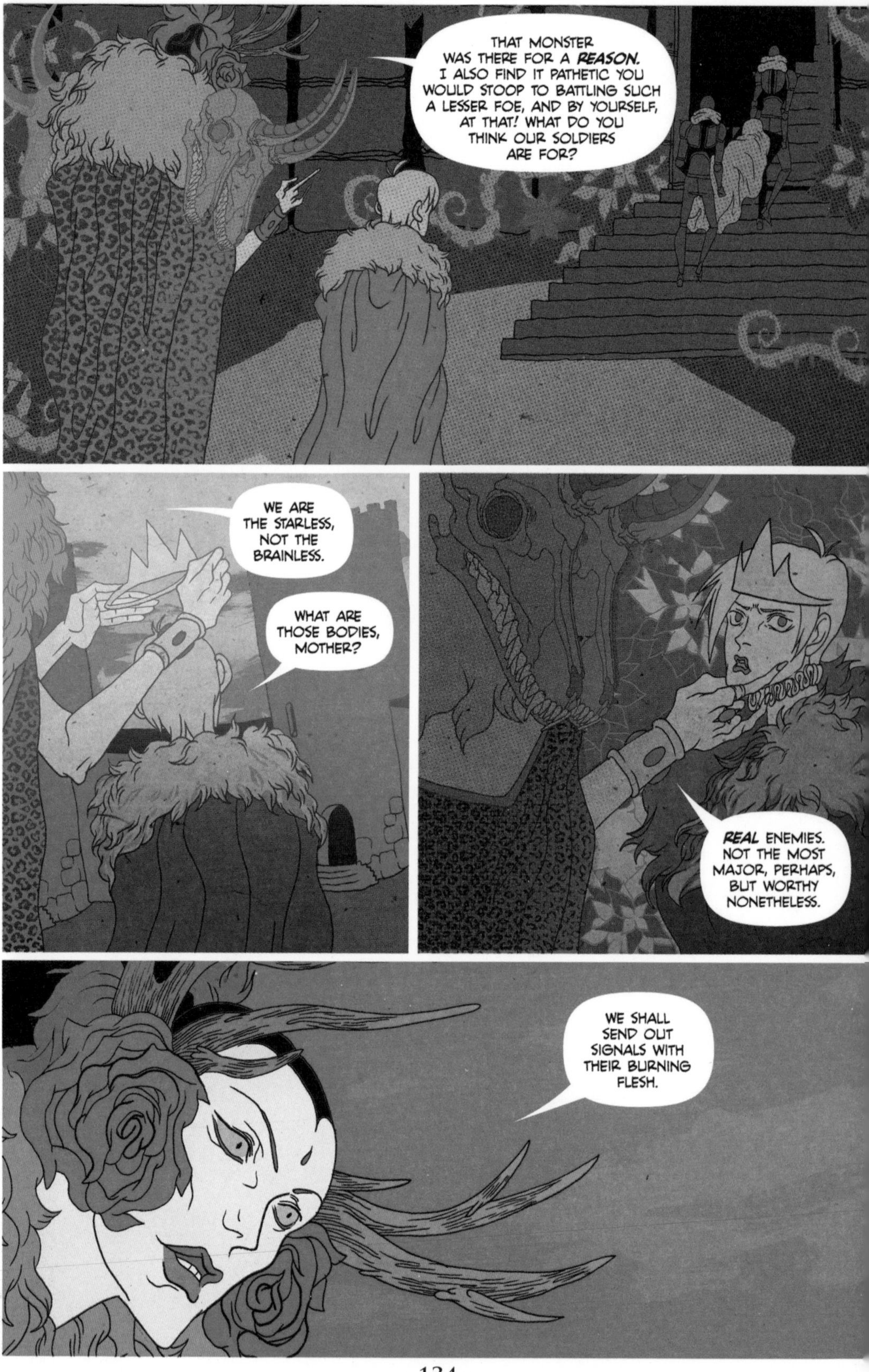
THAT MONSTER WAS THERE FOR A *REASON.* I ALSO FIND IT PATHETIC YOU WOULD STOOP TO BATTLING SUCH A LESSER FOE, AND BY YOURSELF, AT THAT! WHAT DO YOU THINK OUR SOLDIERS ARE FOR?
WE ARE THE STARLESS, NOT THE BRAINLESS.
WHAT ARE THOSE BODIES, MOTHER?
REAL ENEMIES. NOT THE MOST MAJOR, PERHAPS, BUT WORTHY NONETHELESS.
WE SHALL SEND OUT SIGNALS WITH THEIR BURNING FLESH.

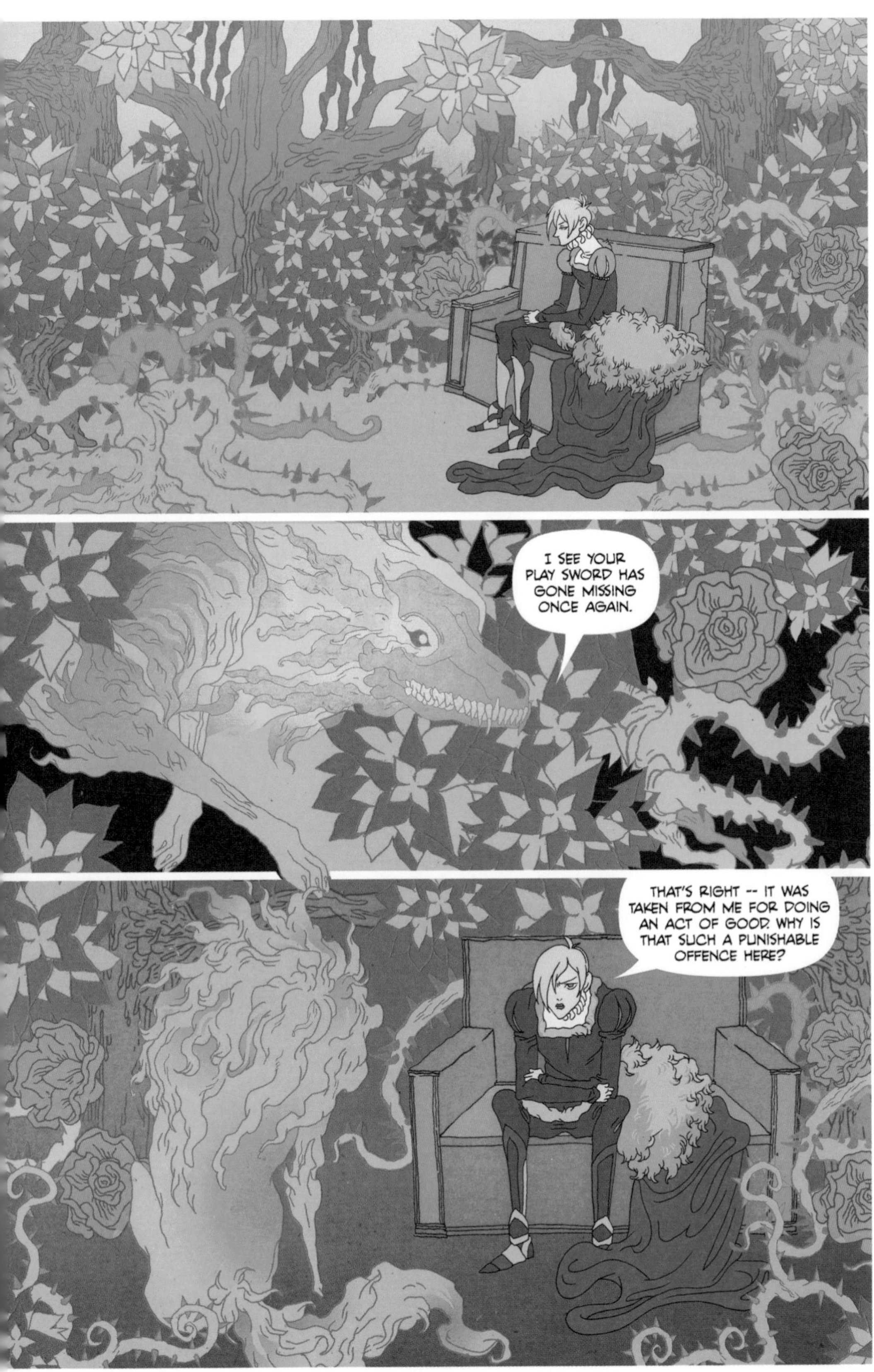
I SEE YOUR PLAY SWORD HAS GONE MISSING ONCE AGAIN.
THAT'S RIGHT -- IT WAS TAKEN FROM ME FOR DOING AN ACT OF GOOD. WHY IS THAT SUCH A PUNISHABLE OFFENCE HERE?

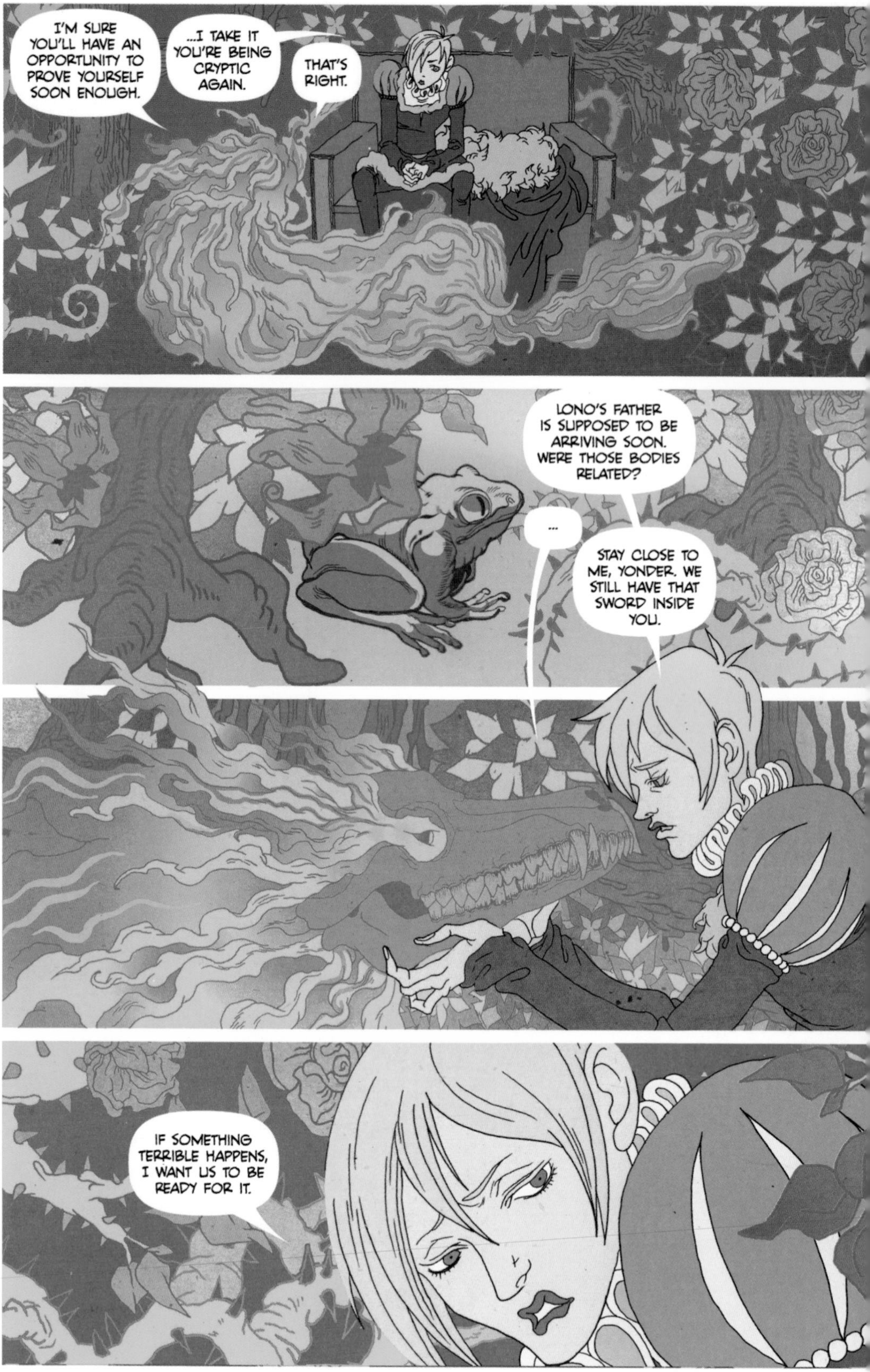
I'M SURE YOU'LL HAVE AN OPPORTUNITY TO PROVE YOURSELF SOON ENOUGH.
...I TAKE IT YOU'RE BEING CRYPTIC AGAIN.
THAT'S RIGHT.
LONO'S FATHER IS SUPPOSED TO BE ARRIVING SOON. WERE THOSE BODIES RELATED?
...
STAY CLOSE TO ME, YONDER. WE STILL HAVE THAT SWORD INSIDE YOU.
IF SOMETHING TERRIBLE HAPPENS, I WANT US TO BE READY FOR IT.

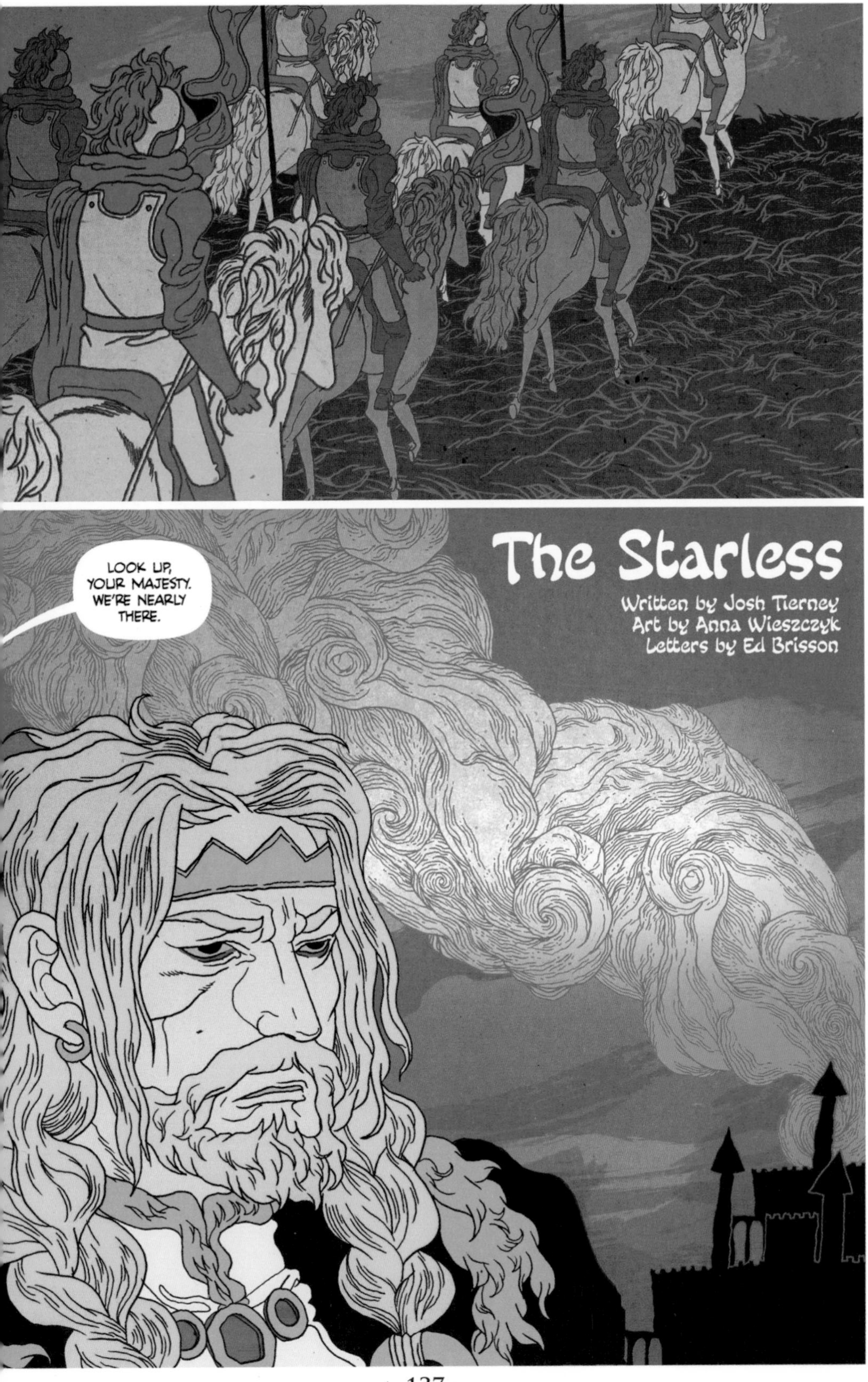
LOOK UP, YOUR MAJESTY. WE'RE NEARLY THERE.
The Starless
Written by Josh Tierney
Art by Anna Wieszczyk
Letters by Ed Brisson

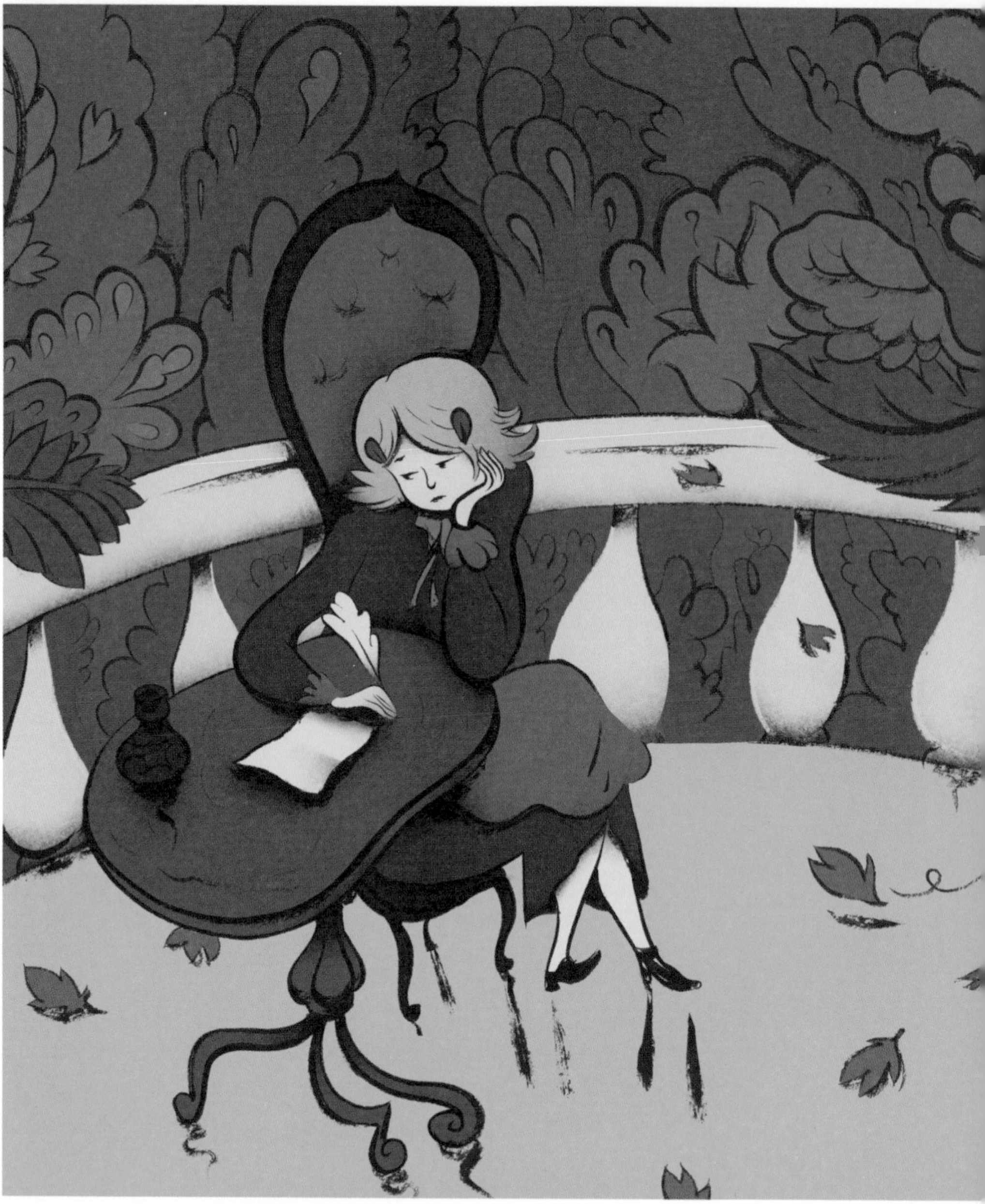

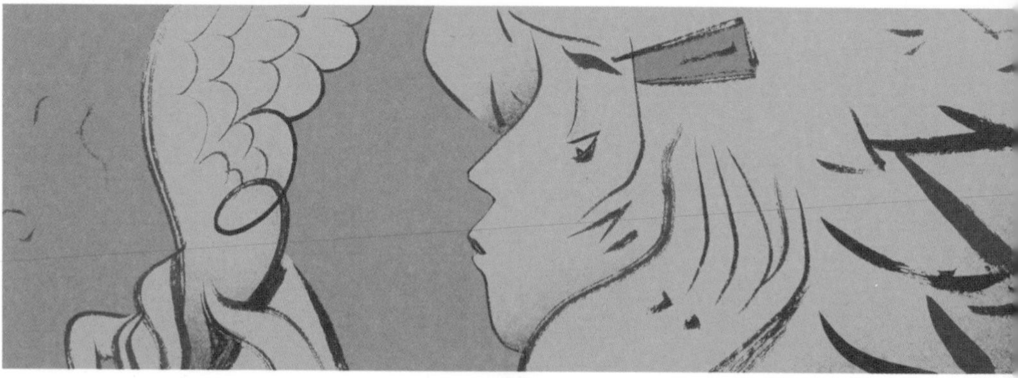

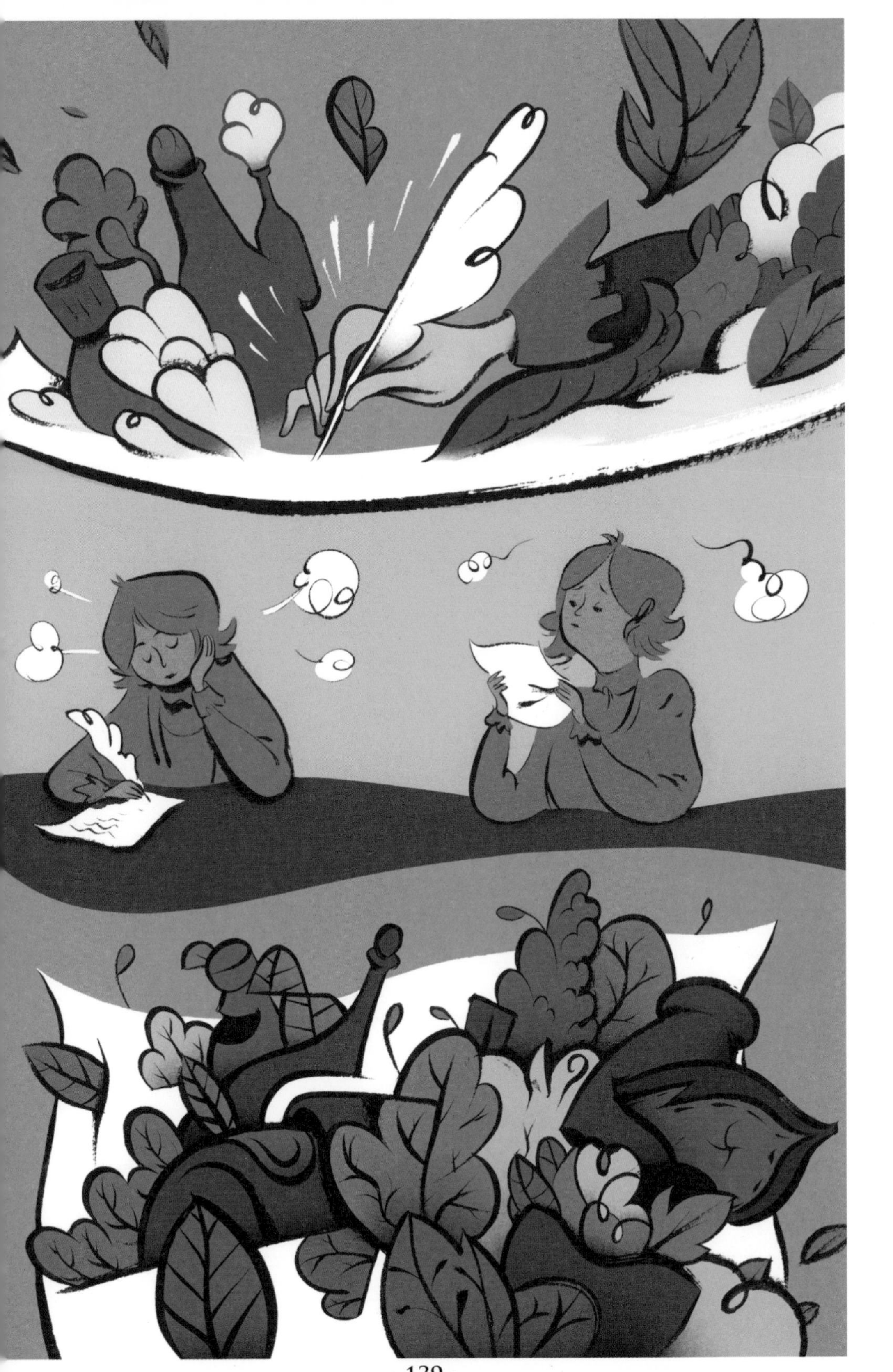

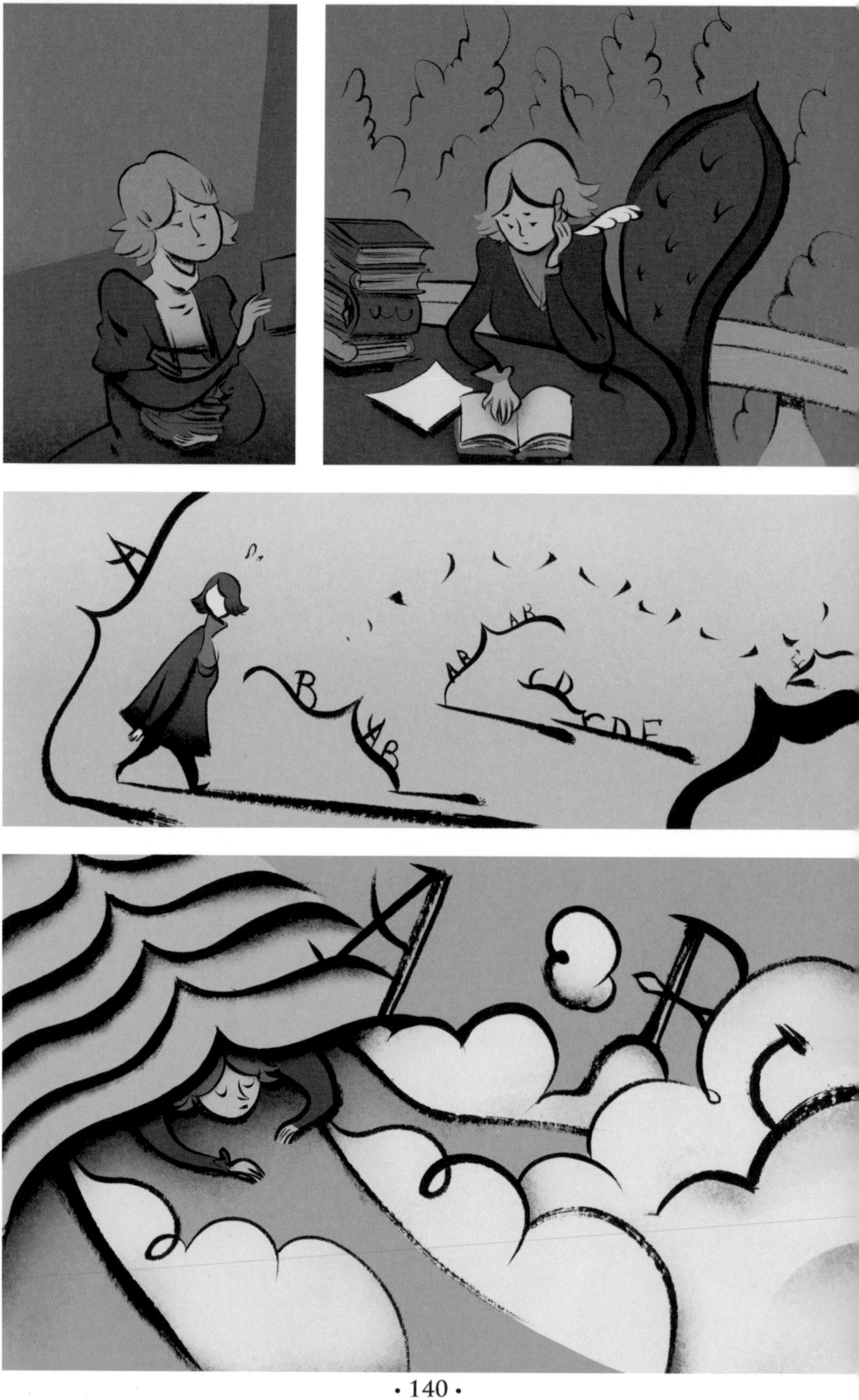

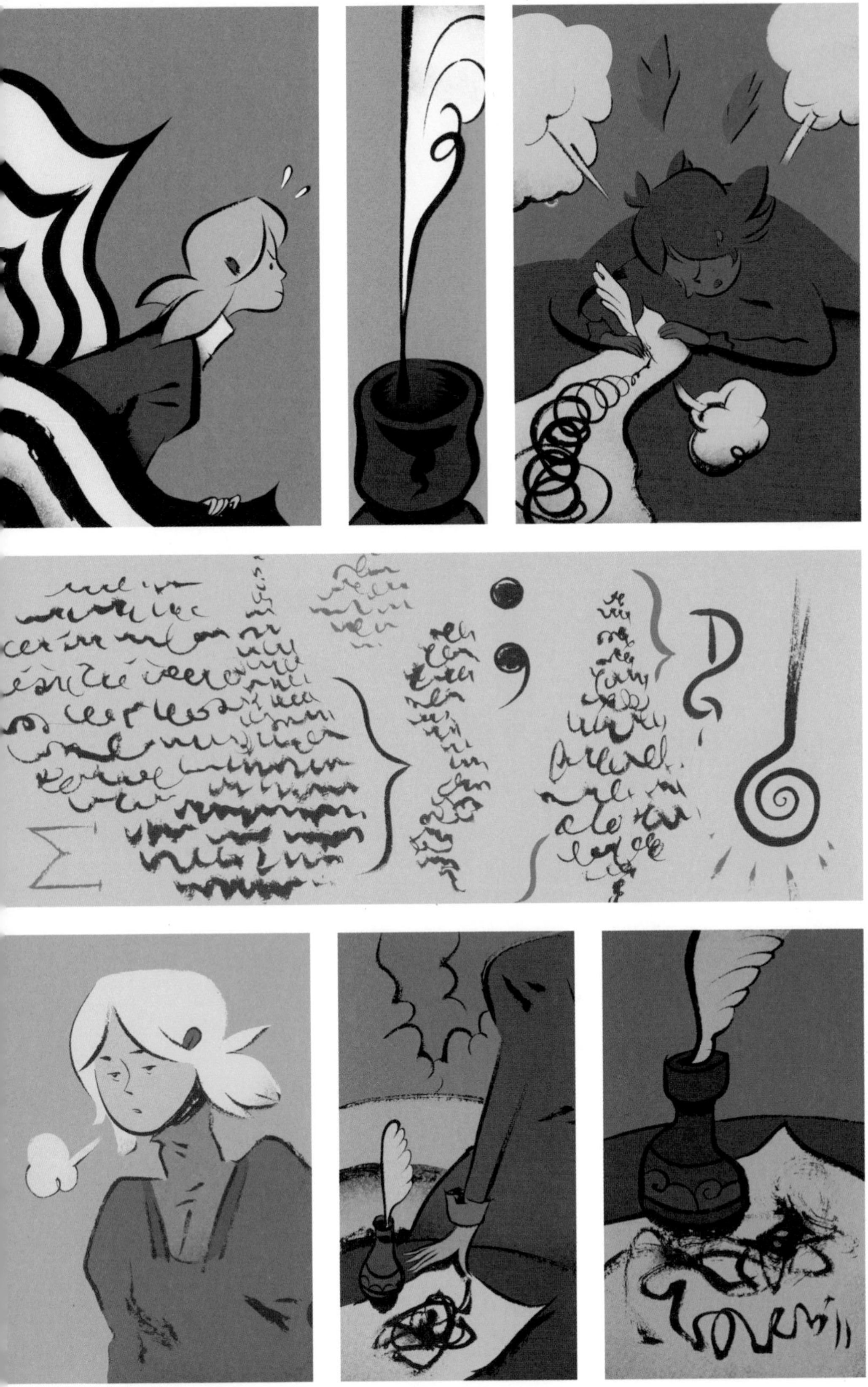

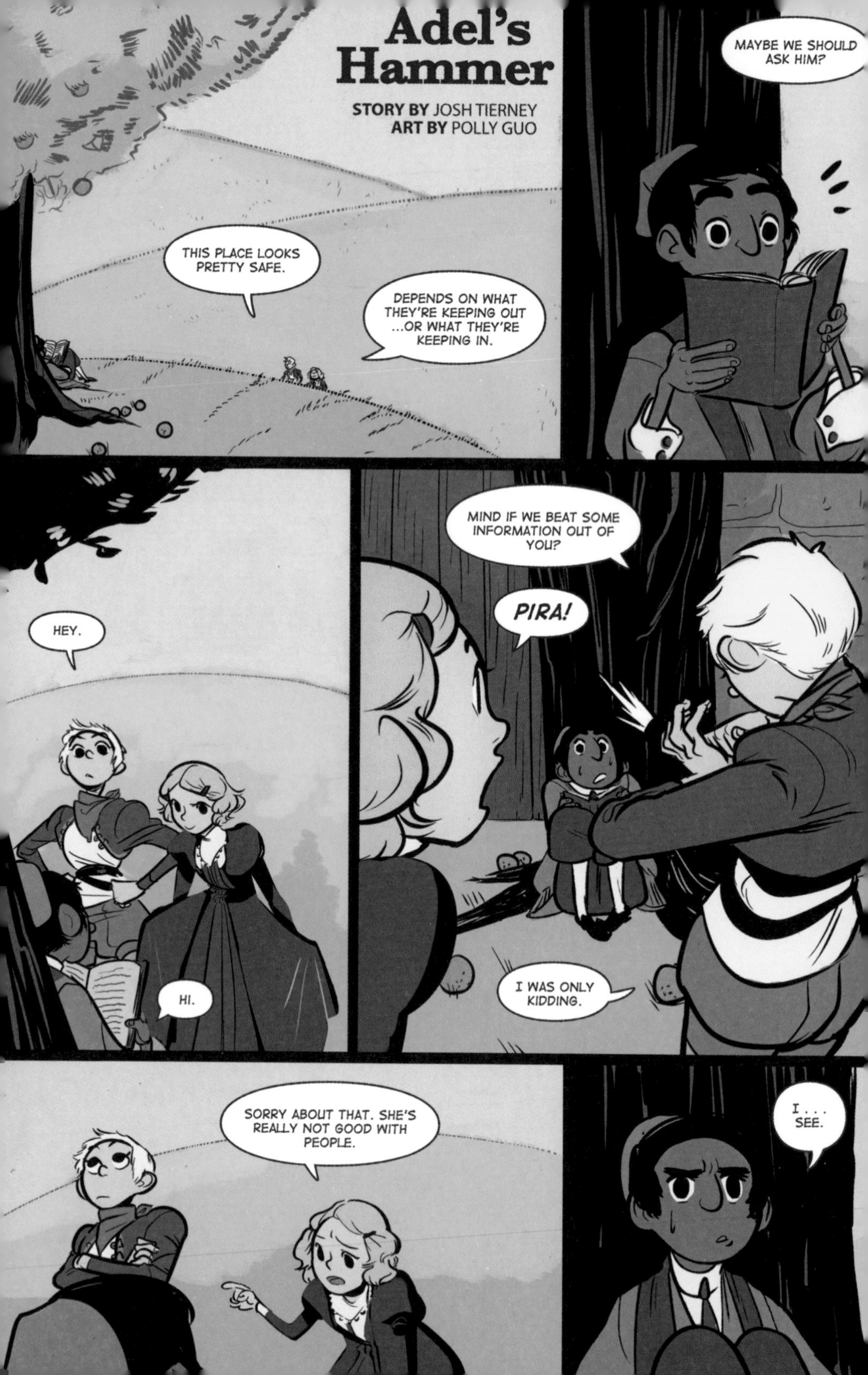
Adel's Hammer
STORY BY JOSH TIERNEY
ART BY POLLY GUO
THIS PLACE LOOKS PRETTY SAFE.
DEPENDS ON WHAT THEY'RE KEEPING OUT ...OR WHAT THEY'RE KEEPING IN.
MAYBE WE SHOULD ASK HIM?
HEY.
HI.
MIND IF WE BEAT SOME INFORMATION OUT OF YOU?
PIRA!
I WAS ONLY KIDDING.
SORRY ABOUT THAT. SHE'S REALLY NOT GOOD WITH PEOPLE.
I . . . SEE.

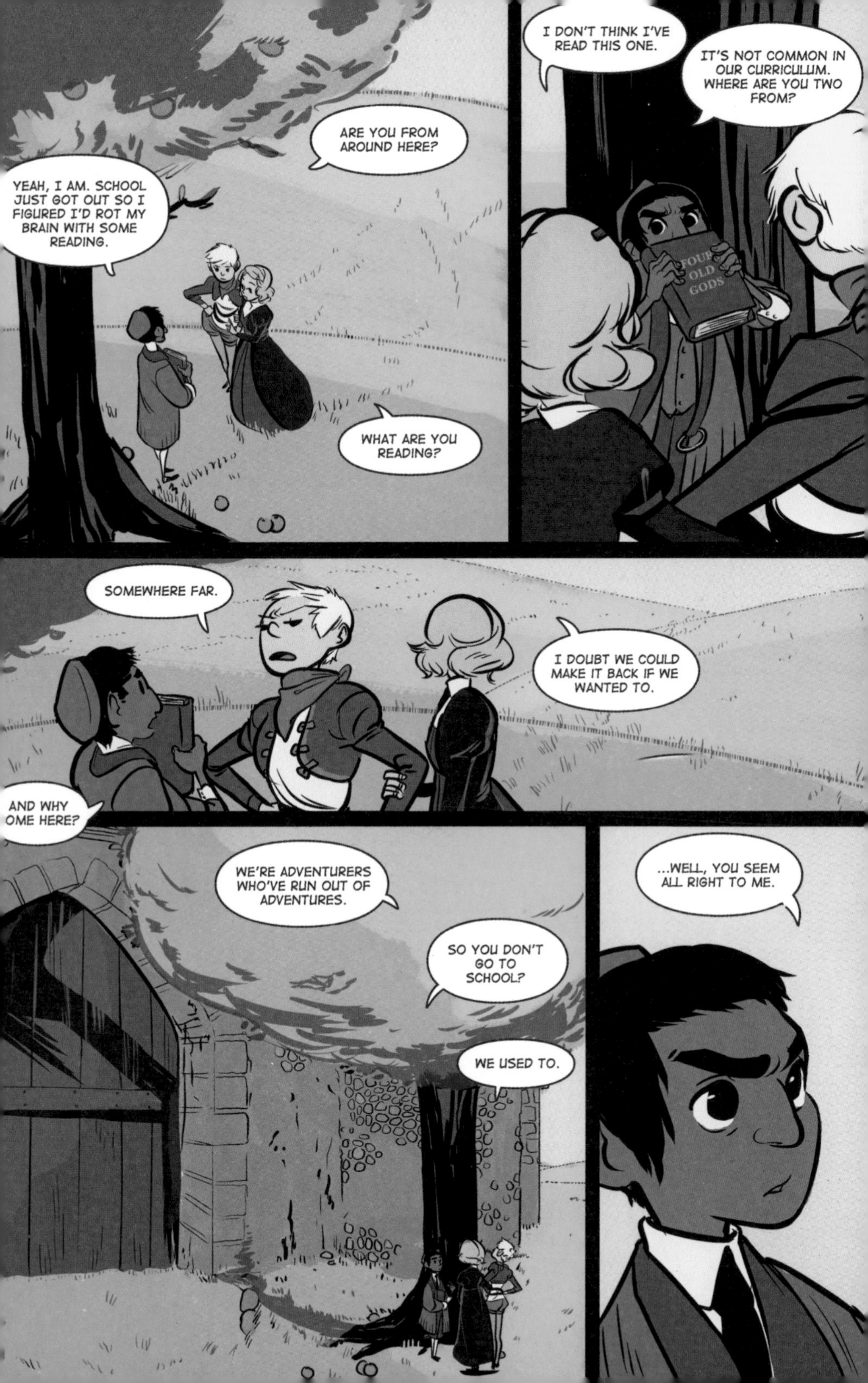
ARE YOU FROM AROUND HERE?
YEAH, I AM. SCHOOL JUST GOT OUT SO I FIGURED I'D ROT MY BRAIN WITH SOME READING.
WHAT ARE YOU READING?
I DON'T THINK I'VE READ THIS ONE.
FOUR OLD GODS
IT'S NOT COMMON IN OUR CURRICULUM. WHERE ARE YOU TWO FROM?
SOMEWHERE FAR.
I DOUBT WE COULD MAKE IT BACK IF WE WANTED TO.
AND WHY OME HERE?
WE'RE ADVENTURERS WHO'VE RUN OUT OF ADVENTURES.
SO YOU DON'T GO TO SCHOOL?
WE USED TO.
...WELL, YOU SEEM ALL RIGHT TO ME.

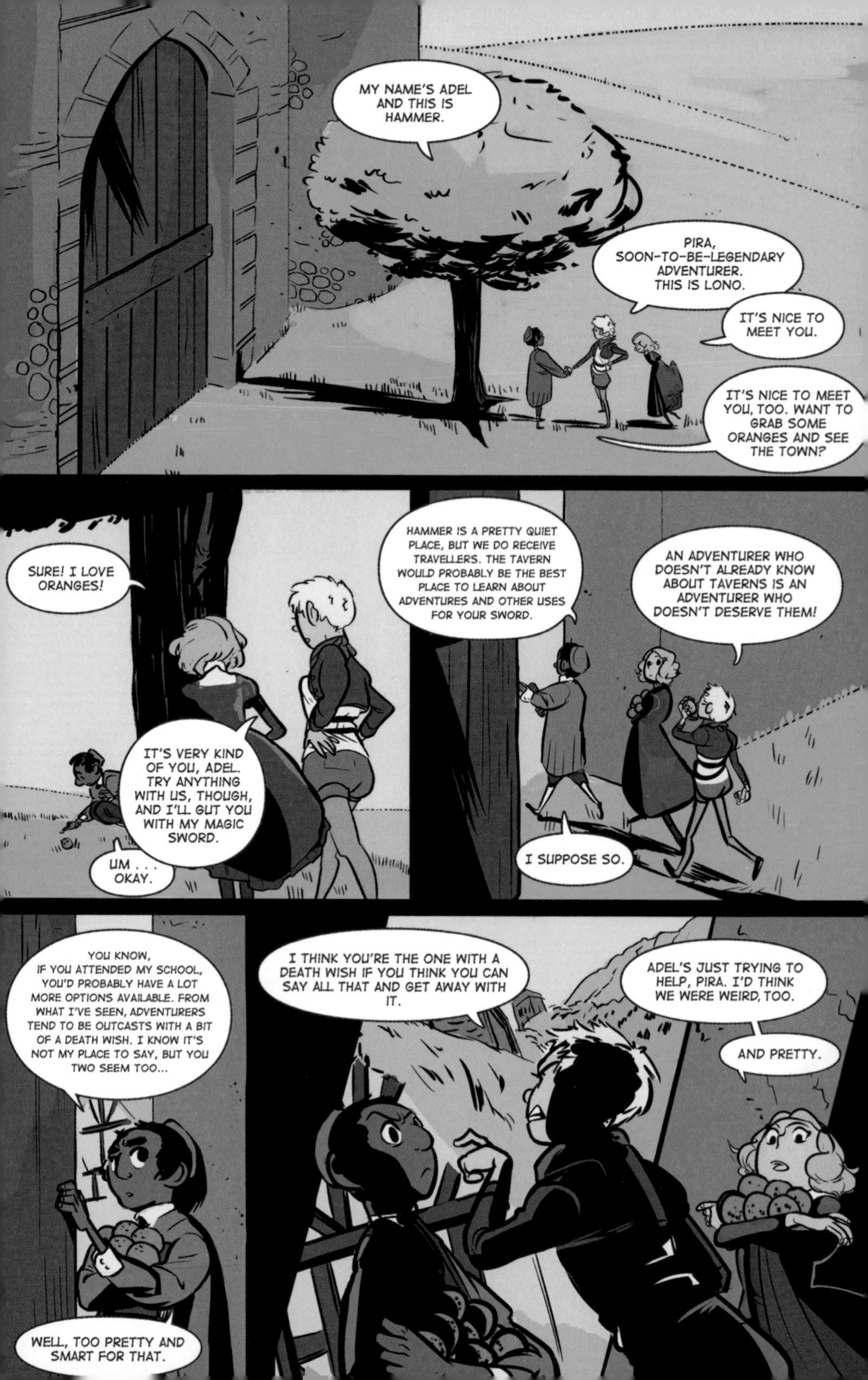
MY NAME'S ADEL AND THIS IS HAMMER.
PIRA, SOON-TO-BE-LEGENDARY ADVENTURER. THIS IS LONO.
IT'S NICE TO MEET YOU.
IT'S NICE TO MEET YOU, TOO. WANT TO GRAB SOME ORANGES AND SEE THE TOWN?
SURE! I LOVE ORANGES!
IT'S VERY KIND OF YOU, ADEL. TRY ANYTHING WITH US, THOUGH, AND I'LL GUT YOU WITH MY MAGIC SWORD.
UM . . . OKAY.
HAMMER IS A PRETTY QUIET PLACE, BUT WE DO RECEIVE TRAVELLERS. THE TAVERN WOULD PROBABLY BE THE BEST PLACE TO LEARN ABOUT ADVENTURES AND OTHER USES FOR YOUR SWORD.
AN ADVENTURER WHO DOESN'T ALREADY KNOW ABOUT TAVERNS IS AN ADVENTURER WHO DOESN'T DESERVE THEM!
I SUPPOSE SO.
YOU KNOW, IF YOU ATTENDED MY SCHOOL, YOU'D PROBABLY HAVE A LOT MORE OPTIONS AVAILABLE. FROM WHAT I'VE SEEN, ADVENTURERS TEND TO BE OUTCASTS WITH A BIT OF A DEATH WISH. I KNOW IT'S NOT MY PLACE TO SAY, BUT YOU TWO SEEM TOO...
WELL, TOO PRETTY AND SMART FOR THAT.
I THINK YOU'RE THE ONE WITH A DEATH WISH IF YOU THINK YOU CAN SAY ALL THAT AND GET AWAY WITH IT.
ADEL'S JUST TRYING TO HELP, PIRA. I'D THINK WE WERE WEIRD, TOO.
AND PRETTY.

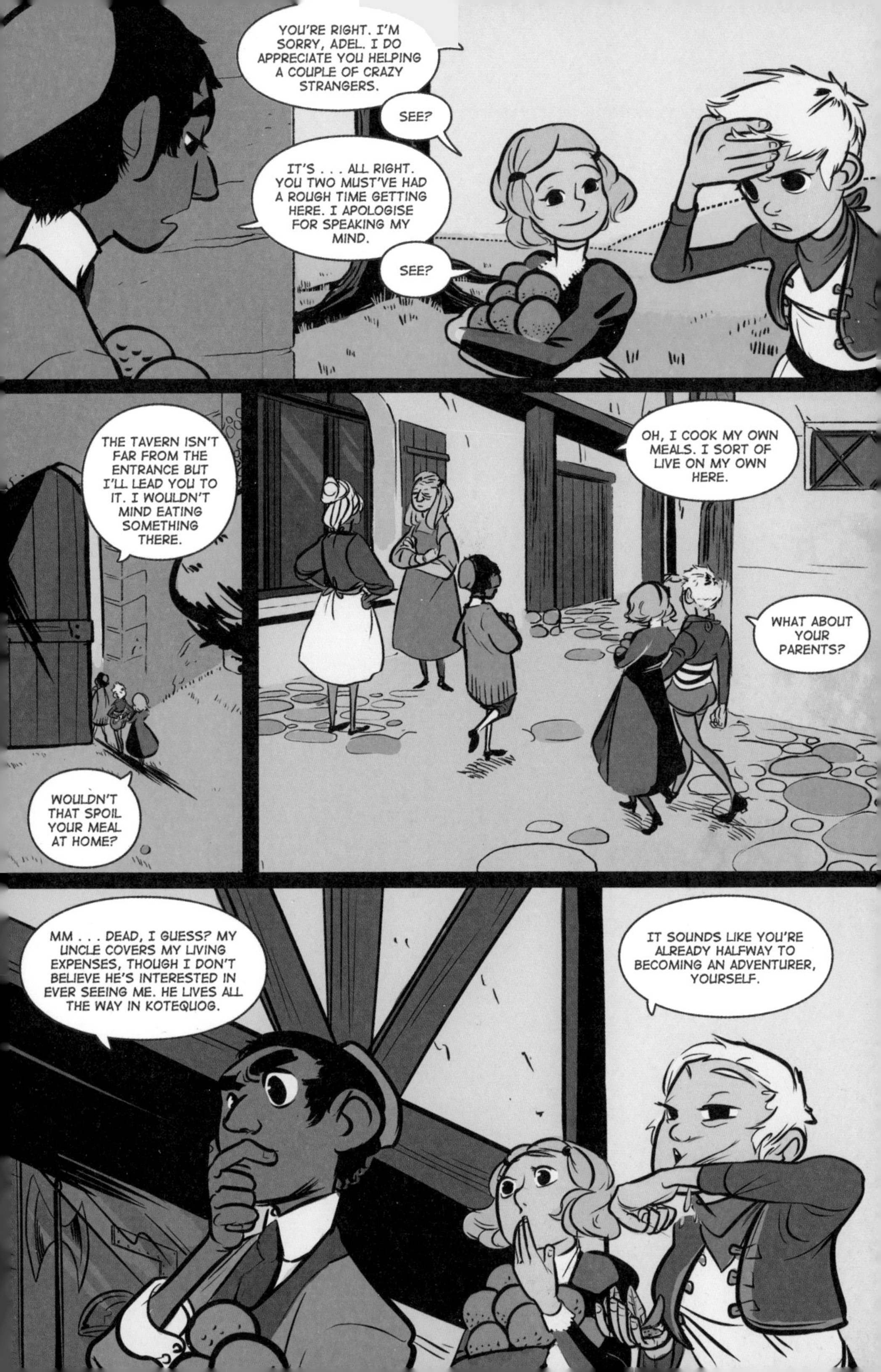
YOU'RE RIGHT. I'M SORRY, ADEL. I DO APPRECIATE YOU HELPING A COUPLE OF CRAZY STRANGERS.
SEE?
IT'S . . . ALL RIGHT. YOU TWO MUST'VE HAD A ROUGH TIME GETTING HERE. I APOLOGISE FOR SPEAKING MY MIND.
SEE?
THE TAVERN ISN'T FAR FROM THE ENTRANCE BUT I'LL LEAD YOU TO IT. I WOULDN'T MIND EATING SOMETHING THERE.
WOULDN'T THAT SPOIL YOUR MEAL AT HOME?
OH, I COOK MY OWN MEALS. I SORT OF LIVE ON MY OWN HERE.
WHAT ABOUT YOUR PARENTS?
MM . . . DEAD, I GUESS? MY UNCLE COVERS MY LIVING EXPENSES, THOUGH I DON'T BELIEVE HE'S INTERESTED IN EVER SEEING ME. HE LIVES ALL THE WAY IN KOTEQUOG.
IT SOUNDS LIKE YOU'RE ALREADY HALFWAY TO BECOMING AN ADVENTURER, YOURSELF.

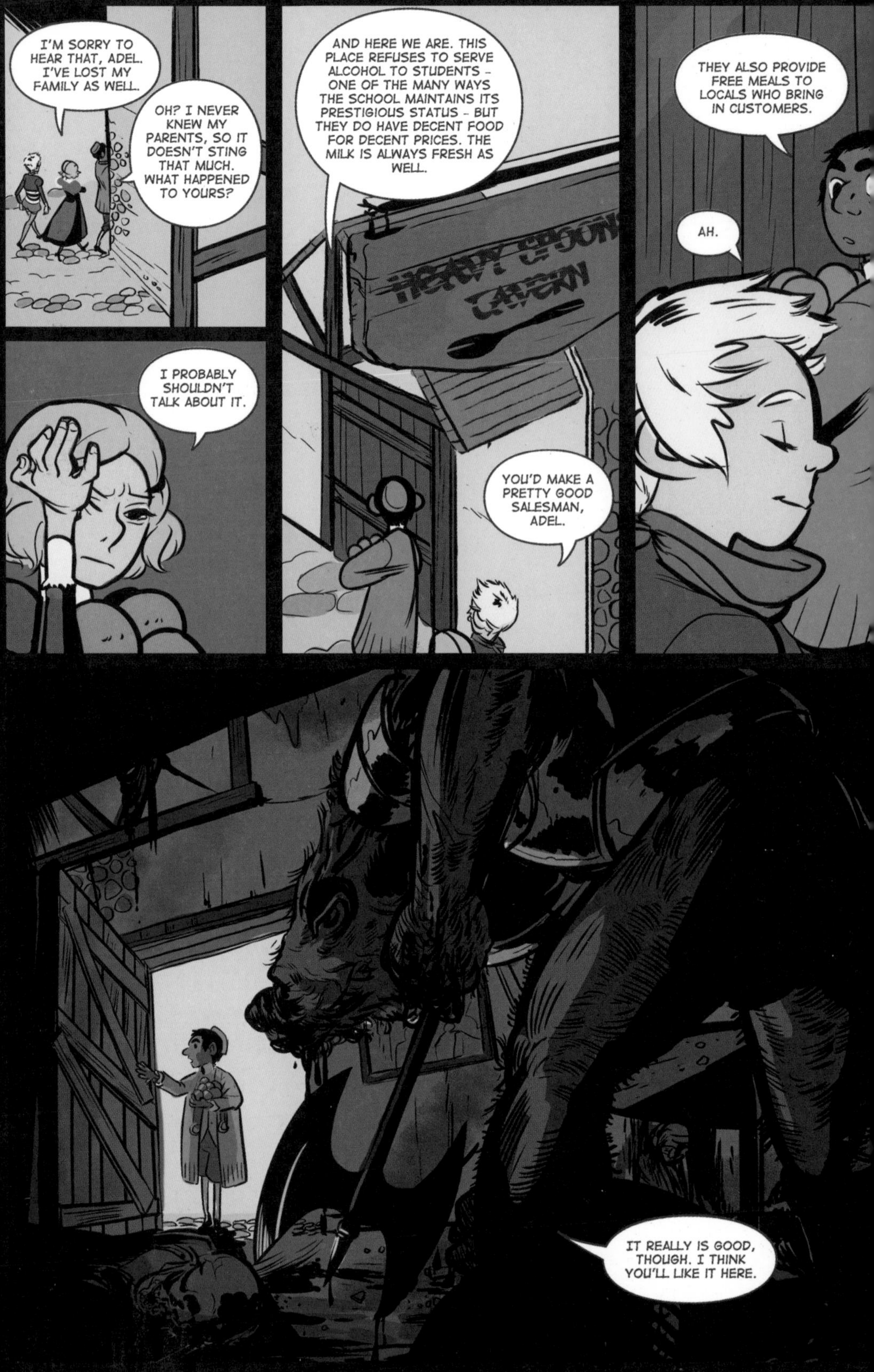
I'M SORRY TO HEAR THAT, ADEL. I'VE LOST MY FAMILY AS WELL.
OH? I NEVER KNEW MY PARENTS, SO IT DOESN'T STING THAT MUCH. WHAT HAPPENED TO YOURS?
I PROBABLY SHOULDN'T TALK ABOUT IT.
AND HERE WE ARE. THIS PLACE REFUSES TO SERVE ALCOHOL TO STUDENTS – ONE OF THE MANY WAYS THE SCHOOL MAINTAINS ITS PRESTIGIOUS STATUS – BUT THEY DO HAVE DECENT FOOD FOR DECENT PRICES. THE MILK IS ALWAYS FRESH AS WELL.
YOU'D MAKE A PRETTY GOOD SALESMAN, ADEL.
THEY ALSO PROVIDE FREE MEALS TO LOCALS WHO BRING IN CUSTOMERS.
AH.
IT REALLY IS GOOD, THOUGH. I THINK YOU'LL LIKE IT HERE.

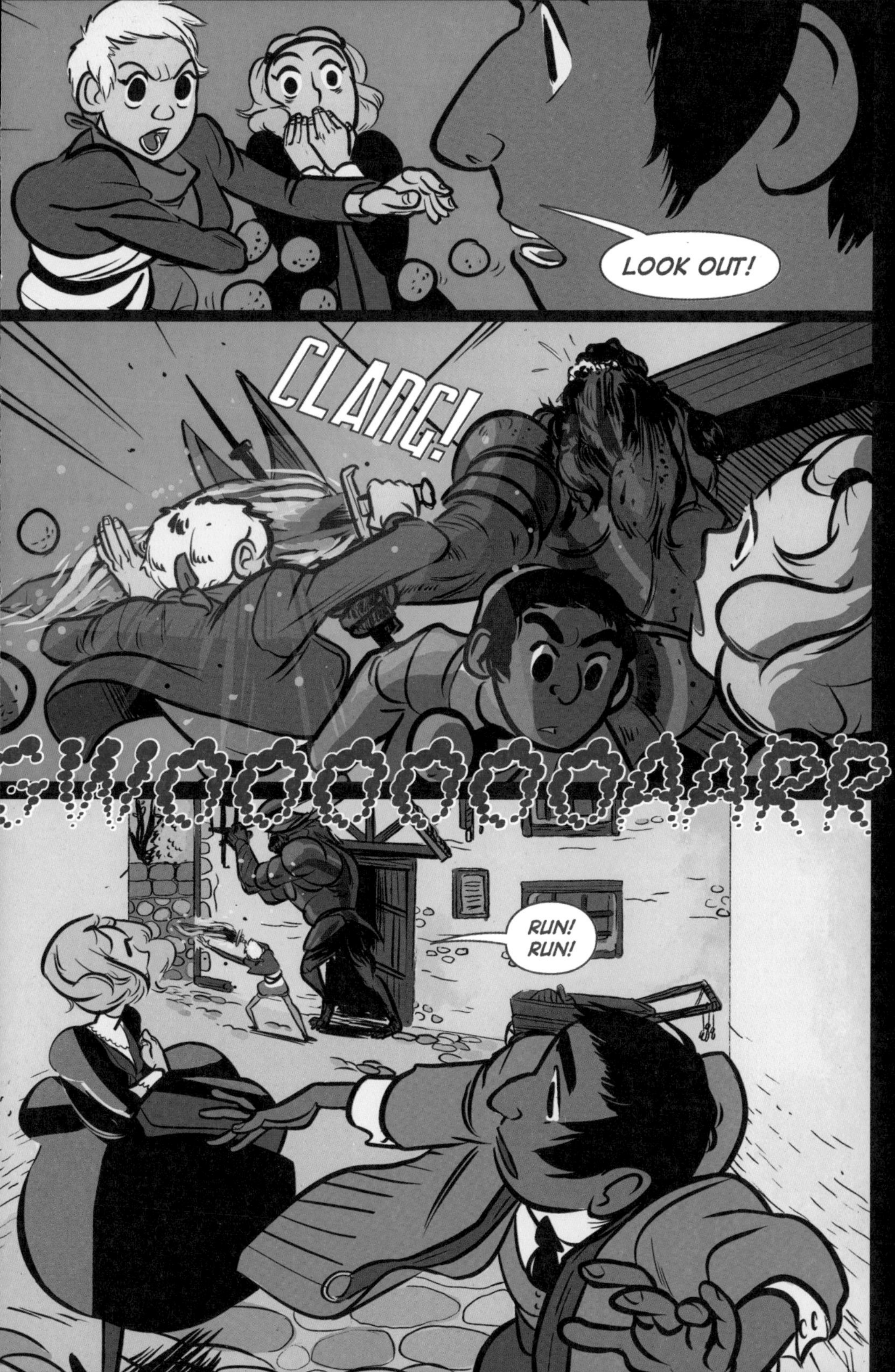
LOOK OUT!
CLANG!
GWNNNNNNNAARR
RUN! RUN!

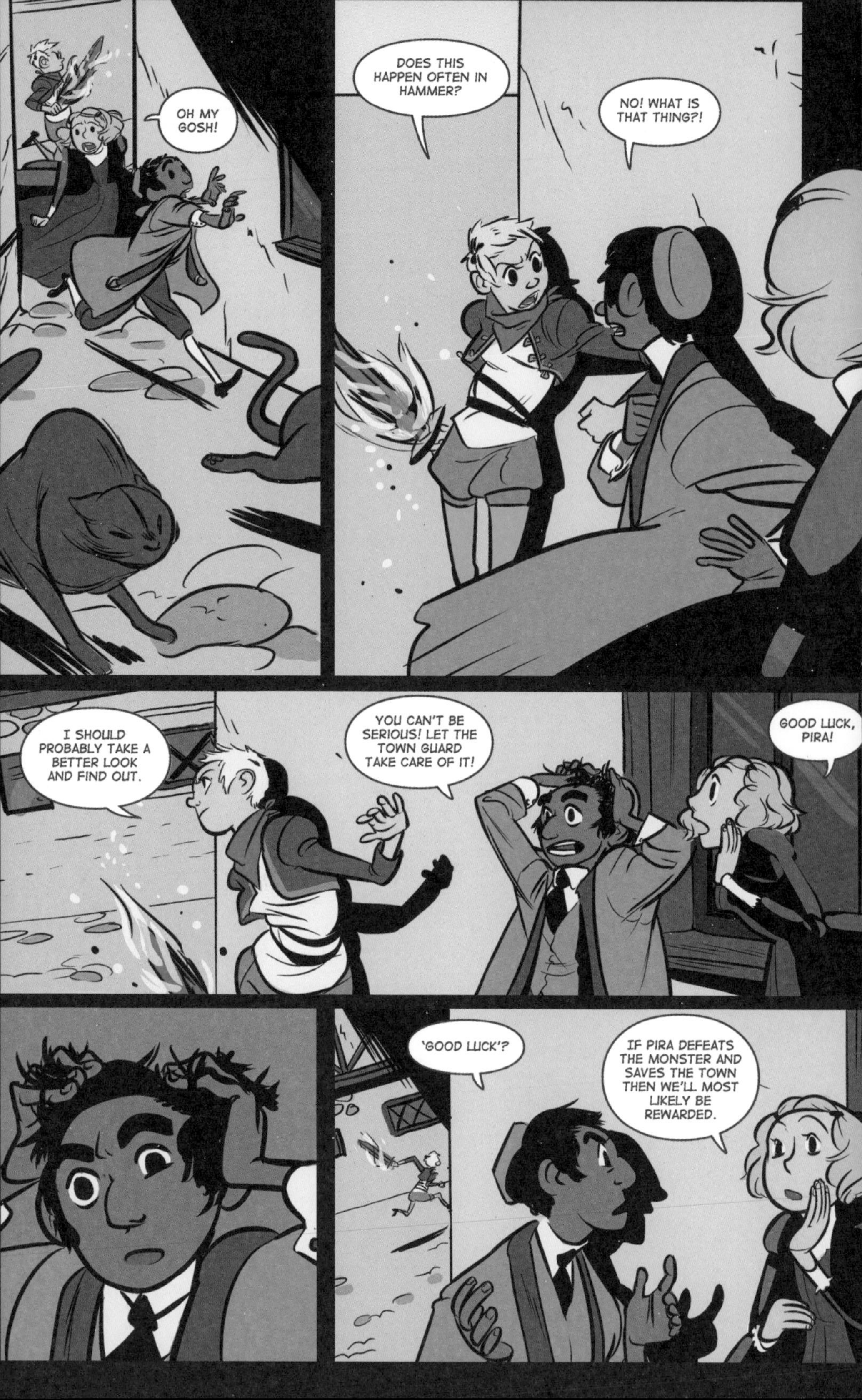
OH MY GOSH!
DOES THIS HAPPEN OFTEN IN HAMMER?
NO! WHAT IS THAT THING?!
I SHOULD PROBABLY TAKE A BETTER LOOK AND FIND OUT.
YOU CAN'T BE SERIOUS! LET THE TOWN GUARD TAKE CARE OF IT!
GOOD LUCK, PIRA!
'GOOD LUCK'?
IF PIRA DEFEATS THE MONSTER AND SAVES THE TOWN THEN WE'LL MOST LIKELY BE REWARDED.

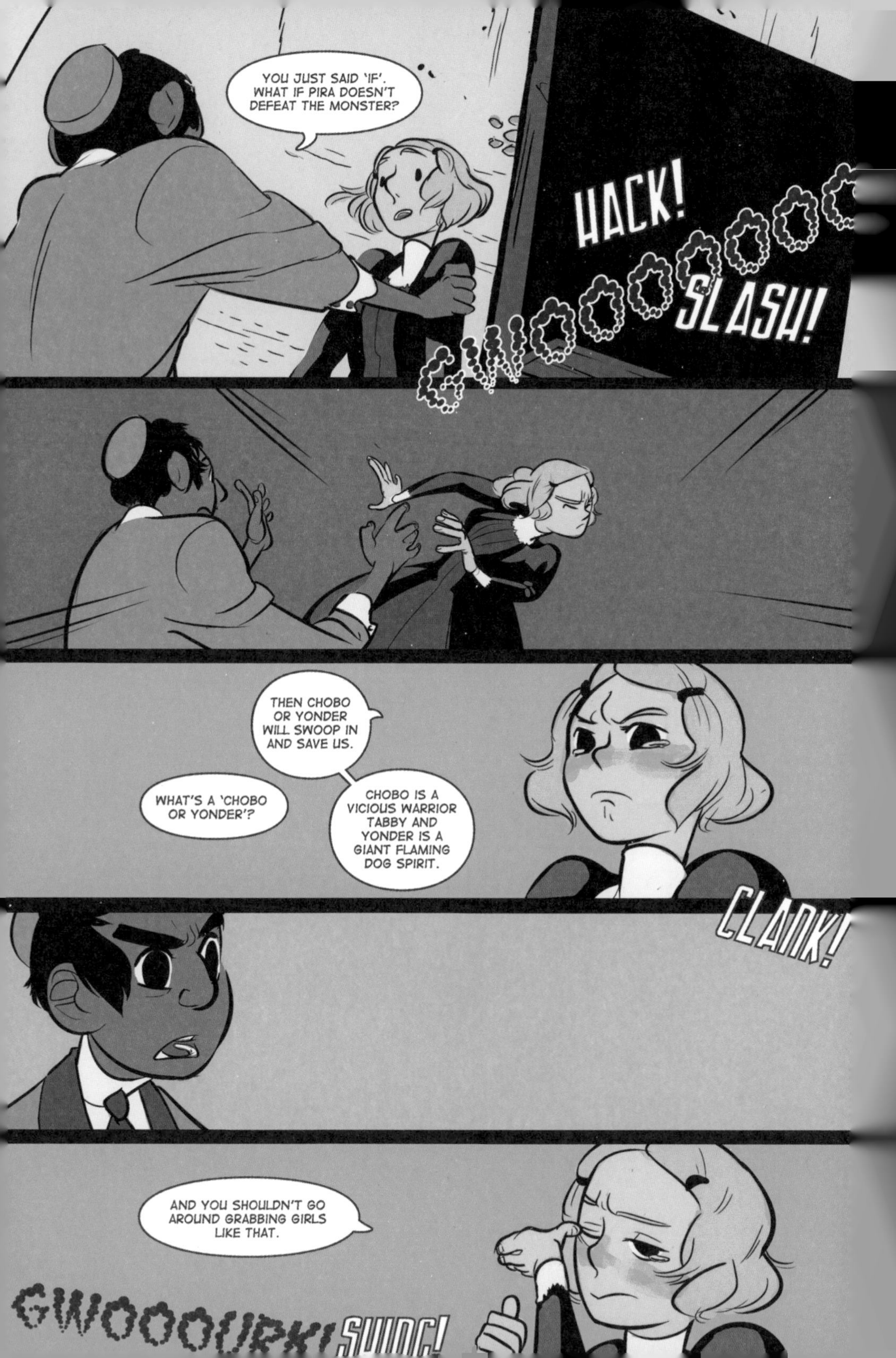
YOU JUST SAID 'IF'. WHAT IF PIRA DOESN'T DEFEAT THE MONSTER?
HACK!
GWOOOOOOOOO
SLASH!
THEN CHOBO OR YONDER WILL SWOOP IN AND SAVE US.
WHAT'S A 'CHOBO OR YONDER'?
CHOBO IS A VICIOUS WARRIOR TABBY AND YONDER IS A GIANT FLAMING DOG SPIRIT.
CLANK!
AND YOU SHOULDN'T GO AROUND GRABBING GIRLS LIKE THAT.
GWOOOURK!
SHING!

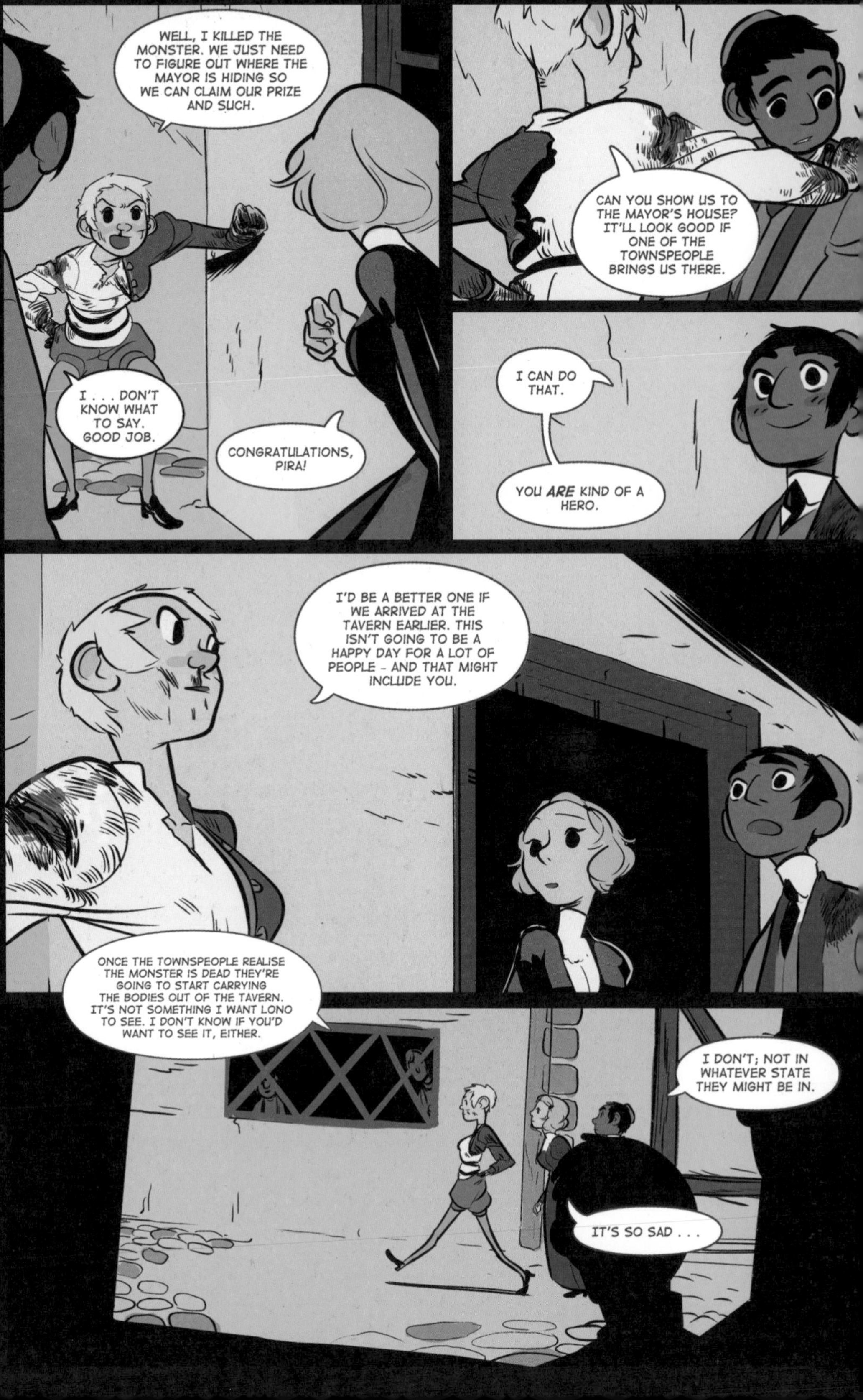
WELL, I KILLED THE MONSTER. WE JUST NEED TO FIGURE OUT WHERE THE MAYOR IS HIDING SO WE CAN CLAIM OUR PRIZE AND SUCH.
I . . . DON'T KNOW WHAT TO SAY. GOOD JOB.
CONGRATULATIONS, PIRA!
CAN YOU SHOW US TO THE MAYOR'S HOUSE? IT'LL LOOK GOOD IF ONE OF THE TOWNSPEOPLE BRINGS US THERE.
I CAN DO THAT.
YOU ***ARE*** KIND OF A HERO.
I'D BE A BETTER ONE IF WE ARRIVED AT THE TAVERN EARLIER. THIS ISN'T GOING TO BE A HAPPY DAY FOR A LOT OF PEOPLE - AND THAT MIGHT INCLUDE YOU.
ONCE THE TOWNSPEOPLE REALISE THE MONSTER IS DEAD THEY'RE GOING TO START CARRYING THE BODIES OUT OF THE TAVERN. IT'S NOT SOMETHING I WANT LONO TO SEE. I DON'T KNOW IF YOU'D WANT TO SEE IT, EITHER.
I DON'T; NOT IN WHATEVER STATE THEY MIGHT BE IN.
IT'S SO SAD . . .

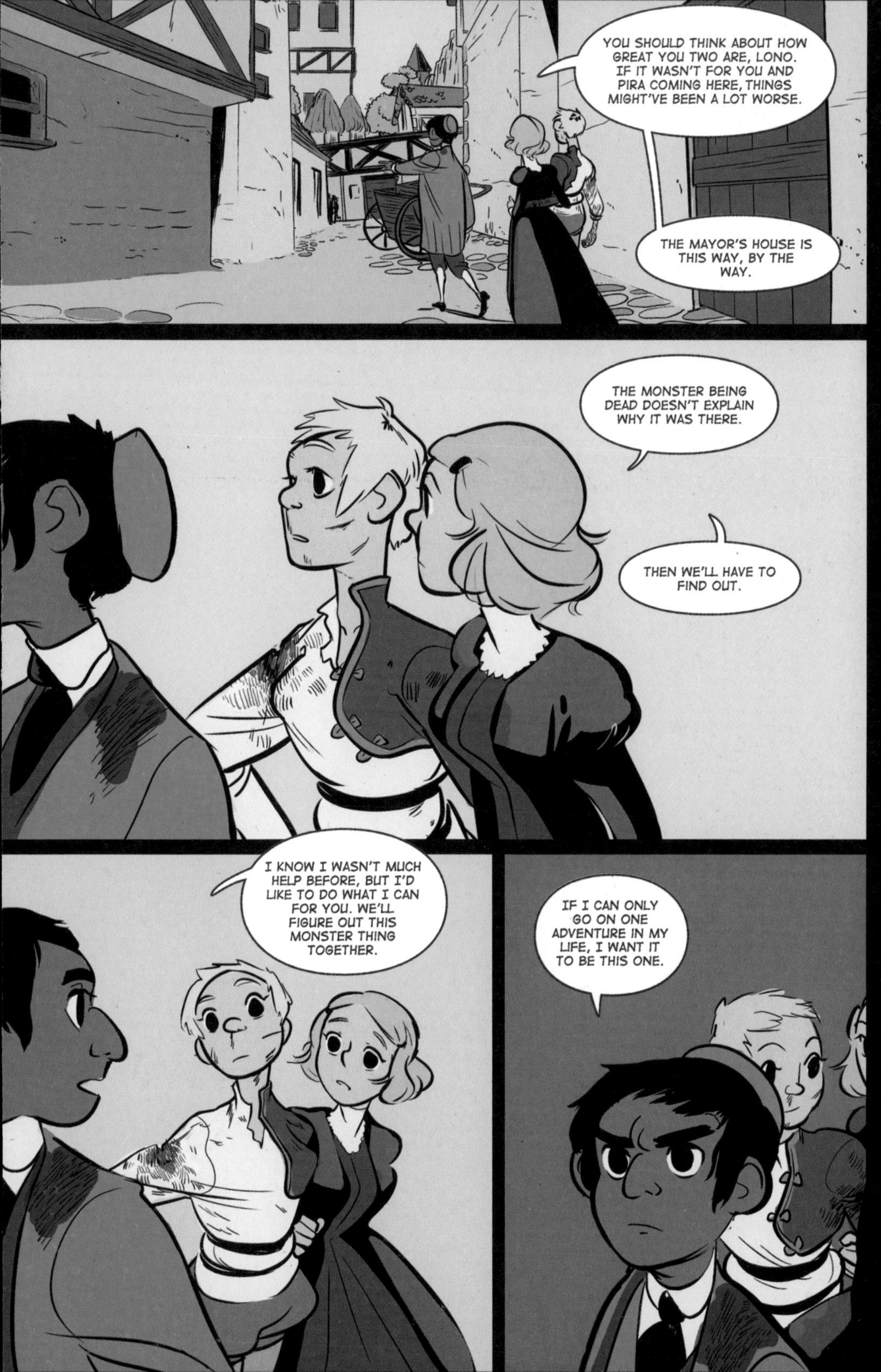

YOU SHOULD THINK ABOUT HOW GREAT YOU TWO ARE, LONO. IF IT WASN'T FOR YOU AND PIRA COMING HERE, THINGS MIGHT'VE BEEN A LOT WORSE.
THE MAYOR'S HOUSE IS THIS WAY, BY THE WAY.
THE MONSTER BEING DEAD DOESN'T EXPLAIN WHY IT WAS THERE.
THEN WE'LL HAVE TO FIND OUT.
I KNOW I WASN'T MUCH HELP BEFORE, BUT I'D LIKE TO DO WHAT I CAN FOR YOU. WE'LL FIGURE OUT THIS MONSTER THING TOGETHER.
IF I CAN ONLY GO ON ONE ADVENTURE IN MY LIFE, I WANT IT TO BE THIS ONE.

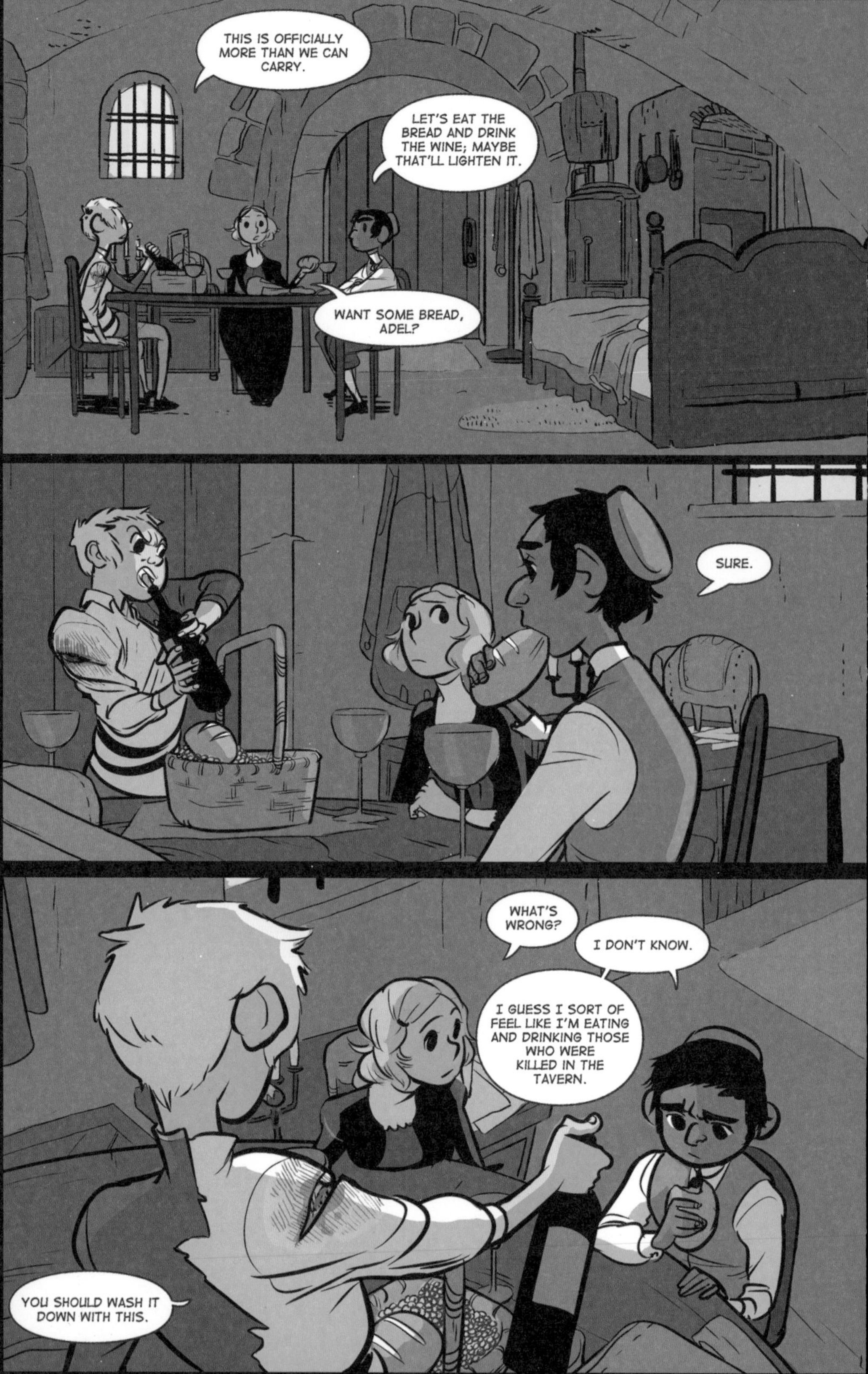
THIS IS OFFICIALLY MORE THAN WE CAN CARRY.
LET'S EAT THE BREAD AND DRINK THE WINE; MAYBE THAT'LL LIGHTEN IT.
WANT SOME BREAD, ADEL?
SURE.
WHAT'S WRONG?
I DON'T KNOW.
I GUESS I SORT OF FEEL LIKE I'M EATING AND DRINKING THOSE WHO WERE KILLED IN THE TAVERN.
YOU SHOULD WASH IT DOWN WITH THIS.

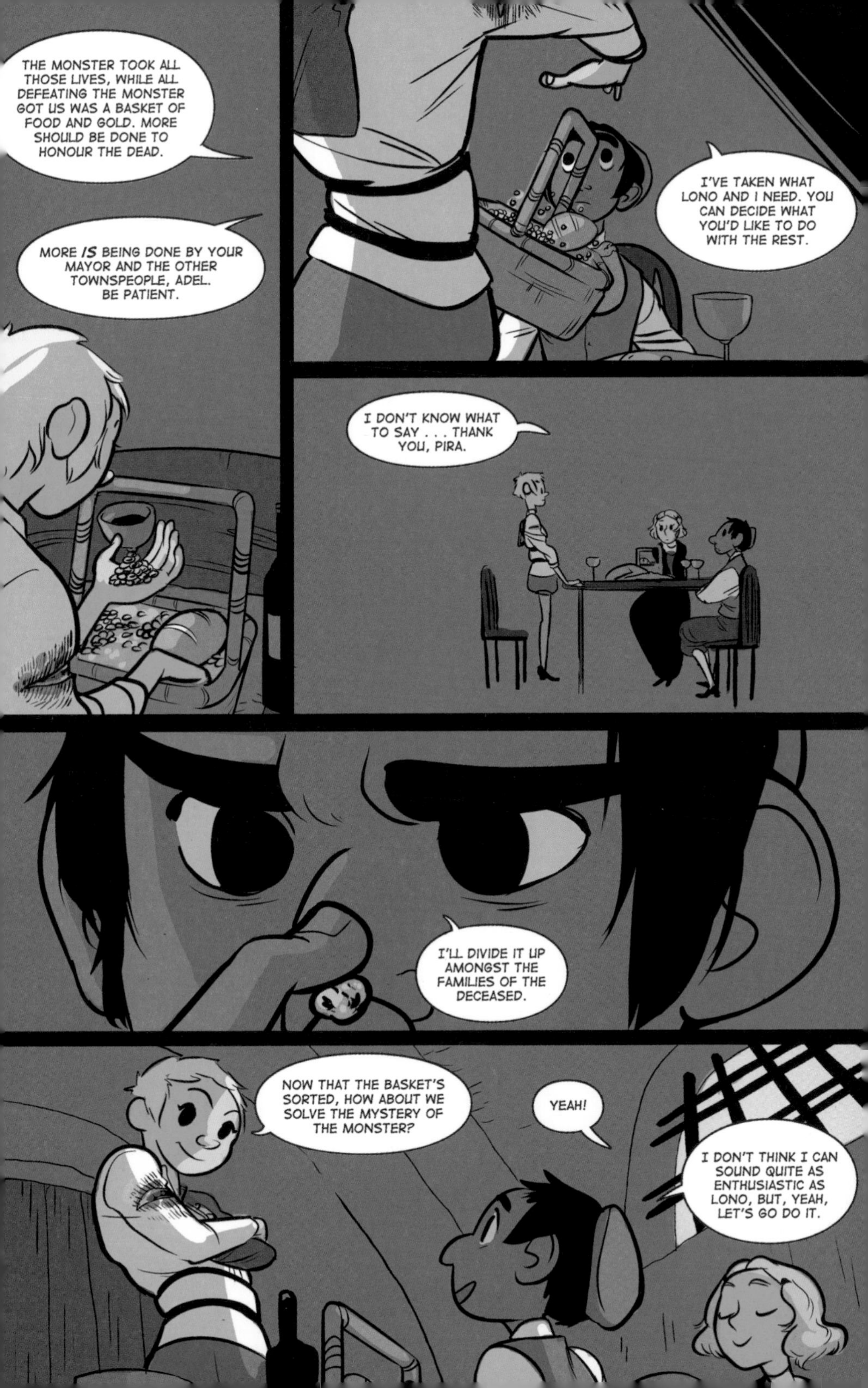
THE MONSTER TOOK ALL THOSE LIVES, WHILE ALL DEFEATING THE MONSTER GOT US WAS A BASKET OF FOOD AND GOLD. MORE SHOULD BE DONE TO HONOUR THE DEAD.
MORE *IS* BEING DONE BY YOUR MAYOR AND THE OTHER TOWNSPEOPLE, ADEL. BE PATIENT.
I'VE TAKEN WHAT LONO AND I NEED. YOU CAN DECIDE WHAT YOU'D LIKE TO DO WITH THE REST.
I DON'T KNOW WHAT TO SAY . . . THANK YOU, PIRA.
I'LL DIVIDE IT UP AMONGST THE FAMILIES OF THE DECEASED.
NOW THAT THE BASKET'S SORTED, HOW ABOUT WE SOLVE THE MYSTERY OF THE MONSTER?
YEAH!
I DON'T THINK I CAN SOUND QUITE AS ENTHUSIASTIC AS LONO, BUT, YEAH, LET'S GO DO IT.

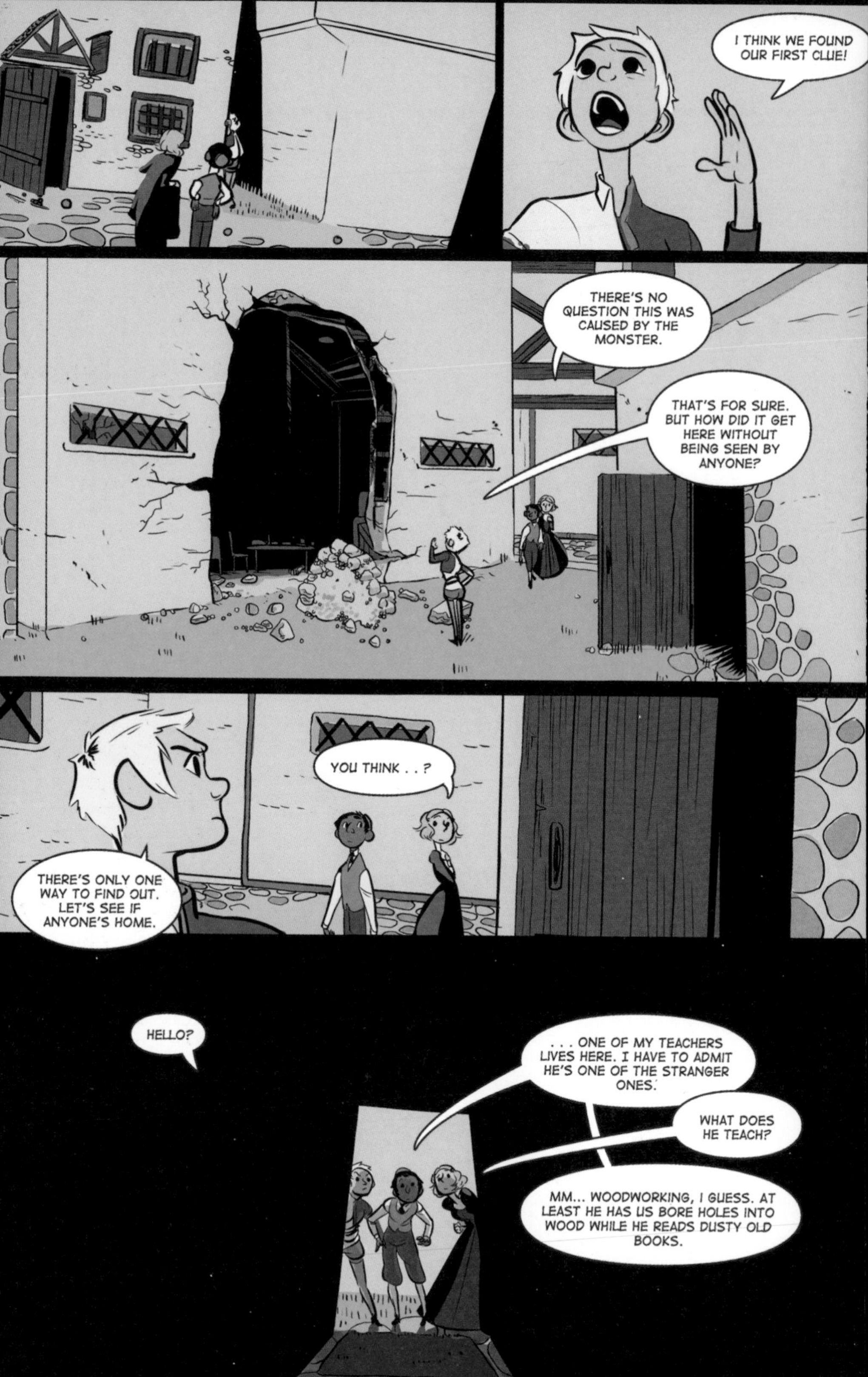
I THINK WE FOUND OUR FIRST CLUE!
THERE'S NO QUESTION THIS WAS CAUSED BY THE MONSTER.
THAT'S FOR SURE. BUT HOW DID IT GET HERE WITHOUT BEING SEEN BY ANYONE?
YOU THINK . . ?
THERE'S ONLY ONE WAY TO FIND OUT. LET'S SEE IF ANYONE'S HOME.
HELLO?
. . . ONE OF MY TEACHERS LIVES HERE. I HAVE TO ADMIT HE'S ONE OF THE STRANGER ONES.
WHAT DOES HE TEACH?
MM... WOODWORKING, I GUESS. AT LEAST HE HAS US BORE HOLES INTO WOOD WHILE HE READS DUSTY OLD BOOKS.

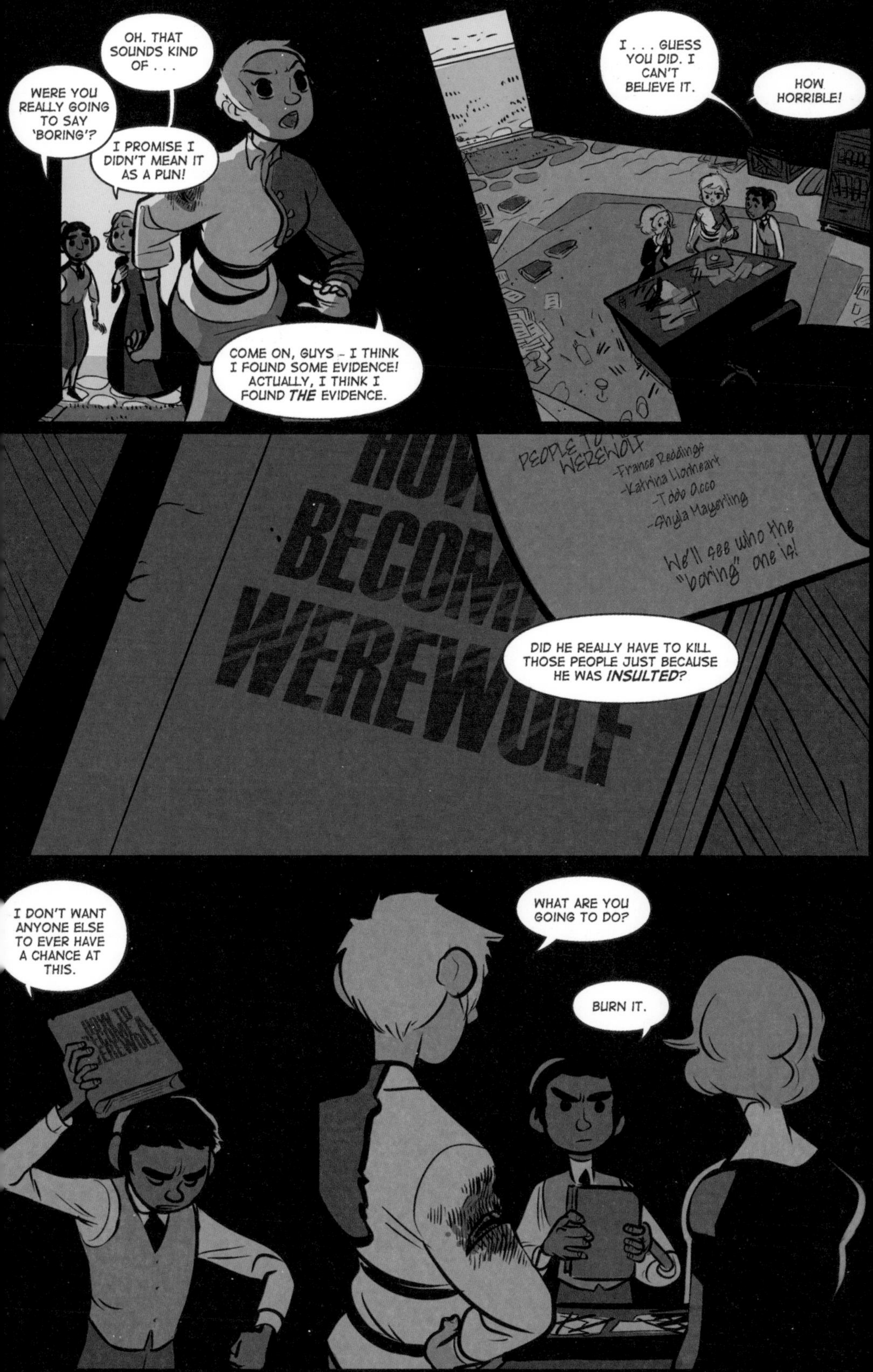
WERE YOU REALLY GOING TO SAY 'BORING'?
OH. THAT SOUNDS KIND OF . . .
I PROMISE I DIDN'T MEAN IT AS A PUN!
COME ON, GUYS – I THINK I FOUND SOME EVIDENCE! ACTUALLY, I THINK I FOUND ***THE*** EVIDENCE.
I . . . GUESS YOU DID. I CAN'T BELIEVE IT.
HOW HORRIBLE!
BECOM
WEREWOLF
PEOPLE TO
WEREWOLF
-France Reddings
-Katrina Lionheart
-Todd Acco
-Shyla Mayerling
We'll see who the "boring" one is!
DID HE REALLY HAVE TO KILL THOSE PEOPLE JUST BECAUSE HE WAS ***INSULTED***?
I DON'T WANT ANYONE ELSE TO EVER HAVE A CHANCE AT THIS.
WHAT ARE YOU GOING TO DO?
BURN IT.

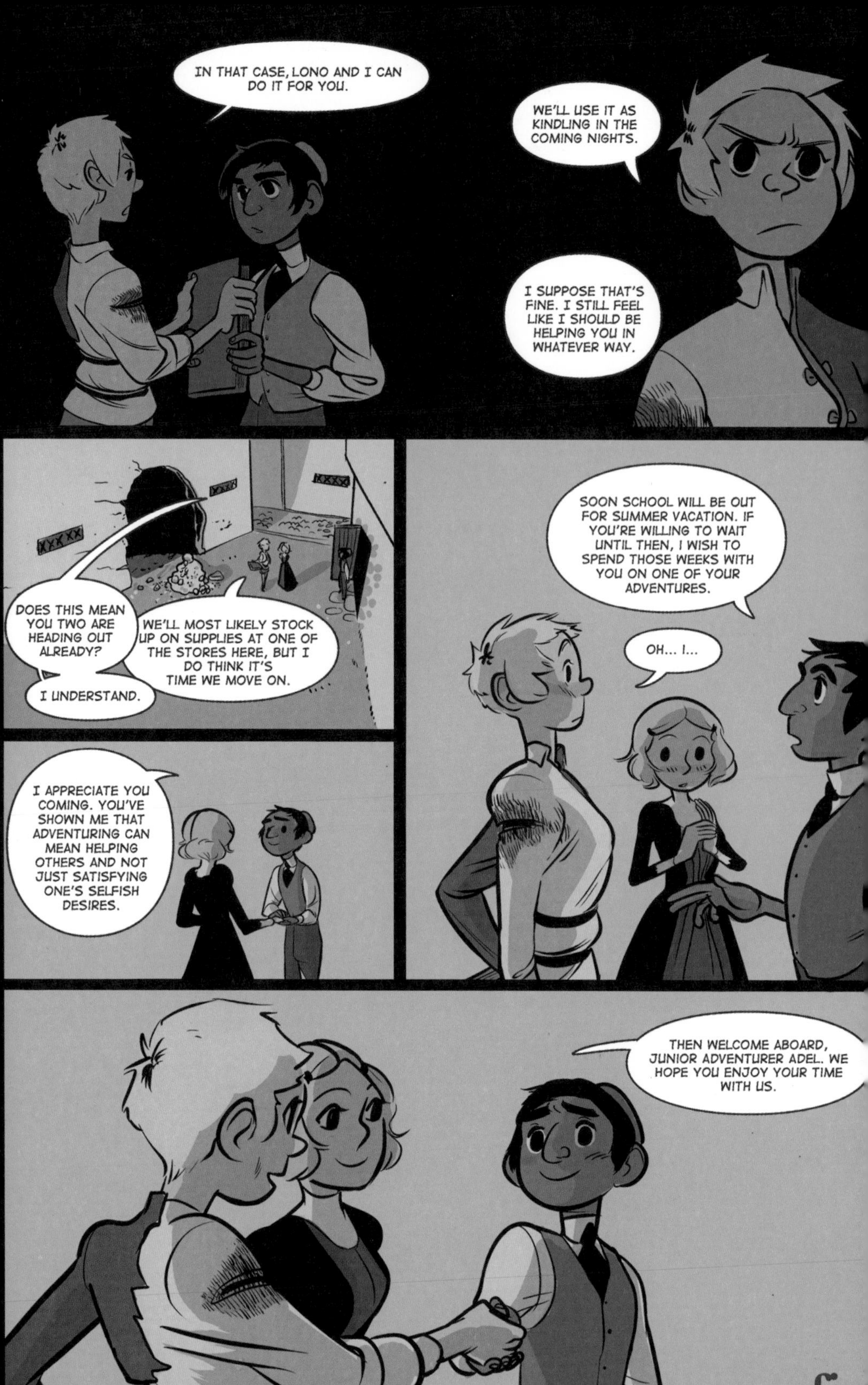
IN THAT CASE, LONO AND I CAN DO IT FOR YOU.
WE'LL USE IT AS KINDLING IN THE COMING NIGHTS.
I SUPPOSE THAT'S FINE. I STILL FEEL LIKE I SHOULD BE HELPING YOU IN WHATEVER WAY.
DOES THIS MEAN YOU TWO ARE HEADING OUT ALREADY?
WE'LL MOST LIKELY STOCK UP ON SUPPLIES AT ONE OF THE STORES HERE, BUT I DO THINK IT'S TIME WE MOVE ON.
I UNDERSTAND.
I APPRECIATE YOU COMING. YOU'VE SHOWN ME THAT ADVENTURING CAN MEAN HELPING OTHERS AND NOT JUST SATISFYING ONE'S SELFISH DESIRES.
SOON SCHOOL WILL BE OUT FOR SUMMER VACATION. IF YOU'RE WILLING TO WAIT UNTIL THEN, I WISH TO SPEND THOSE WEEKS WITH YOU ON ONE OF YOUR ADVENTURES.
OH... I...
THEN WELCOME ABOARD, JUNIOR ADVENTURER ADEL. WE HOPE YOU ENJOY YOUR TIME WITH US.
fin

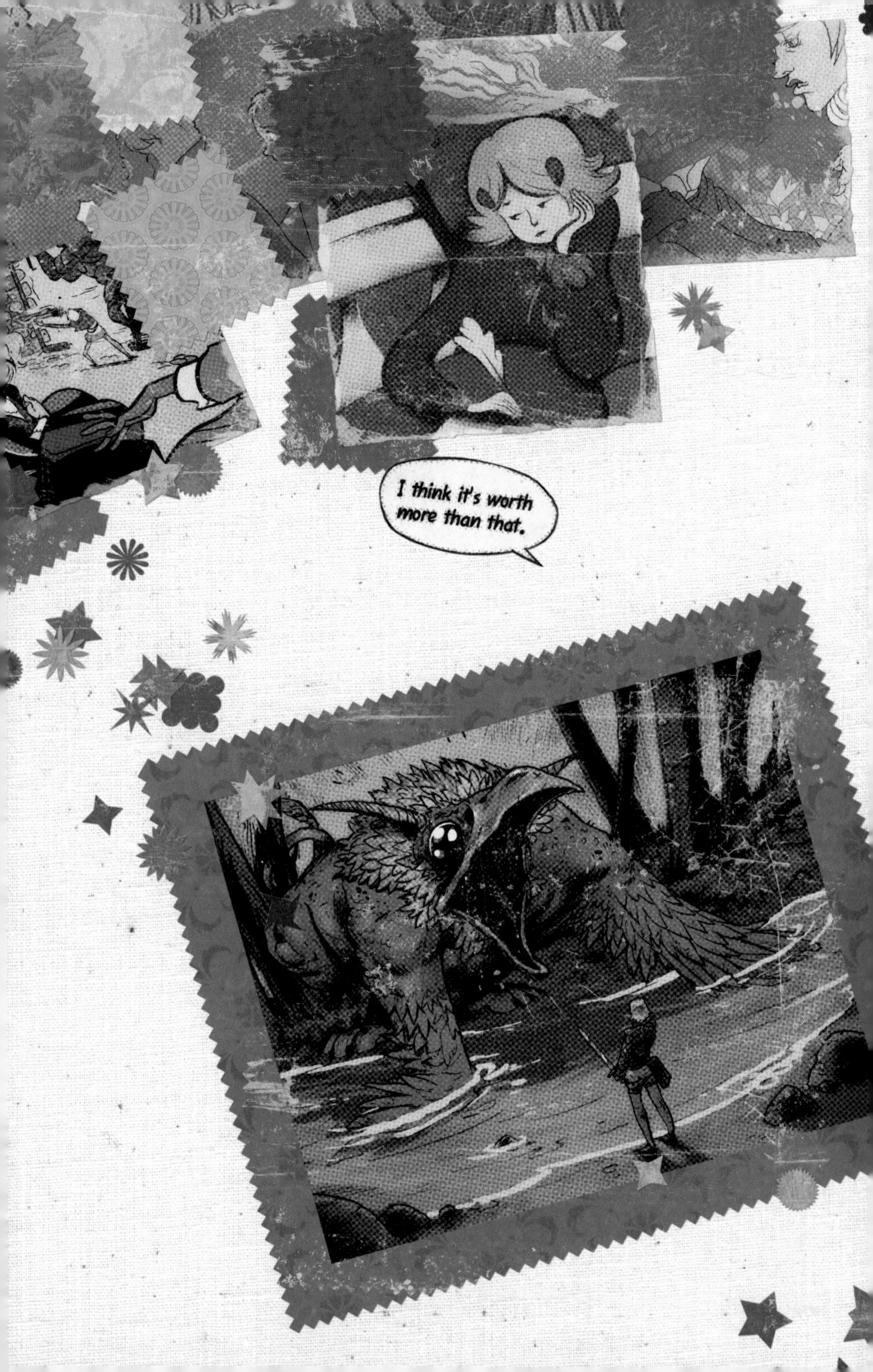
I think it's worth more than that.

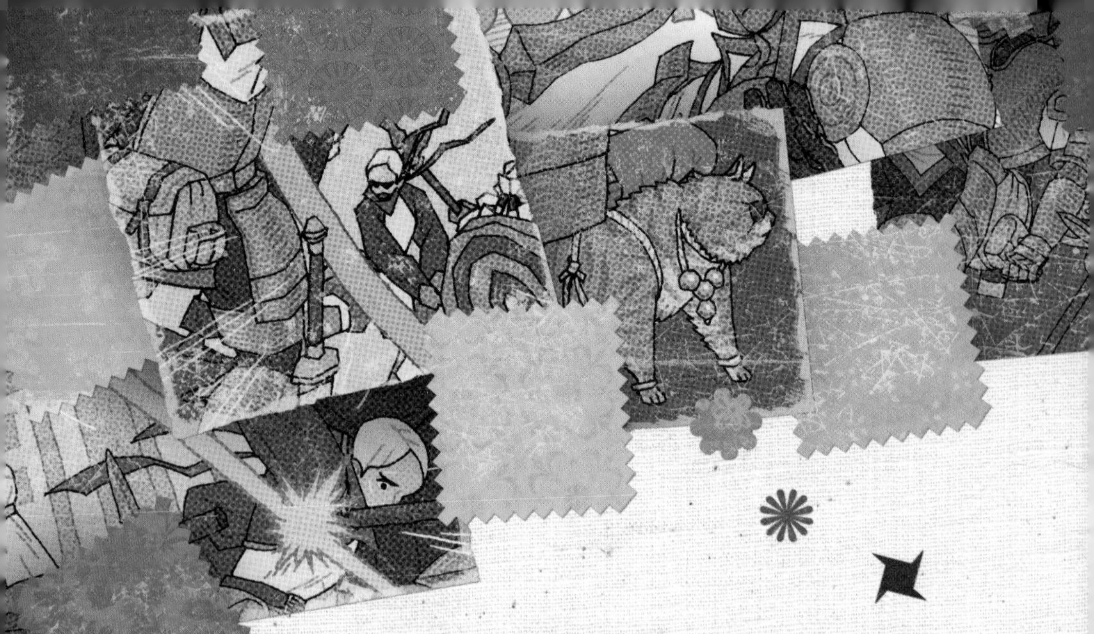

CHARACTER GALLERY

character designs and illustrations by
AFU CHAN

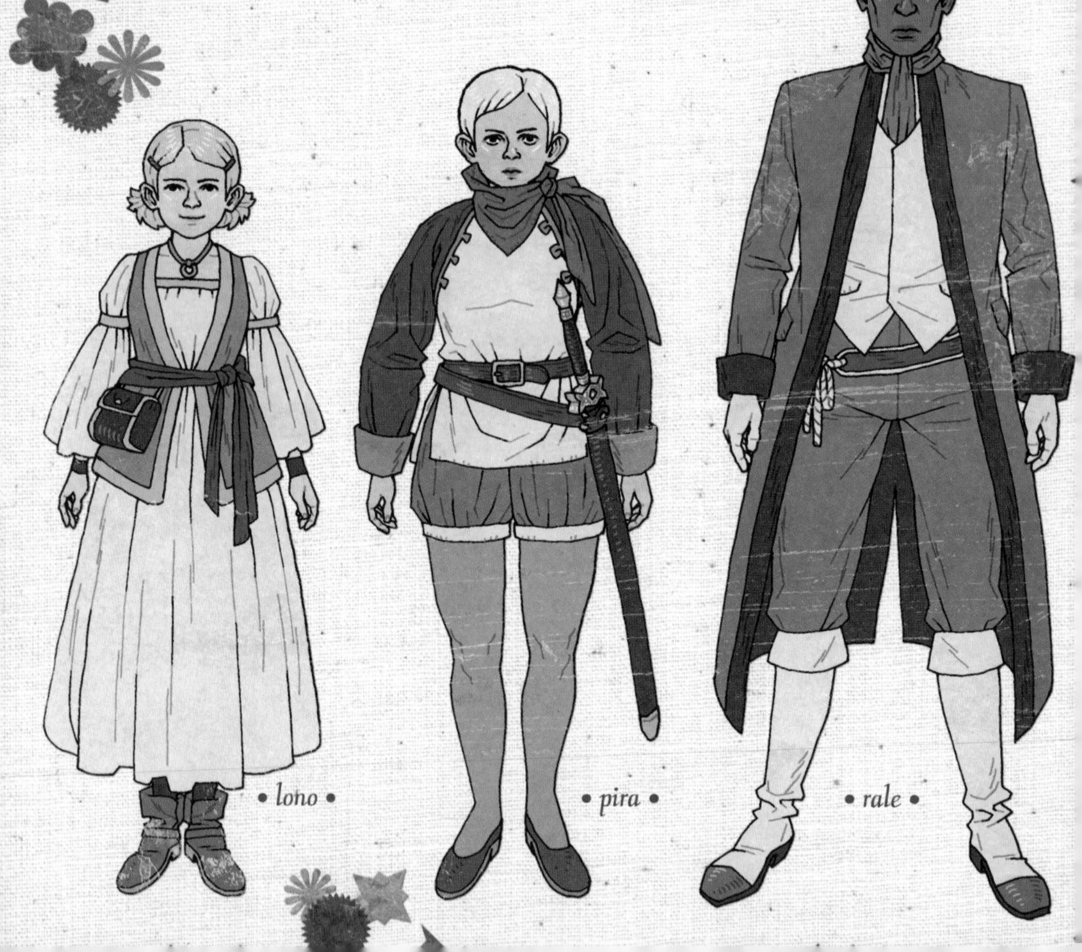
• lono •
• pira •
• rale •

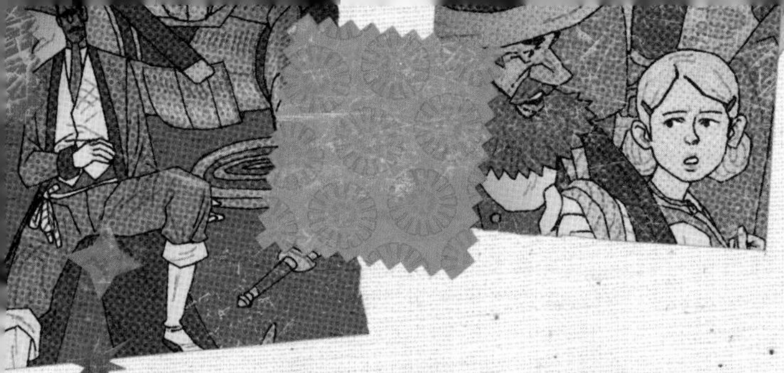

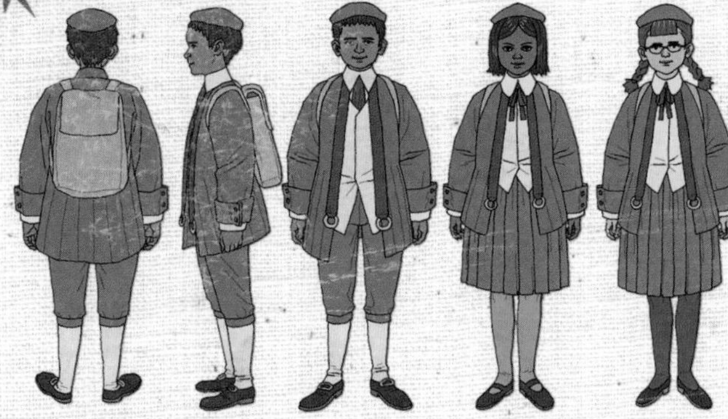

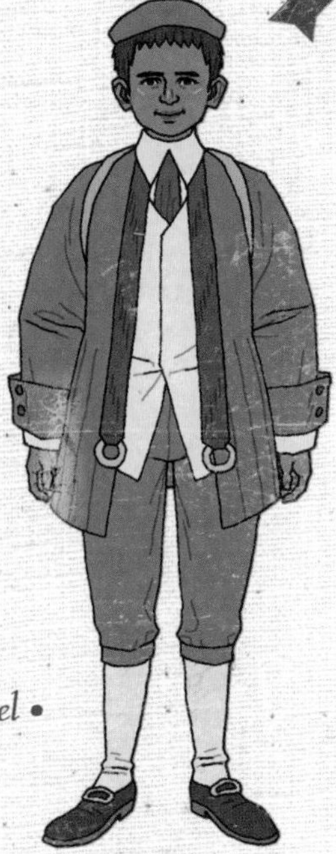

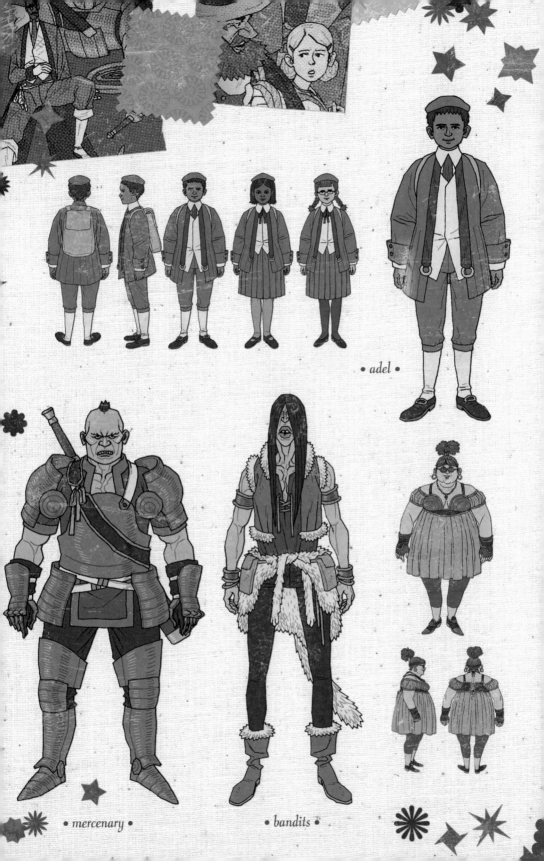

• *adel* •

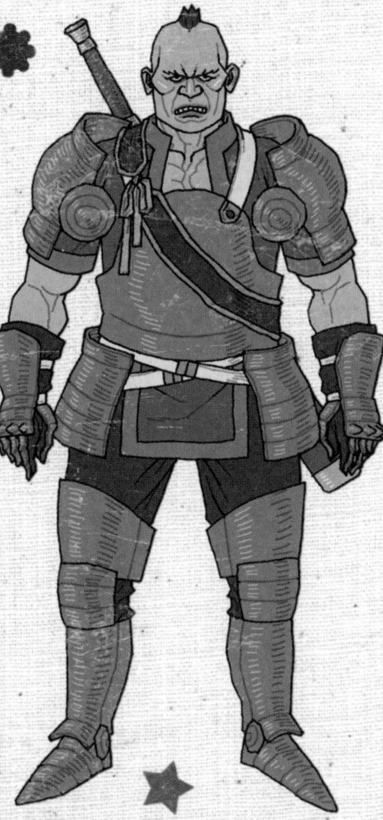

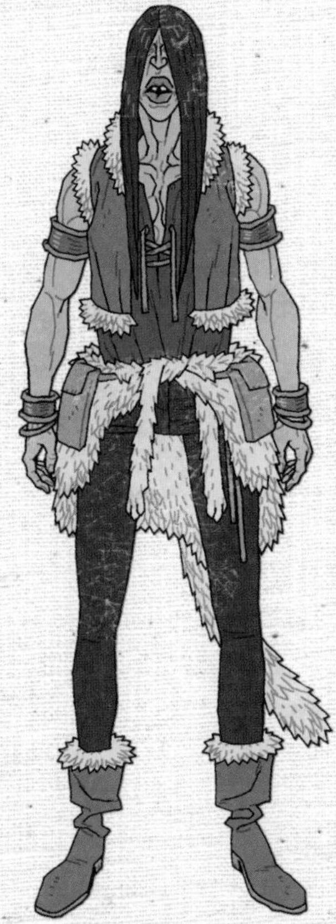

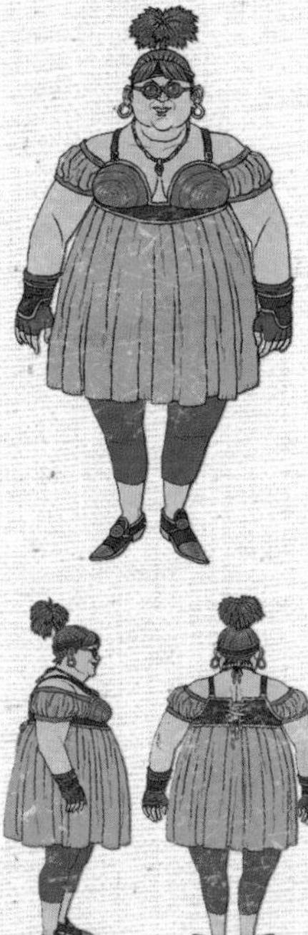

• *mercenary* •

• *bandits* •

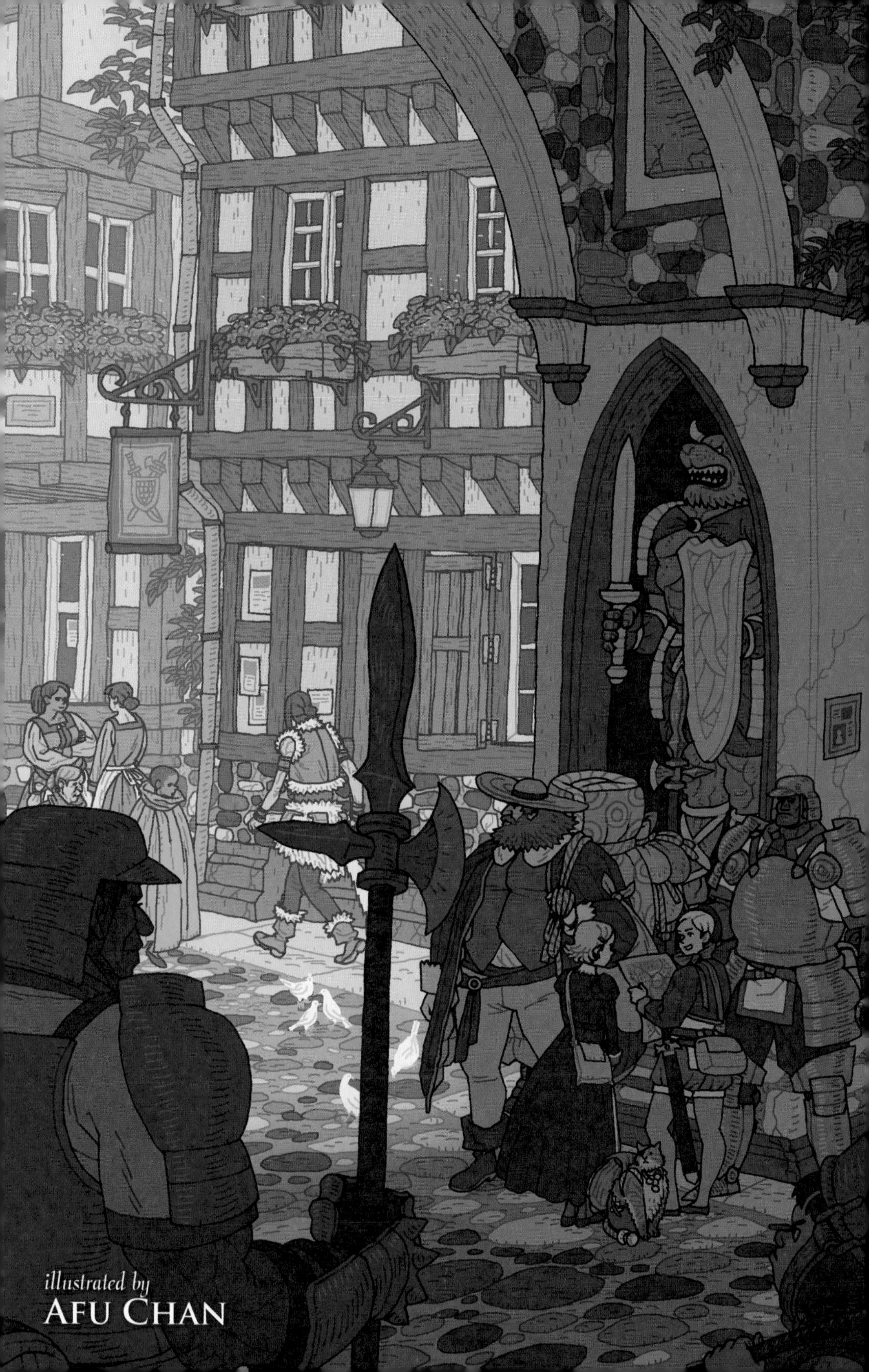

illustrated by
AFU CHAN

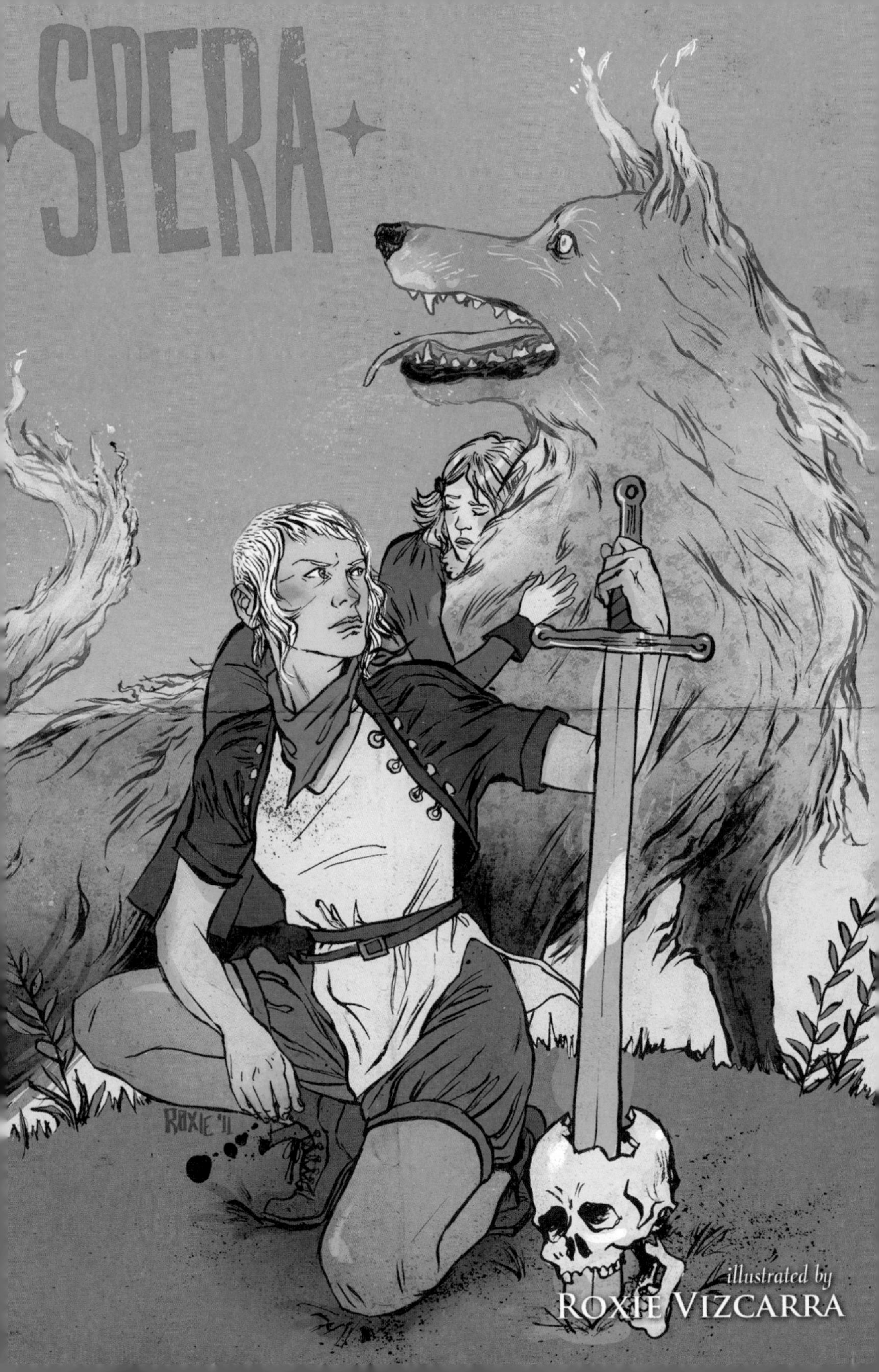
SPERA
ROXIE '11
illustrated by
ROXIE VIZCARRA

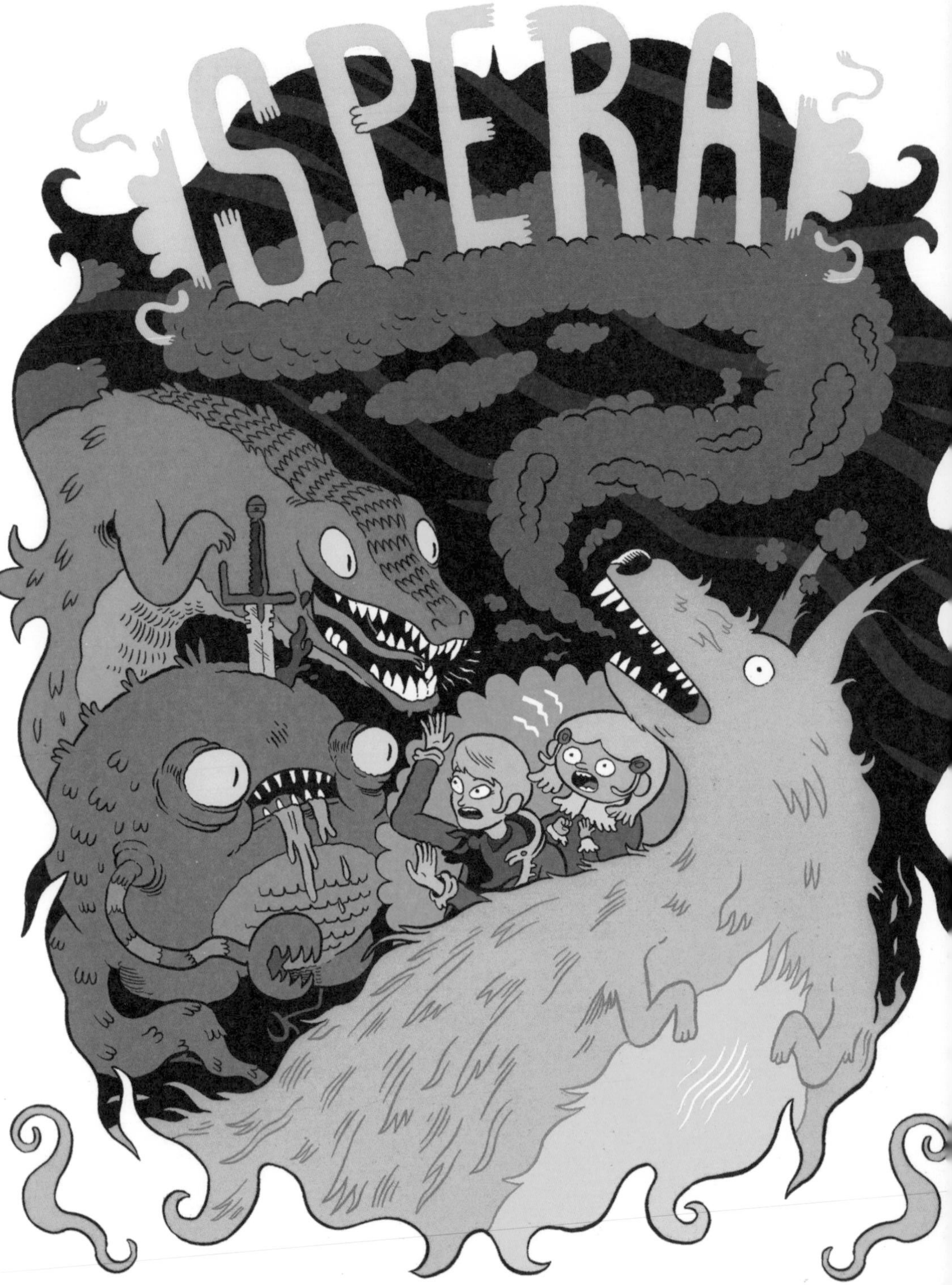
SPERA

illustrated by
NICK EDWARDS

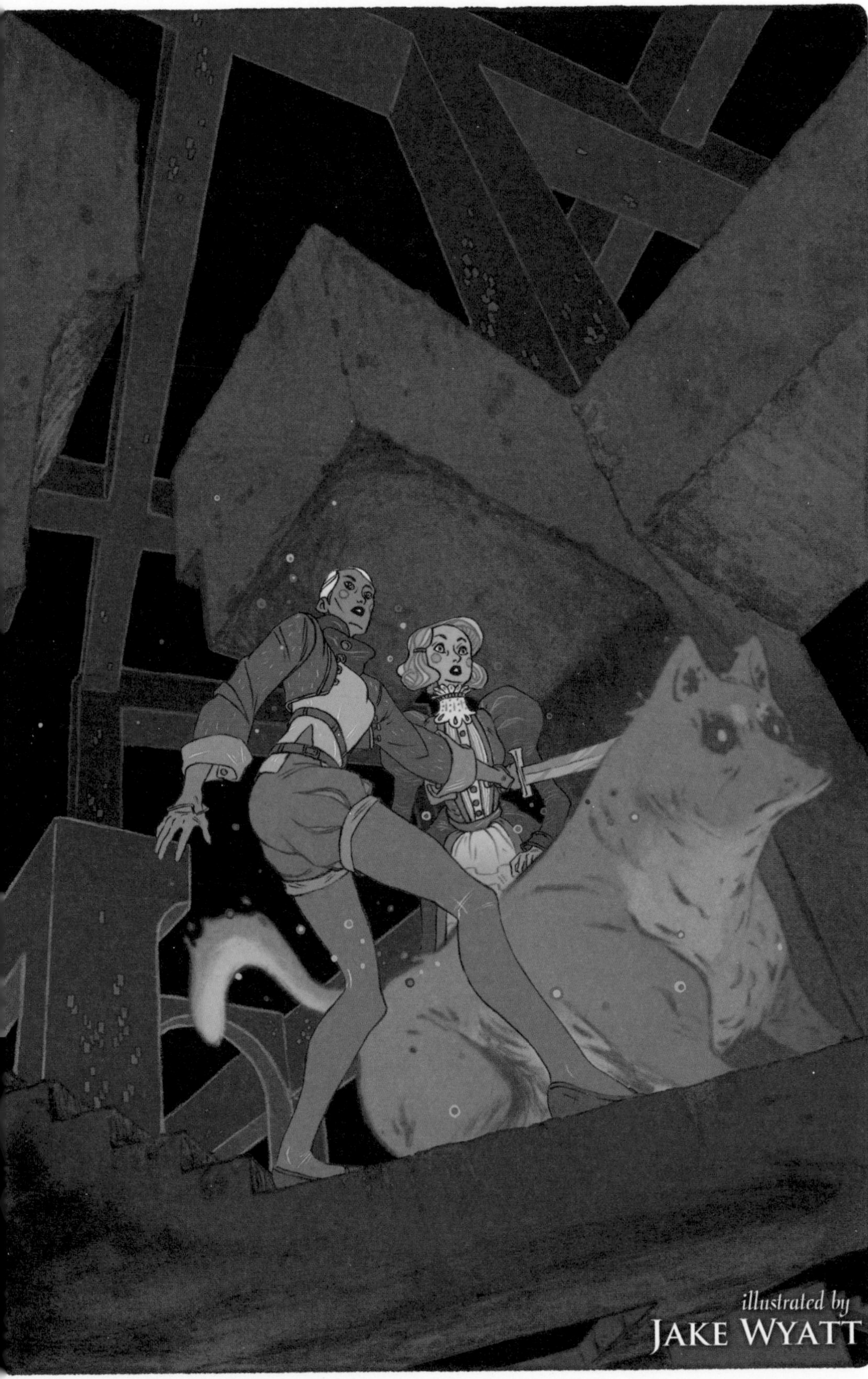
illustrated by
JAKE WYATT

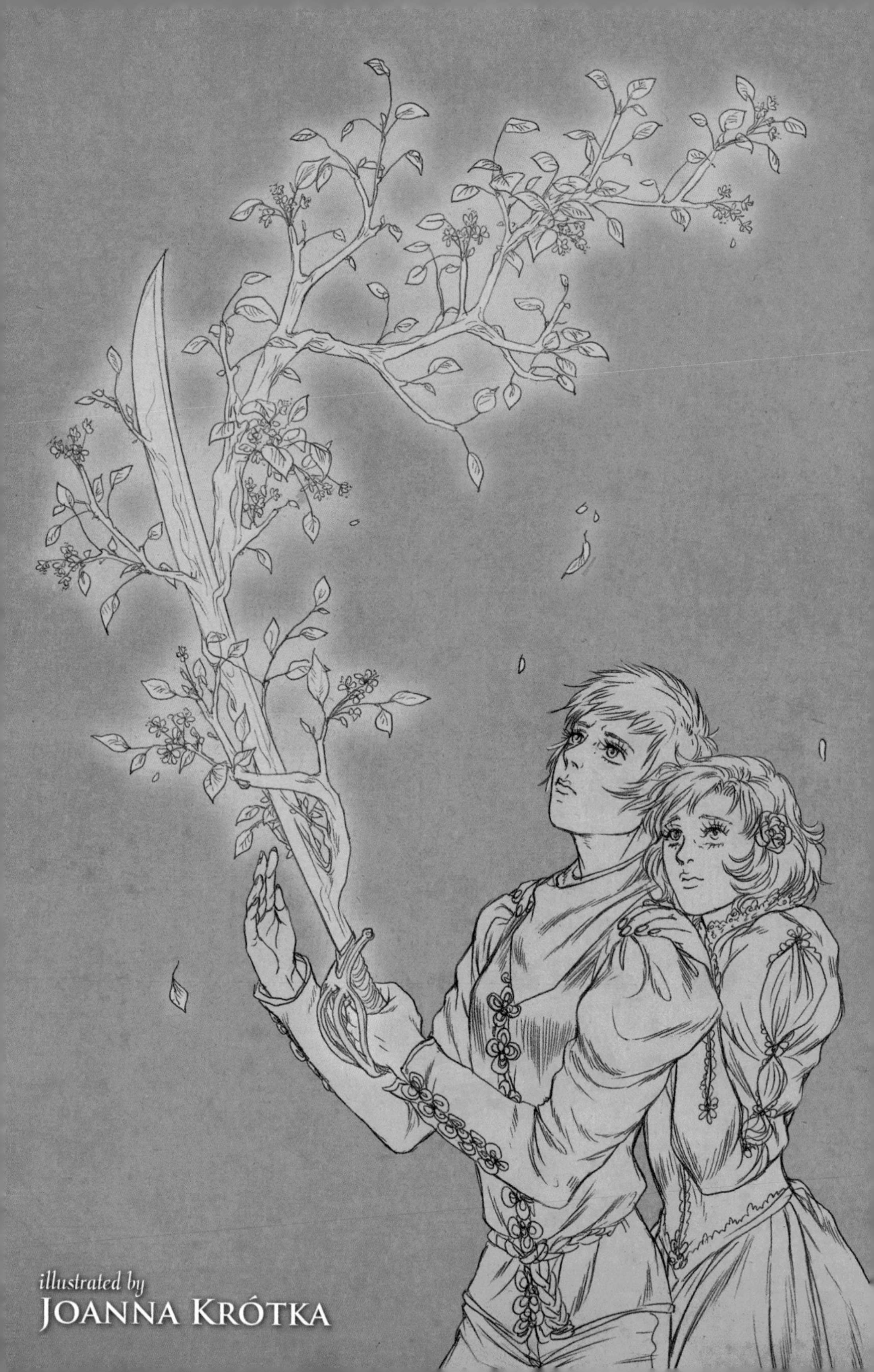
illustrated by
JOANNA KRÓTKA

ABOUT THE AUTHORS

the storytellers who have spun our tales...

JOSH TIERNEY resides in Ontario, Canada with his wife, daughter and cat. In addition to writing and editing the *Spera* series of books for Archaia, Josh runs *Spera-Comic.com* with the help of Olivier Pichard. There you can find a new *Spera* story every month, each illustrated by a different artist from around the world.

GIANNIS MILONOGIANNIS has been writing and drawing comics since 2006 and is the creator of the cyberpunk thriller ***Old City Blues*** (**Archaia**, 2011). Currently living and working on stories out of the second largest city of the fifth largest island in the Mediterranean. More of his work may be found at *milonogiannis.com*.

KYLA VANDERKLUGT is a Toronto-born freelance illustrator and comic artist now working out of her ramshackle little studio in the country. She takes inspiration from her surroundings, and mostly the things she is surrounded by these days are animals and trees – and the tottering piles of books of her overflowing library. You can visit her online at *www.kylavanderklugt.com*.

AFU CHAN is an illustrator and freelance artist. He is a fan of the films of Wong Kar Wai and Johnnie To due to their quirky storytelling and distinctive styles, which serve as some of the biggest inspirations for his work. Afu designs the characters and creates the covers for *Spera*.

TIMOTHY WEAVER is an illustrator and comic artist from the U.S. He finally graduated from school and is now at a tiny little desk in Savannah, GA. He likes to draw creepy self-portraits and mostly does memoir-based comics, but he's working on some other stuff, trust him. His favourite colour is turquoise. His website is *timoillo.com*.

MIKKEL SOMMER is a Berlin-based comic book artist from Copenhagen. After quitting his second art school, he started freelancing in 2009. He's done a few comics here and there; among them are **Obsolete** for British publisher **Nobrow**, the comics **Z** and **De Gale** for Danish publishers, and works in a number of anthologies.

MICHAEL DIALYNAS is an illustrator and comic artist that resides in Athens, Greece. He has published his collection of mini-stories called **Trinkets** and a series by the name of **Swan Songs** through **Comicdom Press**. When he is not planning on bigger and better stories to draw, he loves to play hide and go seek with his cat, Shiro, or just relax with his sweet girl. You can find more about his work at *WoodenCrown.com*.

PAUL MAYBURY is an artist that moves once a year. His work has appeared in books from **Marvel**, **DC**, **Image**, **Archaia**, **Heavy Metal** and **Smartercomics**. His favourite food is Chilean Empanadas. For more relevant information about Paul, visit *paulmaybury.com*.

KRIS MUKAI is a cartoonist living and working in Brooklyn, NY. Her favourite breakfast is cold pizza with black coffee. You can find her work at *www.krismukai.com* and *krismukai.tumblr.com*.

ZAC GORMAN is a cartoonist with a warrior cat of his very own. He draws videogame-inspired comics for **Magical Game Time** as well as the popular game culture site **Kotaku**, and has been featured in a number of publications like this one which makes his parents very proud.

LOUIS ROSKOSCH is a comic artist and illustrator from the UK. He is the author of **Leeroy and Popo** published by **Nobrow Press**.

RACHEL S. (a.k.a. 'Baru'), is a reclusive, troll-like creature who lives in the UK. She enjoys drawing, comicking and animating. You can see more of her work at *rachels.web.fc2.com*.

JULIA SCOTT is an illustrator and comic book store minion living in Richmond, Virginia. Her most recent work is the short ***Sink Slow Down***, as seen in the **RVAnthology**.

ANNA WIESZCZYK is a freelance illustrator and comic artist from Poland. If you look carefully you'll be able to find her published works here and there. You can also check her out at *muckcracker.deviantart.com*.

ED BRISSON is a professional comic book letterer, by day. By night, he hones his craft as a writer. His online crime comic series for adults, ***Murder Book*** (*www.murderbookcomic.com*), was nominated for a **2011 Joe Shuster Award**.

ROMAN MURADOV is an illustrator/cartoonist from Russia. His drawings & comics have appeared in the **New Yorker**, the **New York Times**, **Village Voice**, **Washington Post**, **Nobrow** magazine & other nice places. He loves tea and dislikes most other things. *www.bluebed.net*.

POLLY GUO is an animator and cartoonist from the USA. She loves funny people and good food, and her favourite things to draw are bromance and punching. Her website is *pollums.com*.

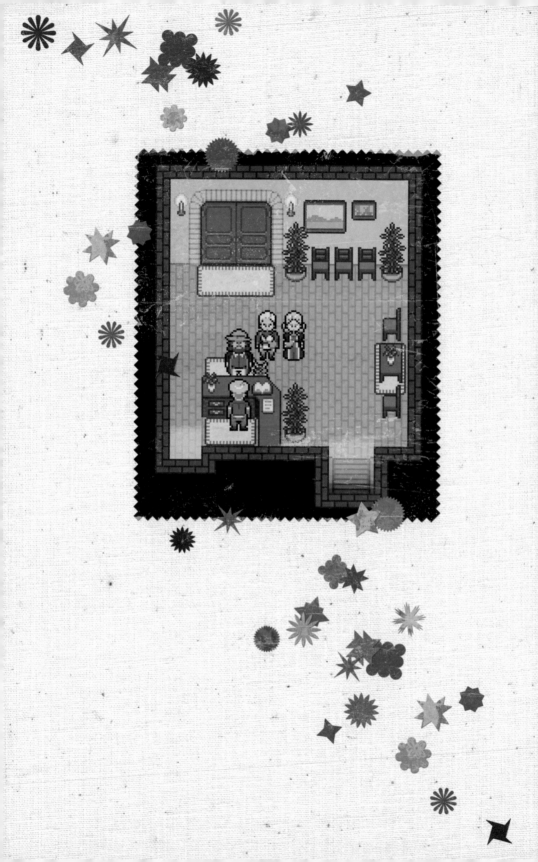

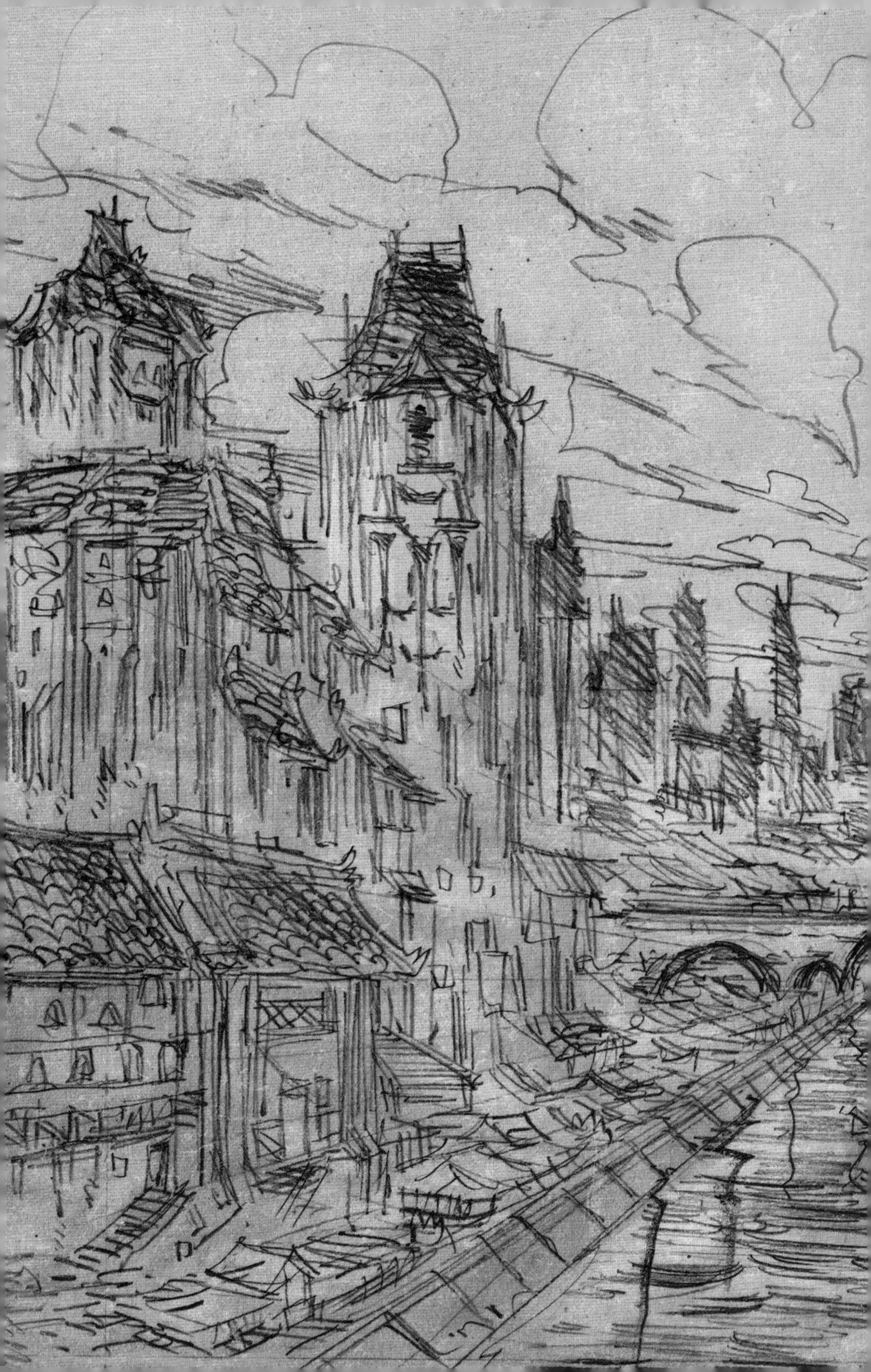